Louise Cooper began writing stories ...... school to entertain her friends. She continued to write and her first full-length novel was published when she was only twenty years old. Since then she has become a prolific writer of fantasy, renowned for her bestselling *Time Master* trilogy. Her other interests include music, folklore, mythology and comparative religion. She lives in Worcestershire.

'One of our finest writers of epic fantasy . . . Never has the battle of order and chaos been better recorded than in Louise Cooper's magnificent trilogy. She has a sharp understanding of human ambiguity, a gift for narrative and a wonderfully original imagination'   Michael Moorcock

'Louise Cooper is one of the finest storytellers of her generation'   Tanith Lee

'The writing skills she evinces should keep . . . readers enthralled'   *Publishers Weekly*

'Well drawn and beautifully written'   *Fantasy Review*

'A beautifully wrought, deceptively simple tale that has the texture of legend'   *Kirkus Reviews*

'One of fantasy's finest talents . . . Ms Cooper melds rich, imaginative concepts, superlative language skills and intense emotional colouring into a stunning reading experience'   *R*A*V*E Reviews' Magazine*

The King's Demon

Louise Cooper

HEADLINE
FEATURE

First published in 1996
by HEADLINE BOOK PUBLISHING

First published in paperback in 1997
by HEADLINE BOOK PUBLISHING

A HEADLINE FEATURE paperback

10 9 8 7 6 5 4 3 2 1

ISBN 0 7472 5371 4

Printed and bound in Great Britain by
Cox & Wyman Ltd, Reading, Berks

HEADLINE BOOK PUBLISHING
A division of Hodder Headline PLC
338 Euston Road
London NW1 3BH

The King's Demon

Prologue: Before the War

The labour had been protracted and difficult, but at last the travail was over. The midwife, heavy-eyed from nearly a day and a half without sleep, took the newborn infant and, with a practised but fond hand, wrapped it in the shawl set ready, noting with satisfaction that its limbs moved easily and its breathing was sound. Then she glanced towards the narrow embrasure of the bedchamber window, where a dim, green-blue glow filtered through the darkness.

'Past midnight, if I judge the moon correctly,' she said to her apprentice, keeping her voice low. 'Go you downstairs; tell the good master that his first-born is safely in the world and he can come now and see for himself that all's well.'

The apprentice, who was only fifteen but had potential, said, 'Yes'm' and hurried from the room. In the bed the mother stirred, and though her voice was weak, it was suffused with hope and the beginnings of pride.

'Is my child healthy?'

The midwife looked at her sweat-soaked hair and drawn face, but saw from her eyes that, for her, the suffering had been worthwhile. She smiled. 'Healthy and strong, madam, and perfect in every way.'

The mother sighed with relief. 'A son, or a daughter?'

The midwife opened her mouth to answer. But before she could speak she was pre-empted by a sudden, sharp cry.

'*Ahh!*' The woman in the bed tensed violently, then her body twisted into a contortion and her face became rigid with shock.

Hastily the midwife laid the child down on a folded blanket and started towards the bed. 'What is it? What's amiss?'

'P . . . *pain* . . .' The word choked out through violently clenched teeth. 'Not like before – this is worse, it is *worse!*' Another convulsion shot through the woman, as though someone had stabbed her. 'Ah, no, no – help me, *oh, help me*—'

The words swelled into a throat-tearing scream. In all her fifty years the midwife had never heard a sound of such raw agony; the woman was writhing, arms and legs thrashing as she strove to escape from something that her body couldn't endure. Footsteps in the corridor outside; they quickened abruptly and a man's voice was raised in alarm, counterpointed by the apprentice's shrill tones. The door smacked open as the midwife managed to get a grip on her shrieking patient's wrists and struggled to stop her from hurling herself from the bed in a frenzy of pain.

'Kessie!' the midwife shouted. 'The quiet-leaf, girl, *quickly!*'

With commendable self-possession the apprentice ran for her mistress's scrip and snatched out one of the calming leaves which the stricken woman had been given to chew on through her ordeal. But as she ran towards the bed with it the mother went suddenly and violently into a new contraction, and her wild expression changed to a look of bewildered astonishment that under other circumstances might almost have been comical.

'Preserve me from all evil!' The midwife's eyes widened as she stared. 'There's a second child in her!'

The patient's husband, who had frozen on the threshold unable to do anything more than stare in horror at the scene, said, 'What? But there were no omens—'

'Omens or none, sir, your lady has another life to bring forth! You'd best leave me to—' And she stopped.

One further contraction had surged in the woman – and in that single moment the child had emerged. It lay on the stained sheet, not moving. But it was alive. Against all justice, it was alive.

The mother made a sound halfway between a gasp and a moan, and fainted. Which, the midwife thought as she continued to stare at the second newborn, was a powerful blessing. Her mouth worked but no sound would come, for the words in her mind could not, *must* not be spoken.

Kessie said softly, 'Oh, ma'am, what *is* it . . . ?'

A violent gesture silenced her, and the midwife steeled herself to look up at the father.

He knew. She saw it in his eyes as their gazes met, and realised that he understood all too well the nature of the curse that had fallen, without rhyme or reason, on himself and his wife.

The second-born child was no normal infant, but as translucent as a ghost. It had hair, a spider-web white nimbus about its skull, and its body too was white, like fresh snow. Only its eyes displayed colour; a hard, unnatural blue. And its gaze was so steady, and there was such an abominable, calculating intelligence in the look it gave to the world around it, that the midwife felt nausea rise from the pit of her stomach.

Then, as they all watched, the child's form began to fade. Like the ghost which it so resembled, it shimmered, evaporated . . . and vanished. A cold breath skittered across the room, brushing icily against the midwife's face, ruffling Kessie's hair; the curtain at the window stirred briefly and then the small disturbance was gone. There was a sound, a faint echo, as though a fine wineglass had cracked and rung a small discord. Then nothing.

For a long time they were all silent. Kessie had pushed a clenched fist against her mouth and was too shocked and frightened to utter a sound; her glance darted nervously from her mistress to the unconscious woman in the bed and back again. And the woman's husband stood with head bowed and both hands covering his face.

At last the midwife broke the thrall and moved slowly to where the first child – the natural child – lay on its blanket. Healthy and strong, a fine infant which, but for this, would have brought its parents great joy. It waved its limbs vaguely at her as she approached; its tiny mouth seemed to be trying to smile, and her heart constricted with grief.

'Drowning,' she said very softly, 'is the kindest way. And no other living soul need ever know.'

The man's hands fell away from his face. 'No,' he said. 'I won't countenance it. I won't countenance murder.'

'But sir—'

'I said, *no*.' He moved with sudden energy, as though some paralysis within him had abruptly snapped. A glance at his wife to ensure that she was still unconscious and could not overhear, and he continued, 'I know you mean it for the best, midwife, but murder is what it would be. The infant can't be held to blame for its own misfortune and should not be forced to suffer. This is a random and senseless stroke. Besides . . .' He sighed heavily. 'It is my child. It is *my* child.'

Kessie was listening, face stricken, and for a moment the midwife thought to send her out of the room. But the damage had been done now; and besides, she thought, lessons learned young tended to take deeper root. She had learned that from bitter experience.

'But sir,' she said gently, 'you cannot keep it. Your Fellowship . . . your business . . . it would be impossible to bring up such a child in accordance with the life you must lead; if the secret were ever to be discovered – and that is far more likely than not – it would mean your ruin,' she glanced sadly at the bed, 'and that of your lady.'

He sighed again, but now he sounded calmer, resigned. 'I know that. But I still won't stand by and see the infant die.' A pause; he seemed to be steeling himself to say what was in his mind. Then: 'Take it away. Find a good, respectable household in a more fitting Fellowship. A man and wife who can have no children of their own, and who will love and care for this little one.'

The midwife nodded. There were many such couples and the search would not be difficult.

'I will provide generously for the child's every need,' the man continued. 'It will want for nothing, and neither will its new parents. But they must not be told the truth.' He glanced at the midwife, a look that hovered uneasily between hope and doubt. 'It is possible that the curse will never awaken and that the child will live a natural life. I shall hope with all my heart that that is so.'

The midwife cast her own gaze down. 'Yes, sir,' she said. 'As will I.'

'And my wife . . .' He turned towards the bed. 'I shall tell her that she did indeed bear twins. The second child was stillborn, and the first died in a sudden convulsion after appearing at first to be healthy. I'll break the news to her gently . . . she will recover from the loss in time. And if fate is not too unkind, we shall have other children.'

The midwife and her apprentice left the room a few minutes later. Kessie carried the scrip, while the midwife held the child, carefully and warmly wrapped, under the folds of her voluminous cloak. Outside in the passage Kessie opened her mouth to speak, but the midwife shook her head. This was not the time for words. Later she would tell Kessie the whole truth of what she had witnessed tonight; but not now. The shock of it was too strong and too sharp as yet, and she wanted time to shake off the memory that it had brought to mind, an incident years in the past now but one which she still relived in her dreams. Another birth, another horror, another spiteful turn of chance. She didn't know what had become of that other child; whether it had thrived or died, whether the plague that invaded its soul had ever stirred from dormancy. There had been a certain rumour, but that was long ago and, cowardly though it might be, she had never sought to discover the truth. This child, too, she would put out of her mind as best she could. She would tell Kessie, then that would be an end to it and they would both try to forget.

But tomorrow, she thought, it would be a kindness, not to

mention the smallest charity, to go to a hallowed place and say a luck-blessing for this little one and its uncertain future.

Chapter I

When the storm broke she was genuinely frightened, and that answered another small conundrum. Afraid of lightning. It explained the uneasy tension that had been haunting her since the wind started to rise and the first rain fell, and which had grown stronger as the elements began to assault the landscape in earnest. The weather had worsened rapidly, but even with the wind screaming and the rain driving horizontally and ferociously against her she had kept on walking, because there was no other choice. No shelter, not even a rock or bush of sufficient size; just the huge, empty moorland stretching away in all directions, a featureless grey blur in the streaming dark. Head down and shoulders hunched, butting and stumbling into the onslaught of wind and water. Clothes sodden and hair and face streaming, struggling to see the faint contours of the track beneath her feet, and striving to stay on it because in a strange country to stray aside could be worse than dangerous.

When the first flash of lightning came she jumped as though she had been shot, and an involuntary yelp broke from her throat. In that instant the unease jerked into focus. Her skin crawled, her stomach churned, and she felt her heartbeat quicken to the painful, arrhythmic thumping of outright terror. One thought, animal and primal, filled her: *Get away from it, hide from it, I don't want to have to see the lightning, because I'm so afraid that the next bolt will strike me . . .*

Thunder answered the flash seconds later, an ominous, echoing rumble that briefly eclipsed the turmoil surrounding

7

her. Feeling sick, she tried to find a spar of reason in the churning sea of her mind. She could stop, crouch down, shut her eyes and try not to think about it. Or she could keep moving. Was a moving person less likely to be struck? She didn't know. But if she did press on, there was at least some chance of finding shelter.

She chose the second option because it was less passive and thus less frightening, but she cupped her hands around her eyes like a horse's blinkers and kept her gaze fixed steadfastly on her moving feet. The second flash didn't affect her so badly, though the thunder was louder and closer. Maybe before the third came – or perhaps the fourth – she could find the courage to look ahead, in the hope that the momentary brilliance would give her an idea of where she was now. So *many* questions. So *much* she couldn't remember. The one certainty that stood out was that she had escaped from something – or someone – that had been a dire threat. When that had happened, or where, or how it had led her here, she didn't know, because at some time during the escape something had happened; a fall or an attack or suchlike; something that had left her unconscious for a time. And when she woke, memory was gone, including even the knowledge of who she was. Whether it would come back was a question she couldn't answer. But until and unless it did, she could only follow where instinct led, observe her behaviour and thus learn about herself, and wait for the answers to come.

The third flash was a triple one with the thunder immediately on its heels, and though she felt a fool for doing it, she screamed. It put paid to any idea of trying to see what lay ahead, for the fear that she might glimpse the next blue-white fork was too great to allow room for courage. Just keep going. It was all she could do.

There had been a closed carriage, without windows. It was dimly lit inside, and moving very fast. And they had been taking her to . . .

There the fragment of memory broke off but it left echoes

8

of another kind of fear. And dread, and desperation. *Where* had they – whoever they were – been taking her? To a town, she thought; yet instinct told her that the name of the town wasn't especially significant. Not the place that mattered, but the *event*. And she had been so very frightened, because when they reached their destination they were going to . . .

She stopped on the path. *Kill her. They were going to kill her.*

She didn't see the next flash of lightning because she was standing rigid with her hands over her eyes, and the rain battering down on her, as a shock far colder than anything the weather could inflict sank in. Whoever had been in the carriage with her was a murderer. Or were murderers, because she was certain there had been more than one. Someone had wanted her dead.

She wanted to cry but found she couldn't; tears simply wouldn't come. And after perhaps a minute, and two more flashes of lightning, a kind of calm settled on her. Well, she had had one revelation and, however great the shock, she had survived it. More would follow. Absorb this, she thought. Don't try to understand it all yet but just let it settle. There would be an explanation that fitted with the things she felt about herself, and then she would comprehend. For now there was the storm to fear and the path to follow, and coping with those was enough.

She began to move again. The going was becoming harder, for the track was rutted and potholed, and now the rain had filled the holes. Several times she stumbled knee-deep into water, and once lost her balance altogether, and measured her length in a pool that stretched right across her path; though the wetting made little difference as she was already soaked through. And all the time, *all* the time, the terror of the lightning was in her, churning, sickening, inescapable. Somewhere, even in this bleak and grim landscape, there must be shelter. If only she could find it . . .

The thunder was bawling in a renewed onslaught, a gargantuan voice that seemed to fill the world, when the horse came up on her out of the darkness. She knew nothing of its approach, for the colossal flash that preceded the thunder had snapped the last of her spirit and she was kneeling on the track, hands clamped over her face, sobbing tearlessly as panic reduced her to craven helplessness. No human ear could have heard the thud of hoofs anyway; but amid the storm's din the dark shape loomed suddenly, and there was a shout that mingled shock, alarm and outrage as at the last moment the rider saw her. The horse slewed, rearing; belatedly realising the danger she jerked up, her hands falling from her face, and there was time for an instant's impression of a horrifyingly solid shape toppling towards her, hoofs flailing, a figure crouched in the saddle and wrenching on the reins.

'Damn you to perdition and back, what do you think you were *doing*?' The rider had jumped from the saddle and was running towards her, dragging the horse after him. She was sprawled amid stones and heather and hummocks of grass at the track's edge, there was a hot pulse of pain in her left thigh, and she was going to be sick with it and with the shock.

Hands grasped her as she tried to roll over and she retched helplessly, miserably. But there was nothing in her stomach to be rid of, and when the hands pulled her into a sitting position it occurred to her in a strange, blind way that at least she didn't have that to shame her as well as everything else.

'Are you badly hurt?' The voice's tone changed as the rider's initial anger gave way to other considerations. A man's voice, though in the darkness she could see only a silhouette wrapped in a heavy cloak.

'Nn . . . no.' She could speak. She had thought so, but hadn't dared put it to the test alone. 'Just m-my leg . . . but I don't think it's broken.'

'Bruised, more likely. It was only a glancing blow from a forefoot; hardly touched you.' He had raised his voice, almost shouting to be heard as the thunder roared again. 'What in the name of five hundred demons. are you *doing* out here? Where have you come from?'

'I d-d—' She was trying to say, '*I don't know*', but yet another flash cracked the sky in half at that moment and the attempt collapsed in a cry of terror. Instinctively her hands clutched for his arms and she choked out, 'I'm so *frightened* . . .'

He swore, she thought, though thunder drowned the words. 'Get up. Come on, on your feet. Can you ride a horse?'

'I d-d—'

'Never mind; if you can't, I'll hold you on. Up in the saddle, and we'll get out of this abysmal filth before we worry about anything else.'

He heaved her up with as much ceremony as if she had been a sack, and remounted behind her. Smells of leather and of wet, sweating animal; the man clamped one arm firmly and a little painfully around her waist, while with his free hand he gathered up and flicked the reins, saying something sharp to the horse. They began to move, a jolting trot turning to a smoother canter, and she hunched down as far as she could, too shocked and fearful to be anything other than passive.

The ride wasn't a long one, and in a glare of lightning, when she had made the mistake of daring to look up at the wrong moment, she saw their destination: a tower, grey and squat and solitary, standing incongruously beside the track. She had shut her eyes again, so she sensed rather than saw the stone wall looming; then suddenly there was a feeling of enclosure and the storm's racket faded to a muffled background bellow.

She felt the man behind her loose his hold and dismount, then the sound of a wooden door slamming started her out of her paralysis. Blinking, hair dripping over her face, she opened her eyes and stared into dimness that smelled of straw and horses. A stable? In a tower, in the middle of nowhere?

She opened her mouth to try to say something, though she didn't know what, but her companion pre-empted her.

'Get down.' He had reached up, emphasising the command by catching hold of her arm, and she let herself slide from the

11

saddle and be caught. Her left leg didn't want to support her weight and pain stabbed through her again; he saw the reaction she tried to hide and said, 'Sit there, on the hay bales – can you see them? I'll care for the horse first; it's probably more deserving of consideration than either of us.'

Flint and tinder scraped, and she watched silently as he lit a lantern that seemed to have been left ready. A warm glow pressed the darkness back as he turned up the wick, and she saw that they were, indeed, in a stable of sorts. Wooden partitions had been built on the tower's ground floor to make stalls for three or four horses, and beside the bales of hay on which she was sitting were two large corn bins and a water barrel. Above her head was a raftered ceiling covered with cobwebs, which she put at about the height of two men, suggesting a floor or floors above. What *was* this place? Someone's home? Impossible to imagine; impossible to guess. But at least she could no longer see the lightning, and at this moment that was all that mattered.

She looked obliquely at her rescuer. He had unsaddled the horse and was briskly rubbing it down with wisps of hay; only his back was visible but she could see that he had light-coloured hair which fell in a rough, uncombed mane to his shoulders. He was tall, and the hands that worked on the horse's coat looked strong. No rings. A practical man, then. What had he been doing out on the moor? Where had he been going? Not here, surely; she sensed intuitively that the tower had not been his destination.

Then he turned and looked at her, and she saw his face for the first time. A narrow but strong face, with prominent bones and a full, expressive mouth; but not, she thought, overly pleasant. It was hard to imagine him smiling; not because he carried any great sorrow but simply because – intuition again, and she was inclined to trust it – he would see no reason to put himself out to be agreeable to anyone. She couldn't judge the colour of his eyes in this light, but he had a confident, steady, faintly condescending stare. It made her feel uncomfortable. And she had an instinct – though without a mirror to confirm it, it was nothing more than instinct – that he was considerably older than she was.

He saw that she was watching him, and she turned her head away.

'Can you walk?' he asked.

She tested her leg. 'I think so.'

'Good. Then bring me a measure of corn from one of the bins.' He snatched up a wooden bowl, held it out to her, and abruptly the glimmer of a smile made his mouth a little less unfriendly for a moment. 'Then we'll see if there's anything in this place fit for human consumption.'

She obeyed him, handing the bowl back silently, and listening to the sound of the grain hissing into the manger. He filled a bucket with water from the barrel, set it beside the manger, then brushed his hands together and gave the horse a last, satisfied look.

'He'll last the night out on that.' Then he nodded towards a corner of the tower and a narrow door set into the wall. 'The stairs are that way.'

She said, 'Stairs?'

'To the living floor. Unless you want to stay in the stable all night?'

In truth she would rather have stayed in the stable, for its windowlessness and proximity to the ground made her feel further from the lightning. But his manner was too dominant for her to argue with him in her present state, so she inclined her head acquiescently and limped in the direction he indicated.

Stone stairs, a narrow flight that curved up and ended at another door. He had brought the lantern, and when its light spilled into the room above the stable she stared about her with a mixture of curiosity and disappointment. Whatever this place might be it was certainly no one's home, for the chamber that formed the tower's upper floor was furnished only with a narrow bed, a table, stool, two chests, and a rack of wooden shelves set crudely into the wall and empty but for a small cooking pot and two half-burned candles. There was a brazier in the middle of the room but it was dead and empty, and the atmosphere was one of cold, dank disuse.

Her companion set the lantern down on the table, surveyed the room briefly and said a word that she didn't recognise but which sounded like an extreme profanity. 'Damn the keepers! It must be months since anyone was last here, and they've not troubled to replenish any of the stores . . .' He took three strides to one of the chests, wrenched it open and started to rummage among the contents. Another profanity, and he slung a bundle of thin twigs into the middle of the floor. 'That's the sum total of our fuel, and it isn't worth burning for the five minutes' heat it will give us. So we'd best resign ourselves to the prospect of a cold night, and a hungry one unless you've got food.' He looked at her, raised fiercely querying brows, and she shook her head.

'I was carrying nothing. You saw that for yourself.'

A disparaging grunt was her only answer, and he moved to the second chest. 'At least there are two blankets, if the moths haven't been eating better than we will. Here.' He flung a bundle; she fended it off reflexively and it dropped to the floor at her feet. 'Best get those sodden clothes off and wrap yourself, or you'll have the wet-fever to contend with by tomorrow.'

Her expression collapsed into dismay and she said, 'Here? Now?'

'Here, now. Yes.' Then his mouth twitched in a hard smile. 'Don't worry, I won't watch you. I doubt you've got anything to display that I haven't seen before.'

Before she could react to that he had turned his back and started to strip off his own garments without any ceremony. Hastily she swung round and unfastened her cloak. Under it she was surprised to find herself wearing clothes that by rights should have been a man's; trousers and a loose-sleeved shirt with a jerkin, unbelted, over it. The revelation was startling,

14

for until this moment it hadn't occurred to her to notice her apparel. The fabrics were coarse, and a flicker of memory went through her mind like the lightning flickering outside. *They had taken her own clothes away from her and dressed her in these, because . . .*

But the *because* didn't come to her, neither did *their* identity. More conundrums; the mystery grew more entangled. But she was learning, slowly, to bear her ignorance and be patient. It would come back, in time.

She undressed as best she could with the cloak still on her shoulders, not entirely trusting the truth of his last disparaging remark. Once, she couldn't resist the impulse to glance covertly and very swiftly at him, to see if he had lied and was watching her. He wasn't, but she caught a glimpse of his naked back view. Very lean. Thin, almost; as if he hadn't eaten a sound meal in a long time. But his body looked strong and sinewy, and well proportioned. Narrow hips, long legs. Small, shining runnels down his back where his hair, darkened to the colour of soiled straw by the rain, was dripping. And on his right arm, just above the elbow, he wore a band made from some kind of bright metal, with the device of a crown on it. The overall impression was brief but profound, and embarrassed, she returned her attention to herself.

At last they were both wrapped in blankets, and she sat down a little uneasily on the hard bed while he took the stool beside the table. Now he was watching her and she refused to meet his gaze, said nothing, waited for him to break the hiatus, if he intended to. The tower room had two narrow windows, but to her relief the shutters were closed and the storm muffled; only the light of his lantern relieved the gloom.

At last he spoke.

'Well. As it seems we'll be here until dawn at least, you'd better tell me your name so that I can address you if I need to.'

Her head lifted; with the gesture her hair flicked across her cheeks and she realised that it was short. She wasn't sure of its colour – dark, possibly black, though it was now so wet that that impression could be misleading. But it had been cropped. And that didn't fit with her instinct about herself . . . Then the frisson passed and the dilemma posed by his casual question came back to the fore.

She said, 'I . . . would rather not say.'

His fair eyebrows went up. 'Rather not? Why? Is your Fellowship so high-ranking that you fear I'll hold you captive for an unhealthy ransom?'

Fellowship? She was baffled by the term. Then she saw that his eyes and mouth betrayed sarcasm behind the words and she felt the skin of her face prickling with chagrin.

She said, 'I don't know what a Fellowship is. In fact I've no idea what you mean, because I . . .' *ah, damn him!* She met his steady eyes and finished, 'Because I don't know who I am. Not even my name. I – seem to have lost my memory.'

That did surprise him, and in a perverse way she found his surprise gratifying. A lapse; a crack in the wall of his supercilious confidence. But it lasted only a moment before the cool mask was back and he asked simply, 'When?'

She made a vague gesture with one hand. 'Not long before you found me – I think.' A shake of the head; water spattered from her hair onto the blanket. 'The first thing I can recall is walking on the moor, and the storm beginning.' She frowned. 'I'm afraid of lightning.'

'Afraid of lightning.' He considered that for a few moments. 'So are a good many other people, and some with good reason; that tells us nothing worthwhile. So; you simply found yourself walking, alone at night in the middle of nowhere.'

She nodded. 'I think I must have been unconscious. Before, I mean.'

'Then you woke, and started out along the track before you came properly to your senses? It's possible, yes. But you've no thoughts of where you might have come from or where you were going? No images, no glimmerings?'

'No,' she said. She didn't want to tell him about those, for she didn't trust him, and before he could ask any more questions she took refuge in one of her own. 'But if I know little about myself, I know even less about you.' She ventured a small smile. 'I would at least like to be told the name of my saviour.'

An odd light gleamed briefly in his eyes at the word *saviour*, but then he returned the smile, though his had a hard edge.

'It's Grendon.'

'Grendon.' It might be a common name or a rare one; she simply didn't know. 'Then I thank you, Grendon, for what you did.' She paused. 'Though I find it hard to guess why anyone should be riding alone at night in this weather.'

The smile faded. 'My business is entirely private, and I'm not in the habit of discussing it with friends, let alone strangers. I accept your gratitude, and I've told you my name; but your curiosity can stop at that, for I won't tell you any more.'

Stung, she looked away. 'I didn't mean to pry.'

'I'm glad to hear it. Because the fact that you're in need of help and I'm not gives me a far greater right than you to ask questions and expect to have them answered.' The hard smile twitched again. 'Where possible.'

'Very well. I take your point, and I apologise.' His tone angered her somewhere very deep down where she couldn't take a proper hold of it, and she added under her breath, 'As might you, for making your point so rudely.'

She hadn't intended him to hear that, but he did, and rose suddenly to his feet. '*Rudely?*' The word snapped out. 'I beg your pardon, madam! But I'd remind you that this situation is of your making, not mine! When I set out on my business I had no intention of being distracted by someone else's problems, and no desire whatever to waste the remainder of the night sitting in this tower! Quite frankly, you're a nuisance!'

Her cheeks flamed furiously and she stood up, almost throwing the blanket off before she remembered that she was naked beneath it. Snatching dignity and the blanket back she said savagely, 'Then I won't put you out any further!' and

17

started towards the door and the stairs beyond.

His voice stopped her in mid-step. 'Don't be ridiculous!'

She looked over her shoulder. He had shut his eyes and was pinching the bridge of his nose between thumb and forefinger. He looked extraordinarily tired.

'I'm sorry,' he said. Clearly it took an effort to force the words out. 'What I said was churlish and unnecessary; I apologise for it. And whatever impression I might have given, I'm not *quite* so callous as to be entirely indifferent to your plight. Sit down.' A hesitation. 'You're in no fit condition to leave, and if you'll only believe a selfish motive, I don't want your death from exposure or fright or both on my conscience for the rest of my life.' His hand fell away from his face and his eyes regarded her wearily. 'Please.'

The word, the small courtesy, dissipated her anger. Even if he didn't mean it he had at least said it, and her shoulders relaxed a little. 'Very well.' A shrug; the wet ends of her clipped hair made new dark stains on the blanket. 'I've nowhere else to go anyway.'

For a moment tension persisted. Then he smiled. It wasn't entirely a renouncement of his irritation, and it certainly wasn't a submission in any form, but it put them on a faintly kinder footing.

'Well, we've reached one small understanding,' he said, and the edge in his voice was lessened just a little. 'One obstacle overcome. Shall we tackle the next, and see about our sleeping arrangements?'

She couldn't decide at first whether she was more afraid of going to sleep or of staying awake. Wakefulness meant awareness of the storm, and though the shutters at the tower windows were sound there were enough cracks and knot-holes in the wood to make the lightning all too visible. He wouldn't allow her to leave the lantern burning; there wasn't enough oil in it for such profligacy, he said, and as he couldn't conjure more out of thin air she would simply have to endure the flickering dark. Sleep, then, would take that fear away. But there was another fear to which sleep only added extra potency, for the room had just the one bed. One of them could have spent the night on the floor, but the prospect of any rest would be slender. Besides, one blanket apiece wouldn't be enough to keep the cold from settling into their bones. The logical solution, as Grendon pointed out, was for them to share the bed, with both blankets on top of them, and let propriety be damned. And, he added, if she imagined that his desire or intention was for anything other than a night's sleep, she was wrong. Which was all well and good, but she couldn't bring herself to trust it. Words were easy; he had a clever tongue, and something – instinct, intuition, possibly even bitter experience which she couldn't now remember – urged her to distrust. But Grendon's will was stronger, so they settled at last, back to back and at as great a distance as the bed's width allowed, and she shut her eyes, burying her face in the thin pillow and trying not to let weariness overcome her.

But for all her nervous suspicions she did sleep, and what woke her was not the danger she had anticipated, for suddenly, breaking into an uneasy dream, a segment of her memory came back.

She sat up in a flurry, eyes wide as she stared into the dark. Her name was Sefira. It had come to her as though a voice had spoken it in her mind. Sefira. And with the name another memory had returned, which sent a shock through her as though someone had stabbed her in the stomach and then twisted the knife.

The closed, fast moving carriage and the captors who intended to kill her. But they were not murderers. *She* was.

She had been on her way to her own execution.

The silence that seemed to enclose the tower like a shroud was broken abruptly as Sefira began to breathe. She hadn't realised that she was holding her breath but now the sound intruded harshly; a rapid, hectic rhythm. She had killed someone. Murdered someone. And had been condemned to pay with her own life. But . . . she didn't *feel* like a murderess. It wasn't *right*. How had she done it? Poison? A knife? A blow to the skull? She wasn't capable of such things! And who was her victim? What had her motive been? Was she even guilty, or had there been more to the matter; a mistake, or a conspiracy of some kind? Had someone else had a reason for wanting to accuse her, and what could that reason have been?

A faint shiver of lightning came through the shutters and showed a momentary glimpse of Grendon beside her. He was sound asleep, his hair drying patchily and one arm hanging loosely over the edge of the bed. Suddenly panic began to rise in Sefira's mind as she saw for the second time the metal band around his biceps. The crown symbol. Crowns were worn by kings . . . did this mean, then, that Grendon was in service to the ruler of this country? If it did, she was in great danger, for a king's man would be a man of justice and law. And a murderess – her name and description perhaps already posted abroad – was the ultimate lawbreaker.

She must go. Whatever her fear of the storm, the terror of being unmasked was far greater, and if Grendon should have the smallest inkling of her circumstances she had no doubt of his response. She had been condemned once; she would not risk that horror again.

Her clothes lay on the floor where she had discarded them. They would still be wet but no matter. Should she take his horse? She decided against it, for that would give him cause to come after her and, besides, she didn't know whether or not she had ever learned to ride. The storm was further away; the interval between the last flash of lightning and the rumble of thunder that followed had been a long one. She would fare well enough.

Sefira slid from the bed and padded across the floor. A swift backward glance confirmed that her movement hadn't disturbed Grendon; she reached out for her shift.

And froze.

Someone had *spoken*. For a fleeting moment she thought

that the quiet and strangely flat voice had come from outside, that there was a third person in the tower room with them. But that impression was wrong. This had come from within her own mind, and it was speaking to her.

'*Sefi.*' A diminutive of her name. *Why was that voice so familiar?* She raised her head, muscles locking into a tension that she couldn't shake off.

'*Sefi.*'

So briefly that she was unable to grasp it, the image of a face flitted across her inner vision. A girl's face, young, but peculiarly hollow, as if it had no true substance.

'*Sefi.*'

Without knowing why, Sefira turned her head to look at Grendon again. Her eyes had grown used to the darkness now and he was visible as a dim shape in the gloom. His hair looked bleached and colourless. His arm still hung over the bed's edge. Something was happening to her, for she was no longer afraid of him, or of what he might do if he were to unravel her secret. He wasn't an enemy, nor was he her saviour, or even merely a stranger to whom she had taken a dislike.

He was a *victim*.

In her mind, on a level which she could neither comprehend nor combat, the small, toneless voice spoke again.

'*Sefi, I'm hungry. Feed me, Sefi. Strengthen us.*'

Softly, so softly that there was no danger of waking him, Sefira retraced her steps. On a reflexive level she was aware of her limbs moving, of climbing on to the bed and sliding carefully, adroitly across it until she was crouched over his recumbent form. His arm looked pale, limp, *vulnerable*. He was breathing shallowly and evenly, so deeply sunk into sleep that he would not know what was happening until it had begun. And then it would be too late.

'*I'm hungry, Sefi . . .*'

Her fingers curled around Grendon's wrist, lifted it clear of the blanket. Very gently, she lowered her head . . .

Chapter II

The shock ripped Grendon out of sleep, for it was as though his arm had been suddenly and violently plunged into a fire. Dreams smashed into oblivion and with a shout he flung himself upright, twisting with a wild reflex and trying to snatch his wrist clear. But a force he couldn't fight dragged his arm back; whatever had hold of him hung on ferociously, burning, savaging, *devouring*.

In a flicker of lightning through the shutters he saw her. She was a demon, a succubus, hunched over him like a rabid animal as her teeth drove into the flesh of his arm. Her body writhed in mad convulsions and from her throat came a high-pitched snarling sound as she bit harder, deeper, tearing skin and flesh and muscle, seeking the artery and the lifeblood it contained.

And an appalling memory erupted in his mind.

Grendon flung himself from the bed and Sefira went with him, dragged by the impetus. They hit the floor together and with his free arm he tried to knock her away, break her hold. But she clung; her hands, claw like, clamped on his arm and her snarling was rising to an insanely hysterical pitch. They rolled into the middle of the room, and now Sefira's fingernails were slashing for his face, trying to tear at his eyes and blind him. Grendon twisted again and gained his feet; as he came upright she was a solid, struggling weight on his arm and he felt wet heat spill over his hand. He couldn't shake her off; his arm was numb and she was shrieking now, the sound hideously distorted by the blood that filled her mouth. He heard her

22

bare feet scrabbling on the floor's planking; instinctively he knew that she meant to gain the advantage by pulling him off balance towards her, and that if she succeeded there would be a split second movement, a darting, and the teeth that now were ripping into his arm would fasten on his throat.

A few moments' forewarning and he would have known what to do – but there had been no warning, and physical resources were all he had to save him. Pain eclipsed the numbness suddenly, shooting from his wrist to his shoulder and making him swear obscenely, and Grendon knew he had only one chance. His free hand clenched into a fist and – in all his life he had never hit a woman in such a way, but this creature wasn't a woman any longer and the instinct to survive was and had always been far, far stronger than any principle – he drove it straight into her contorted, demented face.

The flesh of his arm tore as Sefira's head snapped back, and he saw a spray of blood – his blood – fly from her mouth in the instant before she went spinning from him. Her hands flailed uncontrollably as the force of the blow flung her across the room; then she hit the far wall and collapsed.

Stillness clamped down on the tower as Grendon stared at her. He was swaying on his feet and could hear his blood spilling on to the floor, a steady and unpleasant sound. On a subliminal level he expected her to move suddenly, to revive and come at him again with redoubled ferocity. But she didn't. She lay motionless, unconscious. And her face, reddened by the impact of his fist, looked like the face of a helpless child.

Abruptly he came to his senses. Her teeth had torn deeply into his arm and the bleeding was serious. Grendon's hands shook as he tore a strip from the bed's single sheet, and by the time he had managed to bind the wound, the strip and both hands were crimson. But the makeshift bandage stemmed the flow; though vicious, the damage hadn't gone too deep. He had stopped her in time.

Trying not to flex the injured arm and at the same time to convince himself that pain was irrelevant, he moved slowly across the room and stared down at Sefira. If the force he had put into the blow was any indication, he doubted if she would come to for a while; time enough to clean her up and remove the evidence of what had happened. If he was right about this – and there was little room for doubt in his mind – then when she woke she would remember nothing. And for reasons of his own, Grendon didn't want her to glean any idea of the truth.

He started to dress, and was fastening his belt when outside, carrying on the sullen aftermath of the wind, he heard a sound. The hairs at the nape of his neck prickled; quickly he crossed to the window and wrested the stiff shutter open.

Rain blew in but it wasn't the downpour of a few hours ago, only a damp spatter accompanied by a rush of chilly air. Daylight hadn't yet come, but a cold, pre-dawn glimmer on the eastern horizon gave a pearly cast to the sky; enough to show the dim contours of the moor and, closer by, the hard-trodden earth at the base of the tower. Around the tower, something was moving.

For perhaps ten seconds Grendon watched the shadow that flickered subtly, indefinitely near the tower's base. Its movements were like the fluttering of an aberrant black moth, and he knew that it hadn't yet found the direction of what it sought, for it was casting about blindly, randomly, unsure of itself and its surroundings. Its shape was unstable; it was too weak as yet to have corporeal form and it still hovered on the borderline between worlds. But it had been drawn unerringly to the tower. And its presence gave Grendon all the confirmation he needed.

Glancing again at the girl to ensure that she was not stirring, he pressed the palms of his hands together, concentrating his mind and closing his eyes. A small, hard point of fire sprang into being at the core of his inner vision, hurting momentarily as it always did; he focused on it, willed it to become brighter, fiercer, brought it under his control . . .

The thing below shuddered, and, mingled with the whistle

of the wind, he heard a faint, peculiar sound, a mewl of anger and frustration. Gathering mental strength Grendon thrust a wave of energy at it, pushing it back into the dark dimension whence it came and adding a savage injunction that he hoped would deter it from trying to return. At least, for the present.

He opened his eyes again in time to see the shadow fade and flick out. A sudden resurgence of the wind threw a flurry of rain into his face; he blinked it away, closed the shutters, then let out a sharp breath and turned to look at the unconscious girl again. This was a development that he could not have foreseen in any nightmare. Another one. And after so many years.

He suppressed a shudder. Whatever memories the revelation conjured, the fact was that fate had dealt him a potentially invaluable hand tonight. Fate also had a sardonic sense of humour, but that was something he had learnt to expect. This girl, whether she knew it or not and whether she liked it or not, would be useful to him. And he intended to make sure that she had no choice in the matter.

'I remembered . . .' But then the words trailed off confusedly and Sefira opened her eyes to find Grendon crouching over her.

Instantly her body snapped taut, and a reflexive thrust of one heel sent her sliding backwards and away from him with a quick, defensive movement.

'What are you doing?' Her voice wasn't steady.

Grendon sat back on his heels. 'Ah. You're conscious.'

Conscious? What did he mean? What had happened? She realised then that the entire left side of her face ached ferociously, and when she put a hand up to feel her cheek she flinched as she felt the bruising.

'Did I . . . ?' But no, she hadn't fallen. This was something else. *Something else.* But she couldn't remember. Her last recollection was of waking suddenly, sitting up in the unfamiliar bed in the unfamiliar room with lightning still flaring intermittently through the shutters. A piece of her lost memory had snapped back into place. And then . . .

'You . . .' Hostility saturated the word as her mind started to jump to a conclusion, then fury flared in her look. '*You tried to rape me!*' For all his disparaging comments and professed uninterest, he must have woken when she did – or more likely been lying awake, awaiting the right moment – and he had assaulted her. She had resisted, they had fought, and . . .

Well, he must have hit her hard enough to knock her senseless for several minutes at least. Her aching face was proof of that. He had lost his temper, no doubt, when she had refused to let him have what he wanted from her, and the blow had perhaps been more violent than he had intended.

Or perhaps not.

She said a word that she thought she must have learned in a gutter, injecting it with all the venomous disgust she could summon. Grendon had risen to his feet and was standing by the bed, his back towards her, and Sefira sent a mental flare of loathing that she hoped he would feel like a knife in the spine. His only reaction was to fold his arms, but if she could have seen his expression Sefira would have been surprised. He was relieved. While he had cleaned the blood from her mouth and waited for her to regain consciousness, he had asked himself how he would explain what had happened to her and what he had been obliged to do, and had been unable to find a plausible answer. Unwittingly, Sefira had come to his rescue by jumping to an entirely wrong conclusion; that she should think what she did offended Grendon's pride, but in the circumstances pride took second place to pragmatism.

He said coldly, 'Whatever I might or might not have *tried*' – he gave the word a derogatory emphasis – 'to do, you're unsullied. And don't fear that any such thing will happen a second time, for I assure you that it won't.' No; for next time he would have enough warning to stop the seizure before it was beyond her control. He would make very sure of that.

Slowly Sefira stood upright. What he said was true, she realised; he might have hit her but he had done nothing worse. She would have been able to tell. Surely she would?

Watching him covertly and suspiciously, alert for some further mischief, she reached for her clothes and pulled them on. As she wrapped the cloak, which was still damp and unpleasantly clammy, around herself he turned at last, abruptly.

'Where do you think you're going?'

Sefira laughed, a short, derisive bark. 'Where am I *going*? Away from this place, of course! Away from you!'

She started towards the door, and had taken two paces when Grendon stepped into her path.

'You,' he said, 'are doing no such thing.'

She stared back at him, outraged. On a detached level it occurred to her that, realistically, if he meant to force her to stay she would have no choice in the matter. He was far taller and stronger than she was, and recent events had proved he had no scruples whatever. But she pushed that reasoning away down a dark well in her mind and said defiantly, 'I said I'm leaving, and I mean it. Don't *dare* try to stop me!'

He interrupted her. 'You mistake me, lady. I have no intention of staying here either; my business has already been disrupted for long enough by this little interlude. But when I leave – which I intend to do as soon as possible – you're coming with me.'

'*No*,' she said.

'Yes.' Then Grendon's mouth twitched with amusement. 'And there's no need to look at me as if I was both mad and dangerous. I'm neither, so unless you push me beyond the limits of my patience, you'll come to no harm. But I won't take any argument from you. I intend to find out who you are and where you come from. And until I can do so, logic suggests that you'll be considerably safer in my company than roaming the countryside alone and unprotected.'

Sefira thought that logic didn't suggest anything of the kind.

27

Perhaps her fear of him was unjustified in one sense. But she had every justification for the other, greater fear – that if she went with him to any town or settlement, he was sure to discover the appalling truth which had come so suddenly and shockingly back to her during the night.

'Thank you for your concern,' she said with a caustic smile, 'but I shall manage perfectly well alone. And after . . .'

'After what?' Grendon prompted.

She looked away angrily. He knew very well what she meant and she wasn't going to give him the satisfaction of hearing her say it aloud.

'I'm going now.' She met his gaze again, though it was an effort to hold it. 'Kindly get out of my way.'

'I'll do no such thing.' Grendon watched her steadily. 'And I don't think you're in any position to argue with me, my lady, for one very good reason.'

Ah, yes; that quick glimmer of apprehension. She thought she had disguised it soon enough, but she was wrong. She *had* remembered something, and as she regained consciousness had almost given it away. Her fear that he would find her secret out was far greater than her dread of any more immediate danger, and that, in conjunction with the blatant sign that she didn't even realise she displayed, was enough to allow Grendon to gamble.

'Do you know,' he asked her, 'why your hair has been cropped?'

Sefira looked at him warily. 'No . . .'

'I thought not. Well, I'll tell you. The hair of certain felons is cropped as a matter of course once guilt has been established and sentence pronounced. It's a convenient and practical measure when preparing the convicted person for execution.'

Before she could stop herself Sefira put a hand to her mouth. 'Ah no—'

'Ah *yes*.' Grendon stepped towards her. 'That's what you've remembered, isn't it? You're a criminal. And, by one means or another, you've escaped from justice.'

She couldn't deny it; she had given herself away and any pretence now would be a pointless exercise. But even if he knew a part of her story he could only guess at the greater detail. There *was* a chance to evade the whole truth, and she turned her head aside.

'I don't know what my crime was. Perhaps I merely stole food, or . . .'

He broke in. 'In this country only two crimes carry the death penalty, even now. One is treason, and the other is murder.'

On a subliminal level she took in the cryptic words *even now*, but consciously they didn't register; she was too terrified to think of anything beyond his obvious implication.

'Which was it?' he asked. A pause. 'There's no point in pretending that you don't understand. I know you do.'

Hope withered. He was right; she could gain nothing by trying to lie. In a small, crushed voice she said, 'Murder.'

Grendon nodded. 'Who, how, and when?'

'I don't know.' Sefira's lower lip trembled, then her head jerked up and her expression mingled defiance and angry appeal. 'I don't even know if I *did* kill anyone. All I remember is that I was being taken to . . . to . . .'

'To the stake.' He saw her quick, shocked reaction and added, 'Burning is the usual method, and these days it's a popular public spectacle, so doubtless you were being taken to one of the more sizeable towns in this district. Chalce possibly, or Emelian. Or even' – something odd flickered momentarily in his eyes – 'Tourmon itself.'

'Tourmon . . . ?'

'The king's city.'

Sefira shivered but didn't speak. For a few moments more Grendon continued to look at her with a thoughtful, calculating steadiness which unnerved her further. Then he said,

'I should, of course, return you to the custody of the justices so that your sentence can be carried out. As a king's man – oh yes, I saw you look uneasily at my device, and now I know

29

why – that is my duty. Not to mention the fact that no one in their right mind would savour the prospect of a dangerous criminal left loose to wreak whatever further havoc might take her fancy.'

'I didn't wreak—'

'You apparently haven't the least idea of whether you didn't or whether you did,' he interrupted. 'But the law is the law, and it is adamant. If you want to escape the fate ordained for you – and I assume you do – then you have only one option, and that is to comply with my wishes.'

'Your wishes . . . ?' Sefira was baffled.

'Yes. For reasons which I have no intention of explaining to you at present, I don't think justice would be served by your execution. I can keep you alive – but only if you put yourself entirely in my hands.' Suddenly a smile, hard as before but with an underlying strangeness that she couldn't begin to interpret, curved his mouth. 'In other words, a bargain. My protection in exchange for your compliance. I'm offering to be your salvation a second time. And it's an offer that I don't think you're in any position to refuse.'

They left the tower under a pale, watery sky made colder by a sharp north wind. Sefira rode pillion behind Grendon; the saddle wasn't designed for two riders, and to have any modicum of comfort she was forced to press close against his back, which she resented. But she didn't complain. Under the circumstances, she couldn't afford to antagonise him.

I'm offering to be your salvation a second time. Fine words; but, as he had said, it was an offer that she was in no position to refuse. Impotent anger filled Sefira as she thought how easily she had been trapped. One paltry clue: her hair. Were there no other circumstances in which a woman's hair might be cut short? Presumably not, or Grendon wouldn't have jumped so easily to the right conclusion about her. Unless, of course, he had simply gambled on a guess; in which case she had fallen straight into the trap.

She pushed her thoughts down and tried to distract herself by concentrating on the countryside around them. In daylight, and with the sun breaking weakly through, it was a very different prospect from the black mayhem of the previous night. True, there was a bleak and grim edge to those unending and featureless acres of flat moor. But the colours of the moor were soft and subtle – purple, gold, and many, many shades of green mingling and blending with them to form a misty patchwork. Far in the distance, to the west judging by the angle of the sun, a range of mountains showed pinkish-grey and bare. They looked a formidable barrier, and she wondered if they marked the boundary of this kingdom. But when she searched her mind for any snippet of knowledge, there was nothing.

It surprised her, however, to find that she knew the names of the moorland plants. Heather, gorse – near the end of flowering, for its gold was faded and dull – whin, sedges, and a tall tough grass called cockaigne which something told her was particularly favoured by horses. Strange, to recall petty details; but she reasoned that, perhaps, such knowledge was a little like the knowledge of language. She hadn't lost her understanding of speech, so presumably there were many other fundamentals which her memory still retained.

Intrigued and a little heartened by that, she started to search through her mind for familiar things, compiling a small mental list. She was engrossed and had all but forgotten her dilemma when Grendon suddenly spoke.

'You'll need to change your appearance.'

'What?' She lifted her head.

'I said, you'll need to change your appearance. Anyone who sees you as you are now will take one look at your hair and draw the obvious conclusion. So it must be hidden.'

Sefira frowned. 'Why should that pose a problem? Do women not cover their hair?'

'Only certain women.' He twisted round to look at her, the unexpected movement almost pushing her backwards out of the saddle. 'Married women.'

Sefira stared back. 'You're saying I should pretend to be your wife?'

'Yes.'

'I'll do no such thing!'

'You will, if you don't want to create more trouble for yourself than either of us can cope with.' He smiled coldly. 'Don't worry. I won't expect you to play the role to the full.'

She made a sound of disgusted scepticism. 'Oh, won't you? After last night—'

'Last night was an aberration.' Grendon still didn't feel at all comfortable with her assumptions, but – *ah, damn it*, he thought; *let her believe what she pleases. There are more important matters at stake*. 'This is simply the most practical means I can think of to ensure your safety. However, if you have a better suggestion I'd be interested to hear it.'

She shrugged resentfully, aware – as he was – that she had no suggestions at all, yet still determined not to capitulate entirely. 'Why should I pretend to be *your* wife? Why not your married sister; a widow, maybe?'

'Because people ask questions. Fall into any company – which we will, it's unavoidable – and before long you'll find yourself the subject of well-meant enquiries about your husband, your family, your home, your background. You won't be able to answer the questions, that will arouse suspicion, and—' He drew one finger malevolently across his own throat, making further words unnecessary.

Sefira thought he was exaggerating, but nonetheless the point went home. She averted her gaze and Grendon added, 'As my wife you won't be expected to say anything; all the friendly questions and small-talk will be directed to me.'

She scowled. 'So I simply play the part of the meek woman.'

'Precisely. Smile and nod, give me an adoring look once in a while' – he ignored her snort – 'and keep a still tongue. It shouldn't be that great a blow to your pride.'

Sefira only curled her lip in reply and Grendon turned his attention to the track ahead once more. The look of the moorland was changing, Sefira saw, as the sun climbed and the cloud cover began to break up in earnest; swathes of light and shadow moved across the landscape, brightening some colours, dulling others. And the land was sloping gently but perceptibly downwards now. In fact, if she screwed up her eyes and looked hard, she thought she could glimpse a thin shimmer of water far in the distance, winding like a dormant snake towards the mountains. A river, then. Rivers meant towns, civilisation. People. A shiver went through Sefira as for the first time the reality of her situation, and her dependence on Grendon's goodwill, truly came home to her. Her fate, as he had taken no pains to hide, lay entirely in his hands, and the full comprehension of her own vulnerability lodged queasily in her stomach. Something close to panic flickered like a small, hot flame, and—

'*Sefi. I don't want . . .*'

Sefira started violently and blackness slammed briefly across her eyes as the words skimmed through her head like a sudden, cold breath. *That voice! What*— But it was gone, vanished, as if it hadn't happened. She felt the skin of her face tingling with shock, knew instinctively that she had paled. Then her eyes refocused and she saw that Grendon had turned in the saddle and was looking hard at her.

'What's the matter?' he demanded. His voice sounded uneasy; Sefira swallowed, and caught an unpleasant taste at the back of her mouth.

'N . . . nothing. Just a . . .' Then she shook her head, neither able nor willing to explain. Had she heard it at all? She couldn't even remember, now, what its tone had been or what it had said; all she recalled was one word: *Sefi*. A variation, almost affectionate, of her name. It didn't make *sense*.

Grendon was still staring, and his eyes were cold with suspicion. 'If you've remembered something—' he began.

'I haven't.' She heard the defensiveness in her own voice and struggled to overcome it. 'It was just a feeling, as if – as if I was about to. But I couldn't grasp it, and now it's gone.'

She could see that he didn't believe her, and he had opened his mouth to press her again when suddenly a high, distant wail sounded from behind them. Grendon's head jerked up; he looked back and in shock Sefira looked too.

A coach drawn by four horses was heading towards them along the track. Though still far off it was moving fast and would overtake them within minutes; Sefira could make out the figures of two men on the driving box, and as she watched, one man lifted a horn to his lips. The warning wail rang out again, and Grendon's fingers took a ferocious hold of her shoulder.

'Pull your cloak over your hair! *Quickly!*'

Terror struck her and she scrabbled to obey, dragging the damp fabric up and close around her face.

'Don't speak,' Grendon said curtly. 'Not a word, even if you're addressed directly. You don't yet know enough to be trusted.'

Her heart thumped. 'They might not stop.'

'They will.' Now the rumble of hooves and wheels was audible; Grendon was guiding his own horse off the track to allow the coach room to pass, and Sefira saw that it was already beginning to slow down. The second man on the box was drawing something from the well at his feet, and metal glinted as he laid it across his lap. A weapon of some kind . . .

Grendon's horse whinnied loudly and the leading coach horses answered. A voice shouted, '*Ho-aaa!*' and the rattling bulk drew level with them and came to a halt. Peering surreptitiously through lowered lashes, and keeping a tight grip on her makeshift hood, Sefira saw the two men sweep suspicious gazes over them. Then the coachman extended an arm, displaying something in the palm of his hand, and said curtly, 'Facilitant; licensed from Emelian. What's your destination and business, travellers?'

Sefira could smell the sweat of the horses and she tried to concentrate on that rather than looking at the coach, which was big and dark and had curtained windows and made her think of another closed carriage with another, more brutal purpose. She heard Grendon reply, 'We're for Chalce, and our business is private.' Then, as though as an afterthought, he added carelessly, 'Communicant,' and let his cloak fall back far enough to reveal the device on his arm.

The driver's tone and manner changed instantly. 'Your pardon, sir; I didn't realise.' Grendon nodded lofty acknowledgement, and the man continued, ingratiating now, 'It'll please you to hear then, sir, that there's another Sanctified been found in Chalce. The news was abroad yesterday, before I started my homeward run, and the Purging's to take place in three days.' He paused. 'As an Arraigner, sir, I thought you'd wish to know.'

'Your diligence is appreciated,' Grendon said, then glanced at the coach. Someone inside was coughing loudly. 'How many passengers do you carry?'

'Six, sir, all vouched at Emelian. If you wish to—'

'No, no; it's not necessary. I'll detain you no longer; good speed and the king's peace to you all.'

'The king's peace, sir. And thanking you.' The reins twitched, the horses started to move and the coach gathered speed along the road ahead.

Sefira, staring mutely after the dwindling vehicle, was about to let her cloak slide down from her head, but Grendon snapped, 'Leave it. The guard's looking back and his kind have eyes like eagles.' He touched his heels to the horse's flanks; it started to follow in the coach's wake, and silence fell between the two riders.

For perhaps a minute Sefira watched Grendon's shoulders. They were tense; in fact he radiated tension, and that she didn't understand. They had been safe enough; the coach driver had not suspected her secret. Why, then, was he still uneasy?

She mulled over the brief conversation that had taken place, and focused on the terms and names she had heard. Emelian and Chalce were towns, she knew, for Grendon had mentioned them before. But other words were unfamiliar. And two in particular had aroused her curiosity.

She said suddenly, 'Why did you say "Communicant" to the driver? What did it mean?'

There was a slight but noticeable pause before Grendon replied, 'When strangers meet, the protocol is for each to announce his Fellowship. The driver is a Facilitant; I am a Communicant.' Another, briefer pause. 'As are you while you're masquerading as my wife, so I'd advise you to memorise the word.'

He had spoken of Fellowships when they first met, Sefira recalled, and she asked what they were and what they meant. But Grendon shook his head impatiently. 'I'll explain later, when we stop for the night. I'm not in the mood for a long discourse now.'

Silence fell again. The horse plodded stoically on and the sun was in Sefira's eyes, making them water. Then she asked, 'Is Arraigner another Fellowship?'

He sighed to show that he found her persistence irritating. 'No. Arraigner is an office, not a Fellowship; Arraigners are king's men, and that transcends any other considerations.'

'Must I pretend to be an Arraigner?'

'No. There are no female Arraigners. Women are too compassionate – and too squeamish.'

A worm of disquiet shifted in Sefira. 'Squeamish? Then what does—'

Grendon interrupted, at the same time giving her a quick, sour glance over his shoulder. 'I told you, I'm not in the mood for discourses. I don't want to answer any more questions, so hold your tongue.'

Sefira wetted her lips. She had obviously touched a raw nerve, but for all his intimidating tone she wasn't willing to let the subject drop.

She said: 'What's a Sanctified?'

Instantly the atmosphere between them was spiked with a tension so palpable that she could almost have grasped it in her hand. She heard Grendon draw in his breath, then he pulled sharply on the reins, bringing the horse to a halt, and twisted round in the saddle until he was facing her directly.

'There is only one thing,' he said ferociously, 'that you need to know about the Sanctifieds, and that is that they and their ways are anathema to any living soul who values his life and his future. Fear them, hate them, and never stint in declaring the depth of your hatred to everyone you meet.' He waited to see that the message had sunk in. 'Do you understand?'

She didn't, but saw that this time any further argument would lead to real trouble. So she said, 'Yes.'

'Good. Then have the sense to pay heed.'

He slapped the reins viciously against the horse's withers and, with a snort of protest at the rough treatment, it moved on. Sefira stared at the moorland, but its bleak, shifting beauty didn't register in her mind. She had learned a few salient facts. But the knowledge she had gained was far outweighed, now, by new enigmas. And the answers to those were, she suspected, far more complex – and possibly far more dangerous – than she could yet begin to imagine.

Chapter III

The road turned eastward with the river which Sefira had earlier seen in the distance, and for some time they followed the valley of the sullen, murky-brown current, into countryside that, though lusher than the moorland, had little else to commend it. Reeds and sedges replaced the heather; the ground was growing softer and within a few miles the river began to encroach on the land in small but treacherous-looking creeks and pools. At last they reached a low, stone-built pack bridge. Ruts and hoof prints showed where others had taken this route before them and they crossed over the river and began to follow the track to higher ground on the other side.

The wind had changed, and as they rode along the crest of the valley slope it blew in their faces, bringing a sharp and unpleasant chill that made Sefira shiver and huddle deeper into the folds of her cloak. She was hungry, uncomfortable and bored. For the past five hours Grendon had spoken only to the horse, and she had no intention of sparking further hostilities by addressing him if he didn't choose to address her first. So there was nothing to do but endure the hollow feeling in her stomach, and the increasing ache in her back and thighs, and try to glean what little information she could from her surroundings.

This higher land, she realised, was farming country of a sort, for flocks of sheep wandered on the scrubby grass and buildings were visible in the middle distance to her left. But everything had an air of desertion. The buildings were dilapidated; several had no roofs, just rafters protruding stark and bare to the sky. The sheep, pausing in their grazing to stare with witless yellow eyes at the passing strangers, looked unkempt and untended. Though there were traces of burning on some areas of ground, there was no sign of any human presence. It was as if, Sefira thought, the entire district had been abruptly abandoned and everything in it left to fall into decay. And nothing about it stirred the smallest whisper of familiarity in her vanished memory.

The sun was westering and losing the last of its warmth when Grendon abruptly turned the horse off the road. Sefira was by this time half dozing in the saddle, and her eyes opened with a start as she heard and felt their mount's change of stride from earth on to uneven turf. Blinking, she stared around her and saw that they were following a grass track, overgrown but still just visible. And at the far end of the track was a house.

Unconsciously her hands tightened on Grendon's waist, and he must have felt the movement and known the reason for it, for he broke his silence and said, 'There's no need for that. The house is empty.'

Relief vied with another kind of trepidation. 'Then why—'

'Because the next available shelter is the town of Chalce, and it wouldn't be sensible to take you there until you're better disguised. We'll find all we need here; we'll stay the night and continue on in the morning.'

This made sense and Sefira's apprehension subsided. The house, she realised as she peered around Grendon's back, was large and had clearly once been the home of someone wealthy. But as they drew nearer she saw that of the two wings only one still stood intact; the larger wing was a burned out shell of blackened stone and timber, and the well-tended courtyard that had once fronted the place was choked with rubble in which weeds ran riot.

She said, half to herself, 'The sheep, and the barns . . . does no one live in this district any more?'

Grendon hesitated, and she thought that he was going to

respond with another curt order to hold her tongue. But after a few moments he said indifferently, 'This area was one estate, belonging to one family.'

'What happened to them?'

'They were executed for treason last year.'

A cold shaft went through her. '*All* of them?'

'Vipers breed vipers, and in matters of treason the guilt of one is the guilt of all. Especially in a time of war.'

That came as a greater shock, and Sefira echoed '*War . . . ?*' She hadn't known, of course. Irrational to think that she could have done. But the depth of her ignorance made her feel suddenly more vulnerable than ever. Who had fought whom? What had been the cause of it? Which side had triumphed – or had there as yet been no victory, and did the fighting still continue? The questions boiled in her mind as they rode up to the smashed wall that marked the courtyard's boundary, but she couldn't find the words with which to ask them. Past the wall, then they stopped in a wilderness of withering vegetation; the damaged house stared blindly down at them, a dead, empty hulk that seemed to bring the cold of evening suddenly closer.

Grendon slid from the saddle with a grunt of relief, but Sefira sat where she was, staring.

'Come on,' he said sharply, 'I want to get a fire lit before nightfall.'

She didn't move. 'Is the war over now?'

'It's been over for nearly two years.'

Nearly two years . . . 'Then the family who lived here . . . they were executed afterwards?'

'Yes.' Grendon's voice was becoming more impatient.

'They were the king's enemies.' At last she looked at him, a strange, searching look. 'So they must have been your enemies, too.'

'Of course.'

She paused. 'Did you know them?'

Grendon's eyes narrowed angrily. 'No, I did not. And if

you're now asking yourself how in that case I know so much about the fate of this house and its occupants, the short answer is that it's my business to know. It's a necessary part of my work. Now, will you get down from that horse before the wind cuts all three of us to ribbons?'

She still didn't move but continued to look at him. 'What do you really want with me?' she said softly.

'Oh, by all that's—' Grendon cut the rest of the oath off and sighed exasperatedly. 'I *want* nothing. I've told you before: I merely think there's more to your supposed crime than meets the eye, and I intend to find out the truth.'

'For the sake of justice.'

'Precisely.'

'I don't believe you.'

Grendon felt his temper tipping over the brink. 'Then invent another motive and believe that, if it satisfies you! I've said all I'm prepared to – and I've also told you your choices. Stay with me, or walk away and court certain disaster. But kindly decide *now*.'

For perhaps five seconds his eyes and Sefira's locked combatively. Then, as he had expected, she looked away, set her mouth in a tight little line and slid reluctantly down from the saddle.

He said: 'Go into the house and look for dry wood.' She hesitated and he added, 'Don't worry; the cleansing was thorough. There's no one, human or ghost, lying in wait.'

She shot him a look of cold hostility, then walked towards the broken front door as he led his horse towards the empty stables.

With most of its contents destroyed, damaged or gone altogether, the house had the atmosphere of a chill and desolate cavern, but within two hours they had created a comfortable enough oasis within the desolation. Smashed furniture provided ample wood and kindling, and Grendon lit a fire in the grate of an upstairs room that overlooked the courtyard.

Two torn but still usable feather mattresses from an adjoining chamber made beds for them both, and there were blankets in plenty left from the looting or confiscations of the past.

While Sefira prepared the makeshift indoor camp, Grendon killed a scrawny, half-wild fowl from a small flock inhabiting the stables. Sefira found that she instinctively knew how to pluck and draw it, and it was set to roast on a makeshift spit over the hearth. Grendon then found his way to the house's kitchen, searched it and brought back a flask of wine. The smell of it made Sefira's nostrils curl, and when he offered her the flask to drink from she shrank back.

'You don't like wine?' Suddenly there was an odd note in Grendon's voice; as if, she thought, this was some kind of a test and he was anticipating the result.

'I don't know.'

'Then taste it.' He pushed the flask into her hand. 'It might trigger a memory.'

The thought overcame her sense of aversion and Sefira tilted the flask to her lips. The liquid warmed her tongue; it was slightly bitter, but—'

NO!

Sefira dropped the flask and choked on her mouthful of wine, coughing and spitting. Firelight and shadows were momentarily blotted out by blackness; she felt Grendon grab her arm as she lurched sidelong towards the fire, then he slapped her back, hard, to stop the choking, and the echo of the single, ferocious, silent word ran through her head and slid away into nothing.

'Sefira. *Sefira.*' Grendon shook her. 'Open your eyes. Look at me!'

She did, wiping her mouth as the coughing subsided, and he demanded, 'What happened?'

Sefira didn't answer him. Instead she reached out to the flask, righted it – by sheer chance little had spilled – then lifted it up again. Grendon didn't repeat his question but watched like a hawk as she raised it to her mouth. Inwardly,

Sefira was shivering as though with a terrible ague. *Something*, she knew, was trying to stop her from drinking, and a part of her wanted to fight that something with all the strength she possessed. Wild thoughts of grave wights, vengeful spirits of the house, flooded through her mind – but it wasn't that, she knew it wasn't. It was something *else*. Something to do with *herself*.

'*Ahh!*' The sound was almost a gasp of defiance as she forced herself to swallow. In the same moment Grendon felt a sense of oppression close in; a feeling of menace and malice and thwarted anger. The fire spat suddenly and shadows stretched and flickered, and with an old, sure instinct he knew that something else was in the room with them. It couldn't reach them, couldn't make itself tangible, but it was there as surely as they were. It had tried to stop Sefira from touching the liquor, and Grendon knew why. He knew, too, that this was probably the first time in her life that Sefira had defied it. There would be repercussions. He was in no doubt of that.

Sefira lowered the flask and stared at it with a surprised, almost childlike expression that in other circumstances Grendon would have found amusing. Then she said, 'I *think* I like the taste. But I don't remember it.'

Whatever coercion the presence had tried to use against her, she had already forgotten it, and that, Grendon knew, was another sure sign of its influence. He took the flask away, knowing the need for caution at this early stage, and said, 'We'll have more with our meal. It can have a heady effect on an empty stomach if you're not used to it.'

Sefira nodded. The one taste had warmed her and made her feel almost mellow, and the relief of being warm and comfortable, and having the prospect of food, was easing her hostility and her suspicion. Grendon, reading the signs in her face, continued, 'While we wait for the fowl to cook, I may as well tell you some of the facts that you'll need to know from now on.'

A slight frown creased her forehead. 'About Fellowships?'

'Those and other matters.' But not, he appended silently, the single most vital element of all. That he would keep from her for as long as he possibly could.

Mentally, he probed the atmosphere. The oppressive feeling had faded and he thought that the other presence had withdrawn. Not that that left any room for complacency; it was surely aware of him now, and it would have marked him instantly as a potential enemy. Chances were it would try to return when he least expected it. That would pose no problem, for he knew how to protect himself. But vigilance must be his watchword now. Vigilance for himself, and also for Sefira. For if fate had chosen to place such a potentially valuable asset in his hands, he would be worse than a fool if he risked losing it through a moment's carelessness.

Sefira was waiting for him to begin. Her small face within its frame of black hair looked very young and almost painfully innocent. Reminding himself of the power of illusions, Grendon said, 'Very well. I suppose I'd best start with an outline of the war, and of how King Karel came to rule . . .'

Much later, lying with her back to the fire and staring into the dark, Sefira turned the facts she had learnt over and over in her mind. Grendon was stretched out on the other mattress; she thought he was probably asleep by now but didn't want to look at him to make certain. Not that it mattered. He wouldn't make another attempt on her honour, she felt that instinctively. Last night had been an aberration; either that or, disliking her, he had lost his initial interest and preferred now to leave her alone.

So, then, consider what she had learned. The history lesson had been straightforward enough: a country plagued by what Grendon called injustice and inequity, ruled by an old dynasty which for generations had taken the greatest care to keep power in the hands of a small, hereditary and self-serving elite. Grendon had spoken of the old regime with fine contempt, using terms such as 'corruption', 'avarice', 'decadence'; Sefira had no opinions on the rights or wrongs of it all, but his rhetoric was certainly impressive, if at times, she thought, a little glib.

Then had come the rebellion. It was led, he said, by a landowner from the south-western territory, who in youth had trained and served with the king's own militia and become greatly disillusioned as a result. He quickly became a popular figurehead, and within a year of his rise to popularity outright civil war had begun.

The war lasted for three years, and at last the rebels triumphed. The old king, besieged with his few remaining loyal followers in the city of Tourmon and knowing that his cause was lost, poisoned his wife and children before taking his own life, and with his fall came the final victory.

The rebel leader, though protesting his unfitness and unwillingness to rule, was swept to power on a tide of jubilation as champion of the common people, installed in the royal residence, and offered the crown. For half a year he refused to accept it. He was no king, he said. His title would be, simply, Elector, and the idea of dynasties would be consigned to the past where it belonged. But – and Grendon had smiled an odd, almost bitter smile at this – for all the changes that the war had wrought, old habits died hard. The people in whose name the battles had been fought and won had lived through three years of upheaval and confusion. Now, they wanted the comfort and reassurance of familiarity, and those closest to the new leader urged him to listen to what was being said in the towns and villages and farms. What did a title matter? they argued. Elector or King; it made no difference to the man behind the name. It made no difference to his ideals, nor to his plans for reform. If the people truly wanted a king, was it right to deny them their wish? So at last the Elector gave way, and as the next spring came and the crops began to grow, King Karel was crowned with great ceremony at Tourmon, and the entire land celebrated.

Sefira had listened carefully as Grendon spoke, taking in every detail and hoping that something in the story he told would bring a recollection to mind. She was disappointed; there was no sudden jolt of memory, nothing familiar, nothing to recognise. It was as if, for her, the world and everything about it had only begun to exist during the thunderstorm on the moor.

Then, as she tried to disregard her frustration, Grendon had told her about the Fellowships; which were, it seemed, the one immutable fact in the life of every man, woman and child in the land. Or rather, they had been until King Karel came to power.

Everyone, Grendon had told her, was born into a Fellowship, and that Fellowship dictated all major aspects of their lives, from the trades they were permitted to follow to the marriages they were permitted to make. The child of Artisan parents had no choice but to become a stonemason or wheelwright or metalsmith or some other Artisan calling; the law simply did not allow him to work outside the bounds of his own Fellowship. Nor could he marry outside those bounds; an Artisan must wed another Artisan and not a Scholarly or Lander or Creative. High-born or low, Grendon said, it made no difference; each individual must remain in his Fellowship from birth until death, and under no circumstances could it ever be changed. And that principle, set hard as granite in both tradition and law, was one which the new king intended to abolish. The Fellowship system had kept power in the hands of a chosen, hereditary few – now, that would change. And as a loyal king's man, it was Grendon's task to see that those who resisted the change, and sought to bring down the new regime and restore the old, had no chance to put their plans into practice.

The fire was dying now, allowing shadows to encroach further from their corners and into the room. Sefira watched their slow, creeping progress and again tried to push away her feeling of helpless depression. She was as ignorant of the world as a newborn child, and nothing seemed to be capable of stirring her memory into life.

And yet . . . she moved restlessly on the mattress as an unpleasant disquiet squirmed in her. Two things she *was* certain of: her name, and the fact that she had committed murder. Both those snippets of knowledge had come to her unexpectedly and from nowhere – perhaps, then, if she didn't try to force the pace the rest would follow before too long.

But could she be content with that? Already, she thought, there was a strange and unsettling paradox in the little she had learned about herself. On a deep-rooted and instinctive level the idea of killing repulsed her, and she found it impossible to believe that she could be capable of taking another human life. Yet she knew she had done so, and felt no pangs of guilt or remorse. *Why?* Was her indifference because her memory of the actual deed was lost, or might there be some other reason? Had the killing been an accident? Or had someone made an attempt on her own life, leaving her with only one option if she was to save herself?

Sefira shifted fretfully again, biting back a sigh of frustration at her own impotence. Grendon claimed to suspect that some injustice had been done, but she trusted neither Grendon's honesty nor his motives, and if it wasn't for the fact that he was her only hope of protection from what the law would otherwise do to her she would have left the house and slipped away into the night at the first opportunity. She had no answers, nor any clear instinct of what to do for the best. And there was something else at the back of her mind now; something to which she couldn't give a name but which nagged at her like an aching tooth. It was to do with the wine she had tasted; that much she was certain of. A reaction, a momentary spark of recall; but it had lasted only a moment and now even the memory of how she had felt in that instant was gone. Yet as she stared at the slowly pervading shadows, Sefira felt a chill creep over her that had nothing to do with the dying of the fire. The shadows seemed to call to her, like something familiar yet which had its existence in the hinterland of dreams. If only she could *remember* . . .

Outside the wind was rising, whistling hollowly among cracks in the stonework and rattling a loose pane in the window. Sefira shivered, though not with cold, and wrapped herself more tightly in the blanket that covered her. Whether she could sleep or not she didn't know. But she wanted to try.

She closed her eyes, and tried not to see the shadows' after-images behind her closed lids.

The wind was becoming vicious and was booming in the chimney breast when Grendon woke, but he knew at once that that wasn't what had disturbed him. The fire was out save for a few sulky embers, and the lingering aroma of woodsmoke couldn't mask the less pleasant smell of musty damp that clung to the room. But underlying that, Grendon's nostrils detected another scent, and he was instantly alert.

Sefira was a silhouette in her blanket cocoon, so soundly asleep that there was barely any sound or movement to show that she was still breathing. And around her, faint but discernible, a thin, grey aura hung like mist over water.

Grendon rose slowly to his feet. His purse, which he had kept at his waist, touched the buckle of his belt and clinked noisily, but Sefira didn't stir. That added weight to his suspicion, and he moved carefully closer until he could look down at her face.

Sefira's lips were curved in a smile which would have looked more fitting on an ancient and evil crone than on a young woman barely in her middle twenties. It was a rictus, unnatural and ugly, and to either side of it two spots of feverish colour burned on her cheeks. Her nostrils flared as she breathed, as though with some unconscious excitement, and as Grendon drew close to the aura that surrounded her he felt the temperature of the air drop sharply.

He stepped back, still watching her. He could wake her out of this trance – there was a method – and that would put paid to any potential trouble. But, for the moment at least, he held back. It was possible that the presence might show itself more clearly, and if it did, anything more he could learn about it could prove valuable. So he moved away again, across the room to the tall window. Outside, moonlight diffused through a thin cloud cover cast a dim green haze over the courtyard, enough to show shapes and angles if not detail. For a few minutes Grendon gazed out, watchful for anything untoward, as had happened at the tower. He saw a rat scuttle furtively across the flagstones but nothing else showed itself, and at last he turned back to the room once more.

When he looked at Sefira he saw that her aura had vanished. And a tall, thin shape made of mist and darkness was bending over her.

Grendon froze. The shape was vaguely human but it lacked substance; in the last of the firelight it wavered and shimmered, and the contours of the door were clearly visible through its indistinct outline. But he saw the slender arm that reached out towards Sefira's sleeping face; saw the hand curve and the fingers curl, as though beckoning. Sefira twitched in her sleep and muttered a word that he couldn't catch. The shape bent lower, closer . . . then paused.

Grendon knew it had sensed his presence. He stayed motionless, and after a few seconds that seemed to drag on forever the figure slowly raised its head and looked directly at him.

He had one glimpse of its face, of the deathly whiteness, the colourless lips, the huge, deep-set eyes and the awful intelligence they contained. Then, so fast that he was caught unawares, it flew at him. Grendon jerked back; he had an instant's wild impression of clawing hands, whirling hair, a snarling, demented expression – then, like a blast of wind, it rushed past him and hurled itself at the window. There was no impact, nor even the slightest sound; it simply flowed through the solid wood and glass, and vanished as though the night had sucked it away.

Heart pounding, and inwardly cursing himself for the momentary terror that had made him lose his self-control, Grendon swung to the window and stared down. He thought he saw a shadow flit rapidly across the courtyard, but breaks in the cloud were playing tricks with the moonlight and it was impossible to be sure. Nothing else stirred, and at last, murmuring an imprecation under his breath, he moved back across the floor to look at Sefira again.

The ugly smile and high colour were gone from her face, and she was sleeping peacefully. She had known nothing of the incident, had had no awareness of the visitation, and for that at least Grendon was thankful. Not for her sake, but for reasons of his own. In time, she would find out the truth; it was inevitable. But for now, she remained blissfully ignorant. And that suited his own plans very well.

He returned to his bed and sat down with his back against the warm wall of the chimney breast. Wiser not to sleep now; it was unlikely that there would be any further incidents but safe was better than sorry, and the knack of staying awake without suffering for it the next day was one he knew well. Tomorrow, they would go on to Chalce and Sefira's first significant test. And then Tourmon. The king's city.

Where the *real* work would begin.

Chapter IV

The mirror hung in deep shadow and was cracked right across, but enough of its surface was still intact to show Sefira her own reflection. She stood very still, staring, trying to take in every detail of her appearance – and what she saw appalled her.

She was confronting a total stranger. Not for one moment had she expected to see such a small, sharp face; defined cheekbones, pert nose and full lipped mouth with a quirkish downturn at one corner. Her skin was very pale, and her eyes, deep set and a very dark brown, had a hunted look to them. Perhaps that was just a result of her predicament, but Sefira suspected not.

How old was she? She looked younger than she felt; barely more than twenty, in fact. Turning slowly before the glass and watching the sluggish movement of the clothes that Grendon had found for her, she wondered uneasily if she was too young to pass convincingly as a married woman. This garb looked alien on her small, slight frame; the heavy woollen dress, heavier tunic and cumbersome linen wimple rightly belonged to someone far older. The wimple in particular she loathed; it made a severe mask of her face, and only a few black wisps escaping on to her forehead and cheeks proved that she had any hair at all. But all this was necessary, Grendon had stressed again, when he brought the garments to her shortly after dawn and told her to put them on. She must pretend to be his wife, and she must pretend to like it.

Sefira shivered abruptly as she wondered who had worn

these clothes before her. Stepping into a dead woman's shoes – quite literally, for Grendon had included those too – made her feel unclean, and at the back of her mind was a half-formed fear of retribution from an angered and vengeful spirit. And there lay yet another conundrum, for this fear didn't fit in with the image of herself as a cold-blooded murderess.

A footstep behind her made her turn quickly, and she saw that Grendon had come into the room. He looked her critically up and down, then gave a curt nod of satisfaction.

'You'll pass well enough. Have you memorised what I told you?'

He had given her a brief but thorough lecture this morning on how she must behave when they reached Chalce: what to say and what not to say, whom to speak to and whom to ignore, and an outline of the Communicant Fellowship to which she must feign to belong. Hoping that she could remember at least the gist of it when the need arose, Sefira said, 'Yes,' and then added edgily, 'but I don't like these clothes. And the shoes are too big.'

'Like them or not, you must suffer them until I can find you something more suitable.'

'When will that be? In Chalce?'

'No. We'll stay only a day in Chalce and I've no intention of wasting my time there haggling with merchants. You'll have new clothes in Tourmon, and not before.'

Sefira stood very still. '*Tourmon*? The king's city? Is that where you mean to take me?'

He frowned at her. 'Yes, it is, and there's no call to look so horrified. It's simply a city like any other; the fact that the king is there doesn't give it any special significance.'

'But—' she began.

He interrupted brusquely. '"But" nothing. My home is in Tourmon, my work is in Tourmon; so it's to Tourmon that I'm taking you. In fact you can comfort yourself with the thought that you'll probably be safer there than you would be anywhere else. So kindly stop arguing and get ready to leave.'

For a few seconds Sefira stared at him; misery, anger and uncertainty vying for precedence in her mind. But there was nothing she could do. She was in his hands.

She gave a shrug, and turned away.

They reached Chalce at midday, in foul weather. The rain had begun an hour after their departure, then the wind dropped and they rode in a steady, dismal downpour that quickly turned the road into a morass. The sky was a blank grey bowl, and scarves of darker, thinner cloud scudded beneath it, obscuring the summits of the distant hills and enclosing the landscape in a close, claustrophobic shroud.

Sefira was surprised when she first glimpsed Chalce ahead. It was not the fine city she had anticipated but only a haphazard and sprawling town, uncontained by any wall, which straddled the road as it rose towards the crest of a gentle ridge. Rooftops punctuated by occasional squat towers lay jumbled against the skyline, and spreading out from the town's borders was a patchwork of cultivated fields and allotments.

Two tall wooden poles from which hung limp and sodden banners marked Chalce's official perimeter, and they rode between them on into the heart of the town. Silent and wide-eyed, Sefira gazed at the wooden buildings: houses, stables, barns, small parades where goods were on sale under leather awnings, a larger structure which, from the painted sign outside, she surmised must be an inn; all jostling together in a maze of streets and alleys. The river had curved back from its meandering and now ran past below the town, the gaps between the buildings showing occasional glimpses of its dully gleaming ribbon, with flat, barge-like boats drawn up at a wooden jetty.

And everywhere there were people.

Though reason argued fiercely against it, Sefira couldn't shake off the conviction that every man, woman and child they passed would, if they only looked up, see into her soul and know her secret. She gripped Grendon's belt until her knuckles turned white, struggling not to panic; but no one spared the plodding horse and its passengers more than the briefest of glances. Traders in the parade huddled morosely under their coverings, more concerned with staying dry than with soliciting customers. Those whose business forced them into the open scurried past with heads down and shoulders hunched against the rain, and only once did they have to move aside as a cart laden with wood and drawn by two oxen lumbered past.

The centre of the town was marked by a large square surrounded by taller buildings. Grendon guided the horse towards the wide gateway of a house with a painted sign depicting a bottle and a drinking cup. A wooden board hung beside the gate, and he pointed to it.

'Can you read that?'

Sefira looked. The board bore words, etched in a stylised script.

'"Good wine and the finest food. Rooms let at moderate terms to persons of orderly disposition only,"' She blinked. 'I *can* read.'

Grendon gave a short, sardonic laugh. 'Well, that's a small mercy. It would be hard to pass you as a Communicant if you didn't know your letters. And it's another clue to your background.'

'Is it?' The horse's hoofs clattered hollowly as they passed under the gate, and Sefira had to raise her voice to make herself heard.

'Certainly. If you'd been born a Functional, for instance, you'd never have been taught. It wouldn't have been permitted.'

She frowned. 'That seems very unfair.'

'Which is why the king intends to change it. Now, be quiet – your first test's about to take place.'

They emerged on the far side of the gateway, into the stable yard of the inn. As the horse halted, a boy of about fourteen came running out. He touched a finger to his forelock and took hold of the reins.

'Welcome, sir and lady, welcome! I'll take your horse, sir, I'll tend him, thank you, sir!'

Grendon slid from the saddle and turned to lift Sefira down, but didn't trouble to speak.

'Foul weather sir, but only to be expected this time of the year,' the boy rattled on. 'Go you in, sir, thank you sir, and you too, good mistress, into the dry. Innmaster has a side of beef just delivered and roasting, and—'

Grendon cut him short. 'Give the horse a hot mash, and don't stint when you rub him down.'

'Yes, sir, be assured, sir!' The boy hovered, and Sefira saw Grendon slip something small into the palm of his hand. His eyes lit up and he said, 'Thank *you*, sir! Your servant, sir; king's peace to you and your lady . . .' His compliments faded as, without any further acknowledgement of his existence, Grendon led Sefira away. They reached the side door of the inn and she started to look back, but he nudged her, hard. 'Don't do that. He's a Functional; you're a Communicant. You give him his instructions, tip him, but otherwise you ignore him utterly.'

'What about the innmaster? Is he a Functional too?'

'No. He'll be a Facilitant, or possibly at a pinch even a Mercantile. In either case you're still of a higher station, so treat him with courtesy but don't be over-familiar.'

They entered the building, and as the door closed behind them a sense of warmth and a smell of well-cooked food enveloped them like a thick cloak. There was a buzz of noise in the distance; they followed it along a short corridor and found themselves in the entrance hall. Across the hall another door stood open, allowing Sefira to glimpse a large room – the source of the noise – that seemed to be filled with people.

'That's the taproom,' Grendon told her under his breath. 'Stay away from it; you don't yet know enough to be trusted in there.' He turned to where, on a table, a small metal gong and gavel stood. Picking up the gavel he rapped the gong once, producing an awful and discordant noise that set Sefira's teeth on edge and momentarily stopped the hubbub in the taproom. In the brief silence there was a scuffle of feet, and moments later the innmaster appeared.

Grendon nodded to him and displayed his arm device. 'Communicant,' he said. 'The king's peace to you, innmaster. Do you have a room available for me and my wife?'

The man bowed. 'Mercantile, sir, and the king's peace to you both. We've a choice of rooms, any one of them at your disposal. May I ask how long you mean to stay?'

'Only one night.' With his eyes Grendon indicated the taproom. 'Are there bargers for Tourmon among your customers?'

'Three, sir; and a fourth expected this evening if he keeps his usual pattern.'

'Good. Find the most reliable of them, and tell him I'll see him in the taproom an hour from now.'

'Very well, sir.' The innmaster paused. 'But the Purging, sir . . . it's not set for tomorrow, but for the day after. Won't you need the room for two nights?'

'I shan't be attending the Purging.'

The man looked puzzled. 'But—'

'But you recognised my device and thus assumed that I have official business here,' Grendon finished the sentence for him and smiled thinly. 'Even the king's Arraigners are allowed *some* leave from their duties, innmaster. And as a newly married man I intend to make the most of mine, without allowing official matters to blur my pleasure.'

As Grendon spoke he raised an eyebrow and flicked a knowing sidelong look in Sefira's direction, and the innmaster's face relaxed into a broad grin.

'Of course, sir – I understand you perfectly.' Now he too looked at Sefira, and the lascivious humour in his eyes made her seethe inwardly. She took a grip on her temper, casting her own gaze down, and the man continued, 'I'll take you to your room at once. He gave Sefira another appraising look, and the tip of his tongue touched his lower lip. 'If you'll be so good as to wait one moment while I fetch the key . . .'

The room seemed comfortable enough to Sefira, though Grendon said that there were probably rats in the wainscot. But, for reasons which she couldn't start to fathom, the innmaster's suggestiveness continued to rankle.

'You're overreacting,' Grendon told her dismissively, whilst mentally and privately filing away the clue her attitude gave him. 'Newly married women expect ribaldry from outsiders and learn to ignore it.'

'Then stop pretending that we're newly married,' Sefira retorted. 'I don't like it. It . . . disgusts me.'

Grendon's lip curled. 'Fine sensibilities, for a murderess,' he said, and started to pull off his wet outer clothes.

Sefira slumped on to the bed, feeling ruffled and resentful. Whatever convention might dictate, she couldn't quell the anger that seethed inside her. It felt like a hot cauldron that at any moment might boil over and spill scaldingly in any and every direction. She *despised* the innmaster. *Hated* him. It would give her enormous pleasure to . . .

The vicious urge, which had come shockingly from nowhere, flicked out of existence and left Sefira sitting bolt upright and gaping blindly at the far wall. Grendon had his back to her and hadn't seen the brief lapse, so quickly she lay back and turned on to her side, away from him. *Where had that moment of savagery come from?* Not from within; surely not from within her? She wasn't *like* that. It didn't *fit*.

'What's amiss?' Grendon spoke suddenly, startling her, and she glanced at him before she could stop herself.

'Nothing.' Sefira collected her wits, hoping she didn't look furtive. 'I just . . . feel sick. And my head aches.'

'Unused to travelling or living rough?' He raised his eyebrows. 'Perhaps you're a lady after all.'

'Perhaps I am. In which case you should be more chivalrous.'

Grendon stared at her for a moment. Then he uttered a soft, odd laugh, almost as though her acerbic comment had brought some unexpected thought to mind. But he only said, 'You'll feel better for a bath and a few hours' sleep. I'll have one of the inn girls bring water, and you can have some time to yourself while I see to my business downstairs.'

Surprised by the change of tone, and wondering if he might just have taken her words to heart, Sefira said stiffly. 'Thank you.'

Grendon shrugged, suggesting that her thanks were neither here nor there to him, and left the room.

A thorough wash improved Sefira's mood considerably, and she slept most of the afternoon away. Grendon returned shortly before sunset, and informed her that arrangements had been made for their journey to Tourmon. They were to travel by water, on one of the barges that plied the river carrying cargo between towns; with the autumn rains setting in in earnest the road would be hard going and they would save both time and a great deal of travail. Sefira accepted his decision unconcernedly, grateful only for the fact that there would be no more dreary and uncomfortable horseback hours to endure, and tried not to think about what might await her in the king's city.

They took an evening meal in their room – the beef was excellent but the innmaster's flowery message that he hoped his guests would have a most *pleasant* night brought a brief resurgence of Sefira's irrational anger – and then Grendon pointedly took a pillow and two blankets to make a separate bed for himself on the floor. Sefira sank almost at once into a second deep sleep, and the night passed without incident.

In the morning, the rain had stopped. Grendon predicted that the respite wouldn't last, but for now at least the skies were dry and the square outside no longer awash.

There was a good deal of activity in the square. No market stalls today; instead, men were erecting what looked to Sefira like a wooden tower in the centre of the arena, roughly twice the height of a man. Grendon saw her staring out of the window, and came to see what had captured her attention.

'Ah.' His voice gave nothing away, but she saw a slight frown on his face. 'That. I'd forgotten. Well, we'll be away by noon, so they won't embroil me in the affair.'

'What affair?' Sefira asked.

'The Purging. Or, if you prefer, execution.'

She remembered suddenly what he had said to her about the preferred method of execution, and her face blanched. 'They're going to . . . burn someone?'

'Mmm. But not until tomorrow, so as I say there'll be no need for me to become involved.' He glanced at her. 'And you won't have to see what you so narrowly escaped.'

Sefira shivered violently. 'What crime did the . . . person commit?'

'Murder or treason; I don't know which and I'm not particularly interested in finding out.' Yet something in his voice suggested to Sefira that that wasn't entirely true. And his face . . . a thoughtful look had crept into his eyes, and behind it was a hard edge. His attitude, she told herself, wasn't *quite* as indifferent as he liked to pretend. And she wondered why.

They shared a silent breakfast in their room, then packed up their few belongings and made ready to leave. The innmaster greeted Sefira, when she came downstairs, with a knowing smile; she in turn looked at him and through him and followed Grendon out into the square. She didn't spare a glance for the growing tower, though a number of townsfolk had gathered and were watching its completion, but waited on the wooden pavement while Grendon dumped his saddlebag and went back inside to settle the bill. In one sense only the tower was a welcome presence, for the idlers in the square were more interested in it than in her. Or so Sefira thought, until she saw the brown-haired man, dressed in better clothes than most, watching her from a short distance away.

He was standing outside a small parade of covered shops and stalls, and even when he realised that she had noticed him he made no attempt to hide his scrutiny but instead studied her all the harder. Sefira felt a cold, numbing fear form in the pit of her stomach and begin to crawl towards her heart and brain. The man seemed to recognise her, or at least see something familiar in her appearance. Desperately she told herself that her face was not memorable, that the wimple was a sure disguise and that her terrors had no foundation. But still the man watched. And her fear was taking an ever-increasing hold . . .

Then Grendon reappeared, and at the same moment a woman emerged from one of the shops across the square and moved to join the man. Behind her came a servant carrying several boxes, and the man's attention was distracted as the woman – his wife, presumably – started to show him her purchases. Sefira turned sharply on her heel as Grendon picked up his saddlebag, and said, 'Is the horse ready?'

'It's being brought round.' He paused, frowning. 'Why the sudden haste?'

She indicated the couple across the square with an expressive movement of her eyes. 'That man. He was watching me. Staring.'

Grendon glanced, without seeming to, at the couple. 'The well-dressed one, with the woman?'

'Yes.' She quelled a shudder. 'It was as if he recognised me.'

'Probably just has a roving eye. Nonetheless, we'll leave for the harbour as soon as that stable boy arrives with the horse.' On cue as he spoke, hoofs clattered under the arch beside the building, and Grendon saw Sefira's palpable shiver of relief. 'All right,' he added. 'Walk on my left as we go; you'll be less conspicuous.'

A second tip to the boy brought more effusive thanks, and

they started across the square, Grendon leading the horse. As they passed the now all but completed tower, Sefira's watcher abruptly moved to intercept them.

'Sir. Your pardon.'

Grendon stopped and inclined his head courteously. 'I don't believe we're acquainted, sir.'

'No. No, indeed. But I recognised your arm device, and I – ah – 'The man coughed. 'My name is Perlion; Lander.'The woman had followed him and he touched her arm, encouraging her forward. 'My wife, Isbel.'

'Madam.' Grendon bowed more formally to the woman. 'I am Grendon, Communicant. My wife, Sefira.'

A hot, prickling sensation coursed over Sefira's skin at his use of her real name; then she rationalised it with the thought that doubtless the world held many Sefiras. Taking a grip on her roiling nerves she inclined her head gravely. Where did a Lander rank in the hierarchy? The lessons Grendon had drummed into her had suddenly deserted her when she needed them.

Grendon, however, was unperturbed, and was asking Perlion how he might be of assistance. The Lander smiled self-effacingly.

'It's a trivial matter, but . . . the Purging tomorrow. You will be officiating?'

'No.' Grendon leavened the word with a smile. 'We're leaving now for Tourmon.' He gestured towards Sefira. 'Despite my calling, it's not a spectacle for a woman of gentle sensibilities.'

'Quite . . . quite. My own wife, too . . . we probably won't be attending the actual . . . ah . . .' Perlion was increasingly discomforted, and seemed to be groping for an excuse to continue the conversation. After a few moments' awkward pause he added, 'Tourmon, you said . . . yes. I can't say that I know the city well.You have your home there?Yes, of course; as a king's man . . .' Suddenly he smiled at Sefira. 'I imagine that life in our good ruler's own citadel is a far cry from our modestly rural existence here, mistress. Is that so?'

His eyes, Sefira noticed for the first time, were very dark. And there was a sorrow in them, a sad yet innocent look almost of craving, that unexpectedly touched her. Surprised by her own reaction, she returned his gentle smile and replied, 'It has its charm sir, yes. But so does Chalce.'

He seemed pleased by her answer, and his wife, Isbel, laughed softly. 'Mistress Sefira is a true courtier, I think.'

Whatever it was about her that had attracted the Lander's attention, Sefira realised, Isbel did not share his curiosity. That, she thought, was strange, and she studied the pair more carefully, seeking answers to the conundrum. They were in middle age, both handsome people but not startlingly so. He dark eyed, slightly florid but with an open, generous look; she with blue eyes, hair which under a gauzy wimple looked darker than her husband's, and delicately pale skin. Well-to-do; probably even wealthy. Why, then? *Why* was Perlion so interested in her?

A stilted silence had fallen. Perlion seemed to have run out of conversation, and at last Grendon said, 'Was there some particular reason for your original question, sir?'

'My original question . . . ? Oh – yes, of course . . . No, no; it's of no relevance now. If you're not to be officiating, it's of no relevance.' Perlion clasped his hands together and rubbed the palms vigorously. 'I apologise for detaining you. Good day – the king's peace to you both.'

They bade him a polite farewell and moved on. Sefira could almost feel Perlion's gaze boring into her back, and as soon as they were out of earshot she whispered, 'Well?'

'He was interested in you; no possible doubt of that,' Grendon said. 'But as to why . . .' He shrugged. 'Probably it means nothing. You could have met at some time in the past.'

'Then why did you tell him my name?' Sefira hissed furiously.

He shrugged. 'To see if it provoked a reaction.' A glance at her horrified face. 'Which it didn't. So even if you have met, he obviously doesn't remember it clearly.'

Sefira sucked in her breath. 'That was a *monstrous* risk to take!'

He gave another shrug. 'I used my judgement, and it was accurate. You'll simply have to learn to trust me.'

She said something soft but vicious, in which he caught only the word *arrogant*. It didn't seem worth replying, and they continued on towards the harbour in unfriendly silence.

The barge nosed out from the jetty just before noon, easing into the current and heading north-eastwards with the flow of the river. There were quarters – surprisingly comfortable – for eight passengers in all, and Grendon and Sefira were to share the voyage with a young couple and their baby son. Despite the alarm in the square, Sefira was beginning to gain a little confidence and would have made conversation with their fellow passengers, but Grendon ordered her to feign a headache and stay out of sight in their cabin. He wouldn't explain his reasons to her. But he had witnessed the momentary, rabid look that had crept into her eyes when she saw the child in its mother's arms. A look she was unaware of, but which had said: *so young . . . so fresh to the world, and filled with life . . .* It had shocked him to the core, for it had been more blatant than anything he had anticipated, and it warned him that for all the precautions he might take there were always, *always* dangers, and he must be constantly alert. Thankfully, the child's parents had noticed nothing untoward, and he was able to get Sefira to their deckhouse cabin before any suspicions, her own included, could be aroused. He left her sitting sullenly on the bunk bed, locked the cabin door behind him and walked slowly along the deck to the barge's prow, where he stood staring at the churning brown slide of the water. Two days to Tourmon and sanctuary. He only hoped that he could keep control of her until then.

By mid-afternoon rain had begun again, and this time looked

set to last. In the cabin Sefira slept, but Grendon was restless and divided his time between gazing at the passing landscape from the shelter of a tarpaulin, and pacing from end to end of the barge asking idle questions of the crew. He was well aware that the presence of an Arraigner on board had unsettled them, as if they feared he could see into their minds and would at any moment impeach them for some small breach of law, either in deed or in thought. But he ignored their unease; he was used to such reactions from the low Fellowships, and at this moment had a dire need for the distraction of trivial talk.

He discussed winds and currents with the bo's'n, cargo manifests and the difficulties of maintaining profits in the face of unscrupulous competition with the skipper, and described the glories of Tourmon to a wide-eyed ship's lad who had seen the city from a distance but had thus far never been allowed to disembark there. The Functionals and Facilitants of the crew found it unsettling that their high-ranking passenger should be so affable, but they did their best to hide their disquiet. Times were, after all, changing.

Every so often Grendon would return to the cabin to check on Sefira. She still slept, and he woke her only when a meal was served at sunset. She ate well enough, but there was a distractedness about her that kept him wary. And much later, when night had closed in on the world in a dead, heavy shroud unrelieved by moon or stars, he lit a taper in the darkness, and listened to the slap and rumble of the barge's steady progress. He saw her eyes open and another alien intelligence crawl into them. He saw the hunger buried deep in her sleeping mind, beyond the reach of her knowledge but stronger, far stronger, than any conscious thought. And an old, familiar chill seeped into his bones as he thought of the couple in the adjoining cabin, and their child . . .

The barge had rats. It was inevitable, no matter what steps were taken to eradicate them or how many skippers protested their vessels' cleanliness; and at night they were active, scuttling furtively above and below deck in their ceaseless hunt for food.

Catching and killing one proved easy, and Grendon took it back to the cabin. Sefira was turning and twisting in her bunk, as if in the grip of a nightmare. Pressing her back against the mattress, he pushed the rat's limp corpse into her right hand. Her fingers clenched convulsively on it; suddenly still, she started to make a peculiar little noise that hovered between a whimper and a snarl. Grendon straightened, and backed soft footed across the cabin. For a moment he watched her, watched what she was doing. Then he went out on to the deck, taking the greatest care to lock the door again behind him.

Chapter V

The voyage took a little over two full days. There were no more incidents; the rat, it seemed, had served its purpose well enough in keeping trouble at bay. Sefira knew nothing of what had happened and Grendon took great care not to drop the smallest hint. He had cleaned the blood from her mouth and jaw, consigned the remains of her transgression to the river with no one the wiser, and kept careful watch to ensure that no shadow or mist-like wraith made an unwanted appearance, as had happened at the watchtower and the deserted house. Nothing did come, but he was nonetheless deeply and heartfeltedly thankful when, as a foul grey afternoon gave way to a filthier dusk, the towers of Tourmon loomed out of the murk ahead.

They docked among an assortment of other vessels, at a wharf overshadowed by tall storehouses. Emerging on deck and blinking in the rain, Sefira wrinkled her nose at the mingled stinks of a working port and peered into the gloom, trying to get a glimpse of the city beyond the wharfs. Bar a few glimmering lights between the crowding buildings, however, she could see nothing, so she waited with increasing nervousness while the horse was led from its makeshift stall in the fo'c'sle and they made ready to disembark.

Tourmon was a far busier place than Chalce had been. Lanterns and torches bobbed everywhere on the docks as Functionals, Facilitants, Artisans and other low Fellowships went about their work with a hectic energy that to Sefira seemed like a constant race against time. A few wealthier-looking figures – Mercantiles for the most part, Grendon told her – gathered in twos and threes under the shelter of doorways or awnings, discussing or arguing or exchanging money. A fight between two rough-faced, heavy-booted men was broken up by a bigger stevedore wielding an iron-banded club, and Grendon steered Sefira clear of the scene as other unkempt figures, attracted to the fracas, started to take sides. They left the wharfs behind at last and, with the horse's hoofs echoing between walls, walked down a narrow street – almost an alley – that cut through the jumble of lanes and buildings towards the city proper.

They emerged from the alley into a wide thoroughfare, and Sefira stopped, staring at the scene before her. To the best of her knowledge this was her first sight of Tourmon, and she simply couldn't assimilate it all in the space of a few moments. Noise and bustle; buildings of every imaginable size and shape; horses and carts and carriages; all illuminated to a daylight blaze by torches on long poles set at intervals along the street. And so many people. She had thought Chalce crowded, but this . . . it sent a cold spike of fear through her, filling her, perversely, with a sense of appalling isolation. There was nothing familiar, nothing reassuring in the hum and flurry of activity, and involuntarily she took a step backwards, wanting to shrink into the shadows of the alley once more and not become a part of the tumult.

Grendon glanced at her and said curtly, 'It'll be quieter when we reach the upper district. Get up on the horse; we'll make better progress if we ride.'

She swallowed, nodded, and allowed him to give her a leg-up into the saddle. He mounted in front of her and they forged into the living stream.

It took an hour to reach their destination. Progress was slow at first – this, apparently, was a market day, and the markets traded until midnight – but at last the crowds began to thin, and the torches became fewer, until they were riding in semi-darkness along a road that wound gently but steadily upwards, towards the city's heart.

The buildings here were larger and more affluent than those they had left behind. No stalls or shops now but houses, many with iron bars at the lower windows and some even having a servant with a pike or staff set to guard the door. Sefira wondered why, in a time of peace, such things should be deemed necessary, but when she asked him, Grendon only said that peace was one matter but theft and jealousy quite another, and in an area that housed the wealthiest citizens it was wise to be cautious.

Then ahead of them she saw the wall.

It was built of stone and stood at least three times the height of a tall man. The road divided at its foot, veering away to either side so that the wall effectively blocked any further progress. Braziers burned on its rampart, looking like dull, sluggish eyes in the hissing rain, and by the hot light Sefira saw rows of spikes set into the top of the stonework. Here and there the wall had been damaged at some time in the past, and rebuilding wasn't yet complete, for the gaps were filled in by rough wooden palisades. In one such palisade was a makeshift postern gate, and to Sefira's alarm Grendon rode towards it.

Her fingers clenched on his waist. 'What is this place?' she demanded shrilly. 'Where are you taking me?'

'Keep your voice down!' One hand knocked her grip loose and Grendon shot her an angry look over his shoulder. 'And calm yourself. You've nothing to fear, provided you do exactly as I tell you.'

Sefira's heart had started to pump painfully. Licking her dry lips, she said, quietly but urgently, 'But this place—'

'Is the royal quarter.'

Panic surged in her. '*Where the king lives?*'

'I said, keep your voice *down*! Yes, it is where the king lives, just as the old king and countless other kings lived here before him! There's nothing arcane about it; it's simply safer and more secluded than anywhere else in Tourmon. And as well as containing the royal palace, it also houses everyone who works for the royal court. In other words, it's where I live, too.' Another sour glance. 'Satisfied?'

She wasn't, but they were too close to the gate now for her to say so. Two men wrapped against the weather in heavy hide cloaks were stationed at the postern, warming their hands at a brazier; as the horse approached one of them moved to intercept it.

'The king's peace, sir. What's your business?'

Grendon displayed his arm device, then drew a small, tightly rolled scroll from his purse and held it out. The guard took it back to the brazier, inspected it in the flickering light then brought it back. 'Thank you, sir.' His companion was opening the gate, the rain-swollen wood grating back with a noise that set Sefira's teeth on edge. 'Goodnight, sir; though good's not the word, is it?'

'Hardly. But a goodnight to you, nonetheless.' Grendon touched his heels to the horse's flanks. Sefira saw both guards watching her as they passed; one smiled, but she only returned the smile with a blank look. Then they were through and the gate was being dragged back into place behind them. She heard the latch fall, the noise echoing through the rain's hiss, and something in her lost memory seemed to stir briefly and momentarily. As if, just for an instant, she had recalled the sound of a prison door closing.

The royal quarter, as Sefira soon saw, was like a small, discrete city within the greater sprawl of Tourmon. But from the moment they entered the encircling wall she realised that this enclave had been built with one focus in mind; for its only byways were in the form of long, straight streets radiating out from the centre like the spokes of a wheel. At the wheel's hub, dominant amid a blaze of lights, was the king's palace.

It stood at the highest point of Tourmon, square and solid and regular, with flat facades of pale grey stone, a massive portico and tall, mullioned windows that glared out at the world like a hundred insensate eyes. Around it, looking shapeless and peculiarly organic in the uneasy torch- and lamp-light, a network of smaller, lower buildings extended, some lit, others in darkness. They made Sefira think unpleasantly of a litter of nightmare young flocking round a monstrous mother, and despite Grendon's warning of a few minutes ago, she said in a voice that hovered between pleading and defiance, 'We're not going there. We're not going to the palace . . .'

'No.' The word was clipped exasperatedly, then Grendon relented a little. 'I'm taking you to the home of a friend of mine. She'll give you sanctuary until better arrangements can be made.' The horse clopped on for a few more paces before he added, 'And don't fear for your secret; Arrine can be trusted not to betray you.'

Sefira pondered the name, Arrine. A 'friend', he had said, and a woman. How old? And what was the nature of their friendship? Arrine might be a relation; or she might be his lover. Or something else again.

'Where does she live?' she asked.

'She has a house in the Scholarly quarter. It's small, but there's room enough for you.'

His tone suggested strongly that any more questions would be unwelcome, and Sefira fell silent. They were nearing the palace precincts now, where the first of the outlying buildings faced on to the street. Some looked centuries old; others were newer, and some, the most simple of all, were as yet unfinished. At last, with the palace itself looming too near for Sefira's comfort, Grendon turned the horse under a wide stone arch between two of the older houses. Through a short passageway, they emerged into a small square of mews-like houses, set around a formal central garden. Some of the houses were in darkness, but others displayed glowing lanterns above their doors, and before one of these Grendon dismounted and rapped at a heavy iron knocker.

A middle-aged woman in the plain garments of a servant answered the door. Sefira noticed her suppressed start, almost a shrinking back, as she saw Grendon's face in the lamplight; noticed, too, the hard look that slid into her eyes before she made a quick curtsey.

Grendon said: 'Is your mistress at home, Getha?'

'Yes, sir.' There was hostility in the woman's voice, though she tried to veil it, and her gaze flicked swiftly, curiously, to Sefira still sitting on the horse's back. 'Come in, if you please.'

Grendon turned to help Sefira down from the saddle, and led her through the door into a narrow hall. The woman said, 'Jeram will take care of your horse, sir. I'll tell the mistress that you're here.'

She disappeared up a flight of dark-panelled stairs. A minute later, quicker, lighter footsteps sounded above, and another woman, older than the servant and wearing a silk gown with a woven shawl thrown around her shoulders, came skimming down.

'Grendon . . .' She stopped halfway to the hall, giving Sefira, who stood in the shadows, the chance to gain a first impression of her. In her youth Arrine had been beautiful, and even now there was a graciousness, a delicacy to her features that spoke not only of aristocracy but also of kindness and warmth. Her hair, largely grey but still showing trace of its original auburn, was looped up in an elegant style that framed a wide mouth, high cheekbones and large, deep-set grey eyes. She smiled a welcome that mingled genuine affection with a hint of old sorrow.

'Arrine.' Grendon stepped forward and, to Sefira's surprise, made the courtliest of bows over her hand.

'My dear, I'm so glad to see you back again.' Arrine laid her own hands over his, clasping his fingers as though he were a long-lost son. 'How have you fared? How has it gone? Have your duties been—' Then she saw Sefira, and abruptly the flow of words stopped.

Grendon said: 'Arrine, there's a very great deal to explain and to tell you. But for now . . .' He drew back and took Sefira's arm, the grasp appearing gentle but in actuality no such thing. 'This is Sefira. I'm sorry to bring her to you without warning, but she needs your help.' Then, before Sefira could make a move to stop him, he reached for her wimple and pulled it off.

Arrine looked at Sefira's shorn hair, and with commendable self-possession said only, 'I see . . .'

'The story's complex.' Grendon was looking at Arrine again, and so Sefira couldn't see the message his eyes gave her, though she detected Arrine's brief, silent flicker of understanding response. 'Sefira needs shelter first and foremost, but she also needs something more. You see, she has lost her memory.'

'Ah . . .' Arrine studied Sefira, warily but with growing interest. 'Then does she know . . . ?' A gesture towards Sefira's hair expressed the rest.

'Yes; though not what happened, or how or why. That's what interests me, for I suspect it's not as straightforward as it seems. And it's the reason why I impose on you now.'

'I understand.' Arrine's tone suggested to Sefira that perhaps her understanding went a good deal deeper than she implied. Something private between her and Grendon . . . Sefira's dark eyes looked from one face to the other, but she couldn't fathom it.

'Well,' Arrine continued, and suddenly her manner was brisk, 'you must both be tired and hungry. How did you reach Tourmon? By river? I'm sure you'll want to freshen yourselves, and my house is at your disposal. And you, my dear,' she smiled at Sefira, 'may stay here for as long as you wish. Whoever you may be, or whatever you may or may not have done, if Grendon vouchsafes you that is good enough for me.'

Arrine gave Sefira a bedroom at the top of the house, reached by two flights of steep, narrow stairs. Like the rest of the rooms it was small but comfortable, panelled in dark wood and a little overcrowded with equally dark furniture. But to Sefira it felt like a haven. She could hide here; she felt safe.

The servant, Getha, brought her a tub and filled it with

hot water so that she could bath herself, and when she was done she was lent a gown of Arrine's to wear. Silk after coarse wool was a welcome luxury, but though Sefira searched her memory, the finer fabric was no more familiar to her than the rougher, and gave her no clue to her past.

An hour after the bath she was called down to take a meal with Grendon and Arrine. Getha, tight-lipped, served it, and they sat at the polished table, by the light of candles and a well-made log fire, making small talk. Sefira said very little. She was aware that her presence inhibited the other two, and the tone of the conversation would doubtless have been very different if they had been alone. But she listened carefully, and was able to learn at least some facts about her new benefactress.

Arrine was a widow. How or when her husband had died wasn't mentioned, but from her references to him it was obvious that they had been close. There were, it seemed, no children, and Sefira had the distinct impression that Arrine looked on Grendon as a surrogate for the son she had never borne. Her late husband, Lendrer, had clearly been fond of him too – though for some unknown reason Grendon seemed uncomfortable with that fact, and reluctant to talk of it.

No wine was served with the meal. Sefira thought nothing of it and was content to drink the water offered to her. She also drank one of the three small cups of fruit juice that Getha brought in when the dishes had been cleared, unaware of the extra ingredient which, at Grendon's request, Arrine had instructed the servant to add to her measure. She only knew that a short while later she began to feel weary to the bone, and when Arrine gently suggested that she might wish to retire, she accepted gratefully and climbed the stairs to bed.

Arrine listened to the closing of the attic door – sound carried in such a small house – and then nodded to Getha, who was hovering and waiting for instructions.

'I shan't need you or Jeram again tonight, Getha. Thank you; you may go now.'

'Madam.' Getha slid Grendon a brief, inscrutable glance and went out, closing the door quietly behind her. Arrine sat back in her chair and said,

'Now. Tell me.'

Grendon stood up and moved to the fireplace, where he stared into the flames. They had had a little private time together while Sefira was bathing and he had already given her the bare bones of the tale: his meeting with Sefira on the moor, the few details of herself that she had been able to remember, and his decision to bring her with him to Tourmon. But there was one thing, one central thing, which he had not yet revealed. And now that the moment had come he found himself reluctant to say what must be said.

After perhaps half a minute's silence Arrine prompted gently, 'Grendon. You must have a very good reason for taking such trouble with this girl. By rights, and by common sense, you should have returned her to the justices and left her to her ordained fate. That would have been the *dutiful* thing to do.'

'Yes,' Grendon said. 'It would.'

'Then your reasons for not doing it must be personal.' He didn't reply and she probed: 'You're surely not in love with her?'

'In lo—' Then, as he turned sharply to face her, Grendon saw the wry humour in her expression and his protest turned into a laugh. 'No. Oh no, I'm most certainly not in love with her. But I . . .' Another hesitation, then abruptly he took a breath and forced himself at last to broach the crucial subject. 'I want her. Because, you see, I've discovered what she truly is.'

Arrine frowned. 'You say "what", not "who" . . . Grendon, what *is* afoot here?'

So at last Grendon related the events of the night in the watchtower. He left out no detail, and he also told her about the other, smaller incidents; what he had seen when they sheltered in the abandoned mansion, and what Sefira had done to the rat. Arrine listened in absolute silence, and when he finally stopped speaking she said nothing at first, only sat very still, her eyes focused on his face but seeing a far more private vision.

Then, softly, she said, 'Another one . . . I didn't think it possible. I truly believed . . .' The words tailed off.

'You believed that such plagues were gone for good. That the one Lendrer exorcised twenty years ago was the last.'

'Yes,' Arrine said hollowly. 'I believed that.' A memory stirred in her eyes, and for a moment her face looked stark and old. Then: 'But you're sure? There can be no doubt?'

He smiled without humour. 'I still have the scars of her attack.'

The hope in Arrine's eyes died; she nodded, swallowed and said softly, 'The circle comes round again.'

'Indeed. But this time, with a difference. This time – and perhaps for the first and only time – the plague might have a purpose.' He paused. 'Or be made to have one. If we are extremely careful.'

He had turned away and so didn't see Arrine tense, but he felt the sudden charge that came into the room's atmosphere as she realised the direction that his thoughts and plans were taking. Then, explosively, she said, 'Grendon, you can't—'

'I think I can. I think it can be done.'

'But to control something like that—'

'Lendrer succeeded.'

'But that was to *exorcise* it! If what you have in mind is to *use* what the girl has within her, in the way that I think you mean . . .'

He turned his head and met her gaze challengingly. 'Isn't it the opportunity we've been waiting for? We'll never have another chance like this!'

She stood up, went to the fireplace and put her hands on the mantel, her knuckles whitening with the grip. 'I understand what you're saying. And yes, in a cold and pragmatic sense I can't argue with you. But the *risk*—'

'Do you think I care about the risk? Do *you* care about it?' Suddenly there was fierce emotion in Grendon's voice, and real anger. 'After what was done to Lendrer and to you; after what *I* did—'

'You had no choice!'

'But I *did* have a choice!' Then with an effort Grendon brought himself under control. Scrubbing at his face with one hand he added in a more subdued voice, 'I could have refused what was demanded of me. That would have been the honourable course to take.'

Arrine's shoulders heaved, and she wiped at her own eyes. 'And what if you had refused?' she countered gently. 'Lendrer would still have died, and other lives would have been lost, too. At least *something* was salvaged.' Abruptly she came back to his chair and touched one hand to his hair, stroking it as though trying to soothe or comfort. 'You know I don't blame you for what happened, my dear, and you shouldn't go on blaming yourself. There *was* no choice for you, and Lendrer would have been the first to tell you so.'

Grendon didn't reply, and after a few moments she sighed and sat down once more. 'The past can't be changed,' she said. 'And it achieves nothing to brood on it. That's a lesson which perhaps you'll learn with age, as I did.'

He made a gesture of acquiescence, the fires of his anger dying down. 'I know. But this opportunity . . . we can't let it elude us, Arrine. Not after all our work, and our searching.'

'We've never searched for this.'

'No. But it has come our way. We *must* use it.' He looked up. 'Not just for our own sakes, but for the sakes of all the others.'

There was silence for several seconds. Then Arrine said, 'If you do use it, Grendon, you know what it will do to the girl herself. Do you care about that?'

'No,' he replied. 'I don't.' He watched her face carefully. 'To paraphrase your own words, Arrine: one life lost; how many saved?'

He had turned her own argument back on her, and immediately she knew that she wasn't going to dispute it any further. With the knowledge came a sense of relief as emotions which for the past year and more she had done everything in her power to suppress came suddenly back to the surface. The anger; the bitterness. Above all, the *hatred*.

Grendon saw her feelings reflected in her eyes, but decency and the love she knew he had for her stopped him from letting his knowledge show. Arrine said, 'Then we shall do what needs to be done.' She clasped her hands together, studied them. 'I pity the girl; she's little more than a child and her likely fate isn't pleasant to contemplate. But if it achieves what we dream of, if it rights the wrong that was done to us . . . it will be recompense.'

Grendon took hold of her hand. 'Recompense . . .' he repeated thoughtfully. Then his mouth curved into a hard, cold, almost cruel smile, and his fingers gripped hers suddenly in a way that hurt. 'I would prefer to call it revenge.'

Chapter VI

That night, Sefira dreamed that she was hovering above the bed in which she slept, gazing down from somewhere near the ceiling at her own recumbent form among the blankets. At least, she knew that the figure lying there so still and peaceful was herself, but, bizarrely, it did not *look* like her. This person, this stranger, had white hair, not black. And there was something wrong with her face; something missing that should have been there. Sefira tried to recall what features a human face should have. Mouth, yes, that was as it should be. Nose, jaw, cheekbones; in the irrational way of dreams she counted them off one by one, and all was well. Ears. Eyebrows. But . . .

No eyes. That was it. The sleeper in the bed had no eyes, for she couldn't see even the curve of closed lids or the shadow of lashes. This *thing*, which was and yet was not herself, was blind.

Suddenly she felt affronted. She could see well enough; otherwise how could she possibly be gazing down from where she floated? Yet someone had had the temerity, the *arrogance* to steal her eyes away from her, so that when she woke . . .

What, when she woke? She didn't know the answer and wondered if she should rouse the sleeping Not-Sefira, to learn what would happen. But when she tried to propel herself down towards the bed, she found she could not move but stayed suspended in mid-air. And the walls of the bedroom were starting to close in, and the panels were growing smaller and darker and more claustrophobic, like the interior of a closed carriage.

She did wake then, with a rush of her pulse that sent a jolt through her. The eyeless figure and the crushing walls melted into the reality of the attic in Arrine's house, and as they fled they seemed to carry the echo of a voice with them; a sing-song voice, light and sweet as a summer breeze.

'*Sefi* . . .'

But it was only part of the dream. Outside, the rain was still streaming down, hissing on the ground and gurgling in gutters with a sound like quietly mad laughter. Light from the great lantern still burning above the house's entrance impinged on the room, making a shadow pattern of the window mullions, and the soporific draught that she had unwittingly swallowed had not yet entirely worn off.

Sefira closed her eyes again, smiling at her foolishness for thinking, albeit briefly, that someone had stolen them, and drifted back to sleep.

She stirred only when the unsmiling Getha came into the room bearing a basin of hot water and telling her that breakfast was almost ready and the mistress awaited her. Sefira dressed hurriedly, eschewed a wash (she had bathed only last night; what was the necessity?) and made her way downstairs. She expected to find Grendon in the dining room but, to her surprise and unease, Arrine was alone. Grendon, it seemed, had business elsewhere this morning, and until he returned Arrine would be glad of Sefira's company. And, the older woman told her, of the chance to get to know her better.

At first they made little progress. Sefira was cautious and mistrustful of her hostess, despite the apparent kindly intentions; there were too many enigmas in this situation for her to let her guard down even for a moment. But at last, when they had both eaten meagrely of a breakfast which neither really wanted, Arrine took matters into her own hands.

She prodded the fire with an ornate metal poker and said, apparently casually, 'Grendon tells me that you have been posing as his wife while you travelled together.'

Sefira tensed. 'Yes.'

'A sensible precaution, under the circumstances. And one which I think it might be wise to continue.' Arrine glanced meaningfully at Sefira's hair, and Sefira realised that she had forgotten to put on the hated wimple.

Arrine saw her chagrin and gave a small, tight smile. 'It's of no moment to me, my dear, as I don't doubt Grendon has told you. However, others are less sanguine. Getha, for example, is more than a little alarmed by the knowledge that we have a convicted felon under our roof.'

Fear came to Sefira's face. 'She won't—'

'No, no; she'll say nothing, you can rest assured. But it might be kinder, not to say more prudent, to wear your disguise indoors as well as out. Just as a precaution.'

It was both a rebuke and a warning, and Sefira suddenly felt very vulnerable. 'I'm sorry,' she said. 'I didn't think . . . you see, I'm not accustomed . . .'

'To wearing it; I quite understand. And I suppose it tells us that you are in fact single, which is one small snippet of information in a wilderness of uncertainty.'

Sefira said nothing to that, and Arrine stirred the fire again. 'So, you were convicted of murder, were you?'

From the corner of her eye she saw the girl start as though someone had pinched her. Sefira's look became defensive and she said, almost angrily, 'Grendon told you . . .'

'I asked him. And he also told me that you remember nothing of it. Not the name of your victim, nor the reason why you did what you did.' She straightened up. 'Oh, child, don't look so hostile! I'm inclined to share Grendon's view that there was more to the matter than meets the eye, for the more I see of you the less likely I think it is that you're capable of being a cold-blooded killer!'

Sefira subsided, though she was still very uncertain of herself. 'May I ask you a question?' she said.

'Of course.'

'Grendon doesn't know me. You don't know me. I'm a stranger to you both, yet you're willing to put yourselves at risk to help me. I don't understand that.' She paused. 'And I don't trust it.'

'I quite appreciate your doubts,' Arrine said with a smile. 'And if Grendon has refused to explain everything to you . . . well, I'm afraid he can be a little insensitive about others' finer feelings at times. But for all that, I assure you that he does have a genuine reason for wanting to help you.' She smiled again, this time a little wryly. 'And for all his faults, he can be trusted. You see, in exchange for his helping you, he believes that there may be a way in which you can help him.'

This was a complete revelation, and Sefira's eyes narrowed. 'How?'

Arrine's smile faded into a look of slight embarrassment. 'I'm afraid I can't explain it all, for I promised Grendon that I would leave it for him to do. All I can say is that he *does* have a personal reason for what he has done, and that no harm can come of it – in fact, if he can achieve what he hopes, it will be to your advantage as well as to his.'

Sefira felt her suspicions start to ebb. At last, she thought, someone was willing to admit to the truth. If Arrine had protested some high, idealistic purpose behind Grendon's interest, she wouldn't have believed a word of it. This, though, made sense. It was human nature.

Yet it begged the question of what, precisely, Grendon might want from her; or more to the point, what help she could possibly give to a man who was already so highly placed in the king's service. This part of the conundrum still made no sense. But Arrine wouldn't be pressed, insisting that she had promised to leave the full explanation to Grendon, and could not in all conscience reveal any more.

At last Sefira changed tack and said, 'And what of you, madam?'

'Arrine, my dear. Call me Arrine, for I hope we're to be friends. What of me?'

'Why are you willing to help me?'

'Simply because Grendon has asked me to.' Arrine saw her surprised and puzzled reaction, and gave a soft, gentle laugh. 'No, of course you don't understand; no reason why you should.'

'He isn't . . . your son?' Sefira ventured.

'Oh, no, no. We're not related in any way; in fact I have no children of my own. But to Lendrer and I Grendon was *like* the son that we never had. And in recent times, something . . . happened that has made me indebted to Grendon in a way that I can never repay.'

Sefira gazed at her. 'May I ask what it was?'

'Of course you may, my dear. The spring before last there was a virulent fever in Tourmon. Half the city was stricken with it, and a great many died. Lendrer and I both caught the sickness, and Grendon risked his own life to care for us both. He tended us day and night; he brought us food and medicines from the palace's own supply – the city was quarantined, you see, and rations were desperately short – and he stayed with us even through the height of the fever, when it was at its most deadly and contagious.'

Arrine paused then and put a hand to her mouth, giving a small cough that disguised some suppressed emotion. 'My husband died,' she continued at last. 'Grendon did everything humanly possible to save him; far more than anyone had a right to ask. But even he could not prevail. I survived. For a time, when I knew that Lendrer had gone, I wanted only to follow him. But Grendon wouldn't allow it.' She blinked and looked at Sefira. 'He restored me to health whether I wished it or no, and he gave me back the will to live. And I can never do enough to repay such a great debt.'

Sefira gazed back at her. This side of Grendon's character was one she had never guessed at, and it forced her to view him in a new light.

She said quietly, 'I believe I understand a little better now . . . Arrine. Thank you. Thank you for telling me.'

'Don't fear that it hurt me to do so, Sefira. Time heals, and I have happy memories as well as sad ones. Please, try to think more kindly of Grendon. For all his brusque manner with you, he is a good man, and you can trust him.'

Oh, it had been so easy, she thought. Sefira's small face was sombre as she pondered all she had been told, and her reaction was painfully transparent. She believed it; believed the fiction that Arrine and Grendon had so carefully prepared as they sat up late into the night. And there was no reason why she should not believe. She was young, and youth was gullible. For a moment Arrine felt a stirring in her conscience, but that was something with which she had wrestled in the small hours, and it was resolved. Recompense. *Revenge.* Compared to that, Sefira's fate was of no importance.

She glanced one last time at the fire, using the moment to compose her face more carefully, then said gently:

'I think perhaps we should change the subject, don't you? I've no wish to burden you with the sorrows of my past. What matters now is your future.'

Sefira looked at her uncertainly. 'If you say so, Arrine.'

'I do. Now, I promised Grendon that I would see about getting some more suitable clothes for you. So let us turn our attention to that, shall we?'

Sefira answered with a cautious smile, before repeating, 'If you say so.'

Arrine nodded. It was a good beginning. Better, in fact, than anyone could have hoped. Grendon would be pleased. And the next stage of the plan could proceed without unnecessary delay.

If Sefira had known where Grendon had gone that morning, she would have been struck dumb with terror. But she did not know, and so was content to spend her time under Arrine's apparently benign ministrations, without the least idea of the real purpose behind her interest.

It was only a short walk to the palace, and the route was so familiar now that Grendon knew the contours of every stone that passed beneath his feet. Equally familiar was the man on guard at the side entrance by which he approached the royal residence, and who greeted him with a salute and a sharp, 'Sir!'

Grendon nodded to him. 'Not the best of mornings. Is Arbitrator Cottlas in his office today?'

'Yes, Arraigner. Please to go through.' The door was opened. Giving another nod Grendon entered the vestibule beyond, shook rain from his hair and cloak and turned along a narrow passage – again familiar – towards a more ornate door at the far end. Arbitrator Cottlas was indeed in his office, alone, and when he heard Grendon's request he opened a large appointment book and pored over it.

'Ye-es . . . I believe His Majesty may be able to accommodate you, Arraigner Grendon. Shall we say . . . in six days' time?'

There was a sharp silence. Cottlas was not looking at him, but Grendon could see the tiny, pinched smile playing about his mouth, and a wave of disgust rose in him. Cottlas traded on his position, as he always had done. In the past he had been easy to intimidate. Now, though, Grendon had to tread more carefully.

He tried to keep exasperation from his voice as he said, 'I would prefer an earlier appointment. This is not a routine request, Arbitrator; it's an irregularity and one which will be of great interest to the king.'

'His Majesty,' Cottlas used the title with careful nicety, to differentiate from Grendon's form of address, 'will doubtless decide that for himself. But I'm afraid that, unless it is something of *extreme* import or urgency, he is too busy to—'

'It is of extreme import.'

'Ah?' A glint of triumph; Grendon's annoyance was showing and Cottlas relished it. 'Ah . . . well in that case, perhaps we might make an exception for you.' He made a show of studying the book again, then looked up with a cold smile. 'This afternoon. One hour before sunset. You may have four minutes.'

The slight, the insult, was delivered without any effort at disguise, and to control his temper Grendon stared at a map on the wall. 'Very well,' he said when he was sure he could trust his voice. 'One hour before sunset.' With fine sardonicism he added, 'I'm obliged to you.'

'The pleasure is entirely mine.' Cottlas watched him go, and waited until enough time had passed for him to have reached the outside world. Then he summoned his page, and sent him running with a message for his royal master.

Grendon did not return to Arrine's house but instead paid a visit – rare for him – to his own home; though 'home' wasn't a term he cared to use for the two barely furnished lodging-rooms in another part of the royal quarter. From the first he had not liked his surroundings, nor could he feel comfortable in them. They were not what he had been used to in the old days, and that rankled. But he had had no choice; the decision had been made for him and he had been in no position to argue.

That, however, was a circumstance which might be about to change.

Inside, he went to a cupboard which was not often opened, touched a knot in the wood at the back of a shelf and watched as the sprung lid of the compartment below it, which only he and one other living soul in Tourmon knew of, clicked free. The compartment had been made to exact proportions, and the book that fitted perfectly into it was Grendon's most valued possession. Grendon carried the book to the window, where the sullen daylight was just strong enough for reading, and sat down.

He studied for over three hours, his mind locked and concentrating on what the book contained. Then, satisfied with what he had achieved, he turned to the back, made some notes in a personal shorthand of his own devising, and returned the book to its place in the compartment. He spent another half-hour cleaning the dust that had accumulated during his absence, at the same time making a few other adjustments that would give any prying eyes the impression that he had slept here last night instead of on a couch at Arrine's house, and left for the palace.

Arbitrator Cottlas was no longer on duty, and another, younger official – one of the newer appointees whose name Grendon didn't yet know – consulted the book and escorted him to the door of the audience room. This was not the old audience room, with its decorated ceiling and gallery of frowning royal portraits, from the days of the previous regime; King Karel had made it clear from the beginning that he would have none of the prodigal extravagances of the past. And doubtless the portraits had all been burned anyway. Instead, this chamber had been the personal sitting room of the previous ruler's family, and the fact that its once sacrosanct doors were now open to every citizen with a grievance to air was a joke which the new court appreciated; or pretended to. The official opened the door, cleared his throat to indicate his presence, and announced Grendon's name.

King Karel was sitting on a plain chair at a large but equally plain desk in the middle of the room. He was a stocky but extremely fit man, not many years older than Grendon; and despite the fine clothes that he now felt obliged to wear there was still a faintly military severity about his appearance. His hair had been fair but was now both greying and receding, and he sported a long moustache of a kind that had been in fashion twenty years earlier.

Grendon crossed the threshold and, as protocol dictated waited for permission to approach the desk. Karel acknowledged his presence with a courteous, if apparently distracted, movement of one hand. Then, as though by prior arrangement, the door to an ante-room behind the king opened, and a woman escorted by a servant entered.

Grendon felt a sharp, painful tingle go through him as,

just for a moment, he locked gazes with the newcomer. She was a few years younger than he was, and fair like himself and the king. She in her turn looked at him before quickly averting her gaze, and the servant, whose name and nature Grendon knew very well indeed, set steady, dark eyes on his face, watching his reaction and mentally noting it.

A minute went by. Grendon forced himself not to look at the woman again, and his schooled expression gave no clue to the anger that burned behind the mask. The only sound in the room was the slight scratching of Karel's quill on the paper laid before him; then at last the king signed his name with an efficient flourish and looked up.

'Grendon. Come in, come in. I'm sorry to have kept you waiting.'

Grendon bowed from the waist; it was the only obeisance used these days. 'Sir.' The woman was being ushered to a chair at the back of the room; he heard a faint rustle of silk as she sat down. 'I understand I have four minutes of your time.'

Karel smiled reservedly. 'I imagine that's Cottlas's way of displaying his authority. However, Cottlas has gone home to his worthy wife, and so is not here to exercise his privileges.' He sat back, regarding Grendon fully for the first time. 'Reading between the lines, and judging by my past experience of you, I imagine you have some news for me which might take rather longer to relate.'

Karel, Grendon thought, was catching the mode of speech of the court. In the days of the war he had been renowned for his economy with words, unless he was in the throes of one of his rabble-rousing speeches, but rulership was changing that as it was changing so much else. Under other circumstances the irony might have been amusing; as it was, he found nothing funny in it.

He said: 'What I have to tell you, sir, is something that I think you would prefer to hear in private.' A meaningful glance at the servant.

'Oh?' Karel looked interested, but also, now, a little

unfriendly. 'I doubt that you have anything to say which can't be said in my secretary's hearing.'

'I beg to differ, sir.' Grendon smiled, the smile not reaching his eyes. For a moment they stared at each other, then Karel lifted his shoulders in a disinterested shrug.

'Very well.' He signed over his shoulder to the dark-eyed man. 'Leave us, please, Tomany. And the lady Mischane may go, too.'

The young woman rose and curtsied, though Karel wasn't looking at her. She and Tomany left through the same door by which they had entered, and when it had closed behind them Karel tipped his chair backwards and stretched his legs out under the desk.

'You try my patience sometimes, Grendon. I don't take kindly to being contradicted; especially by you.'

'I wouldn't presume to do any such thing, sir.'

'No . . . No, you wouldn't, would you. You wouldn't dare.' Briefly, a spark of malice showed in the king's light blue eyes. 'Did you have no word of greeting for your sister? She must think you very unfeeling.'

Grendon's fingers clenched involuntarily. 'Anything I have to say to her would be better said in private, Your Majesty.'

'Ah, privacy again. Well, we'll have to see what can be arranged. And don't call me "Your Majesty". It may suit the court sycophants, but from you it's hollow and we both know it.'

Grendon bowed again, faintly. 'As you wish, sir.'

'Mmm.' Karel sounded cynical. 'So, now that we've dispensed with the niceties you'd best tell me what you came to say. I presume it concerns your work?'

'Yes.'

'You've encountered some trouble? A nest of vipers, perhaps? Not that it isn't to be expected; even your especial talents aren't infallible when it comes to dealing with Sanctifieds.'

Karel saw the barb find its mark, and though he took no

personal satisfaction from it, it did no harm to deliver the occasional reminder to Grendon of how matters stood. To give Grendon his credit, he thought, he didn't rise to the bait; in fact he didn't react outwardly in any way at all. But then his kind never did; they were too skilled, and that was a part of the problem they posed.

He continued, 'I understand that another Purging has taken place in Chalce. Is credit due to you for that?'

This time a slight flush of colour did come to Grendon's face, but his voice remained level as he replied, 'No, sir. I was in Chalce three days ago, but I didn't stay for the . . . event.'

'You did, however, oversee two proceedings in – where was it – Endine, I believe. And another in one of those large farming estates in the south-west. Yes, I saw the reports. I gather you were commendably thorough. So, if this new matter isn't about rooting out more Sanctifieds, what does it concern?'

'It does concern the Sanctifieds,' Grendon said. 'But indirectly. I have something to offer you, sir. Something that could make a very great difference to the effectiveness – and the speed of completion – of your campaign.'

There was a pause. Then Karel said, in a carefully neutral tone, 'Go on.'

'On my way back to Tourmon,' Grendon continued, 'I encountered a young woman. The circumstances of the meeting aren't relevant; but I discovered that she has extraordinary abilities.'

'What sort of abilities?'

'Perhaps a better word would be *powers*.'

'Ah . . .' Karel's expression didn't change, but a pursing of his mouth was just discernible. Like a fish, Grendon thought, approaching the bait and feeling the stirrings of temptation.

'Is she,' the king asked at last, 'a Sanctified?'

'I don't believe so.'

'Well, if she is she won't admit it, so the matter's hardly relevant. What Fellowship does she claim to belong to?'

'She makes no claim. She has lost her memory, and knows

nothing whatever about herself. To all intents and purposes she has no family, no home . . . no place in the world.'

'I begin to see the direction your thoughts are taking. And these "abilities" of hers. What is their nature?'

Oh yes; his interest was clear now. And Grendon had planned his strategy carefully. A year ago the lure he had to offer would have cut no ice with Karel, but time and, more pertinently, the king's increasing experience of power, was having its effect.

He said, almost carelessly, 'They are raw as yet; I suspect she's had neither training nor discipline. But her potential is phenomenal.' A pause. 'For example, sir . . . what value would you set on someone who could scry, at will, into any part of your realm and tell you what was taking place there?'

There was a sharp silence. Then Karel said, 'She's capable of that?'

'I believe she is. Among other things.'

'And you, of course, would know . . . Yes. That is, indeed, phenomenal.' Suddenly restless, Karel stood up and paced across the room, stopping to stare at a tapestry depicting a two-hundred-year-old battle. 'So, this talent of hers is an occult talent. A formidable occult talent.' Abruptly he turned to face Grendon again. 'In fact, she has the very same kind of powers that I have spent the past two years trying to stamp out.'

Grendon held his gaze. 'Yes. But I'm convinced that her abilities go far beyond that. If I'm right, this girl has seeing skills that even the most powerful of Sanctifieds couldn't hope to hide from. And, as you yourself have often reminded me, it takes a thief to catch a thief.'

Karel smiled thinly. 'Indeed it does . . . and I won't deny for one moment that I am a great believer in the pragmatic approach. However, this new discovery of yours does beg a number of questions. Firstly the coincidence, for want of a better word, of your encountering her as and when you did – not to mention the fact that she has so conveniently lost her memory.'

'It's the truth, sir,' Grendon said evenly. 'Put the girl to any form of questioning you please; she'll bear it out.'

'Perhaps I will, in good time. For now, though, I'm more interested in the practicalities, which brings me to my second question – the proof of her supposed talents. Can you provide that?'

'I think so.'

Karel nodded. 'Good; for you'll need to if this negotiation is to go any further. Lastly, then, the most pertinent question of all, is what do *you* want in exchange for delivering this prize to me?' His pale eyes took on a harder light. 'We know each other too well, I think, to pretend that there won't be a price. So what is it?'

Grendon said, 'Three things.'

'Ah; three. And none of them money, I imagine. Well?'

'Firstly, my own quarters here in the palace.'

The king inclined his head so that his expression was briefly hidden. 'Which in itself implies an improvement in status. Not unreasonable, if the girl proves worthwhile. Secondly?'

'Custody of the girl herself.'

That, Grendon saw, surprised Karel, but it also laid the false trail that he had intended. The king smiled again, this time with a strong hint of humour, and replied, 'Well, if you have a personal interest I see no reason why that shouldn't be indulged. Although "custody" is not a word I entirely like; it smacks too much of imprisonment. Shall we say "guardianship", instead?'

Grendon bowed his acquiescence.

'Then that leaves only your third condition. Which is?'

Grendon paused for a few moments before answering. Then quietly, he said, 'That if the girl achieves what you require, my sister will be allowed to leave the palace and make a new life for herself without fear of retribution.'

'Ah,' said Karel. 'I thought it might be something like that. You're asking, then, for a full pardon.'

Grendon's jaw tightened at the choice of words but he

controlled his reaction, knowing that at this moment it would not be wise to show it. 'Yes, sir,' he said. 'A full pardon – and freedom.'

In the silence that followed Grendon heard something buzzing at one of the windows; an insect trying to reach the outside world and frustrated by the barrier of the glass. It sounded angry, and the sound it made set his teeth on edge as he waited for Karel to respond. The king was pacing again, very slowly, as if deliberately prolonging the tension. At last he stopped and turned once more.

'You set a high fee, Grendon.' His eyes were steady and hard. 'I don't need to spell out the implications to you, of course. If Mischane were no longer to grace the court, then I would have no further guarantee of *your* loyal service. And I don't think that would be prudent – do you?'

'There are other ways of ensuring my compliance,' Grendon said.

'Perhaps; but this one is particularly effective.' Another long pause, during which Karel turned slowly on one heel, surveying the entire room as though summing up the value of everything it contained. When the survey was complete, he continued.

'On the other hand, if this new protégée of yours is what you claim, it could be that the advantages will outweigh the drawbacks. And that, I think, is the crux of the matter.' Over his shoulder he shot Grendon an intense look. 'Prove the value of what you are offering. If – I say *if* – it is worthwhile, then I'll grant what you ask; though with a condition of my own, which is that you and Mischane will leave this kingdom altogether and for good.'

'That I agree to.'

'Then we have at least the skeleton of a bargain between us.' Suddenly brisk, Karel walked back to his desk, sat down and reached for his quill. Dipping it in the inkwell, he added, 'I'll see the girl for myself two hours after sunset tomorrow evening. Use the west gate and bring her to my private apartments.' He wrote something quickly on a sheet of paper, signed it and added a seal from a ring on his right index finger. 'With this, you won't be thwarted by guards or petty officials. Use it discreetly, and don't answer any questions.' He looked up. 'You'll have one hour and no more to show me what the girl is capable of. And I trust it won't be a waste of my time.'

Grendon took the paper. 'I assure you that it won't.'

'We'll see, won't we? Very well; and we'll meet again tomorrow. You may go.'

'Sir.' Grendon bowed, turned and walked from the room.

Karel waited until the door had closed, then rang a small bell that stood on the desk. The dark-eyed secretary emerged from the antechamber, approached and made a lower obeisance than Grendon had done. 'My lord?'

Karel gestured to the door by which Grendon had departed. 'You heard the gist of that, Tomany?'

'I did, my lord.'

The king rubbed a finger over his own chin. 'How long has it been since Grendon's lodgings were searched?'

'A little over a month, sir. Nothing of any interest was found.'

'Mmm . . . I think it's about time to repeat the exercise. Make the necessary arrangements, and tell the searchers to leave the usual signs. We don't want Grendon left in any doubt of our interest.'

'Yes, sir. Are they to look for anything in particular?'

'No, no. The girl won't be there, of course; Grendon wouldn't be so crass. But it does no harm to give him an uncomfortable moment once in a while.'

'Of course, sir. And should I also make any new investigation of the widow Arrine?'

Karel considered for a few moments, then shook his head. 'Arrine's harmless enough; she hasn't Grendon's skills, and certainly not those of her late husband. Leave her to nurse her grievances in her own way; she's no threat.' It was likely, of course, that Grendon had lodged the girl at Arrine's house, but to root her out now would be to throw down an unnecessary gauntlet. Tomorrow would come soon enough, and then Grendon's claim would stand or fall on its own merits. If it failed, there was nothing to lose. If it stood . . . well, Grendon might have it in mind to bargain hard, but the high cards were in Karel's hands. He would need Grendon to hone and train the girl's talents, but beyond that he was expendable, and once he had completed his task he could if necessary be dispensed with altogether.

Tomany was silently and efficiently gathering up the documents that he had earlier left for his master's attention. Karel watched, then when the last paper was collated and the secretary looked to him for permission to withdraw, he said:

'Ask the lady Mischane if she would do me the honour of joining me in my private quarters this evening. We will have a meal served there in three hours' time.'

The invitation, Tomany knew, was not one that would – or could – be refused. His eyes were bland, his smile less so as he replied, 'Of course, my lord.' Then he moved, soft-footed, from the room, leaving Karel alone.

Chapter VII

'Getha was far from happy about it,' Arrine said. 'But I pointed out to her that the more readily she cooperated, the sooner you and Sefira would be gone from under our roof.' She shrugged. 'I can't hold her to blame for her attitude. She knows the truth, but she's a simple woman; she sees everything in stark colours only and can't understand the subtler niceties.'

Grendon squirmed inwardly at her choice of phrase but suppressed his reaction. 'So she bought these.' He fingered the small pile of clothes that Getha had laid neatly on a chair. 'Hardly the height of fashion but they'll serve well enough. I'll recompense you.'

'Don't. Let it be my contribution to the cause – I can do little enough in a practical sense, and I have more money than I shall ever need again.' With her eyes Arrine indicated the floor above them. 'The girl's asleep; I gave her another soporific shortly after lunch.' She paused. 'I wouldn't advise giving her any more, Grendon. We'll be able to pass it off this time as the after-effects of her journey, but she's no fool; she'll become suspicious before too long.'

'If all goes well there'll be no need for any more,' Grendon said. 'She'll soon be safely under my protection in the palace.'

'Assuming that she passes Karel's test. How sure can you be?'

'Sure enough.' Grendon smiled with some irony. 'And I should know, shouldn't I?'

'Yes. Yes, you should . . . so Karel doesn't distrust your motives?'

95

'Not as far as I can tell. He's an intelligent man but not quite as discerning as he likes to think – as far as he's concerned, my sole purpose is to buy my freedom and Mischane's, and he believes that I'll trust him to keep his part of the bargain.'

'Which he won't.'

'Of course he won't. But by then I'll have extracted payment of another kind.' He gave another harsh smile. 'A corpse can't break promises.'

Arrine nodded with dark satisfaction. 'You're to take Sefira to Karel's private apartments, you said? Mmm. Obviously he doesn't wish too many to know about this.'

'Which can only be to our advantage.'

'Perhaps. Nonetheless, be careful. Don't let your vigilance lapse.'

'It won't.'

Their eyes met, held for a few moments. Then Arrine's posture relaxed. 'Very well. I'll trust your judgement and try not to worry.' She let out her breath as though some unpleasant thought had abruptly loosed its hold on her. 'So then, it only remains to break the news to the girl. She won't like it.'

'She'll prefer it to the alternative – as you said, she's no fool.'

'Then I suggest we don't delay any longer.' Arrine picked up a plain, serviceable green dress which, more by luck than by Getha's judgement, would suit Sefira's colouring very well, and laid over it a finer wimple than the one purloined from the abandoned house beyond Chalce. 'I'll wake her, oversee her dressing and bring her downstairs. Let's get the next obstacle over and done with.'

'The *king*?' Sefira stared in disbelief, first at Grendon and then at Arrine. She looked like an animal that had suddenly and unexpectedly found itself in a cage with no exit. 'Oh, no. Oh, *no*! I won't *do* it!'

Arrine sighed and gazed down at her own folded hands,

and Grendon looked back at Sefira with hard-eyed resolution. 'You'll do it, my lady,' he said. 'Because if you don't, your one chance of redemption will be lost for ever.'

She struggled to accept as, painstakingly but relentlessly, he explained the logic of it to her. She was a wanted criminal with an execution order set upon her. He had shielded her thus far from the perils of recapture, but if she wasn't to remain a fugitive for the rest of her life she must either be cleared of her supposed crime, or pardoned. And only one man in the realm had the power to overrule the verdict against her.

Floundering, she tried to protest that King Karel could have no possible interest in her; that if he knew the truth about her he would simply hand her back to the justices to be executed without any further ado. But Grendon demolished every argument: the king, he said, was her only hope of salvation, and the sooner she acknowledged that fact, the sooner she could learn to live without looking over her shoulder at every turn. Besides, he added finally, there was one very good reason why Karel would be prepared to reprieve her.

That stopped Sefira in her tracks, and she realised that this must be connected to the personal motive at which Arrine had hinted. Abruptly the old doubts and suspicions came flaring back to her mind, and she said combatively, 'There *is* something you haven't told me. Something about me – something you know!'

Grendon said, 'Yes.'

Arrine glanced at them both in turn but didn't speak, and Sefira heard her own breathing become suddenly ragged against the quiet.

'What is it?' Her voice was level, but dangerous.

'You have a talent,' Grendon said. 'One which the king would find valuable enough to override any considerations about your past.'

'Talent?' Something stirred in Sefira; she began to feel sick. 'What talent? What can I do, that the king wants?'

Arrine leaned forward. 'You're a clairvoyant, my dear.' She

looked briefly at Grendon again; he signalled for her to go on. 'A clairvoyant of a very special kind; for you have no conscious awareness of your own abilities. Grendon and I we . . . know something of such matters, and we both recognised the unmistakable signs in you. It's an extremely rare skill, and, you see, to the king it could have inestimable value.' She smiled poignantly. 'The war may be over in name, but in some senses it continues, for there are still those who want to see the old, unjust regime restored to power, and who work in secret to infiltrate and overthrow the new order. And while some of these people have been unmasked, there is a core, a nucleus, who are far harder to root out. They are the sorcerers, men and women with the power to conceal themselves and their deeds behind a wall of secrecy that ordinary mortals cannot penetrate.'

She paused, looked at Grendon again, then continued once more. 'In the days before the war their kind held supreme sway, and they meted out the foulest punishments to any who sought to oppose them. Then when the conflict began, they used their dark skills in an attempt to preserve their dominance, no matter what the cost to the realm. And the cost was high. It was only sheer force of numbers that enabled the rebels to prevail – without that, there would have been no hope for the reforming cause. But even though we *did* prevail, there is still a danger that the sorcerers will try to win back the power they once held. And until the last of them is found and destroyed, there can be no true peace and security in the realm.'

Sefira's queasiness grew stronger. 'But what can that have to do with me?' she said. 'I'm not a sorcerer; and if I was, then the king would—'

'No, no, my dear; you misunderstand.' Arrine reached out and took hold of her hands, squeezing them reassuringly. 'Of course you're not one of their kind! If you were . . . well, to be blunt, if you were, Grendon would not have allowed you to live beyond your first meeting. But you *do* have another skill.'

'As a clairvoyant?'

'Yes. One who can penetrate the darkness in which the sorcerers shroud themselves, and see the secrets which they keep. In other words, you have the ability to be the king's eyes, to enable him, finally, to erase the scourge of the Sanctifieds.'

The Sanctifieds . . . Sefira's mind sprang back to her first day under Grendon's wing, and the meeting with the coachman on the road to Chalce. In the wake of that encounter she had asked an innocent question, and Grendon's savage response had confounded her. 'They and their ways are anathema to any living soul who values his life and his future,' he had said. 'Fear them, hate them, and never stint in declaring the depth of your hatred to everyone you meet.'

Arrine spoke again. 'To erase the Sanctifieds is King Karel's most fervent wish,' she said. 'Help him in that task, Sefira, and he will be ready to grant you anything you want.' She paused, then added pointedly, 'A full pardon will only be a small measure of his gratitude.'

Sefira looked from Arrine to Grendon, saw that he was smiling and didn't like the smile. This, she realised, was blackmail, and for all her overt kindness Arrine was as much a part of it as Grendon was. Which could only mean one thing – that they both had something to gain.

She bit back the angry retort she would have liked to make and instead demanded, 'And what do *you* want, Grendon? Whatever your reasons for doing this, it isn't for my sake, so don't pretend that it is!'

Arrine's face remained neutral, but Grendon's smile broadened. 'I've no intention of pretending anything, my lady.' He used the term, she knew, because he was well aware that she disliked its derisive overtone. 'Yes, of course I have something to gain. Or rather, two things – status, and payment.'

'You're *selling* me!'

'If you care to put it that way. At least, I'm selling your talents. But don't forget that you'll benefit from it too, and to a far greater degree. You won't only earn from this in a material sense; you'll also earn your life. And I imagine that's worth more to you than mere pride.'

The resentful glint in Sefira's eyes told him that his words had stung, and he wondered briefly if she had yet begun to ask herself just why he was so often unpleasant to her. She still seemed to assume that it was simply a fact of his nature, and he needed to maintain that deception a little longer. It was a matter of fine balance; provoking that *other*, without making the mistake of also arousing her conscious suspicions.

She had calmed down, though her anger still simmered. Suddenly and sharply, she asked the question he had been waiting for.

'How do you know that I have this power?' she flared at him. '*I'm* not aware of it, so how do *you* know?'

Grendon laced his fingers together with the air of a patient teacher confronted by a dullard pupil. 'I'm trained to know,' he replied. 'Trained to recognise the signs.'

'What signs? What have I done, that makes you so certain you know more of me than I do?'

He regarded her steadily. 'Do you remember the night we spent in the old watchtower?'

Sefira's eyes narrowed. 'Only too well.'

Arrine looked puzzled, and Grendon turned to her with faint amusement in his expression. 'Sefira and I had a minor misunderstanding that night,' he said. 'In the small hours of the morning she woke to find herself lying on the watchtower floor with a bruised face, and me standing over her. She jumped to the conclusion – quite erroneously – that I had attempted to rape her and then hit her when she tried to resist.'

Sefira's cheeks had turned scarlet with mortified fury. 'And isn't that the truth?' she demanded.

'No, it is *not* the truth. Quite frankly, you flatter yourself if you think it is. What actually happened was that you had a psychic episode.'

She stared at him, nonplussed. 'A what?'

'To put it more bluntly, a fit. Your voice woke me; you were standing in the middle of the room with your arms outspread, staring at nothing and speaking aloud. A few minutes later you became hysterical, and I had to knock you unconscious to stop you from harming yourself. But before that, you uttered some clear predictions.'

Sefira blinked. She was suddenly very unsure of herself. 'What did I say?'

'You predicted the meeting with the coachman on the road the following day, and the news he would pass on. You also gave the name of the Sanctified who had been arrested in Chalce, and a description of the circumstances under which he and his family were taken. I took time to check the facts while we were there, and your revelation was highly accurate – you gave a number of small details which you couldn't possibly have known except by psychic means.' Grendon leaned back in his chair. 'You proved your abilities beyond any shadow of a doubt. And now, they will be your salvation.'

'And your enrichment.'

'Do you find that so offensive?'

Sefira frowned. Did she? After all, without him she certainly would not have survived this far; she owed him something, and if he profited from this it would only be fair repayment. What rankled, she admitted to herself, wasn't the idea of paying, but the simple fact that the debt had been incurred in the first place.

He was holding her gaze with more than a hint of challenge in his eyes, and abruptly Sefira looked away. 'No,' she said. 'I don't.'

Grendon and Arrine exchanged a glance which she didn't see, and Arrine spoke. 'You've nothing to fear from the king, Sefira, and nothing to fear from your own abilities. I assure you again that you're *not* one of the sorcerer caste; your talent is a natural accident of birth, albeit very rare. Take this chance, my dear. Take the reprieve and the freedom that it offers you.'

She was wavering, still unsure but desperately wanting to

believe the words. 'But if I fail . . .' she said.

'You won't fail. Grendon knows, and he can help you. Trust his judgement.'

Sefira wanted to say that she trusted nothing in which Grendon had any hand, but the protest was fighting a losing battle with the gentler logic of Arrine's argument. She wavered, hesitated . . .

'All right.' Her voice sounded remote to her own ears, as though someone else were speaking for her. And somewhere very, very deep inside her was a stifled anger, almost fury, that hurt like a sharp stone lodged in her gut. 'I'll do what you want.' She blinked rapidly. 'I don't think I have any choice, do I?'

Neither Arrine nor Grendon answered, but she felt their tension ease and realised on some semi-conscious level how important her favourable answer had been to them. It occurred to her to wonder why, but she couldn't quite cope with the thought and so pushed it away into a dark cranny where it wouldn't haunt her. Aloud, she said, 'What must I do to prepare myself?'

'Nothing, except have a sound night's sleep,' Arrine told her.

She laughed hollowly. 'That won't be easy.'

'Of course; I understand. If you like, I can give you something that will help.'

'Yes.' Sefira shivered involuntarily. 'Perhaps that would be a relief . . . Thank you.'

'Then I think we'd do best to close the subject. We'll spend the evening quietly, retire early and be fresh for the morning.' She took Sefira's hands again, smiling kindly into her eyes. 'Don't be afraid, Sefira. All will be well. You'll see.'

Rain was still falling, closing the house and the world beyond it in a leaden and dismal pall. Getha had doused the lamps and gone to bed, and the manservant, Jeram – seldom seen and still more seldom heard – had gone silently out into the saturating night to close the house's heavy shutters before making his way to his own lowly quarters in the stable mews. Grendon and Arrine had waited a further hour, passing the time with a desultory card game, and now, with all as secure and private as it could be, they went quietly up the stairs by the light of one candle, and eased open the door of Sefira's room.

At a nod from Grendon, Arrine snuffed out the candle. It took a few moments for their eyes to adjust to the dark, but as faint outlines began to form out of the blackness Grendon touched Arrine's shoulder in a silent alert, and she dimly saw him nod towards the bed and its occupant.

Sefira was dead to the world; Arrine's offered sleeping draught had done its work and nothing would stir her for some hours yet. But something else was awake. At the moment it manifested only as a faint, chilly smudge of radiance, like the afterglow of some peculiar and deceptive marsh-light hovering over swampy ground. But it was moving, drifting between bed and window, and its movement had an air of purpose.

Arrine drew a long, soft breath, tasting the unnatural cold in the air. She made as if to whisper something but Grendon stilled her with a warning gesture and, putting his lips close to her ear, mouthed,

'*Look for the face.*'

To Arrine there seemed to be no face, nor any other feature in the shifting glimmer, but when she narrowed her eyes in an effort to focus the better, she saw it. And instantly twenty years slid away leaving the past a raw and open wound in her mind.

Every instinct Arrine possessed impelled her to shrink back and leave the room, fastening the door and shutting this and all it implied away into blank, black forgetfulness. She fought the impulse, aware of, and thankful for, the presence of Grendon's hand still on her shoulder, and forced her gaze to stay on the slowly moving light and the face within it. So white, so barren . . . it was a thing devoid of humanity, with its great, glistening eyes and its white mouth moving soundlessly, ceaselessly, pitilessly, and a shudder that felt like a knife-thrust went through her.

'It hungers . . .' The sickness she felt was betrayed in her whisper.

But Grendon shook his head. 'No. It was sated on the river, and as yet it expends little energy; it wants no more sustenance for the present. It's merely exploring its surroundings. Growing accustomed to them. Learning.'

Arrine shuddered again, and when Grendon reached to close the door, she was grateful to withdraw into the warmer, kindlier dark of the small landing. She heard the latch fall into place and closed her eyes momentarily in relief.

'I thought . . .' Her voice caught; she touched a hand to her throat and tried a second time. 'I thought I would never see such a thing again.'

Grendon took the candle from her and re-lit it. 'I'm sorry you had to see it.'

'No. No, don't be sorry; I was the one who insisted. I think perhaps I needed proof, for I couldn't quite believe . . .' She looked to right and left, quickly, like a nervous animal. 'I would prefer to go downstairs now. If you'll forgive me . . .'

They returned to the ground floor as quietly as they had come, and Arrine went to the fire to warm her hands, which felt pinched and numb. Facing the flames, she said:

'Sefira has no knowledge of this?'

'As far as I can tell she's completely unaware of it. She probably never has known.'

'Poor child. Poor *child*.' Suddenly she looked at him over her shoulder. 'Grendon, my conscience isn't easy. To subject her to the full power of this; to use her for our own ends – when I think of the past, and the pain and terror of that—'

'It's a part of herself, Arrine. She was born with it and she can't escape from it, and I haven't the power to help her.' Grendon paused. 'I'm not Lendrer. I can't do what he did.'

Arrine sighed. 'No. That's true.'

'With or without us, the outcome for her will be the same,' Grendon continued. 'This thing won't abandon its claim to her. It can't, for its existence depends on her. One way or another, it will bring to her ruin; at best she'll face insanity and at worst, if it overreaches itself, she will die.'

'Which would be a mercy.'

'Quite – and not just for her. We can't change that, Arrine. It's her destiny, and has been since the day she was born. But this way, at least something worthwhile will be achieved through it.'

Arrine moved away from the fire, pacing slowly to a deep-cushioned chair. She sat down heavily.

'You're right. I'm a fool and a sentimentalist if I think that there might be some chance for her. There isn't.' She was silent for a few moments, then made an odd little gesture halfway between a shrug and a shiver, as though casting off something unpleasant that had settled on her shoulders. 'So, then – tomorrow.' Her voice had changed; it was almost brisk. 'Will you be able to exert enough control? And do you know precisely what you'll need to do?'

'I've no fears on either score. Sefira is malleable, and the other thing isn't yet independent enough to act on its own account. By the time it is, I shall have the upper hand. As for what I need to do, I've made all the necessary preparations. It'll be a simple demonstration, nothing more.'

'Enough to convince Karel?'

Grendon smiled reservedly. 'I doubt it; he's not that susceptible. But it will intrigue him beyond the point where he can turn down my proposal out of hand.'

Arrine nodded. 'Then there's no more to be said or done until morning.' She looked at him. 'Will you stay here tonight?'

'If I may.' An expressive glance upwards in the direction of the attic. 'It might be advisable.'

'Yes . . . yes, perhaps it would. Well, then . . . before I retire, there is one more thing. If you will.' She got up, moved to a shelf and took down a small brass cup, one of a pair that stood half hidden beside some books. Looking at it, she frowned. 'I have no unguent. These days, I use an oil from the kitchen; it seems safer.'

Grendon, too, had risen to his feet. He was smiling, and one hand went to an inner pocket of his coat, from which, wordlessly, he produced a small phial and held it out to her. 'From my quarters,' he said.

Arrine stared at the phial, then at him. 'You still keep some? That's a dangerous risk, Grendon! And to carry it about you—'

He closed his hand over hers, pressing the phial into her palm. 'Hush. You don't need to fear for my safety; I know how to avoid trouble. But if you'd prefer not to use it—'

'No.' She said it emphatically, and her eyes were warm. 'I'll use it. Thank you.'

Silence fell again as she measured nine drops of the thin, sweet-smelling oil from the phial into the brass cup. Then they moved to the fireside and knelt down, facing each other. A log crackled and sparks spiralled upwards, disappearing into the chimney and hissing as they met a flurry of rain coming down. One lamp burned on a table near the hearth; Grendon reached to turn down the wick until the small flame died and there was only the firelight. Then, together, they dipped the smallest fingers of their left hands into the cup, withdrew them and traced a symbol on the other's brow, then on each cheek just below the eyes. Their skin tingled where the unguent touched them; the feeling revived old memories and Arrine smiled poignantly, a smile which Grendon could not quite bring himself to return. Then they raised their hands; their fingers touched, entwined, and Arrine intoned three words in an old language, a language understood by few and now forbidden and slipping into obscurity. Grendon repeated them softly after her, then, as one, they began to speak the ritual that they both knew so well.

* * *

'As night to day; as sun to moon. As brother to sister; as parent to child. Ours is wisdom and the hidden way. In wisdom there is power; in power there will be justice. We who are Sanctified pledge trust unwavering. We who are Sanctified pledge loyalty undying. And we who are Sanctified pledge vengeance unsleeping . . .'

Chapter VIII

Perlion was thankful that the courier arrived while his wife was out visiting one of her friends. It wasn't that he wanted to keep any secrets from Isbel; that was not his way. But Isbel had never known of this. To tell her now, when it was more than likely that he was mistaken and that his enquiries would lead to nothing, would be cruel. In truth, Perlion told himself, he was probably an utter fool to pursue this in the first place. But he couldn't get that girl's face out of his memory and he knew he would have no peace until the questions in his mind were resolved.

When the courier came he was at his desk, attended by a steward and discussing next year's spring plantings for his estates. The loud rapping resounded through the house; a minute later footsteps thudded on the stairs and there was a knock. The steward answered it, low voices were audible, and the steward returned with a sealed letter in his hand.

'Thank you.' Perlion took the letter, looked at the writing and the seal. Both were familiar, and with a quickening pulse he glanced up at the steward. 'Leave me for a few minutes, Kayse, if you please. Take some refreshment in the kitchen.'

'Sir.' The steward bowed and departed. Trying not to fumble in his haste, Perlion opened the letter.

His man had been successful. The woman he had originally set out to look for was, it seemed, no longer alive – but he had traced her former apprentice, herself now middle-aged and practising in her own right in Tourmon. No direct contact had been made with her. But the letter gave her address.

Perlion put the sheet of paper down and stared through the window into the wet afternoon. Tourmon. Pure coincidence, of course. But somehow it fitted into place; almost as though it were an omen. He couldn't let it rest here. He *couldn't*.

There was a sudden noise in the passage outside; scuffling of feet and the sound of youthful voices. Then abruptly the door flew open and his two youngest children appeared.

'Father!' His twelve-year-old daughter, who had inherited his complexion and her mother's temperament, ran towards him, ignoring his frown at the unlooked-for interruption. 'Mother's home, and she asks that you join us at table so she can tell you all her news!'

Perlion smiled, at the same time slipping the letter underneath a ledger away from curious eyes. 'Yes, yes, tell her I'll come in a little while,' he said. 'And I have some news of my own for you. Tell me, how do you like the thought of taking a journey?'

'A journey? Where to?'

'Somewhere you've not been before.' He had been promising them this for some time, Perlion reminded himself, seeking to justify the impulse. 'To Tourmon.'

'Tourmon?' The girl's face lit up, and her younger brother whooped with delight. 'Tourmon! I've always wanted to see Tourmon!'

'Yes, well; it's not the best of seasons for it but I've a little time to spare at present. And I have a relation who lives in Tourmon – you've heard me talk of Cousin Vinor, haven't you? He supplies grain to the king's own household and has a home in the royal quarter itself. We'll be welcome to stay with him. So if your mother's agreeable we shall all go.' Perlion smiled. 'Does that please you?'

It did, and he suffered their joyful hugs and kisses and thanks before dismissing them with an assurance that he would be down in good time for the meal; there was just a little more business to be finished first. As they left, talking and planning excitedly, he drew the letter from its hiding place, folded it, and tucked it into an inner pocket. Tourmon. To do it this way would at least salve his conscience, for Isbel would enjoy the visit and would have plenty to keep herself and the children occupied while he pursued his quest a little further. Even if the midwife could not help him, he might find the girl again. He would see her face. He would learn more about her. And, one way or the other, he would be *sure*.

As they walked the last stretch of road, their heads and shoulders covered against the rain, Sefira refused to look at the bulk of the palace rising ahead of them but, in an effort to calm herself, mentally repeated the instructions she had been given. She must curtsey to the king – Arrine had taught her how. She must not sit unless invited to do so. She must not speak until directly addressed; and if she was addressed she must call the king 'Sir' or 'My Lord' and not 'Your Majesty'. Above all, Grendon had said, she must not stare at him, but should keep her gaze lowered except when answering a question. As for the rest of the coming ordeal – well, that was a matter for others, Grendon had told her, and she need do nothing whatsoever. Put yourself entirely in my hands, he had said. The thought did nothing for her confidence, but she had no choice but to comply.

They arrived at the palace, not by the imposing main entrance – for which Sefira was profoundly thankful – but through a wicket-gate that led to a sprawl of lower buildings behind the massive frontage. Grendon led her down paths and between high walls until she was hopelessly lost. Finally, they reached a small door which seemed to abut on to the kitchens. This, like every other entrance, was guarded, but Grendon showed the king's seal and they were instantly admitted. They passed through a maze of corridors, with Sefira staring, awed, at the splendour of wall-hangings and carvings and the soft glow of polished wood and bronze. People passed them by, some in livery, others in richer garments; one long-faced man in black, with a scarlet and gold sash across his shoulder, stopped them and imperiously demanded to know their business; Grendon showed the seal again and, reluctantly, the questioner withdrew.

At last they were in a quieter passage which led straight as an arrow to a single, ornate door. There were no guards this time; Grendon simply knocked on the door, and after a few moments it was answered.

'Arraigner Grendon.' Sefira took an immediate and intuitive dislike to the servant, whose voice and dark eyes she found too soft to be trustworthy. 'You are punctual. The king is expecting you.' His gaze fell on Sefira and lingered speculatively.

'Tomany.' Grendon nodded but didn't trouble with any further courtesies, and they went into the ante-room. Facing them was another door into which a crest had been set. The crest looked new, and there were faint marks in the wood of the other, older device that it had replaced. Tomany walked silently before them to the door and then, indicating that they should wait, opened it.

Arraigner Grendon, sir. And his . . . protégée.'

'Send them in.' The voice sounded younger than Sefira had expected. Tomany bowed, gestured to Grendon, and they were admitted into the king's presence.

This was Karel's private sitting room. The floor was carpeted, the chairs looked comfortable, and a fire burned hugely and cheerfully in the vast hearth, driving out shadows and the dismal wet of the outside world. It was possible that Karel had chosen this setting to put his visitors at their ease, but as she looked quickly into the king's eyes before casting her gaze down, Sefira doubted it. This was a shrewd man, and a ruthless one. And his smile, which she could just see through her lowered lashes, had no genuine warmth in it.

'Well, Grendon, so this is the girl? Not what I had expected.' She heard him rise, heard the tread of his feet on the soft carpet as he walked relaxedly towards her. 'What's your name, child?'

She glanced nervously at Grendon, who nodded encouragement. 'Sefira . . . sir,' she said.

'Sefira. You seem very young, Unusually young, I'd have said, to be married. Tell me, Grendon, have you made any effort to trace her husband?'

There was a brief pause, during which Sefira felt that her stomach was trying to turn over inside her, then Grendon said, 'She's not married, sir. It was simply a precautionary device, to . . . avoid complications.'

'And what might those complications be?' Karel enquired mildly.

Heat washed over Sefira and she felt perspiration break out on her skin. As though from an enormous distance she heard Grendon reply to the question, but her mind was paralysed and the words wouldn't register; she couldn't take in what he was saying. Then, to her horror, the king moved to stand directly in front of her, and his hand – she saw it at close quarters, scarred and hardened, with unclean fingernails – touched the edge of the wimple by her left cheek. He lifted it back a fraction, just enough to reveal the colour of her hair, and said, 'I see. Take the veil off, Sefira.'

Her eyes widened and, forgetting her lessons, she stared at him. His eyes were very light and very blue, and the look in them terrified her.

'The veil.' His eyebrows lifted a little as he waited. 'If you please . . . ?'

She couldn't disobey. Slowly, unsteadily, her hands went to her face and the wimple slid back, exposing the truth. Karel's expression didn't change as he saw her shorn hair. Voice still smooth, he asked without any ceremony, 'Murder, or treason?'

'M . . . murder.' Sefira's voice was barely audible.

'And are you guilty of the crime?'

Sefira's mouth worked and she started to stammer, 'I . . . I . . .' but Grendon intervened.

'We don't know, my lord. She might be guilty or innocent; she can't recall.'

'And you, with your skills, were unable to find out? You surprise me, Grendon. Or perhaps you thought it more expedient not to probe . . . and perhaps that was wise of you; we shall soon see. Well, lady,' looking at Sefira again, 'if you are what your champion claims, then I don't think we need to worry overmuch about your past misdeeds, if they exist. You know, I presume, why you've been brought here?'

'Y-yes, sir.'

'Good. Then I suggest we begin.' He looked briefly but intently into her eyes, then abruptly laughed. 'Posing as Grendon's wife . . . how very out of character for him! He *must* value you highly. I only hope he was a little more courteous to you than he would be to a real wife, if he had one.'

He was smiling, and despite her fear Sefira's mouth twitched in response. But she thought better of giving him an honest answer and after a moment he turned and walked back to the couch where he had been seated.

'Sit down, if you wish to.' From a flask near his elbow he poured himself a cup of wine. 'Then show me what you can do. I wait eagerly to be convinced.'

Sefira looked at Grendon, and he said very quietly, 'Sit. That chair, there. Relax your mind' – as if she could under such circumstances, Sefira thought – 'and don't try to obstruct or resist me. You'll remember nothing of this afterwards, but that doesn't matter. Sit, now.'

She obeyed, wishing that she could stop trembling. Since Grendon and Arrine had told her of his plan she had struggled fruitlessly to remember something about the powers that he claimed she possessed. But her efforts had yielded nothing; she couldn't recall, and she didn't even understand exactly what it was he believed she could do. That made no sense, for surely if she had a clairvoyant gift she *would* have remembered that before almost anything else. Yet her mind was a blank, a void. She had no inkling of any special talent. And that made her feel certain that Grendon was withholding something from her. It made her feel certain that something was *wrong*.

But this was no time to argue with him. King Karel was watching them, his expression a blend of the cynical and the bored and faintly tinged with impatience. Sefira tried to settle more comfortably on the chair. She didn't know what to expect, and so when Grendon crouched down before her and took hold of her hands, she was surprised.

'Keep still.' His voice was level. 'Look at me.'

She did, aware on the periphery of her vision that Karel had now sat forward and was observing with greater interest. Grendon's eyes, grey flecked with green – had she ever noticed that before? – were intently focused, the pupils dilated. Experimentally she tried to look away for a moment, and to her consternation found that she couldn't. Then, unbidden, something Karel had said a few minutes ago came suddenly to her mind. 'Guilty or innocent?' he had asked her; and when Grendon had answered for her, claiming – untruthfully – that they didn't know, the king had said: 'You with your skills, were unable to find out?' What 'skills' had he meant? What was Grendon capable of – and why, now, could she not even summon the *wish* to pull her gaze away from his? A well seemed to be opening up in her head, deep and dark, plunging away into depths she couldn't imagine or comprehend. Bigger, and darker . . . why couldn't she control it? What was happening to her willpower? *Where was her mind going . . . ?*

Beads of sweat broke out on Grendon's face as, moving slowly and carefully, he sat back on his haunches. He was aware of Karel's voice saying, 'You work quickly. I'm impressed,' but he ignored the comment, concentrating only on Sefira. Her eyes had taken on the peculiar, senseless yet penetrating look of one in a deep trance, and he knew without needing to test her that she had slipped away into another dimension of consciousness. Nonetheless, to be sure, he said aloud: 'Sefira. Can you hear my voice?'

No response. Karel said suspiciously, 'She's not aware of you.'

'That's as it should be.' Grendon's tone was curt. 'Now, sir – if you please – I need silence.'

Karel shrugged and leaned back once more, and Grendon transferred his grip to Sefira's wrists, feeling for her pulse. It was sluggish but steady; her head turned and her gaze appeared to be following his movements, but he knew that she saw nothing. Well and good; now all that remained was to shift his own consciousness into a dimension that matched hers, and he would be ready.

He closed his eyes, concentrating. Momentarily it occurred to him that Karel might have some treachery in mind – he would, after all, be vulnerable during this – but he dismissed the thought. The king had nothing to gain from harming him; if he had, it would have been done a long time ago. Controlling his breathing, slowing it down and letting it become shallow, he looked in his inner vision for the key that would allow him to slip between dimensions and on to the astral plane. It came; the symbol of an egg, black against softer darkness and striated with silver as though about to crack apart. Grendon waited until its form was complete, feeling rather than seeing it become three-dimensional, then focused his will. The egg shattered, silently but blindingly, and all sense of his physical surroundings vanished as he projected his mind through the broken shards.

He was in a strange, indistinct landscape that shifted erratically and uneasily between open ground and the confines of a town or village. There was no colour; everything was black, grey and silver, and the contours around him changed constantly. One moment a river ran beside his feet; the next instant it vanished and crumbling stone walls loomed where before there had been dim, distant hills. For a few moments it was disorientating, and Grendon took a hard grip on his senses, steadying his mind and assessing what he had found. There was great confusion here, mirroring the unconscious turmoil in Sefira's mind; but the lack of colour was a good augury for it meant that the territory was at least neutral. Now, he must begin his search.

He started to move forward; a strange, light sensation as though he were drifting on a gentle air current. And as he moved, he watched the perpetually altering landscape. Time, he knew, ran differently here; an hour might pass, or seem to, while in the physical world only a few minutes or even seconds had slipped away. No need to hurry. Haste tended to make one careless, which was a mistake he couldn't afford.

He could hear someone breathing. Himself, Sefira or Karel; whichever of them it was, it provided a link with reality and helped him to concentrate the better. Still moving, still searching. A horizon was visible now as another stone wall melted away into nothing. And the sky – or what passed for sky – was growing darker.

Then he saw a single spot of red smearing the ground ahead of him. It stood out starkly in the monochrome, and it was the sign he had been waiting for. The colour of blood. Apt. And an indication that *it* was aware of his presence.

Abruptly, everything changed again and Grendon found himself standing in a long, dark hall with doors leading off on either side. He could still hear breathing, and now it was augmented by the deeper throb of someone's heartbeat – probably, he thought, his own. The red smudge was still visible as a bright stain on the chequered floor, and as he moved towards it he felt a psychic tingle that warned him he was no longer alone here. Something had noted his presence and was waiting for him.

One of the doors stood open. Its shape was unstable and altered its dimensions each time he looked at it, and he slowed, approaching cautiously. He didn't think there would be a surprise attack – it didn't yet have the strength or confidence for that – but it would be looking for any weakness in his defences. Drawing level with the open door he halted and turned fully to face it. The fluctuating outline steadied, and beyond the frame a scene came into focus: an empty room, with stone walls and stone floor, and a cold shaft of light slanting in through a single slit of a window.

And in the light, like a player on a stage, his quarry was standing.

They stared at each other, and as Grendon took in the full impact of the thing's appearance, a memory which he had spent twenty years trying to erase swelled violently into his mind and heart. The creature was white as a newly buried corpse, and as thin; he could see the gaunt outlines of its frame beneath the filmy shift that clothed it, and its hands, their long fingers clawing restlessly, were nothing but skin and bone. Ashen hair fell to its shoulders in a ragged halo, and the face framed by the hair, though not beautiful, had a horribly and dangerously alluring vitality about it. There was *life* in that face. Alien life, but keen and vibrant and eager. And the huge eyes, their hard blue contrasting shockingly with the monochrome scene, glowed with a monstrous intelligence that made him feel sick to the core.

Time crawled while they gazed at each other. Grendon knew that the thing was assessing him just as he was assessing it, and he waited, knowing that whichever of them made the first move would be at a disadvantage. His patience, it seemed was the greater, for at last the thing blinked – the movement made him think of a predatory snake – and its tongue appeared, flicking over its lower lip. That startled him, for the tongue was a brilliant red and the sight of it against the sickly pallor of the creature's face was almost obscene. He had forgotten so much, he told himself.

Then it spoke, in a thin, husky voice. It said: 'I know your name.'

Grendon didn't answer. Again it blinked, and then it smiled, showing small, perfect teeth and a scarlet cavern of a mouth beyond. 'I know what you are. I know what you did.'

Ah, yes; hatred was creeping into its tone now. It had recognised the truth about him and it was angry.

'You destroyed one of us. Long ago. But I do not forget.'

Grendon spoke then for the first time. 'Neither do I,' he said.

It hissed, angrily, like a sullen cat. 'You will not destroy me.'

'I could.'

'*No!*' It spat the word. 'You could *not*.' Then its expression grew sly. 'I have Sefi. Sefi is my sister.'

'And if she should die?'

Silence. It put its head on one side, as though it wanted to appraise him from a different angle, but he knew that was a ploy to buy time while it considered. Then: '*You* will not kill her. If you meant to kill her, you would have tried to do so by now.'

'Possibly.'

'Not possibly. I see your mind. I know. So . . .' The evil little smile appeared again. 'You do not want to destroy me.' It giggled. 'That is foolish of you.'

'I have my own reasons.'

'I do not care about your reasons. You cannot harm me. You are too weak. And if you try to kill Sefi, I will destroy you.'

'I don't think so.'

'*Yes.* I saved Sefi from death before.'

'By driving her to murder.'

A shrug. 'I was hungry. When I am hungry, Sefi feeds me.' Its eyes shone suddenly with a hot glow. 'That makes me stronger, and so it makes her stronger, too. She depends on me.'

'Oh, yes,' Grendon said. 'But then, you also depend on her, don't you? Without her you could not feed, and you would wither away into nothing. Sefira could live without you – but you can't survive without her to sustain your filthy existence.'

That hit its intended target, and he felt the psychic thrust of fury that emanated from the being as it hissed at him a second time. He knew its weakness, and it was aware that he knew it. It was time, he thought, to begin bargaining.

'Sefira is in danger now,' he said. 'And only I can help her.'

The thing spat, and a ripple of disturbance went through its bloodless frame. 'Not true! *I* protect Sefi!'

'Not from this. You haven't the power.'

The taunt had the desired effect, for it tore its gaze from him and looked around, its tongue darting as though tasting the atmosphere. Grendon felt the momentary slip between dimensions as it probed, and hoped fervently that nothing of its form would manifest in the material world. But there was no alarm, no sudden tugging at his mind, and after a few moments the being faced him again.

'One man.' The words were contemptuous. 'He is nothing; we can overcome him.'

'He is a king,' Grendon said, 'and kings have servants and men-at-arms to protect them. If you goad Sefi into killing the king, she might succeed, but then the king's men would take vengeance on her, and you would not be strong enough to stop them.'

It frowned, resentful and suspicious and yet aware that he was right. Before it could think beyond that, Grendon continued, 'If Sefira does what the king expects of her, her crime will be pardoned and she will continue to live and sustain you. But if she fails, she will die. Do you want her to die?'

It uttered a peculiar, soft growl. '*No.*'

'Then you must do as I tell you.'

'*You?*' This time the psychic shock was painful, and left his consciousness tingling. 'I will give nothing to *you*. Only ruin. Only death.'

'There will be only ruin and death for you if you refuse.'

It turned its head again, rapidly, its mouth working, and he knew that it was seeking for another option. But he had driven it into a trap from which there was only one exit, and at last it had no choice but to acknowledge the fact.

It demanded, sullenly, 'What do you want?'

'Answers to questions that the king will ask Sefira. She does not know those answers, but it will be a simple matter for you to find them and place them in her mind.'

It considered this. 'How will that help Sefi?'

'It will earn the king's gratitude. That is what will keep her alive.'

Yes; he had it snared. However much it might loathe him, it couldn't refuse without putting Sefira's life, and thus its own, in jeopardy. Grendon felt the palpable tension as it struggled one last time to find an escape route, but he had won the battle and they both knew it.

'Very well.' Hostility and malice spiked its voice like vitriol. 'I will do it. *This* time.'

'There will be other times, if you want her to live.'

'Perhaps there will. But not always.' It blinked in its slow, menacing way, and the cruel little smile appeared on its face again. 'Not always, Grendon. I have time. I am patient. And I never, *ever* forget.'

Though as yet the threat was an empty one, Grendon felt a cold spike go through him. For as long as this monstrosity continued to exist, he knew, it would be looking for any and every chance to take retribution, and in time, if he made the smallest mistake in his dealings with it, it would be strong enough to strike. On the material plane his body broke out in a chilly sweat. On the astral, he pushed back the thick, choking fear that came roiling out of his past.

The being was watching him intently, still smiling. 'Ask your questions,' it said, almost sweetly. 'Ask, and I will give you what you need.' Then it giggled once more. 'We are *all* linked now. Sefi depends on you. I depend on Sefi. And *you* depend on *me*. Don't you, Grendon? Don't you? That amuses me . . . but it will not always amuse me, and when I no longer find it amusing *I* will come to *you*, when you least expect it. And then *you* will be the one to die!'

Grendon didn't reply; he had nothing to say.

'Ask your questions,' the being repeated. 'Go back to your king, and we shall all play the game with him. But remember me, Grendon. My name is Xai. Remember that. For I *shall* kill you one day.'

The unstable walls of the hall shuddered, lost their form and collapsed into the contours of a vague, bleak open vista. Briefly the shaft of light lingered, shining now through a window that hung bizarrely in mid-air. Then it flickered, faded, and sank into darkness, and the creature called Xai was gone.

Chapter IX

Sefira's legs failed her halfway to Arrine's house. She had been feeling disorientated since they left the palace but had thought she would be able to walk the distance; she was wrong, however, and suddenly the strength went out of her. She felt it go, but there was no time to save herself, and like a puppet with its strings cut she sagged helplessly and ungracefully on to the streaming pavement.

Grendon, who had belatedly reached out to stop her fall and had been too late, said, 'In the names of all the—' then broke off the oath and bent to catch hold of her arms. Sefira looked up at him, her eyes bemused. 'I'm sorry . . .'

'Never mind that. Have you hurt yourself?'

'Nn . . . no. I'm just wet.'

He hauled her unceremoniously to her feet and, when she seemed incapable of doing it herself, tried to shake the worst of the water from her skirt. She tottered; he steadied her, then frowned. 'What happened?'

'I don't know.' Her legs were supporting her now, but Sefira felt chilled through to the bone and couldn't stop shivering. 'Suddenly I just . . . had no strength. I couldn't walk; I couldn't even stand.' She shut her eyes. 'I feel so *tired*.'

'That's hardly surprising under the circumstances.' Grendon had been so preoccupied with personal considerations that he hadn't given a thought to the effects the past hour had had on her. His conscience twinged and he adjusted her cloak on her shoulders, pulling up the hood which had slipped off as she fell.

'Come on. A warm fire and something to eat will soon set you right again. Can you walk the rest of the way?'

She nodded, but didn't demur when he put a supporting arm around her. They moved on again, and Grendon pushed away other, darker thoughts as he speculated on what might be happening in the palace at this moment.

That demonstration had gone better than he had dared hope. With Sefira still in a trance Grendon had pulled his own consciousness back to the physical world, to find that a little over ten minutes had passed and Karel was becoming sceptical and bored. The encounter with Xai was sharply uppermost in Grendon's mind, but with an effort he had thrust it aside and told the king that he might ask any question he chose of Sefira. Karel had deliberated for a few moments, then demanded to know how many rooms there were in the palace. Sefira's response had surprised him and amused Grendon, for her answer gave the true number, including various chambers whose existence was known only to the most senior members of the court and whose purpose was not, and never had been, a matter for public disclosure. Karel was impressed, but guardedly so, and his next three questions were more obscure. Sefira answered each without hesitation, and finally the king had only one more to put to her. There was, he said, a certain man by the name of Ruethe, of whom nothing had been heard for more than a year. He was very anxious to discover Ruethe's whereabouts, but all enquiries had so far failed. What, he asked, could Sefira's clairvoyance achieve in that matter?

There had been a long pause; so long that Grendon began to fear that he had overestimated Xai's powers. But suddenly, in her trance, Sefira smiled.

'The Sanctified you are looking for lives in a village called Ishen. He goes by the false name of Nimre, and claims to be of the Mercantile Fellowship.' A pause. 'And his true name is not Ruethe. It is Rueshe.'

Grendon doubted if he would ever forget the look that

123

came to Karel's face at that last statement. He had tried to trick Sefira – or, rather, Xai – and the ploy had failed. He would check the information, of course, but Grendon had no doubt whatever that it was correct, for Xai and her kind were abominably effective in tracking on the astral planes. Another Sanctified would be found and put to a barbaric death, and Karel's position would become a fraction more secure. Rueshe. Grendon didn't know the name, and he gave silent thanks for that small mercy.

So, then: Xai had fulfilled her part of the bargain, and Sefira was none the wiser. She would ask him what had happened, and he would tell her enough to allay her fears but not enough to give any hint that the 'clairvoyance' had been anything other than her own. Within a few days a second summons would come from the palace. And while they waited for it, Grendon had a great deal of work to do – not least of which was contending with Xai herself. In the wake of this she would be hungry, and it was vital that her feeding should be controlled. Arrine would do what she could, Grendon knew, but she had never followed the sorcerer's path as her husband had done and so her ability to help was limited. The time had come to map out and act upon the next stage of the plan. And when that was completed . . .

Sefira stumbled then, and as he reflexively caught her and tightened his hold, Grendon broke the chain of his thoughts before they could go any further. His mind was running too fast; the future was still very far from assured, and to plan ahead when the first foothold was not yet secured was dangerously complacent. One step at a time. He had learned that lesson many years ago, from Lendrer. Anything else was too great a risk.

Sefira said, her voice muffled by the cloak, 'I feel ill.'

'Exhaustion. The episode was draining for you; such things always are.'

He felt the movement as she nodded. Then, at last, the questions came. 'What happened to me back there? What did

I *say*?' Her body twisted suddenly and she tried to pull back from his grasp enough to look up at him. 'What will the king do now?'

'Peace,' Grendon said. 'You've nothing to fear. The king was impressed.'

'What did he—'

'I'll tell you everything when you're dry and rested,' he interrupted firmly. 'No questions for now. Just be assured that it went well.'

Though he would have denied the fact to her face, he pitied Sefira. She was too young for this; an innocent, almost a child, and the fact that her soul was the sustaining nucleus that gave vitality and power to a demonic parasite made no difference. She knew nothing of it, not yet, and though in time to come that would inevitably change, to Grendon it was cause for compassion rather than loathing. But, as he had said to Arrine, this compassion must give way to the greater need and the greater cause. There was no room for doubt or hesitation.

They had reached the square of houses, and over Arrine's door the great lamp burned like a guiding beacon. The rain seemed to be abating, though possibly that was mere wishful imagination. Hooking his arm more firmly around the flagging and now silent Sefira, Grendon turned towards the warm, dry haven of the house.

In her nightmare, a voice was saying to Sefira over and over again, '*I'm hungry . . . I'm hungry . . .*' She tried to tell herself that it was only a dream and that she should not listen, but the words had an awful compulsion in them and something within her was beginning to respond.

'*Feed me, Sefi. Feed me. Strengthen us. Feed me . . .*' Sefira's stomach was gnawing, aching with a strange, hollow pain that seemed to spread not only through her body but through her entire being. Hungry. *So* hungry. She had to eat; she had to *feed*, or the pain would grow too great to bear.

In her sleep she cried out aloud then, a plea and a demand

in the night for the sustenance she craved. In her was an anger which was threatening to swell into blind fury. *She would not be thwarted! She would . . .*

Then another presence loomed into the dream, and out of the darkness something was pushed into her flailing hands. What she did then she could not later remember, but the fresh, warm taste of blood in her mouth was a balm that soothed the snarling and craving thing writhing in her head, and it loosed its hold on her, and the pangs began to fade, and Sefira's body relaxed into the realms of a deep and almost comatose sleep.

Grendon disposed of the bird's drained carcass, while Arrine cleaned the tell-tale spatterings from Sefira's face and hands and slipped a clean pillow under her head. Through all this Sefira didn't stir, and when all was done Grendon and Arrine stood watching her for some minutes in sombre silence.

Xai had not shown herself. Grendon had felt the sense of intense cold around Sefira, and the grey aura had manifested again, but the thin, spectral shape of the soul-invading parasite had not appeared. This time she had been easily satiated, but Grendon was aware that her satisfaction would not last for long. Each feeding gave her strength; and as her strength grew, so her demands would become greater and more frequent. He would have to maintain tight control if her predations weren't to get out of hand before the time was right.

Arrine seemed to know what he was thinking. She looked at him, an uneasy, searching look, and said softly, 'Are you sure you're strong enough for this?'

Grendon continued to look at Sefira. 'No,' he said. 'No one could be sure beyond any doubt. But I believe I can do it.' He took a step back, towards the door. 'I've nothing to lose, Arrine. Even if I fail, and die of it, it's better than the alternative.'

She had no answer to that. She turned, went out, and he followed her wordlessly down the stairs to the ground floor.

* * *

Several days passed without any word from the palace. Sefira had woken with no memory whatever of Xai's visitation, and the episode was not repeated; but the tension it had sparked in Grendon and Arrine soured the atmosphere and made Sefira – who misinterpreted the reasons for it – increasingly nervous.

Then, on the sixth morning after the interview, a courier arrived with a letter bearing the king's seal.

The fact that the letter was delivered to Arrine's house was a clear and deliberate signal from Karel that his spies hadn't been idle. The king knew that both Grendon and Sefira were under this roof, and by displaying his knowledge he was giving Grendon a none too subtle warning against any trickery. That was no less than Grendon had expected, and he smiled wryly as he broke the letter's seal.

The message was brief: merely an instruction to bring Sefira to the palace that afternoon, with arrangements as before. No hint of what Karel might or might not have unearthed as a result of her 'clairvoyance'; for all Grendon knew, the information could have proved false and she would simply be arrested without any further ceremony. But if that was the case, Karel wouldn't have troubled with the charade of a letter. Armed men would have come for Sefira, and that would have been an end of the matter. The fish, Grendon was certain, had taken the bait.

So, another walk along the straight, paved road, with the bulk of the palace poised like some unpredictable nemesis ahead of them. There was a sporadic respite from the autumn rain, and a number of people were about in the streets, but Sefira was too nervous, and Grendon too preoccupied, to notice among their number the middle-aged woman who passed by with two children at her heels. Isbel, however, saw them, and recognition glimmered in her mind. The tall, fair man, and his wife who looked so young . . . she had seen them somewhere before, but couldn't place them. Possibly, she thought, Perlion would remember. Not that it was important, but she would mention it at dinner tonight. The man could be a business acquaintance, in which case Perlion might wish to call on him while they were in Tourmon.

'Mother! Mother, look at *that* house!' Her son grasped hold of her hand and tugged, eagerly pointing out yet another piece of Tourmon's elegant architecture. His pleasure at being in the king's own city knew no bounds, and Isbel wondered if Cousin Vinor might find a way to let him see King Karel in person, even if only from a distance.

'Yes, my dear. Isn't it all splendid?' She smiled indulgently, and they went on their way.

Karel was waiting, as before, in his private sitting room. This time, though, no fire burned in the grate, and from the king's brisk manner when they entered Grendon knew immediately that this interview was to be more cursory than the last.

Karel had a folded document in his hand; without any preamble he handed it to Grendon and said, 'The Sanctified, Rueshe, was arrested in the village of Ishen two days ago. He has confessed his true identity, and will be brought to Tourmon for Purging. This is my warrant instructing you to oversee the matter personally.'

Sefira saw Grendon's lips turn white at the edges, and also saw the glint of undisguised malice in the king's eyes. She didn't understand – there was clearly some deep antipathy between Grendon and Karel, but the reason for it was impossible to fathom. Before she could explore her puzzlement any further, however, Karel turned to her.

'I owe you thanks, Mistress Sefira. Your prediction proved accurate in every detail, and thanks to you a threat to the peace and security of this land has been exposed and will shortly be eradicated.' He smiled, though the smile didn't quite reach his eyes. 'I am in your debt.'

'Th . . . thank you, sir . . .' Sefira could think of nothing more consequential to say.

'So, Grendon,' Karel swung on his heel, 'as you seem to have proved your protégée's talents, we come to the question of the arrangements that are to be made. I've given your requests a good deal of thought, and I think I can accommodate them . . . with, of course, one or two provisos of my own.'

Grendon said nothing.

'Regarding your living quarters,' Karel went on, 'I see no objection to granting you an apartment in the palace.' He noted Sefira's quick, surprised glance at Grendon. 'And I will also grant you guardianship of Sefira . . . ah.' Now his gaze fastened intently on the girl's face as she drew in a breath of shock and her jaw dropped. Karel smiled. 'Did Grendon not tell you, mistress? He feels that in your somewhat ambiguous position – by which I mean your memory loss and the unresolved matter of the crime you may have committed – you need protection. And I'm inclined to agree with him. So it would be prudent, he suggests, to appoint him officially as your custodian . . . or guardian, or whatever term you prefer to use.'

Sefira swallowed. Grendon had said *nothing* of this, and from somewhere deep inside her a vast anger surged against him and tried to break loose. Desperately she struggled to control it. 'He . . . did not tell me, sir,' she managed to get out. There was venom in her voice, and Karel looked astutely in Grendon's direction.

'That was very cavalier of him. However, when you consider your position . . .' He paused. 'Grendon is also ideally qualified to help you hone your remarkable abilities – and those abilities, of course, are what *I* require from you. So I'm sure you'll agree that it's the most sensible thing to do.'

She realised, then, that the polite words masked a tacit but emphatic threat. Karel was giving her no choice in the matter. He wanted her skills for his own use; Grendon was a part of that usage, and if Sefira did not comply her future would be grim, and brief.

Karel, seeing the bitter emotions in her face, said more kindly, 'Don't forget, Sefira, that *you* will also benefit from this arrangement. After all, it's quite improper for a king to employ a convicted felon in his household; so if you are to enter my service your conviction must be quashed and a full pardon entered in the official records.'

She blinked. 'You would . . .'

'Grant you that? Certainly. In fact my secretary has already drafted the necessary document; it needs only my signature and seal and the thing will be done.'

Sefira's anger collapsed. Grendon had used the prospect of a pardon to gain her agreement to his plans, but she had not expected it to be achieved as easily and quickly as this. To be free of danger, free of fear . . . a small inner voice warned her that that freedom might prove to be only another form of captivity, but at least this way she had time, and a chance. And life in the royal household, even under Grendon's guardianship, would surely have its own rewards?

Then Karel spoke again. 'There is, however, one small problem which must be dealt with before everything is settled.' His attention now was on Grendon, and Sefira saw that a glimmer of amusement was beginning to creep into his eyes. 'Sefira has kept her secret only by posing as your wife. Obviously that can't continue; yet neither can we have her displaying her cropped hair at court for all to see. It seems to me there's one very simple answer that will satisfy convention and keep Sefira's secret into the bargain.' Clearly savouring his amusement now, he smiled broadly at Grendon. 'And that is for you to take her as your wife in reality instead of in pretence.'

Sefira did not know whether she or Grendon was the more dumbfounded. They both stared at the king in disbelief; Karel only continued to smile, and after a time which seemed to crawl by Grendon found his voice, though he clearly had difficulty controlling it.

'You're . . . not serious . . .'

'Oh, but I am. It's the perfect solution, don't you think?'

Something in Grendon snapped. 'No, sir, I do *not*!' he

retorted explosively. 'I have no desire whatever to marry anyone, let alone—'

Karel interrupted, holding up a warning hand. 'Watch your choice of words, Grendon. I'm sure you don't want Sefira to take insult.'

Grendon shot Sefira a furious glare which she returned with cold hostility. 'Whether she does or whether she doesn't, my lord, the fact remains that I have *no* desire to marry her, and I've no doubt she feels the same as I do!'

'I see.' Karel sauntered to a nearby table and fingered a sheet of paper that was lying there. 'A pity, when we were so close to an agreement. And here is the decree of pardon; as I said, completed and ready to be signed. It's unfortunate that it must now be wasted.'

He picked up the paper and made as if to tear it in half. Sefira uttered an involuntary, choked sound – and Karel's hand paused. 'Yes, mistress Sefira? Was there something you wanted to say?'

Sefira glanced desperately at Grendon. His face was like granite, and an ice-cold light burned in his eyes. He didn't speak, and Sefira took a deep breath, struggling to find words.

'Sir – my lord – if this is—' but she couldn't continue.

'If you were going to ask whether this is a part of the bargain I offer you, then the answer is yes, it is.' Karel's gaze flicked from her to Grendon. 'However, as Grendon is clearly immovable in his attitude, then I'm afraid there's nothing more I can do.'

Grendon said suddenly, 'I would like to speak to Sefira alone, sir. With your permission.'

'Certainly.' Karel waved a negligent hand. 'You may use this room. I'll return in five minutes.'

He crossed the floor and went out through an inner door. As it closed behind him, Grendon turned to Sefira. Resentment and anger burned in his look, but it wasn't directed at her – and underlying it was something else. Grendon was cornered, and he knew it.

'The king,' he said at last, tensely, 'has an extremely unorthodox sense of humour.'

For once, Sefira thought, they were in agreement. 'In case you need reassurance,' she told him, 'I'm no more willing to marry you than you are to wed me.'

'I don't doubt it for a moment. However, it seems that unless we *do* acquiesce, your future – and my ambitions – are in ashes.'

Silence. After a hesitation of some seconds Grendon continued. 'There is an answer. Not ideal, and not especially palatable, but it might be the only logical choice.'

'What is it?'

'To do what the king wants.'

Her eyes flared. 'I wouldn't—'

'Wait; hear me out. I mean, to go through the marriage rite, but not to live as man and wife. We would have to share the same quarters, but it would be easy enough to keep ourselves separate from each other.'

'You mean you wouldn't want to . . . claim a husband's rights?'

'No, I wouldn't. Whatever you might think of me, I'm not the kind of man who would take any woman against her will.' He gave her a small, hard smile. 'Nor am I *quite* so repulsive that I need to. We can play one role in public, another in private, and what Karel doesn't know can't hurt him.'

Sefira considered. She knew, now, that Grendon had not tried to rape her in the watchtower, and the knowledge had forced her to revise her view of him a little. She didn't like him and fundamentally she didn't trust him; but in this, at least, she believed she could rely on his word.

Besides, in all her consideration of fine feelings, she was overlooking one vital thing.

'The king implied,' she said, 'that if I refuse, I won't be pardoned. Did he mean it?'

'Yes.'

It was the answer she had expected. Sefira stared at the

floor. 'Then . . . I suppose it's a better choice than death.'

Grendon laughed cynically. 'Thank you for the compliment!'

She glowered at him through lowered lashes. 'For someone who doesn't want to marry, you seem very untroubled by the prospect. You're surely not offering to do this for my sake?'

'No, I'm not,' he retorted. 'As I've already told you, I have my own ambitions and you can do a great deal to help me further them. That's my sole motive, and on balance the sacrifice is worth it.'

Did she believe him? Sefira asked herself. On the surface his arguments had a certain logic to them, but she still found it hard to credit that a man like Grendon cared so much for ambition and advancement. It didn't fit with her own observations over the past days, and she mistrusted it.

But even if there was some underlying purpose behind the façade Grendon put on, the fact remained that she herself had a stark choice. Marriage, or execution. The dilemma answered itself.

She let her breath out in a long sigh and said, 'Very well. I'll do it.' She looked up, challengingly, 'But in name only. If you ever try—'

'I won't. Be assured of it. And if it's any consolation to you, the law allows for an unconsummated marriage to be annulled providing the woman's virginity is proved, so one day in the future we can be rid of each other. That is, assuming you *are* a virgin.'

'I am!' She said it indignantly; for all her memory loss she was certain of that fact.

Grendon smiled an odd, thoughtful smile. 'Yes . . . yes, I don't doubt it either.' Xai would have ensured it, he told himself. An unsullied host was far easier to control. 'So, then; the king will return in a few moments. Do we have a bargain?'

He held out one hand, formally and, she saw in surprise, without any apparent sardonicism. Sefira hesitated for a moment, then quickly, before doubt could get the better of her, took his fingers in a brief clasp.

'Yes. A bargain.'

Grendon hid his reaction, but inwardly he felt a surge of relief. What was it he had said to Arrine a few days ago? He had nothing to lose. The cause that they both served was paramount, and besides that, nothing else mattered. Karel's contemptible and unexpected joke had caught him unawares, but once the first shock wore off it seemed a relatively small price to pay. The king doubtless believed that Grendon had carnal designs on Sefira, and this was simply a piece of petty spite on his part; a turning, or so he thought, of the tables.

Two years ago such a trick would have been beneath Karel's notice, and it was interesting, Grendon reflected, to see how time and the temptations of absolute rulership could alter a man's character. Pleasing, too, to the self-seeking tacticians of the court, who must be finding their master easier to manipulate with each passing day. Well, he too would be in a position to play the game now, though with a very different outcome in mind. In that sense he owed Sefira a debt, and he had a pang of conscience at the thought of how he would be obliged to repay it. She deserved a chance, at least. And it *was* possible, though the odds against it were enormous, that she might survive. If that miracle happened, then he might be able to help her. It had, after all, been done before.

Suddenly Grendon pushed that thought away with an angry inward reflex. It was too dangerous a path to follow, even in his imagination, for by the time Sefira was ready to do what he wanted of her, Xai would be too strong for any such idea to be considered. And in the meantime, Xai would present other problems. She would learn of this latest development soon enough, and when she did, she would resist it violently. He must be ready for that; ready to deal with it. If he wasn't, there would be mayhem. And – until the time was right – that must be avoided at any cost.

Chapter X

Grendon said under his breath, 'She's here. I sense her.'

Arrine glanced at him, then looked back to Sefira's recumbent form in the bed. 'The temperature's dropped. I remember that; it was always a forewarning.' She shivered, but not with cold.

Seconds passed, then a minute, as they waited. Outside, the great lamp over the front door reflected spectrally in the glass of the window. Then among the shadows of the room a paler, colder light began to materialise, forming a dim oval that hovered in mid-air. In her sleep Sefira smiled; not a pleasant smile but the same secretive, malignant expression that Grendon had seen on her face during their night in the abandoned house. And at the heart of the light oval, the tenuous figure of Xai took form.

Arrine stared into the baleful blue eyes and Grendon felt her shrink as though she had touched something foul and polluted. Xai had seen them both; and her momentary curious interest in this new woman, a stranger to her, was eclipsed by deeper malice as she focused her unhuman gaze on Grendon.

'Ah, you . . .' There was menace in the words, and an abiding hatred. 'We made a *bargain*, and now you try to break it. *You have cheated me!*'

The light brightened harshly and Xai's shape seemed to swell and distort. Grendon's hand came up rapidly; he made a sharp gesture, tracing a complex symbol in the air and his voice snapped out, '*Peace!*'

Xai was still. Her scarlet tongue appeared, touching her

135

lips, licking. She had felt the quick psychic surge from his mind and, thus far, it was enough to make her think twice about attempting any real attack.

'You will listen to me,' Grendon said sternly, 'and you will pay heed.' Xai hissed. He ignored her. 'Our bargain stands, and nothing has been broken. If you continue to give me what I want, then Sefira will continue to live and thrive. In the palace, in my care, she will thrive better than she could hope to do without me.'

Xai made a contemptuous sound deep in her throat. '*You* . . . You are nothing!'

'I am *everything*, if you want to maintain your existence. Never forget that, Xai.' He paused for long enough to be sure that his words had gone home, then continued, 'Sefira will become my wife. I do not want it and she does not want it, but it must now be a part of the plan. But I will not touch her. She will remain unsullied—'

'*Lie!*'

'Not a lie. I do not desire her.' Grendon's lip curled. 'I wouldn't desire any woman whose soul is tainted by a creature like you; think on that, and let it be proof enough!'

Xai hunched her shoulders and stared scornfully at him. Then her mouth widened in an unpleasant smile. 'A creature like me was good enough for you once. But you are different now. You are *different*.' Then, snakelike, her eyes flicked to Arrine's face for only the second time. With an effort Arrine held her cold stare, and suddenly Xai giggled.

'Oh, yes . . . *her*. I see. I know. Her man was your friend. He was your saviour. Yet when you killed him, she forgave you.'

Arrine made an awful sound and Grendon snapped furiously to Xai, 'Be silent!'

'Silent? Why silent? It is only the truth. She forgave you. Why did she do that? Was it to share your bed, Grendon? Does she share your bed now? Does she?'

'*I do not!*' Arrine choked out. Xai, licking her own jaw

lasciviously, laughed again. 'I hear,' she said. 'I know. You are summer and she is winter. You do not desire old flesh and bones. But . . .' Slowly she executed a pirouette, turning right around in the light until she was facing him once more. '*But*. You will not have Sefi. If you try, I will tear out your heart.'

Though the words were uttered calmly enough, Grendon knew that this was a surer threat than any she had made before. Clenching his teeth, and not daring to look at Arrine, he replied, 'I've told you. I do not want Sefira, and I will not touch her.' There was a pause. 'It wouldn't be in my interest.'

'Ah. Your *interest*. What is your interest? Tell me!'

This was the bait he had prepared to dangle. 'Something that will please you,' he said. 'But it cannot be done until the time is right.'

She put her head on one side in the odd, birdlike manner that he remembered from their first encounter, and he knew that curiosity had eclipsed her anger, at least for the moment. 'Ah?' she prompted; then again, 'Tell me!'

Grendon met her gaze levelly. 'I want the king to die.'

Silence fell for a few moments. Then Xai made the strangest sound he had yet heard from her; a thin, sweet and musical little noise, almost like a child tasting some rich sweetmeat for the very first time and finding it delectable.

'Kill the king. Kill the king.' She was almost singing the phrase, testing it, enjoying it. Then she stopped and regarded him shrewdly. 'You want *us* to kill him.'

'When the time is right. Yes.'

A faint hiss. '*I* would have killed him before. But you said that if he died, others would kill Sefi. Why is it different now?'

'It is not different; not yet. As I said, the time must be right.'

'Right . . . so there is no danger to *us*.'

'Yes.'

'And then we shall kill the king.'

'Yes.'

That obscenely musical little sound again. 'Why?'

137

Grendon smiled thinly. 'Because of what he is and what he has done.'

Xai watched him for several seconds and he could feel her probing thoughts at the edge of his mind. Then: 'Yes. I see. Because he kills your kind.' Another pause. 'But he does not kill you.' She glanced at Arrine. 'Or her.'

'He has his reasons.'

'*Mmnnn.* Yess . . . The king kills your kind. So we shall kill the king's kind. It is a pretty pattern.' Then suddenly her look flared into ferocity. 'But you have killed my kind, and I do not forget that!'

'So you've told me. But, as *I* have told *you*, while I protect Sefira, any vengeance you take on me would result only in your own destruction.' Grendon shrugged. 'It's a simple choice, and there's no third option.'

Silence again. Then: 'I am hungry.'

He knew from the abrupt change of tack that he had won. 'You will be fed,' he told her.

'The last feeding was not enough. I want more.'

'You'll have enough to sustain you. But you must feed only on what I find for you. If you try to take matters into your own hands, you'll betray yourself to others and Sefira will die for it. Do you understand that?'

She did, he saw, though she didn't like it. Then she made a little gesture as though brushing away something of no consequence. It was a tacit admission that she was prepared to capitulate.

'When is the marriage?' she asked.

'Tomorrow.'

'I might come. I might attend.' A giggle. 'Watch for me, Grendon. You will see.'

'You'll stay away if you know what's good for you!' he said balefully. 'Just keep to the bargain.'

'*I* will not break it.' The oval of light dimmed, brightened, then began to fade gently and steadily away. In the bed Sefira turned over and muttered something. She was sweating. Xai looked one last time at Arrine and smiled a pouting, almost affable smile.

'I am glad you killed her man,' she said. 'He must have suffered as he died. I am very glad of that.'

There was a brief, high-pitched sound that seemed to stab through Grendon's senses and into a deeper part of his consciousness, and Xai and the light vanished.

Sefira sighed heavily as though she was dreaming, but neither Grendon nor Arrine so much as glanced in her direction. Arrine's face was like white marble, fixed, trying not to express what she was feeling. Grendon, bereft of words, started to reach out to her, but she drew away, throwing her paralysis off and shaking her head. 'No.' She was trying to smile, to let him know that the rejection was nothing personal. 'I'm all right. Don't say anything. It's only to be expected that she – the creature – should taunt us when and where she can. Forget it, Grendon. Please.'

Grendon acquiesced, but inside him the knot of his hatred for Xai tightened and became harder. No matter: to feel the presence of that knot would serve to strengthen his resolve. When Karel was dead – which prospect, he reminded himself, was now far more than a fantasy – Xai, too, would die. He would make sure of that.

With no knowledge of what had taken place during the night, Sefira assumed that her light-headed tiredness, and the lingering sense of unreality that accompanied it, was due only to nervousness. Perhaps shock, too; for it was only now that the full implications of what she had agreed to were beginning to sink in.

She walked to the palace at Grendon's side, behaving to all outward appearances as though this were just another unremarkable day. Silently she allowed herself to be led through the maze of corridors (they were becoming almost familiar now) and made no protest when she was taken to a small ante-room, told to wait, and left alone behind a locked door. The last spark of protest, the last urge to change her mind and refuse to go through with this, had been snuffed out. The tide was flowing, and it was too strong for her to swim against it.

She didn't know how long she waited before there were footsteps in the passage outside, then the key grated and the door opened. Two people stood on the threshold. One she had seen before; the other, a woman just a few years older than herself, was a stranger.

Tomany, the king's soft-eyed secretary, gave Sefira an unfathomable look but said nothing, only ushered the woman into the chamber with the faintest of bows, then withdrew. The door closed; the key clicked again. Sefira stared at the stranger.

'Sefira?' The woman, whose fair hair was caught into a single braid that reached well past her waist, smiled. 'My name is Mischane. The king has charged me to help you prepare for the ceremony.'

Her voice reminded Sefira of someone, or something, but she couldn't place it. Could they have met before? She didn't think so, though of course it was always possible. She saw now that Mischane was carrying a bundle of clothing and, realising what would be required of her, she put her hand to her wimple in instinctive alarm.

'It's all right,' Mischane said, setting the bundle down on a chair. 'I know about your circumstances, and you won't shock me.'

Sefira wondered uncomfortably how many other people the king had seen fit to let into her secret, and her look grew defensive. 'I didn't ask for any help. I don't need it.'

Mischane laid the garments down. They were all sky blue, Sefira saw. 'If your memory is gone,' she said lightly, 'then I'm afraid you *do* need help. There are certain ways of dressing, certain rules to be followed, and without assistance you wouldn't know what they are. Besides, bride and bridegroom must each have a sponsor to vouchsafe them, so I am to be yours.'

'Sponsor . . .' Sefira repeated the word bemusedly. Karel, it seemed, was determined that the thing should be done according to protocol. 'Who is to be Grendon's sponsor?' she demanded.

'A palace servant; no one of any significance.'

Sefira was on edge, and the response came out before she could stem it. 'Not one of his friends? Or doesn't he have any?'

Mischane's expression tightened and her eyes became just a little harder. 'My brother,' she said, 'does not choose to make anyone his friend unless he has a good reason to do so.'

'Your—'

'Grendon is my brother. Didn't he tell you?'

Sefira stared. 'No. No, he – didn't tell me.'

'Well. Now you know. Perhaps he hasn't seen fit to mention the fact, but I have an apartment by the king's favour, here in the palace.' Mischane turned away and began to sort through the blue clothing, and Sefira watched her in uncertain silence. She was astonished and chagrined by this revelation, though it explained why she had thought Mischane's voice familiar, and after a few moments she said, 'I'm sorry.'

'For what?' Mischane paused.

'For . . . what I said. About Grendon. I didn't mean—'

'It's of no moment whether you meant it or not; we're all entitled to our own views.'

'Yes, but . . .' Suddenly Sefira felt defensive and her tone changed. 'I don't want this marriage, and neither does he! But the king ordered it, as a condition of the bargain he and Grendon made.'

Now Mischane did stop what she was doing, and turned to look at Sefira as though seeing her clearly for the first time. 'Ah,' she said. 'Yes. I'd heard something about an agreement between them. I gather that you have some talent which is useful to the king, but that you need Grendon's help in exploiting it. Is that true?'

There was a harder note to her voice, reflected in the way she regarded Sefira as she spoke, and Sefira felt a mixture of anger and shame. 'If it is,' she replied, 'it's not of my choosing. I didn't ask for this.'

Mischane said, 'Mmm,' in a non-committal way, then glanced towards the window where a break in the clouds allowed her to see the sun's angle. 'Time's getting on, and King Karel doesn't like to be kept waiting. We'd better get you ready. Take off those clothes.'

Silence then as Sefira reluctantly removed her gown and wimple and submitted to being dressed in the blue bridal garments. It was a complicated process and Mischane went about it with tight-lipped efficiency, catching Sefira's hair as she fixed the looped folds of a veil in place and once, apparently by accident, pricking her neck with one of the pins that held it in place. Sefira suffered her carelessness for a few minutes, but when Mischane stabbed her with a second pin her forbearance snapped and she said bitterly, 'Do you hate me that much?'

Mischane paused. 'I don't hate you. Why should I?'

Sefira thought the answer to that was obvious, and said so. But Mischane only laughed. 'My dear, I don't believe for one moment that you've somehow inveigled Grendon into this! To be blunt, you couldn't. My brother has been a law unto himself for as long as I can remember, and the fact that he's prepared to go through a sham of a marriage to gain advancement doesn't surprise me in the least.'

She put another pin in place, more gently this time. 'No, I don't resent you, Sefira. In fact, I rather feel sorry for you.' Pausing, she stared deeply into Sefira's eyes. 'From what I've heard about you, and what I've now seen for myself, I imagine that you'll find yourself greatly out of your depth here, and that isn't a position to be envied.' Another pause. 'But then, it's a matter of convenience, isn't it? Or perhaps I should say, survival. So, as you don't have a great deal of choice in the matter – and as we're about to become sisters after a fashion, whether either of us likes it or not – I have some obligation to help you make the best you can of it. Now.' She stepped back, pre-empting anything Sefira might have tried to say in response. 'You look well enough. Sit down, and I'll go through the basics of the ceremony with you. It isn't complex, but it's important that you get it right.'

Sefira subsided on to a chair. There was a great deal she wanted to say, to argue, but Mischane's peremptory manner had ridden over it all and cowed her. The flowing tide . . . and there was something else underlying it. She didn't have the courage to challenge Mischane about it, but she sensed the feeling emanating from the other woman and surrounding her like a hard, bright shield: a dislike that bordered on loathing. But it was not aimed at her, or at least, only in the most general and detached sense.

Its real target, or so Sefira's intuition told her, was Grendon.

The wedding of Grendon and Sefira took place in a small, unremarkable and barely furnished room in a little used part of the palace. The ceremony was to be conducted by the king in person, and the only others present were the bride and groom and their two sponsors; Grendon's an elderly palace servant, so self-effacing that Sefira couldn't later recall his name or his features.

To Sefira, the whole thing seemed so horribly unreal as to be almost farcical. She stood at Grendon's side, aware that he was looking anywhere but at her, while Karel, with the short, fur-trimmed mantle of an official justicer thrown carelessly over everyday clothes, spoke the words of the ceremony in a tone as casual as if he had been discussing an evening's menu with the head cook. Grendon's responses to the questions asked of him were just as casual. Yes, his name was Grendon; Fellowship, Communicant. Yes, he was free to marry, and did so of his own will and without duress. (Sefira glanced sidelong at him as he said this, but his face was impassive and he ignored her scrutiny.) Yes, this woman was his chosen bride, of the same Fellowship; and yes, he agreed to abide by the laws and protocols of marriage and be husband, provider and protector until such time as one or the other of them should die. It was as simple, and as spiritless, as that.

Then came Sefira's turn, and with her mind fogged by bemusement she heard herself answering the same questions, only changing the final phrase to 'wife, chattel and companion', which she disliked and resented. The sponsors then said their pieces, Mischane mechanically, the servant barely audibly, and at a nod from Karel Grendon fastened silver bracelets around both of Sefira's wrists while Mischane stepped forward with a blue silk wimple to replace the veil. As it was placed on her head Sefira shut her eyes tightly and thought: *it's too late now. The thing is done. I am his wife. And—*

But the thought got no further, for Karel spoke then in a voice laced with satisfaction.

'My felicitations to you both.' There was amusement, too, in his tone. 'And now, to celebrate your happiness, I've arranged a small reception for you. Just a gathering of a few friends, to welcome you to the court and to your new life together.'

For the first time then Grendon showed some reaction – in a scowl which he quickly masked – but he said nothing, only turned and followed as Karel led the way to the door. They walked down a short passage. Somewhere on the route the elderly servant melted away into the background and disappeared, and the rest of the party entered another room where the guests were waiting to greet them.

Karel had invited some dozen or so people to the gathering. Sefira, naively taking his reference to 'friends' at face value, hoped that Arrine might be among their number. She felt isolated and lonely, and would have given a great deal to find a familiar face in the room. But she was disappointed; Arrine was not there, and the guests were all strangers.

Mischane proffered a few clipped words of congratulation at which Karel, who was in earshot, smiled, then she made her excuses and moved away to talk to someone else. Watching her departing back, which radiated the same cold aloofness that Grendon so often exhibited, Sefira wondered what had become of their parents. Killed in the war, perhaps. Or by the fever that had claimed Arrine's husband. Or possibly they had died long ago. Whatever the case, she was thankful that she did not have to contend with them as well as with Mischane.

Wine was proffered by an unsmiling, liveried servant. Sefira took some but did not drink it, only fingered the stem of her glass uneasily as the guests stood making stilted small talk. For the sake of form a few spoke to her, asking polite, trivial questions which she answered as best she could, but the dominant feeling in the room was that everyone would be thankful to get away as soon as they prudently could. Karel, however, seemed determined to draw the occasion out, and as no one else could leave until he had made his departure, the ordeal dragged on.

The Sefira noticed that a new guest had joined them.

How or when she had entered was a mystery, but she stood alone at one side of the room, where low light made her figure indistinct. She was very slight, almost thin, and wore a dress of some indeterminate material with a dark wimple shadowing her face. As she looked at her, Sefira felt a peculiar, queasy sensation take sudden root in the pit of her stomach – for something about the newcomer frightened her. Her hand started to shake; some of her wine spilled on to the floor, and hastily, thinking to calm herself, she raised the glass towards her mouth.

The other woman looked up, and a pair of eyes as blue and hard as zircons fixed Sefira's face with a stare the like of which she had never seen in her life. It was avid, voracious, *monstrous* . . . Sefira's fingers twitched violently, and before she could

145

regain control the wineglass slipped from her hand and smashed on the floor.

Grendon said, 'What—' and swung round, but the question died as he saw Sefira's expression. She was staring into the far corner, transfixed, horrified, and rapidly he turned to see what she was looking at.

There was no one there. But a cold prickle ran the length of Grendon's spine as his psychic senses picked up a trace of something abnormal, a faint trail deliberately left behind.

Xai had kept her promise.

People were reacting to the incident with faintly pitying solicitude. Was Sefira feeling unwell? A little overwrought, perhaps . . . Wine stains on her skirt; such a shame, but they could be cleaned away. Another glass, perhaps, or better if . . . ? Sefira looked as if she was shrinking into herself, and abruptly Grendon answered for her.

'My wife is tired,' he said curtly. The unsmiling servant was clearing away the broken shards at his feet. 'No doubt the excitement of the day is proving a little too much for her.'

They all noted the irony but no one commented on it. Karel was watching from a short distance away; not far from him Mischane was frowning as though some untoward thought had occurred to her. Then suddenly Sefira said: 'I'm hungry.'

Grendon's head snapped round. Her expression had cleared and the fear she had shown only moments ago vanished completely, as though it had never existed – or, he thought, as though it had been wiped from her mind.

He echoed sharply, 'Hungry?'

'Yes.' The tip of Sefira's tongue appeared, touching her lip in a gesture which he had never seen her make before. 'I want . . . something to eat . . .'

Grendon stared at her. The words, he realised, had come quite involuntarily; it was likely that she didn't even know she had said them, for they were not hers but Xai's. It was a threat – and a challenge.

A young courtier, who had had a little too much wine, said

loudly, 'A hungry bride? That's not the way it should be!' He laughed immoderately. 'Best take her to the bedchamber and do something about it, eh, Grendon – eh?'

Grendon turned furiously, but before he could utter a savage response Karel stepped forward.

'Curb your tongue and your vulgarity, Dendo. *If* you please.' The king's eyes were chilly, and the chill didn't moderate as they focused on Grendon. 'You may both retire if you wish to. If Sefira is hungry, order food to be brought to your quarters.' He paused. 'I won't require her services for a day or two yet, so she may have some time to accustom herself to her new life.'

Grendon looked for sarcasm but, for once, found none. He nodded. 'Thank you, sir. Then with your permission . . .'

'Yes, yes. Oh, one more matter.' Grendon stopped. 'The Sanctified captured in Ishen is due to arrive in the city tomorrow. You haven't forgotten your obligation?'

Grendon tensed. 'No, sir, I haven't forgotten.'

'Good. Then start making the necessary arrangements; I don't want any time wasted over this. And you may take your wife along to witness the proceedings.' He smiled thinly. 'It will serve a useful purpose, I think. To remind her of the narrow margin we all tread between good fortune and bad.'

He cast a quick, disparaging glance around the company, then turned and, without any formality or even another word to anyone, left the room.

Chapter XI

The apartment assigned to Grendon and Sefira was on the east side of the palace, where it would have the best of the morning light and the worst of the prevailing winds. The two rooms were large but otherwise very modest, and the furnishings made few concessions to comfort; it was the kind of accommodation reserved for the lowliest members of the court. This, Grendon knew, was the king's way of reminding him that the new arrangement did not include any but the barest privileges. He had been admitted to the royal circle, but that was all.

There was only one bed, but before Sefira could protest about that Grendon told her curtly that she could have sole use of the bedchamber and he would make his own arrangements in the other room. As he spoke, he suddenly imagined what might ensue if he did break his promise and claim his right to her. She wouldn't be able to defy him, either physically or legally. And her virginity was a keystone of Xai's influence over her.

As quickly as it had formed, the impulse faded. The idea was preposterous; Xai was too important a factor in his own plans for him to risk either alienating her further or hampering her abilities. Though it sickened him to admit it, he needed the demonic creature and the powers she commanded. Besides, any attempt he made to seduce or force Sefira would goad Xai into full fury; and that could be calamitous if it happened too early.

He looked at Sefira, who was standing by the window, back

turned defensively to him as she fingered the unfamiliar fabric of her dress. Preposterous, too, that the fancy should have occurred to him in the first place. He didn't find her attractive, didn't even like her; it had just been a stirring of his natural urges, doubtless fuelled by the fact that he been denying himself such pleasures for too long. Scraping the barrel, Grendon thought cynically. If he wanted a woman there were prettier prospects at some of the city whorehouses, and he had little else to spend his money on.

Irritated with himself – and also, irrationally, with Sefira – he walked out of the apartment without speaking to her and went in search of a servant, to order a meal to be prepared and sent to them. She was in the bedroom when he returned; he didn't intrude on her but waited until the food arrived before calling her to join him.

As he had suspected, Sefira didn't want the meal. She did her best but clearly couldn't stomach it. Nor did she understand her own reaction, though when Grendon tried subtly to quiz her on the subject she refused to be drawn and said only that she was no longer hungry. Grendon probed the atmosphere, but if Xai was hovering there was no traceable sign of her. Nonetheless, he knew that trouble would come if the being's appetite wasn't satisfied to some degree, so he persuaded Sefira to return to her room, and went in search of another kind of sustenance.

It was easy enough. Rabbits were bred for the palace kitchens, and a batch, newly killed but not yet skinned or drained of blood, were awaiting collection at a side door. One wouldn't be missed. Grendon half expected to encounter Xai in one form or another as he went on his mission, but it seemed that one brief appearance at the celebration had contented her for the moment and she had no intention of showing herself about the palace again.

Sefira was asleep when he returned with his spoils – Xai, he suspected, had arranged that in anticipation of the feeding – and he left the dead animal under her hand, knowing that he need do no more. He sat for an hour in the other room, staring at the sluggish fire, then went back to the bedchamber, cleared up the mess and performed a minor conjuration that would ensure Sefira remained asleep.

The fire had a soporific effect, and he was on the verge of dozing off when a sound impinged on his half-dreaming mind. Grendon opened his eyes, frowning, not quite sure whether the noise had been real or imaginary. But then he heard it again. Someone was at the outer door.

He got up, walked quietly to the door and stood listening for a few moments. There was no further sound, but he sensed a presence on the other side, nervous, waiting. Reaching out, he pulled the door open.

Mischane was standing outside. Her gaze flicked swiftly to right and left along the corridor, then she said, 'Grendon, may I come in?'

He stood back, and she slipped into the room with a faintly furtive air. 'I'm sorry,' she said. 'I shouldn't be here, and I won't intrude on you and your . . . wife for long. But I had to come.'

Grendon closed and bolted the door. He was surprised to see her, for he knew that she was closely watched and had little freedom even within the palace. Possibly she had managed to elude the watchers for once. Or possibly Karel was in an indulgent mood.

Mischane walked towards the fireplace and stood warming her hands before the flames. She had looked carefully around the room and now said, 'Isn't Sefira here?'

'She's asleep in the other room,' Grendon told her. 'She was very tired, and felt unwell.'

'Yes. Yes, I rather had that impression at the gathering.'

There was a brief silence. Then, wearily, Grendon said, 'I'm sorry, Mischane. This must have come as a shock to you, and I only wish I could have got word to you, to explain.' He hesitated. 'It was good of you to agree to sponsor her. Under the circumstances—'

She interrupted him. 'The choice wasn't mine. It was strongly suggested, shall I say, that I should oblige.' At last she turned to face him, her eyes candid and a little hard. 'And yes, it did come as a shock. Especially when Sefira told me something of the circumstances.'

Grendon's eyes narrowed. 'I'm sorry that you had to hear it from her. How much did she tell you?'

'Enough to paint an unpleasant picture.' Mischane paused. '*Is* what she says true? Is this marriage entirely at the king's behest?'

Grendon shut his eyes and put the heel of one hand wearily to his forehead. 'Yes,' he said.

'So you're not in love with the girl?'

'No, I'm not in love with her. In fact I hardly know her, and the little I know, I don't particularly like. Which, I might add, is mutual.'

Mischane was silent for a few moments. Then she said: 'Grendon, why have you *done* this? Whatever you might want from the king, it can't be worth a sacrifice of this order! It would have been bad enough to tie yourself to someone you don't love, but a creature like this—'

'What do you mean?' Grendon's voice was suddenly sharp.

'The fact that she's a convicted murderess, of course!' Then Mischane's eyes narrowed. 'What else could I have meant?'

Grendon realised that he had come very close to giving away more than was wise. He didn't want Mischane to know the whole truth, either about Sefira or about his own ultimate plan. It wasn't that he didn't trust her; far from it. But what she didn't know couldn't lead her into danger, and that was the most important consideration of all.

He said, wanting to reassure her and also lead the discussion away from dangerous waters, 'I don't think she's guilty of her supposed crime. There's a great deal more to it than meets the eye.'

'Perhaps,' Mischane acknowledged. 'But even if that's true, it doesn't change the – the *recklessness* of what you've done.'

She bit her lip. 'And it doesn't answer my question.'

A stab of hurt went through Grendon, for he had thought – had *assumed* – that she might have guessed his motive without the need for explanation. 'I married Sefira,' he said, 'for one reason, Mischane: to buy your freedom.'

'My . . .' The colour ebbed from Mischane's face and she put a hand to her face. 'Oh . . .' Suddenly she turned away. 'I didn't know. I didn't *realise* . . .'

He stared at her back. 'You should have done. I thought you knew me well enough.' A pause. 'Why else do you think I've done as I have, lived as I have, these past two years? Doing Karel's bidding, being his puppet, carrying out the work with which he won't soil his own hands? If it hadn't been for you, I'd not have stood it for a moment!'

Mischane stood very still. 'You've done what was necessary to stay alive, Grendon, and *that's* what I'd have expected of you.' Her composure returned, she faced him once more. 'I know the terms on which both our lives were spared after the war, but I didn't ask you to agree to them. I don't like being a hostage against your good behaviour.'

'Would you rather have died, as our parents did?'

She hesitated, then gave a bitter laugh. 'I suppose not. Though sometimes . . . ah, Grendon, please forgive me. I spoke in haste and, I suppose, out of . . . shock. Bewilderment.'

'You can't believe that I'd make this sacrifice for your sake?'

'Oh, I can believe it. I know we were never very close in the past, but . . . blood tells. It's just that I feel . . . *guilty* that you should do this for me.'

'Don't,' he said, and smiled faintly. 'My freedom's part of the bargain, too.'

'Is it? I didn't know.' She managed to return the smile, though with an effort. 'That eases my conscience a little.'

Grendon didn't comment, for his own conscience was squirming. 'Maybe,' he said, 'when this episode is over, we can begin again. As you said, we've never been close, but we have no other family now. It would be . . . good to put matters to rights between us and make a fresh start.'

'Yes,' Mischane said. 'Yes, it would.'

She tried to hide the small shiver that assailed her as she spoke, but Grendon saw it and knew what lay behind it. She still feared him. Despite the fact that the cause of her fear was long buried in the past, and at the time she had been too young to have had much awareness of what was happening, the taint of what her brother had once been was impossible to eradicate completely, and the scar would always remain. She might never be able to look at him without an echo of revulsion. But at least he might be able to redeem himself in other ways.

She said suddenly: 'I should go, before I'm missed.' Her shoulders hunched. 'This life . . . it's like being in a cage, isn't it, Grendon?'

'Perhaps not for much longer.'

'No. No, perhaps not . . . I'll try not to think too hard about that. Try not to hope, in case we're both disappointed.' She raised her gaze to meet his. 'But I thank you for what you're doing, with all my heart.'

He escorted her to the door and watched as she walked quickly away along the passage. Though the meeting had started badly it had ended well, and he felt a sense of relief, almost a kind of contentment, as he quietly withdrew into the room again. A gulf had been narrowed this evening. It was, he felt, the first sign of good to come out of recent days' events.

There was no sound from the adjoining room; Sefira was still deeply asleep. Grendon thought of looking in on her, just to be certain that all was well, but decided against it. Xai wouldn't manifest tonight, for she wasn't yet strong enough to waste the energy gained from the feeding simply for the sake of making a show. He could sleep undisturbed – and for the first time in a long while, he probably would.

He banked the fire down so that its embers would keep the chill from the room until morning, then set about arranging his bed on the couch.

* * *

When Mischane returned to her room in the palace, she found the note with its familiar seal lying on her bed. She broke the seal, read the note and smiled before pouring herself a glass of wine – an old vintage, and very mellow – from a flask. Then she changed her clothes, choosing a low-cut gown of dark green velvet with a tight-laced bodice. The king especially liked to see her wearing it, and that gave her pleasure.

As she dressed she thought over her conversation with Grendon. What he had told her had confirmed her suspicions and her fears. It was so like him, she thought sourly, to do something of this nature; to make a rash and extravagant gesture as a point of principle, and act on behalf of others without troubling to ask whether it was what those others wanted. He should have left well alone; but then Grendon had never been open to reason in that sense. Once an idea was fixed in his mind, nothing would sway him from pursuing it. And doubtless he sincerely believed that he was acting for the good.

She fastened a gold, pearl-studded chain around her throat, then began to twine a matching chain into the piled luxuriance of her hair. Her own face in the mirror looked resentful and faintly petulant, and she schooled it into a calmer expression. Damn Grendon. She wished he had died twenty years ago. She wished Lendrer had failed in what he did . . .

But if what she had heard tonight wasn't what she wanted to hear, at least she had gained her brother's trust. It had almost gone wrong, but at the last she had been able to salvage the situation and avert his suspicions, and that was important. Karel would be interested to hear the details of their talk; though the fact that she hadn't been able to speak again to Sefira was disappointing. But there would be other chances. Time was not of the essence. As yet, it was only *information* that Karel required.

She studied her reflection again, critically, and tucked a stray strand of hair under the twined chain. Then she drained her glass in one economic movement, checked the mirror image one last time and stepped out of the room. No one about in the corridor; well and good, for it wouldn't do to have word of her movements reach Grendon's ears.

Mischane closed her door, and turned in the direction of the king's private quarters.

Sefira woke earlier than Grendon had intended her to, jolting out of a bizarre dream in which a stranger with very blue eyes had been showing her a table laden with food and trying to persuade her to eat. In the dream she had been convinced that some evil would befall her if she touched a morsel, yet her stomach ached with hunger. The stranger was persuasive, almost insistent, and though she knew instinctively that she should not trust the blandishments, she had been reaching out for one of the dishes when, abruptly, a surge of uncontrollable anger went through her. The dream scene flared, vanished, and she opened her eyes to the darkness of the palace bedroom.

It took her a minute or so to piece together recent events and realise where she was, and when she did realise she tensed and groped quickly across the width of the bed, half expecting to find Grendon lying beside her. But he had kept his promise. She was alone.

She sat up. The dream had left unpleasant after-images in her mind and she wanted light, but though the lamp on the bedside table was easy to find, there was nothing with which to light it. For some unfathomable reason that brought back the anger Sefira had felt in her dream, and she got out of bed and felt her way to the window, where she wrenched open the heavy curtains. The dismal grey of a very wet dawn confronted her, together with an unprepossessing view of the kitchen wing, and with a sharp hiss that it didn't occur to her to think of as uncharacteristic, she swung round and paced to the door. Suddenly she wanted to be sure of Grendon's whereabouts, and she pulled the door open and went through to the next room.

In the dimness she could just make out his figure lying on a long couch; she approached, and for perhaps a minute stood staring down at him. He was still asleep, and as she watched him Sefira tried to come to terms with the knowledge that they were now, legally, man and wife. The more she thought about it the more the fact struck her as insane, and her anger, which had settled back to a simmer, suddenly rekindled into blind hatred. She despised him. She loathed him. He had wrecked her life for his own selfish ends; for that he deserved the worst punishment that her mind could conjure, and she would like . . . she would like . . .

Sefira sucked in breath, and her tongue darted over her lips. *Kill.* She would like to kill him. It would please her. It would satisfy her. *Above all, it would be the retribution that she and her kind had craved for so long; ever since—*

She jammed her hands involuntarily to her temples as a stabbing pain shot through her skull. Her body swayed; losing balance she stumbled backwards and found herself wavering unsteadily in the middle of the room. The rage that had possessed her moments ago was gone without trace. All she felt was bewildered, cold, and a little sick.

She looked at Grendon again. The disturbance hadn't woken him, and she wondered bemusedly why she should have reacted so violently. To dislike him was one thing, but this level of hatred was quite another . . .

But it had happened before. She recalled the innmaster in Chalce, and the sudden vicious emotion that had taken hold of her in response to his sly innuendoes. Then, as now, she had felt a murderous impulse that vanished as swiftly as it had arisen.

Her skin crawled, and a question rose starkly in her mind. Was that what had happened when she committed the murder for which she was condemned? Had she felt that same lethal compulsion, and acted on it before she could stop herself? If so, then it meant . . . she shivered, sick with fear at the thought, but forced herself to face it . . . it meant that she was insane.

Sefira took a soft-footed pace backwards, then another and another, wanting to put distance between herself and Grendon. Warily, she tried to recall the feeling that had gripped her, to remember what it was like, but found it impossible. The idea of killing someone, either in hot or cold blood, was anathema. Yet moments ago she had wanted to do it. *Craved* to do it. What was she? she asked herself. *What was she?*

In one corner of the room a patch of what looked like mist, but was not, faded and vanished. Sefira didn't see it, hadn't even noticed it, but as the last traces evaporated she experienced a momentary dizziness that made her sway again and almost fall. Regaining balance, she blinked, then looked in surprise at her surroundings. Why had she come into this room? She couldn't remember. Grendon hadn't summoned her; he was still asleep. She couldn't think what she was doing here.

Her head ached, and her mind was still full of the confused clutter of a dream: feelings of anger, and someone trying to force her to eat . . . She wasn't fully awake yet, Sefira told herself. She wanted – needed – more sleep, and she turned slowly and went back towards the inner door. On the threshold she glanced over her shoulder, but Grendon wasn't awake and staring at her as she had half imagined.

Xai, who had tested her own strength and influence and was content for the moment with what she had found, withdrew the final vestiges of her presence. Sefira shook her head as though to clear it, and went out, closing the door quietly behind her.

Chapter XII

Perlion arrived late at the eating house where the rendezvous had been arranged. His last visit to Tourmon had been before the war, and he hadn't realised the degree to which the once familiar city had changed. Old landmarks were swept away, many of them burned or smashed down during the final siege, and the layout of the streets in the western quarter near the harbour had altered beyond recognition. But after a few wrong turns and a few polite enquiries, he finally reached his destination.

He feared that the woman might have run out of patience and left, and as he ducked under the eating house's low lintel he recalled the description his agent had given and looked anxiously around, blinking in the comparative gloom. She was there, at a table by one of the thick glass windows. A brown wimple covered her hair, edged with a widow's band, and as he approached she rose to her feet, a respectful but uneasy smile on her face.

'Sir . . . I'm glad to see you again.'

She had recognised him, Perlion realised, whereas he had barely any memory of her. But then, when they last encountered each other she had been little more than a child, and it was logical that time should have wrought more changes in her than in him.

'It's been a good many years, Kessie.' He returned her smile with a confidence that inwardly he didn't quite feel, and indicated for her to resume her seat. 'Will you take some refreshment?'

'Thank you, sir. A thornberry tisane, if you please.'

An aproned girl served them – for the sake of form Perlion ordered a tisane for himself, though his stomach was too nervous to want it – and his companion sat politely mute, waiting for him to broach the crucial subject. At last, after some uneasy throat clearing, he said:

'I was sorry to hear that your former employer has died. Was it before the war, or . . . ?'

'The year before, sir. She was old, and I think she was glad to leave the world behind.' Kessie paused. 'In truth, I don't believe she would have liked to live through the troubled times. She was of the old ways, and would have found it very hard to change.'

'It isn't easy to adjust . . . you remained in close touch with her, I understand?'

'Yes, sir. She was a fine teacher, and a good friend.'

'Yes. Yes, I'm sure . . . And . . . you remember, then . . . a little over twenty years ago, when—' He faltered. And suddenly Kessie gave him a very candid look.

'When a first child was born to you and your lady. Yes, sir, I remember it very well. And I know that's why you are here.'

The serving girl returned, and as the hot drinks were set before them Perlion had time to regain his composure. When she had gone, he clasped his mug of tisane and said, 'Kessie, I will be frank. I want your help. I *need* it. You see, I – that is, my wife and I – we have had other children, and they have been a great joy to us. But in all this time, I – I have never forgotten . . . *her*. And now, I . . . I find that I need to know . . . what became of her.' His voice caught suddenly. 'I *must* know.'

There was silence for a few moments. Then Kessie said, in a voice laden with sympathy,

'Sir, what good does it do to rake over the embers of the past? Isn't it better to let such coals burn out?'

He shook his head. 'You don't understand—'

'Forgive me, sir, but I think I do.' She smiled sadly. 'I have children of my own now, and I know the love and care of it. But that babe . . . though you sired her, sir, she was not truly your daughter. She could never have been. And . . .' She bit her lip. 'Again I must ask your forgiveness, but I have to say it. It is more likely than not that, by now, she is dead.'

Perlion's head came up at that, and to Kessie's surprise a smile that was almost beatific spread across his face.

'No, Kessie, you do *not* understand. You see – I believe I have seen her. And I believe she is here in Tourmon.'

Kessie stared at him. 'In Tourmon?'

'Yes. And married.'

'*Married?*'

'Yes!' Forgetting the difference in their stations, Perlion leaned across the table and grasped her hands, squeezing the fingers so hard that she winced. 'I first saw her in Chalce, and as soon as I set eyes on her face, I *knew* her. The family resemblance was outstanding – besides, how can a father not instinctively know his own child? And that, Kessie, is where I need your help. I need to have information which only you, now, are privy to.' Releasing her fingers he touched one hand to the purse which he wore next to a well-honed dagger at his belt. 'I will pay well.' Longing crept into his eyes. 'I will pay *anything.*'

Kessie continued to stare at him. She had known that this meeting must have some connection with the events of the past, but she hadn't expected this – and certainly hadn't expected Perlion to run such an obvious risk in opening his heart to her. He was staking a very great deal, for if the truth should become common knowledge, his family had far more to fear from it now than in the old days.

Lowering her voice, she said, 'Sir, do you know what you are saying? To come to me like this – how do you know that you can trust me?'

'I trusted both you and your mistress twenty years ago, and neither of you have ever betrayed the secret,' Perlion replied. 'That, for me, is proof enough that you will tell no other living soul.'

He didn't add that Kessie would be in equal danger if she did, but she knew without the need for words, and her eyes showed it. Her gaze slid away from his, and for several moments she considered. Then: 'Sir, I . . . I'll tell you what I can. But first, I must ask one question.'

'Ask it.'

'Does the lady Isbel know of this?'

'No,' Perlion said. 'She does not. She still believes that the child – the children – died.'

Kessie nodded slowly. 'Do you mean to tell her?'

'No,' he repeated. 'Not until – and unless – I can do so without harm to anyone.'

She nodded again. That was for the best. 'Then I'll do what I can for you, sir, though it's little enough.' She sipped at her drink, taking a moment to compose herself. Outside it had started to rain again; water ran down the window and the hissing patter blurred the sounds of the street. In a corner of the eating house a solitary figure, heavily muffled against the weather, watched them idly, but neither of them – nor, in fact, anyone else – noticed, or even had seen the newcomer enter.

'After the birth and . . . and what followed,' Kessie said at last, 'we took the babe to Emelian. My mistress thought it better for all that she should not remain in Chalce. We found a couple. Long married, but with no children of their own; for some reason they could never have them. Arrangements were made, and—'

Perlion interrupted. 'What Fellowship were they?'

'Communicant.'

His heart pounded. 'Are you sure of that?'

'Yes. I remember them well.'

It fitted. It *fitted* . . . Shaking inwardly with excitement, Perlion continued. 'They agreed to take her and bring her up as their own?'

'Yes. We told them that her parents had died of a fever and had no kin who would take her in. They were very happy to adopt her, and everything was done properly and officially.'

'They must have given her a name. Do you know what it was?'

Kessie's eyes narrowed as she tried to remember. 'It's close to my tongue, but . . .' Perlion clenched his fists, forcing himself with a great effort not to prompt her, and at last her face cleared. 'Ah, yes; I recall it. They named her Sefira.'

Waves of heat and cold chased each other through Perlion's body. He felt sweat break out on his face, and a mixture of relief, elation and terror filled him. Sefira! He had no doubts now. He had been right – *he had been right*!

'And then,' he said, his voice rising in his eagerness, 'what then? What more do you know?'

'Sir, please!' She hissed the words, her eyes darting nervously to the room at large. But no one was paying them any attention; even the muffled figure in the corner seemed uninterested now.

'I'm sorry. I'm sorry.' He made a placating gesture. 'But you *must* understand—'

'I do, yes. But there's nothing more I can tell you. We heard no more of them, you see. We had done what you charged us to do, and it was not our concern . . .' Kessie hesitated, then suddenly added in an urgent undertone, 'Sir, can you be certain that the woman you have seen *is* your daughter? There may be a resemblance, true, but . . . well, when the heart desires, it is all too easy for the eye to be deceived.'

'The woman's name,' said Perlion, smiling at her, 'is Sefira. She is a Communicant.'

'Ah . . .'

'It is too great a coincidence to be ignored, is it not?'

'Yes. Yes, it is . . . and she is married now . . .'

'Indeed. So it seems that fate has been kind to her, and the curse has not awoken.' He sighed, happiness and wistful sorrow blending in the sound. 'I am so glad of that. So very glad.'

Kessie was glad too, though with reservations. But she felt it kinder not to share them; after all, if the scourge of the soul-invader had not yet touched his child, there was every chance that it never would. Perhaps the luck-blessing that she and her mistress had said for the infant had had some power after all.

Perlion looked down at his mug. He had hardly touched the tisane, and now it was cold and unpalatable. Isbel and the children would be returning to the house in time for lunch; he needed to speak to his cousin in private, before their return . . .

He rose. 'Kessie, I owe you a great debt.' His hand went to his purse, but she reached out and forestalled him.

'No, sir, I'll take no payment. I'm happy that I've been able to help you in some small way.' She looked up at him. 'But I would ask you to remember one thing when you consider what you shall do with your new knowledge. To you, Sefira is your daughter – but to her, you are a complete stranger. Please, think on that when you make your decisions.'

Perlion's face sobered. 'Yes,' he said slowly. 'Yes. I shall. I must . . . Goodbye, Kessie. And I thank you, with all my heart.'

He moved from the bench. Kessie watched him, a small smile of farewell flickering on her face. Rain flurried in from the street as he opened the door, then he was gone.

She sighed. He was a good man; a kindly man who wanted only happiness and to do the best for all. Should she have told him, she wondered, that last small snippet that she had kept back?

For a moment she felt an impulse to run after him, but then reason eclipsed it. It would have been wrong to speak; wrong to raise false hopes in him by confessing the secret, the other secret, that she had kept for two decades. The tale her mistress and mentor had told her after Sefira's birth, of another child born years before with the curse of the demon parasite on his soul. Her mistress had attended that mother, too; but then the story had taken a very different direction. There had been no question of killing the child, or even of sending it away. The secret must be kept, of course, but the family's rank and influence had ensured that that was easily accomplished. The midwife, to whom Kessie's old mistress was then apprentice, had died, coincidentally, within the day, and Kessie's mistress knew that she would surely suffer the same fate. She had fled Tourmon, changed her name and made a new life and livelihood in Emelian.

Though the family might have traced her with little difficulty, it seemed that they were satisfied to let matters rest, for no horror ever came to claim her soul in the night, and in time her fear of discovery faded. At last, in middle life, she had finally found the courage to tell Kessie of what she knew . . . and of a strange tale which, years later, had reached her ears. A rumour had come out of Tourmon of a young man born with the plague of the soul parasite, who had been cured of his affliction by sorcery. Only one Fellowship could command powers of that order, and they would not stoop to extend their help to anyone of a lesser caste. So the young man in question had been a Sanctified. As was the child at whose birth Kessie's mistress had assisted.

Kessie shook herself, as though a hole had suddenly opened in the roof and let the rain in. It was impossible, of course. The Sanctifieds were a thing of the past; King Karel was purging them from the land, and rightly so. But the purge was not yet complete. And if one soul-invader had been destroyed, then surely the thing could be done again . . . ?

She raised her head and looked through the blurred glass of the window. Perlion would have left the square by now, and she had no idea of which direction he had taken. That was just as well. For to speak of this to him would have been mad, and cruel, and dangerous to them both. Better to let it alone. Better to let the past die.

She pushed away her empty mug, picked up her cloak and cast it round her shoulders. As she left the eating house the figure sitting alone at a shadowed corner table registered briefly and meaninglessly on her mind. The woman wore a heavy wimple that obscured the details of her face; Kessie noticed that she had startlingly blue eyes, but that was all.

The door closed behind her. For some seconds the solitary figure stayed still. Then, so smoothly that no one else in the room saw anything remotely untoward, her form faded away and vanished into nothing.

King Karel sent for Sefira two days later. The summons ended a peculiar hiatus during which she had seen almost nothing of Grendon and nothing whatever of anyone else, save for the servant who brought meals to the rooms three times each day. In theory she was free to come and go as she liked, and could have spent her time exploring the palace as she pleased and making the acquaintance of those in it. But somehow she couldn't summon the confidence to try. Whatever theory might say, she still felt like a prisoner.

Grendon, she gathered, was engaged on some urgent and time-consuming business for the king, and from his frame of mind on the rare occasions when he returned he clearly didn't like the commission. Sefira suspected that he might also be suffering from bitter second thoughts over his decision to go through the sham of a marriage, and that this was adding to his moodiness. She hadn't probed. If ambition meant more to him than the freedom to order his own life, she reasoned that he had no one but himself to blame, and thus far he had at least had the courtesy not to vent his anger on her.

So they had nothing to say to each other as they made their way to the king's private room in answer to the summons. Grendon scanned the corridors and turnings for some glimpse of Mischane, whom he had not seen since the night of the wedding, but there was no sign of her, and as they were admitted to Karel's presence he pushed the distraction aside and concentrated on more immediate matters.

Karel's greeting was cursory. He simply ordered them to

sit, then told Grendon to put Sefira into a trance. With cold efficiency Grendon guided her into the dreamlike limbo state that would open her subconscious mind to Xai. He saw her eyes glaze over; saw Karel's nod of satisfaction, and closed his own eyes, searching in his inner vision for the key that would allow him to shift his own consciousness on to the astral plane.

This time he found himself in a white, empty, featureless room. No doors or windows, no furnishings, nothing. And no sign of Xai. Grendon waited a few moments, aware on an intuitive level of Karel's mounting impatience, then projected a stern command.

'I've no time for games. Show yourself.'

She didn't, but abruptly he sensed her presence. And then, in his mind, he heard her voice.

'What do you want?'

She sounded sullen and recalcitrant, and his first reaction was that she was sulking for some reason. But then, on a deeper level, he began to suspect something more. Something was wrong. In her own, warped way, Xai was as preoccupied as he was.

He said, 'What's amiss with you?'

A hiss echoed in his head. '*Nothing.*'

Liar, Grendon's instinct told him. Cautiously he probed, but found a hard, bright wall set up against him. Whatever perturbed Xai, she didn't want him to know about it.

On the physical plane he heard Karel cough delicately and deliberately. It was an implied warning, and Grendon knew he must heed it. Reluctantly he drew his mind back and said, 'The king has another task for you.'

'Your king is a fool. I do not take orders from fools. I do not take orders from any mortal!'

'You'll take that one, if you want your precious Sefi to survive.' Oh yes, he thought; something was *very* awry. He felt the hard knot of silence while Xai considered this retort, and after a few seconds she said sulkily, 'I protect Sefi. I protect my own.'

'Then do as you're told.'

The flare of her hatred was like a physical kick, and he thought for a moment that she might attack him. But then she subsided and muttered instead:

'Sefi had wine. At the marriage. I saw.' A pause. 'Don't give Sefi wine!'

Grendon smiled contemptuously. 'Why not? Because it fogs her mind and puts her beyond your control?'

'*It does not!*'

'Oh, I think it does. But what does that matter? She didn't drink it, thanks to you. Which reminds me – I told you not to show yourself at the ceremony, and I don't want you doing any such thing again. It's too dangerous.'

Xai snorted. 'For you.'

'No; for *you*.'

The being gave the peculiar, unpleasant little giggle he had heard before. 'That is what *you* think. But I know different. I know better.'

'What do you mean?'

'Nothing. Everything. Nothing. I am bored. Tell your king to ask his questions, so I can be done with them.'

There was no point, Grendon realised, in pursuing this; if there was something afoot in the background she wasn't about to reveal it of her own accord and he didn't have the time to force her. He returned his consciousness to the physical plane and said aloud, 'Sefira is ready, sir.'

Karel raised his eyebrows faintly, indicating his annoyance at the delay. 'Very well. Then ask her this . . .'

It was over in a few more minutes. Someone – Karel named no names but Grendon suspected Tomany's hand behind this manoeuvre – had cast doubts on the integrity of one of the court's high officials. There were, it seemed, rumours of fiscal corruption, and though nothing could be proved, Karel wanted the culprit – or culprits – found and dealt with. Grendon knew the official under suspicion, and also knew that he was one of the few truly honest men in the court. But a scapegoat must be found; Xai, with an unerring instinct, knew exactly what the king wanted to hear, and she fed Sefira with the answers that would please him. Grendon was disgusted but not surprised by her duplicity and Karel's obvious satisfaction, and when the thing was done he made to bring Sefira out of her trance, wanting to get away from this room and all it contained as quickly as possible.

Karel, however, raised a hand and said, 'One moment, Grendon, before you wake her.'

Grendon paused. 'Sir?'

Karel sat back in his chair. 'The Purging is set for this evening, I understand?'

'Yes, sir.' Grendon's expression didn't change.

'And you've not forgotten my suggestion.' Not a question but a statement this time.

A muscle flicked in Grendon's neck. 'No. I've not forgotten.'

'Good. I would like you to tell me afterwards how Sefira reacts to the event.'

He heard the slight, sharp intake of breath, and Grendon said, 'Her memory may be lost, sir, but I imagine she's seen the spectacle before. Most people have.'

'Ah, no; that wasn't quite what I meant, Grendon. What interests me is to discover whether the sight of the man she identified and rooted out for us provokes any *unusual* response in her. Specifically, one of recognition. You tell me that on waking from a trance she forgets all that she has done or said. I would like to see how deep that forgetfulness goes.'

The picture was clear enough. Karel didn't like the fact that in using Sefira he was dependent on Grendon as a medium, and he was already beginning to look for ways in which that dependence might be broken. To control Sefira's powers himself . . . oh yes; that would appeal greatly to him. And it would put Grendon in a very precarious position.

Well, Grendon thought, Karel had a great deal to learn. But he schooled his face into careful neutrality and gave no clue to his thoughts as he replied, 'Of course, sir. I understand.

I'll watch her carefully, and report my observations to you in person.'

'Do that.' Cat and mouse, Karel thought. And which did Grendon believe was which?

He rose, stretching his arms and flexing his shoulders, which were stiff from sitting for too long in his council chambers. 'Rouse her now, and take her back to your quarters,' he said. 'Oh, and make sure she knows that she has full permission to walk freely in the palace, within the usual limitations of course.' He smiled. 'I gather she hasn't dared venture past your door so far. I hope you haven't clipped her wings in that respect?'

In truth Grendon had tried to do just that, for the prospect of Sefira – or, more pertinently, Sefira under Xai's influence – roaming the palace's corridors unsupervised wasn't one he cared to contemplate. But he inclined his head and said, 'The choice has been hers, sir. But I'll tell her what you said.'

He brought Sefira out of the trance and they took their leave. Sefira's face was closed and unhappy as they walked back towards their apartment. She didn't speak, and Grendon felt too jaded to break the silence – until, as their door came in sight, she suddenly stopped and stared.

'What is it?' Remembering Xai's peculiar mood, he felt a small spark of alarm.

She licked her lips in that unconscious gesture so unpleasantly reminiscent of the soul-invader. 'I thought I . . .' The words tailed off.

He caught hold of her arm. 'What did you think?'

'I thought I remembered something. It was . . .' But then she shook her head, and one hand came up to rub fiercely at her eyes. 'No. It's gone; it's completely gone.' Abruptly, almost challengingly, she looked at him. 'What did the king ask me?'

Grendon sighed. 'It was too trivial to be worth repeating.'

'But I want to *know*.' Then Sefira's eyes narrowed. 'Did it have anything to do with me? With my past?'

'Nothing whatever. It was a court matter, and a very petty one.'

She seemed to sense instinctively that he was telling the truth, and with an effort she made herself relax a little. 'I heard him ordering you to wake me,' she said, 'and before that I seemed to be ... *aware*, somehow, of what I was doing, though I can't remember it now.' She shivered. 'That didn't happen the first time.'

It was a sign, Grendon knew, that Xai was getting stronger, but he feigned indifference and only replied, 'It's nothing to worry about. You'll find each experience is different; in time you'll grow used to it.'

'I wish I didn't have to.'

Grendon gave her a brief but keen look. 'So do I, Sefira. But it's too late for second thoughts now; we have to make the best of it.' Reaching out, he opened the door. 'If you're tired, you'd better sleep for a while. I have to finalise arrangements for this evening's public entertainment, and as the king expects you to attend, you'll need to be fresh.'

She glanced obliquely at him, wondering why he should give the words *public entertainment* such an acid edge. 'You still haven't told me what's to happen.'

'And I'd prefer not to discuss it now. You'll find out soon enough.' Something very strained in his voice, she noticed, but his expression made it clear that he wouldn't take kindly to being pressed. He was standing back, waiting for her to enter the apartment first; with a shrug she moved past him and into the room.

Chapter XIII

It had become the custom for Purgings to begin an hour before sunset, and by late afternoon a considerable crowd was gathering in Victory Square where four of Tourmon's main thoroughfares met. The square had been the scene of the old regime's last stand, before the late king had retreated with the tatters of his army to brief and ill-fated besiegement in the royal quarter; rebuilt, enlarged and renamed, it was now the venue for Tourmon's largest public events. And though the actual spectacle of a Purging was not pleasant, few ordinary citizens had any quarrel with the principle.

Sefira slept half the day away. She disliked the fact that she was sleeping so much, but didn't seem able to summon the energy to stay awake. The clairvoyant episodes drained her to the point of exhaustion, and even though she rested soundly at night, it seemed to do her little good. She suspected that she was dreaming more and more as time passed, and that the dreams were strange and disturbing. She could never recall them when she woke, but they left her with an uneasy miasma in her mind that haunted her throughout her waking hours.

This time, though, she did remember one dream, or at least a fragment of it. She had heard a voice speaking to her; or rather whispering, for there was no timbre or inflection to it, as though the speaker had no physical substance. And when she woke, she recalled what it had said.

'Sefi, we hate him. We want to see him die. We hate him for what he is. And he will pay the price, Sefi. We will make him pay. We will kill him. One day, Sefi. One day.'

171

The words resonated through Sefira's mind like the cold
ring of icicles. She didn't understand the dream; didn't know
what dark crevice of her subconscious had spawned it.
Something, perhaps, out of her forgotten past?

Or something closer to her new life . . . ?

Feeling disquieted and oppressed, she ventured into the
adjoining room, where she found Grendon sitting at a table
by the window with a sheaf of documents before him. She
wanted to tell him of the dream – there was no rational motive
for it; she simply felt the need to unburden herself to someone
– but his grim expression and distracted manner forestalled
any attempt she might have made. He glanced at her, briefly,
and said:

'You'd best put on outdoor clothes. It's nearly time to leave.'

She must have slept for much longer than she realised.
'Are we to walk?' she asked tentatively.

'No.' He stood up, and she saw to her surprise that he was
dressed from head to toe in a shade of crimson so dark that it
was almost black. Breeches, shirt, jerkin, boots – even the
buckle of his wide belt was enamelled in the same ominous
hue. It looked like old, dried blood, and something in her
recoiled.

Grendon saw her expression and said acidly, 'It's the
uniform of my office. You don't have to like it any more than
I do, but there's no need to react as though I were something
out of your nightmares!'

Her face flushed. 'I'm sorry. I was surprised, that's all. You
look very . . . different.'

He snorted with irony. 'That's one word for it, I suppose.'
Another glance at the documents, and she sensed a surge in
him of some feeling to which she couldn't give a name but
which, peculiarly, made her feel momentarily sorry for him.

Abruptly he swept the documents up in one hand, banged
their edges on the table to align them and turned to face her.

'Come on,' he said. 'Get ready. And look your best; it's
expected.'

'This is something official, then?'

'Yes.' He offered no further explanation, but his grey eyes looked angry and dangerous. Sefira tried to hold his gaze, to see what lay beneath the emotion in the look, but it was impossible. Mutely, she returned to her room to change.

They went on horseback to Victory Square, with an escort of King Karel's own guard at their backs. For once the weather was dry, but the cloud cover threatened rain later and a cold north-easterly wind raked through the streets, hinting that winter was following on autumn's heels. This was Sefira's first excursion outside the royal quarter since her arrival in Tourmon, and as she jogged in Grendon's wake on the placid mare provided for her she felt exposed and vulnerable. So many people, and they all seemed to *stare* so. It took a while to convince herself that Grendon, and not she, was the real object of their attention, and even then she found the interest he attracted very disconcerting. For no one smiled when they saw him; they seemed, in fact, to fear or resent him, and she began to realise that for all the adulation the people of Tourmon might have for their king, his Arraigners were another matter. Grendon ignored it all, riding with a face set like stone and eyes focused on the far distance; then as they neared their destination the throng suddenly increased. Their escort moved smoothly to clear a way through, and they entered the square.

Barring a central arena, which had been roped off and was kept clear by men-at-arms, the square was packed almost to suffocation point. But the sea of faces didn't even register on Sefira's mind. She saw only the towering wooden frame that stood in the middle of the arena and dominated the scene, and a sick jolt went through her as she remembered the similar structure in Chalce, and its grisly purpose. Bundles of brushwood were stacked around the base of the frame, and before it stood a lectern mounted on a raised and railed platform.

Pulse thick in her throat and stomach, Sefira urged her

horse closer to Grendon's, trying to get alongside him. She called his name in an urgent hiss, and reluctantly he turned his head to look at her.

'You didn't tell me it was to be a Purging!'

For a moment the expression on his face was so ferocious that she thought he might reach across and strike her, but either the moment passed or the fact that so many eyes were on them inhibited him, for he brought himself quickly back under control and hissed back, 'What would have been the point?'

'I don't want to see this!'

'You haven't any choice. The king ordered me to bring you.'

Her eyes widened. '*Why?*'

'Ask him; I don't pretend to know.' They were slowing as they approached the arena, and Grendon made a quick sign to their escort. 'Go with the guards, and don't talk to anyone unless circumstances force it.'

She wanted to protest, horrified by the thought of being left to cope with the public gaze alone, but before she could say a word her horse was being steered away to a place near the edge of the arena, from where she would have all too clear a view. She looked back over her shoulder and saw Grendon dismount, hand his own animal to one of the king's men and walk towards the raised lectern. As he stepped up on to the dais, the doors of a large building beyond the pyre swung open, and a party of men came out. Several wore the distinctive sashes of court officials; two others were dressed in grey, with grey caps on their heads, and one . . .

The lurch of nausea went through Sefira again as she looked at the man who walked in the officials' midst. He was probably in his sixties, brown hair whitening in two wings at the temples. And he was dressed in plain, dark clothes; trousers, loose-sleeved shirt and an unbelted jerkin. It was a uniform of sorts, and one she recognised – for she had been wearing just such a garb when she had found herself stumbling across the moor on the night of her fateful meeting with Grendon. The memory punched into her mind, triggered a flare of something else, and she put a hand to her mouth, feeling bile rise suddenly and horribly in her throat.

'Madam?' One of the guards, whose hard eyes masked a kinder nature, turned to her and reached out as though to steady her in the saddle. With a huge effort Sefira fought the sickness back and, throat searing, mumbled an assurance that she was well enough. *Why* had the king ordered Grendon to bring her here? Did he think it might call back her lost memory? Was he trying to punish her in some contorted way? Or was it simply a piece of cold and calculated sport at her – and Grendon's – expense?

Sweat was chilling on her face and neck in the sharp wind. Aware that the guard was still watching her she tried not to shiver, and, without moving her head, slid her gaze over the throng to left and right of her vantage point. So *many* people, young and old and from every imaginable walk of life, all mingling together as though for some great celebration . . . she saw a group of women chattering and laughing together, and elsewhere a small gaggle of children gazed at the wooden tower while listening agog to a lecture from a scholarly looking man. They were enjoying this, treating it as a holiday. It was *horrifying*.

Then, suddenly, she saw two faces that were familiar.

Her hands tightened on the reins, making the mare shift restively. The couple in question were some twenty paces away, among a small party that included several more children: the man was dark haired, stocky and had a florid complexion, while the woman had fine, pale skin and wisps of black hair escaping from under her wimple. They were middle-aged, well dressed and clearly wealthy. *Where had she seen them before?*

Then it came to her: the square in Chalce. The preparations for another Purging. And the Lander who had watched her with such acute interest before approaching and introducing himself on a flimsy pretext . . .

She hadn't realised that she was staring fixedly at the couple until abruptly the man turned his head. He saw her, and to her dismay gave a start of recognition. Sefira felt paralysed; it was too late to look away and pretend she hadn't seen him, and for a moment which seemed endless their gazes locked.

Then, to her astonishment, the Lander's face broke into a smile of pleasure and he made a courtly bow in her direction. His wife, noticing, turned; she saw Sefira and she, too, smiled, though unlike her husband it was merely a pleasant courtesy. Reflex came to Sefira's rescue; she felt her own mouth curve and her head nod in response, but under the surface her stomach was churning and she felt a wild urge to swing her mare's head round and spur the animal out of the crowd, out of the square, anywhere that would take her away from this unwanted encounter.

She was snatched back to reason by the sound of a stentorian voice from the middle of the square. An order, barked out by a man in king's regalia; it startled her and broke the thrall, and abruptly all eyes in the crowd turned to the arena. The official party was moving forward again, and a detachment of armed guards had flanked the prisoner. He was led towards the wooden framework; steps were set in place and the guards helped – or compelled – him to climb them.

On the dais Grendon stood alone, waiting, and as she looked at him Sefira's personal crisis was eclipsed by a shock of another kind. For beneath the veneer of sanguine calm, Grendon's mind was burning with sick, all-consuming fury. How she sensed it Sefira didn't know, but she *felt* his rage, like a violent intuitive onslaught in her own psyche. His hands on the lectern were rigid with strain, and he watched the prisoner's slow progress up the steps as though at any moment his self-control might snap and he would turn blindly and flee from the square as moments ago she had wanted to do.

Sefira risked a swift glance in the direction of the Lander, but he was no longer watching her; his gaze was intent, now, on Grendon's solitary figure at the lectern. The crowd had begun to murmur, a susurrus that rose like wind through the square. The prisoner reached the top step; here on the framework was a small platform, just wide enough for him to stand on, and the guards manhandled him around to face the throng before lashing his body to one of the frame's heavy uprights. The man made no attempt to resist; his face was impassive, almost expressionless, as though this whole affair were a charade that had no meaning.

The guards scrambled down from the frame, then Grendon picked up an iron-headed gavel that lay on the lectern. Only Sefira noticed the slight hesitation before he rapped hard, twice, on the lectern's surface. The sound echoed across the square, and instantly the crowd fell silent again. Grendon glanced left and right, as though testing the crowd's mood; briefly his eyes met Sefira's but slid away before she could read anything in them. Then, steeling himself, he began to speak.

He had memorised the contents of the document. An indictment, in the remorseless language of officialdom, cataloguing the crimes of Rueshe, recent alias Nimre, resident in Ishen and now, by his own confession, exposed as being of the Sanctified Fellowship whose adherents were anathema to all that the king and his people held dear. The list of Rueshe's offences was long and complex, but added up to one straightforward charge, against which there could be no plea. Treason. The evidence, Grendon stated, was sufficient to prove the prisoner's guilt, and Rueshe was to be purged, to ensure that his taint could not live on to spread the seeds of corruption among innocent souls.

Grendon could hear his own voice uttering the words and, as he always did on these occasions, strove to convince himself that someone else was speaking, someone else responsible. The attempt never worked (how could it? he asked himself as the litany went on – he had done this too many times to be deceived) but always he tried. He was aware that the condemned man was watching him, and knew without needing to raise his head what message his eyes would carry. Contempt. Disgust. Hatred. One Sanctified, once, had attempted to launch a psychic attack against him as the charges were read, and in repelling it Grendon had revealed the truth about himself. He had seen the shock of realisation in the man's face, and for the first and only time had curtailed the formalities and given the order for the pyre to be lit at once. He would not forget that day. This, by comparison, was nothing.

The speech came to an end at last, and with a taste of iron and sulphur in his mouth Grendon raised the gavel again. He could see the flicker of torchlight on the periphery of his vision, a livid smear against the dull day. He thought of Rueshe's family, if they still lived, and what would become of them. And he thought of Lendrer, and Arrine, and his own parents. And of Mischane . . .

The gavel came down. The torchbearers stepped forward.

As the first of the brushwood began to catch fire, Sefira saw the Lander and his family turn and begin to forge their way back through the crowd towards the edge of the square. There was no haste about their departure, but it was obvious that, unlike the great majority, they had wanted only to hear the indictment and had no stomach for what would follow. There was a good deal of jostling as others eagerly tried to take the places they had vacated, and she realised that the press of the throng was propelling them closer to her own vantage point. They would pass within a few paces of where she sat, and she turned her head quickly, staring straight ahead at the pyre. She didn't want to watch, didn't want to see this barbarity; but fear of meeting the Lander's gaze again and of being forced to speak to him eclipsed her revulsion, and she forced herself to look steadily at the scene unfolding in the arena.

The flames began to dance; smoke churned from the brushwood and the acrid smell of it tickled her nostrils. The prisoner was moving, shifting in his bonds as his self-control started to disintegrate, and she knew what when the fire touched him the last of his dignity would collapse. He would scream. He would burn. He would die. She didn't want to witness it; didn't want—

Ah, but we want to see! For we hate them! WE HATE THEM ALL, SEFI!

The gleeful, triumphant words punched up from Sefira's unconscious and exploded into her mind with an impact that made her cry out aloud. Heads nearby turned and Sefira snatched at a handful of her horse's mane to steady herself as a wave of giddiness swept over her. The scene blurred into starbursts of fire and shadow, and a huge feeling of pleasure, of hungry *delight*, swamped her. *The Sanctified, the enemy, the destroyer of her kind, burning, dying, consumed and turned to ashes that would be scattered to the four winds – she wanted it, wanted to watch it happen, to shriek encouragement to the fire, to shout her satisfaction throughout the city!*

She didn't see Grendon swing round, a silhouette now against the rising blaze. She didn't see the Lander's look of dismay, or her escort's hands stretching out to help her. There was fire in the square and fire in her head; she heard the prisoner's first inhuman scream as willpower and equilibrium collapsed under the onslaught of searing agony, and she rejoiced at the sound. Her mouth moved, beyond her control, and her voice rose up in a savage, swelling cry of exultation:

'*Yes! Yes! YES*—'

The words cut off at a choking pitch, and the guards were just in time to catch her as she slumped unconscious out of the saddle.

'Your pardon, sir. Let me through. Yes, yes; the lady is known to me. Thank you. Your pardon, sir . . .' Perlion was a well-built man and his manner and dress commanded authority; shouldering through the press of curious onlookers in the courthouse's entrance hall he reached the door of the anteroom and pushed his way inside.

Sefira, still unconscious, was lying on a hastily contrived couch, and a small gaggle of people, mostly court officers, were gathered round her. Someone had sent for a physician but he hadn't yet arrived, and there was noisy debate as to what had happened and what to do for the best. Grendon, in the midst of it all, was trying to make them understand that their attentions, though well-meaning, were unwanted; Perlion summed up the situation in a moment and called out above the hubbub.

'Gentlemen, gentlemen! The lady needs the air you are breathing! Leave the room, sirs, *if* you please!'

The ploy worked; taking him for the physician they drew back, shuffling reluctantly out of the room. Perlion closed the door on the last of them, then looked at Grendon, who was staring at him with narrow-eyed suspicion.

'I don't believe you're the physician, sir,' he said sharply.

'No.' Perlion flicked a quick smile. 'Perlion; Lander. We met briefly in Chalce.'

Grendon remembered the meeting and the name very well, but didn't show it. 'Would you kindly leave.'

Perlion ignored the order and approached the couch. 'Is she hurt? I saw her fall; I heard—'

He was interrupted. 'You'll pardon me, sir, but this is my concern and not yours.'

Perlion wanted to tell him how wrong he was, but stayed his tongue. Grendon was still looking at him, and he realised now that the Lander was genuinely and deeply concerned about Sefira. He recalled their previous meeting, and Perlion's acute interest that had so terrified Sefira, and abruptly he knew with a sure instinct that there was far, far more to this man's intrusion into their lives than met the eye.

Through the window, the view of the square was clouded by smoke. Rueshe was charred bone now, but the fire still crackled loudly, though the sound was muffled by the glass panes. Aware that Isbel, Vinor and the children were waiting for him, aware that he had baffled them all by his impulsive action and that he should not have come here, Perlion dabbed at his suddenly perspiring brow and said, 'Sir, I . . . think perhaps I owe you a word of explanation.'

Grendon's eyes were steady. He said nothing.

'I – ah—' He coughed. 'The smoke; it . . . yes, well; you see, your wife; that is, I wondered if – ah—'

'Perhaps,' Grendon put in a little more kindly, 'it would be better to come straight to the point.'

'Of course. Of course.' Perlion gathered his wits. He had come this far and couldn't turn back. 'The fact is, sir, I believe I know the lady – or rather, knew her and . . . and her family some years ago. We . . . ah . . . lost touch, you see. Before the war.' He was floundering, but suddenly inspiration came. 'And I would so very much like to know what has become of her parents.'

There was silence. Grendon's face remained impassive, but his mind churned with the possible implications of this development. At last, keeping his voice neutral, he said:

'You say you knew Sefira and her family, sir. But, as you saw for yourself in Chalce, she has no recollection of you.'

'No, well; that's likely as not. She was very young, you see. Very young, and—'

'Yet you recognised her.'

'Yes.' Perlion realised how unconvincing he must sound, and again regretted his rashness. 'I couldn't be sure, of course, but her name; and the fact that my friends were of the Communicant Fellowship like yourselves . . . I thought about it a great deal after our meeting in Chalce, and then when I arrived in Tourmon on business and saw you both again—'

'On business?'

'Yes. My cousin Vinor is a grain supplier to the king's household.' With a great effort Perlion managed to smile. 'When I saw you both again, it occurred to me that I might extend an invitation to you to dine with us one evening. Then we could have discussed the matter and found out the truth.

I had intended to speak to you after the . . .' he waved a hand uneasily in the direction of the window, '. . . the proceedings today; and when your wife was taken ill, I was naturally concerned . . .'

The words trailed off, and Grendon wondered how much of this tale was true and how much a lie. He had an intuitive feeling that Perlion was in earnest, perhaps even to the point of naivety. But that same intuition also told him that he was hiding something. If he was, then he could be more than a nuisance; he could be a potential danger.

Wanting to put Perlion off the scent but aware that he needed to tread very carefully, he said, 'Well, sir, I'm afraid that I must disappoint you. I don't know the whereabouts of Sefira's family, and neither does she.' He gave the Lander a wintrily sympathetic smile. 'Her parents died when she was a baby, and she was adopted.'

He didn't get the reaction he expected. Perlion's eyes widened avidly and he repeated, 'Adopted!' in a breathless voice. Then suddenly he came forward and clasped Grendon's hands. 'Sir, this is splendid, *splendid*! You see, my Sefira – that is, the child I knew – she, too, was adopted. Her natural parents died of a fever, and my friends brought her up as their own. They hadn't told her when I knew them, of course, for she was too young to understand. But I don't doubt that when she grew older the truth was revealed.' Shifting from one foot to the other like an eager child, he flung a joyful glance in Sefira's direction. 'I'm in no doubt now, sir; no doubt at all. Your wife and the child I knew are one and the same!'

As though his excitement had penetrated the wall of her unconsciousness, Sefira stirred and muttered something unintelligible. Alarm filled Grendon, and as Perlion seemed about to hurry to the couch he caught hold of his arm.

'Lander Perlion.' His voice was stern. 'I think you had better leave now.'

'Leave? But—'

'If Sefira is waking, I don't think it will be in her best

interests to have a new shock so soon after her recovery, do you?'

'Ah . . . no; no, of course.' A sigh. 'It was the Purging, I suppose. Not a pleasant business.'

'Quite.' If he wanted to believe that, Grendon was content to let him. He could sense Sefira's mind coming back to consciousness, and as quickly as was prudent he steered Perlion to the door. On the threshold the Lander turned round.

'The invitation,' he said, flustered. 'If you would accept—'

'Send word to the palace. Now, if you'll excuse my brusqueness—'

'One last thing. Please. *Do* her parents still live?'

'No,' Grendon said calmly. 'I'm sorry. But they are both dead now.'

Perlion's face fell, but only for a moment as he reminded himself that, even if he could not meet the couple who had adopted Sefira, he could at least learn about them and about her life through all the lost years. His shoulders relaxed; he made a bow to Grendon and said, 'Thank you, Arraigner Grendon. I am more in your debt than you know. Please convey my felicitations to Sefira – and I will look forward to our next meeting.'

There was no one else in the entrance hall; with no more drama left to see, the onlookers had found other distractions. Grendon watched Perlion walk away towards the entrance. Then he shut the door of the anteroom and leaned his back against it, muttering a foul imprecation under his breath.

The crowd in the square was slowly dispersing. The fire had almost burned out, leaving little but char and ash behind, and the mixture of emotions that the spectacle had aroused was also dying down and giving way to the more everyday concerns of the evening.

Amid a small human tributary making its way towards one of the side streets, Kessie, the midwife, looked back over her shoulder at the pyre's macabre remains, but her thoughts weren't on the execution. She had seen Perlion in the square with his family, and had seen him become involved in that odd incident with the girl on the horse. Someone had said she was the presiding Arraigner's wife, and someone else had said she had had a fit or a fever or both, and little wonder if the poor creature was wed to one of *them*. But Kessie had been close enough to hear what the girl cried out in the moments before she fell from the saddle, and it had sent a cold chill through her. Perlion had said that his long-lost daughter was married. And Kessie knew her appalling secret, and what it meant. Her old mistress had told her things about the soul-invaders that were known to few survivors of the war; things that even Perlion would be unaware of. So Kessie knew the signs. And she feared for Perlion's life.

The stream of people around her was flowing on; someone jostled behind her and told her to move her feet or how was anyone supposed to see their own hearth and bed tonight? Realising that she had been standing staring at nothing like a dumbwit, Kessie hastened on, suppressing a second shudder that felt as if cold little fingers were tapping on her spine. All day she had been unable to shed the feeling that someone was watching her every movement, and this evening in the square it had flowered into a nerve-racking sensation that she was being followed. It was nonsense, of course; each time she looked there was nothing untoward to be seen. But she was beginning to wish wholeheartedly that she had refused Perlion's entreaties, and not allowed herself to become involved in matters that were none of her concern.

The sight of an Arraigner's wife taken ill in the square was small beer compared to the greater excitement of the Purging, but nonetheless the tale reached the palace and within a few hours Karel was aware of what had happened. Grendon, he learned, had had Sefira carried back in a closed litter and they were now secreted in their rooms, where she was recovering from her unpleasant experience.

The king was intrigued by the result of his small experiment, and one minor factor particularly interested him. An embellishment to the tattle, that was all. But in the circumstances it had a significant element, and after he had eaten a leisurely and solitary meal – he wanted no company tonight – Karel went to the innermost of his private chambers and unlocked a wooden box that stood on a corner table and in which he kept his most personal papers.

Thanks to Tomany's diligence the records hadn't been hard to trace, and the sealed scroll had arrived from Emelian two days ago. At first Karel had intended to show it to Grendon, but had changed his mind. What Grendon didn't know couldn't hurt him; and the information contained in this document could have all manner of uses that Karel hadn't even considered yet.

He unrolled the scroll and reread the contents. They told a tale that made the charges against Rueshe pallid by comparison – and, unlike those charges, every word of this disposition was true. Murder, Karel thought, was hardly the word for it: slaughter would be a more accurate term. A burgher of the town all but torn apart in his own house, the corpse found in a lake of its own blood and with the killer still attacking in a demented frenzy, trying to twist one arm off with hands and teeth . . . The man had been well known as a lecher and seducer of young women, but this was taking retaliation a little *too* far. Sefira, it seemed, had aspects to her character that Grendon had not revealed. Or possibly even that Grendon did not know. It shed an interesting light, Karel thought, on the nature of her talents. A pity that the only person who might be able to interpret that light was the one person he did not wish to alert.

Or was there another way to approach it . . . ? Karel paused thoughtfully, then rolled the document up again and put it away. A new possibility had occurred to him; one which might well bear fruit. The person in question would not cooperate if approached directly, but a subtler ploy might produce the results he wanted.

He closed the lid of the box, turned the key, then summoned Tomany. When the man appeared, soft footed and unobtrusive as ever, he said:

'Ask the lady Mischane to join me, please, Tomany. I have a small favour to ask of her.'

Chapter XIV

The following morning Sefira was commanded to attend the king again.

Karel's timing, Grendon thought acerbically, couldn't have been worse, for he was very concerned by the effect that the spectacle of the Purging had had on Sefira – or rather, on Xai. He had heard what Sefira cried out before her collapse only too clearly, and it alarmed him to think that the demonic parasite could have had such an influence on her host's conscious thoughts and actions. Sefira, of course, didn't remember what had happened, and he hadn't told her the details. But this was a sure sign that Xai was growing stronger and more confident. And he feared that before long she might start to show her strength in more drastic ways.

To add to his discomfort, he had received a formal but effusive letter from Perlion, expressing his hope that Sefira had recovered from her disorder and reminding them of his invitation to dine with him one evening. No specific day was mentioned, but Grendon knew that he couldn't deter the man simply with a polite rebuff. Perlion would persist until and unless a way could be found to put him off once and for all, and that presented Grendon with a dilemma. He could respond with a flat refusal accompanied by a veiled warning about privacy; that would be enough, for even the wealthiest Lander wouldn't take the risk of crossing one of the king's Arraigners. But if he did that, he would never know the real reason for Perlion's interest in Sefira. And that, Grendon felt, might be a very foolish mistake.

He resolved eventually to let a few days pass before replying to Perlion's letter. It would do the man no harm to be patient, and in the meantime Grendon could set a few private investigations in motion. Perlion's background and history would be easy enough to probe, especially as his cousin had business with the court. And a little digging might unearth something useful.

With that decided he managed to put Perlion out of his thoughts. But the potential danger Xai posed was another matter, and as he and Sefira were admitted to the king's presence he hoped fervently that the creature wouldn't try to make mischief during this interview. He was on edge as he put Sefira into her trance, aware that Karel was watching closely and with rather more interest than usual. He seemed to be concentrating on every detail of the proceedings as though they had some new and particular significance, and Grendon was certain that there must be a connection with what had happened in Victory Square. He had, as commanded, sent the king a report of the incident; or at least a version of it, for he had said only that Sefira had seemed greatly distressed by the spectacle and had fainted shortly after the pyre was lit. Karel no doubt had other spies in the square, and they might well have told a more detailed story. But if Karel was speculating on what he had heard, he kept those speculations to himself.

Again Xai refused to show herself, and it was only with difficulty that Grendon forced her to communicate in any way at all. It was an ominous sign, for it implied that she was conserving and trying to build on her energy – and that in turn suggested some trickery afoot. Grendon could have forced her into the open, but it would have needed the full trappings of ritual, and those practices were something he would not reveal under any circumstances in Karel's presence. For now he must be content with compelling her to do what the king wanted, and anything else would have to wait.

Karel had two questions for Sefira. One was a coda to the

affair he had wanted her to explore two days ago, and the other concerned some new court intrigue and the real motives of the leading figures behind it. Both trivial matters but, as before, the answers Karel received seemed to please him. When it was over, Grendon – thoroughly relieved that Xai hadn't overstepped the mark – made to break the spell on Sefira, who sat gazing at the far wall, oblivious to her surroundings.

And a voice giggled in his mind.

Silently, savagely, Grendon projected, *Go! I'm done with you!*

Xai uttered her ugly little laugh again. *So you think. But what did the Lander see yesterday, Grendon? What did he hear?* An unpleasant, itching sensation went through him, as though something physical and alive was wriggling inside his skull. *You should be careful of Perlion. Who knows what he knows? Who knows what he will find out?* Her soundless presence began to fade, dissolving like smoke. *Could he wreck your ambitions, Grendon? Could he bring them crashing down? It will be interesting to see. It will be interesting . . .*

Then she was gone, leaving Grendon feeling momentarily disorientated. His head clearly quickly, but Xai had slipped a sharp knife of apprehension neatly into his mind, and that left its mark. Something was in the wind; he didn't doubt it now . . .

Suddenly Sefira made an extraordinary noise at the back of her throat, and Karel raised his eyebrows. 'Is she unwell again?' he enquired mildly.

It was the first reference he had made to yesterday's incident. Grendon didn't look at him, only said stiffly, 'No, sir,' and placed a hand, splay-fingered, on Sefira's forehead, exerting his will. Her skin felt unhealthily hot, and perspiration had dampened the edge of her wimple. Briefly Grendon seemed to feel Xai's presence again, but then it flicked out and cognition returned to Sefira's eyes.

'Did I—' she started to say, then stopped as she saw the king.

Karel leaned forward and smiled at her. 'Did you what, Mistress Sefira?'

She swallowed. 'Nothing . . . sir. I – must have had a dream, I think.'

'Can you remember what the dream was?'

She hesitated, then: 'No. I'm sorry . . .'

If Karel was disappointed he didn't show it. 'Well, you're awake now. And, as always, you've done your work well. You may both go.'

Grendon and Sefira returned to their rooms in their customary silence, and with a sense of depression Sefira felt the now familiar weariness washing over her. For once she wanted to stay awake instead of retreating into the sanctuary of her bedchamber and the oblivion of sleep. She wanted to think, and she wanted to talk. Or, more precisely, to get answers to some questions that were nagging at her like a sore tooth.

Yesterday she had seen Grendon at work for the first time, and had loathed what she saw. He was little better than an executioner, carrying out work in the king's name with which the king would not dream to soil his own hands. The realisation of it had triggered some ugly thoughts in her mind – she, too, had been in Rueshe's position not long ago, though she had no memory of it, and doubtless her death would have been presided over by another Arraigner; another man like Grendon.

Yet for all the instinctive revulsion that Grendon's work aroused in her, a deeper realisation was flowing against the tide. For it was clear to her that Grendon abhorred his work. Firstly there had been the hint implicit in his behaviour before they left for Victory Square. And then, before her own collapse (the circumstances of which she now had no memory whatever) she had felt that searing wave of bitter fury emanating from his mind; fury, and utter repugnance at what his office obliged him to do. Though it went against the grain after her early experiences, she was beginning to change her view of him.

But that posed another conundrum, for if Grendon detested his calling, the obvious solution was to resign from the king's service. Why hadn't he taken that path? she asked herself. Logic suggested that ambition was the key; after all, he had proved his ruthlessness by marrying her for the sake of preferment. Yet to Sefira's mind, something about that reasoning didn't ring true. It was as if, in his most private self, he was driven by something else entirely; something more complex and possibly even more relentless than his apparent desire for status and influence. And whatever that inner drive was, she had the feeling that it was costing him dearly to pursue it.

He had walked to the window and was staring out at the grey day. Sefira studied his back view, noting the tension of his posture. He seemed constantly on the alert, as if he expected some treachery to strike at any moment – and not only from her, she suspected. She wished she could persuade him to drop his defences, even if only for a short while, and talk honestly to her. She would, she thought, discover the answers to some very enigmatic questions.

Suddenly she yawned, and though she tried to swallow it quickly Grendon must have seen her reflection in the glass, for he turned round and said, 'You'd better sleep for a while.'

Angry with herself, Sefira replied, 'I sleep too much. I'd rather stay awake.'

He shrugged. His eyes were very distant and aloof. 'As you please; though I doubt if you'll succeed.'

He was right, and that added to her annoyance. She had wanted to tell him that she had lied to the king, that she did remember the dream she had had during her trance and had been frightened by it. She had wanted his advice and reassurance. But suddenly there seemed no point. Her fear seemed trivial now, anyway; she had simply dreamed that she was lying on a couch in a strange room, and the Lander from Chalce had come in and had stood staring and staring at her, and when she tried to tell him to stop, she found that she could neither move nor speak. Foolish. Meaningless. *Forget it*, she told herself.

Grendon was still looking at her, and though it might have been imagination she thought that there was suddenly a tinge of weary sadness in his face. Less brusquely, he said, 'Go and sleep, Sefira. It's for the best.'

It probably was. Feeling defeated, Sefira turned and went into the inner room.

When Sefira woke, it was past noon and Grendon was not in the apartment. Suppressing a vague and sourceless feeling of annoyance at his absence, she was just beginning to realise that she felt hungry when someone tapped discreetly on the outer door.

To her knowledge they had had no unexpected callers since the day of the wedding . . . Sefira answered the knock, and her surprise doubled when she saw Mischane standing outside.

For a moment the two women stared at each other, then, a little uncertainly, Sefira said, 'Mischane . . . I'm sorry, but Grendon isn't here.'

Mischane smiled. 'I know; I saw him leaving the palace. In fact, that's why I came. I was hoping to talk to you.'

'To me?' She was nonplussed, and suddenly a little alarmed. 'Why?'

'Because I was unfair to you the last time we met, before the marriage ceremony. I didn't fully understand the circumstances, and I should have been kinder. So I wanted to apologise – and also to get to know you a little better.' Mischane paused. 'May I come in, or are you busy?'

The prospect of inviting her in made Sefira feel very uncomfortable. This was a completely unforeseen development, for at their first meeting she had thought Mischane disliked her and had also had a strong impression that she had little love for her brother either. So why this sudden change? She didn't trust it. But she had been caught off guard and there was no time to think of an excuse.

'No,' she said helplessly, 'I – I'm not busy.' She stood back, opening the door wider. 'Please . . .'

Mischane stayed for nearly an hour, and by the time she left Sefira was thoroughly confused. The woman was, it seemed, very anxious to make a friend of her, and equally anxious to put her at her ease. She had asked no personal questions, only kept to everyday pleasantries, and Grendon's name had hardly been mentioned. As they parted she had expressed her hope that they would see a good deal more of each other from now on. The meeting had been, to all intents and purposes, simply an agreeable social interlude. And Sefira had no idea what could have caused Mischane's change of heart.

Only one small incident had struck a peculiar note. Mischane had been talking of some people in the palace and Sefira's attention was wandering a little, for she wasn't particularly interested in the doings of complete strangers. Then suddenly Mischane's expression had changed. She had frowned, and said a little uneasily, 'Would you like me to fetch you something to eat?'

'To eat?' Sefira didn't comprehend. 'Why, no, thank you. I'm not at all hungry.'

'But you just said you were.'

'No.' Baffled, Sefira shook her head. 'I didn't speak. I didn't say anything at all.'

Mischane gave her such an extraordinary look then that Sefira wondered momentarily if she was ill, or a little mad, or both. It seemed to mingle curiosity with foreboding . . . and a small, inexplicable hint that some private thought or viewpoint had been vindicated. But all she said was, 'I'm sorry, I must have been mistaken. Please forgive me. Now, where were we . . . ?'

Though the episode had puzzled her, Sefira thought little more of it. But to Mischane, as she walked quickly through the palace's corridors, it had been the most significant moment of their encounter. And what it told her set an old, deep fear clawing at the pit of her stomach.

There was a covert way to King Karel's private apartments; a passage leading from a false panel in one of the archive rooms. It was known only to a very privileged few, and Mischane took care to see that she wasn't observed before sliding the panel back and making her way through. Karel was waiting for her, and rose from his chair as she entered his sitting room. He held out one hand; Mischane went towards him and he took hold of her fingers, drawing her towards him.

'Well, my sweet.' She turned her face up to his and he kissed her in a way that combined affection with a hint of lasciviousness. 'You were quicker than I'd expected.'

Mischane returned the kiss, but he detected the underlying unease in her and felt the tautness of her body as she touched against him. Drawing back a little, he looked at her face, read the expression in it, and his grip on her hand tightened. 'What happened? Tell me.'

Mischane drew a deep breath. 'I had enough time to learn all I needed to know,' she said. Her heart was thumping and her voice wasn't quite steady.

Karel frowned. 'Sit down. There, on the couch.' He waited until she had subsided then sat next to her and added, 'Take your time – but I want to know everything.'

She nodded, swallowed. 'Firstly,' she said, 'I don't believe that she's a Sanctified.'

Karel pressed a finger to his own chin. 'That's as we thought. You tested her?'

'As best I could – some pertinent questions, a hint or two; there was no response. I know she's lost her memory, but the *instincts* of a Sanctified weren't there.' She met his gaze a little uneasily. 'Which, of course, I would recognise.'

'Of course you would.' Karel smiled reassuringly.

'She also believes that Grendon's – our – family is of the Communicant Fellowship. And she knows nothing about the circumstances of . . .' She hesitated, and Karel supplied with wry delicacy, 'The circumstances that make Grendon so loyal in my service, shall we say? I'm pleased to hear he hasn't told her about that; it could make matters rather inconvenient for us both.' His hand was still holding hers, and one finger traced an intimate little pattern on her palm. 'So, then; there's no barrier to your cultivating her friendship.'

'No.' Mischane glanced quickly, involuntarily it seemed, over her shoulder, then suppressed a shiver. 'At least, not in that sense. But . . .'

'Ah.' Karel leant forward, his eyes suddenly intent. 'Then the other suspicion – there *is* evidence?'

In her mind Mischane went over the incident again, but there was no room for doubt. It was exactly as had happened at the wedding celebration; Sefira had said suddenly, 'I'm hungry,' and as she spoke, the look on her face had flung Mischane back to her early childhood. How often had she heard those words; seen that look? Her parents had told her what it meant, warned her to keep away when it happened, and she had learned to dread it, and so much else. She had learnt to hate her brother.

Now, even after so many years, she remembered this sign, this symptom, only too well. Sefira knew nothing about it, that was certain. She hadn't even realised that she had spoken, for the *thing* eating at her mind and soul was still taking great care to hide its presence from her. When Mischane was a child the circumstances had been different. But in those days, Sanctified families were privy to knowledge that was denied to lesser Fellowships.

Karel was waiting for her to reply. She recalled the document he had shown her; the deposition from Emelian and the story it told. That, too, was horribly familiar. There was *no* room for doubt.

She spoke at last, and her voice was barely audible. 'Yes,' she said. 'There is evidence. There is more than enough.'

* * *

Grendon returned to the palace in the late afternoon, soaked through from a sudden downpour and in a thoughtful mood. Sefira wanted to tell him about Mischane's visit, but before she could broach the subject he ordered a bath and hot water to be brought to the apartment, and propriety drove her to the inner room while he washed himself. She suspected the bath was a deliberate ploy to get her out of his way, and she was right – though not for the reasons that she assumed. Grendon merely wanted some time to himself to consider his afternoon's investigations, and the conundrums they had raised.

Finding out the basic facts about Perlion had been easy; a call at the Office of Records had furnished him with all he needed. A wealthy man, with a large and productive hereditary estate outside Chalce; married twenty-six years ago; four children, all still quite young. During the civil war Perlion had apparently been very circumspect, speaking up for justice and tolerance but avoiding any extreme point of view; though in the latter days of the fighting his estate had been quietly responsible for some provisioning of Karel's troops. He had neither sought nor received any preferment under the new regime, but his cousin, Vinor, was now well established as a supplier to the palace and had profited handsomely and, it seemed, honestly from it. There was nothing exceptional about Perlion, nothing to hint at any secrets or mysteries, and no clue whatever to his eager interest in Sefira.

So, then, if the public records yielded no answers they would have to come from the man himself. Grendon's early fear that Perlion's attentions might have some connection with Sefira's crime was gone now. From the records it was obvious that he was an upright, decent and almost naively straightforward citizen; if he wanted to unmask a felon, he would simply do so without any subterfuge. So possibly his story was the truth. And the best way to find out would be by a blunt approach. Grendon had no intention of taking Sefira to dine with him, at least not yet. But a meeting between himself and Perlion, to establish the ground a little better, might be very useful.

He got out of the bath, and while he dressed worked out the wording of the reply he would send to Perlion's letter. He would say nothing to Sefira; for the time being, the less she knew the better, so he wrote his message quickly, sealed it, then called to tell her that she could emerge from hiding.

She came out of the bedroom at once and seemed about to say something, but he didn't give her the chance.

'I have to go out again,' he said to her. 'I'll be no more than an hour.'

Again Sefira had been about to tell him of Mischane's visit; again she was disappointed, and as she heard his footsteps diminishing down the passage she felt a surge of frustrated anger. Trying to get through to Grendon was like trying to demolish a stone wall with nothing but her bare hands. He wouldn't communicate with her, wasn't interested in listening to anything she had to say. He gave her no *chance*. She felt the anger swell.

We hate him, Sefi . . .

Sefira blinked, started, and looked down at what she held in one hand.

A crushed piece of tawny-coloured fabric. And another piece lay on the floor . . . for a few seconds she didn't recognise what it was, but then she realised that her head felt oddly cool and light. As if something was missing . . .

With a gasp she put her free hand up to her skull and felt the short, rough locks of her hair. The wimple – she had pulled it off, and ripped it clean in two. Sefira's heart began to pound painfully under her ribs. When had she done this? Surely, only a moment had passed since her rush of anger at Grendon: there wouldn't have been *time*.

But it had happened. She couldn't deny the evidence; she was *holding* the evidence. Yet she didn't remember. She didn't remember a thing.

Very slowly she reached down to where the other half of the wimple lay. She had to force herself to touch it, part of her fearing that it would suddenly come alive in her grasp. As she picked it up she felt momentarily dizzy; straightening, she shook her head in an effort to clear it.

We are getting stronger, Sefi. Much stronger. But soon I will be hungry . . .

She didn't hear the voice, not consciously. But the anger in her seeped away suddenly, like water soaking into dry ground. She blinked, stared at the fabric she held. It didn't mean anything. Just scraps of material. She didn't even know why she had them.

She was only half dressed, and hadn't yet put her wimple on. That was foolish of her, and if Grendon returned and saw her like this she'd feel the sharp edge of his tongue for her carelessness. Giving another shake of her head – her mind *was* a little fogged; possibly it was lack of food – she turned and walked peaceably into the bedchamber.

Chapter XV

Candlelight made a haze of shadows that encroached from each corner of the room and, to Mischane's overwrought mind, seemed to be trying to touch them where they sat at the table. There were no servants to wait on them; this, as always, was a very private encounter, but though normally she enjoyed the privacy, tonight something in the atmosphere felt ominous.

As Karel rose to pour her more wine she shivered and, yet again, glanced uneasily towards the far side of the room where the shadows were deepest. He saw the involuntary movement, and his eyes hardened with a tingle of irritation.

'Mischane, I understand your terrors, but you should try to overcome them.' The flagon went back on the table with unnecessary force, and the thump of it made her start. 'I've no intention of endangering myself, or you. But I also have no intention of allowing this opportunity to slip through my fingers.' He paused, and the hard look intensified. 'Or of allowing your brother to maintain any advantage over me. Which is, I assume, an issue that still matters to you?'

Mischane fingered the stem of her glass, then stopped lest in her nervousness she might snap it. 'You know it is. But to tamper with something like this – Karel, it's *dangerous*! Forgive me, but . . . you haven't the knowledge, the – the skill . . .'

'You mean that unlike Grendon, I'm not a Sanctified.'

She flushed. 'No, that isn't what I mean. It's too dangerous for *anyone*.'

'Your old family friend Lendrer succeeded well enough. He destroyed one of these parasites and lived to tell the tale.'

'Lendrer was lucky – and it nearly killed both him and my brother.'

'Whether it did or whether it didn't, the fact remains that he *did* succeed,' Karel said. 'So there is a precedent, is there not?' He smiled, a hard smile. 'Besides, I have no wish to destroy the creature. I have something else in mind entirely.'

A shaft of cold foreboding struck through Mischane but she suppressed any outward sign of it. She knew that Karel was becoming impatient with her, and that impatience could lead to anger. Yet she had to try to dissuade him from taking this reckless path. He didn't understand what he was dealing with.

Abruptly, Karel pushed his unfinished meal away, rose and, taking up his glass, paced to the fire, where he stood staring into the flames. 'I understand your concern,' he said. 'I appreciate that you're thinking only of my safety, and' – he turned and regarded her more favourably as his annoyance ebbed – 'I'm fully aware of your reasons. But, my dear, *I* must think of my own interests in a wider context. A king, and especially a king who has come to power as I did, is never entirely safe. I may be popular, but I still have enemies – and some of those enemies are capable of wielding powers which make them exceptionally dangerous. Your own family being a case in point.'

Something akin to fear crept into Mischane's eyes. 'I'm not like Grendon and my parents! You know I'm loyal—'

'Of course. Don't think for one moment that I doubt you.' Karel smiled again. 'After all, you could have told Grendon the truth about our little arrangement a long time ago, and that would have lost me a valuable if unwilling servant. But Grendon's unwillingness is a perfect illustration of my problem. While he believes that his beloved sister is a hostage against his allegiance, he'll continue to do as he's told. But if he starts to suspect the truth, that allegiance will vanish in an instant . . . and with a creature like Sefira under his control, Grendon will become a considerable hazard.'

Mischane saw the logic of his argument, but still couldn't overcome the deeper, shrivelling dread lodged in her. 'Grendon may be able to control Sefira,' she said restively, 'but Grendon learned his skills from a master. You have no such protection.'

'Ah, but I have no intention of trying to control her, Mischane. That approach, as you say, is for the likes of Lendrer and his pupils.'

She recalled his words of a few minutes earlier and ventured uneasily, 'You said . . . you have something in mind?'

'Yes. I've read a little about these soul-eating parasites, you see, and it's my belief that Grendon must have made a bargain of some sort with the creature. Well, if he can bargain, so can I – and I can offer Sefira, or rather that which lurks inside her, *far* more favourable terms than your brother could hope to do.'

Mischane stared at him. 'A *bargain*?'

'Mmm. Why do you look so shocked? It makes perfect sense. This thing obviously has a strong desire to survive, and to do that it will need my goodwill far more than it will need Grendon's – especially once it realises that I'm aware of its presence. I, in my turn, want something that the creature can give me.'

'Its powers . . .'

'Precisely. I won't say that they'll make me invulnerable or omnipotent . . . but it will be the next best thing.' Suddenly Karel's look became wolfish. 'And then neither I nor you will need to worry about Grendon, for he'll no longer have a hold over either of us. Think about that, Mischane. Think about what it would mean to you.'

He saw the slow gleam of hunger that crept into her eyes and knew he had won her over. Grendon had been a liability to Mischane since the day that she had decided her own interests were better served by loyalty rather than opposition to the new king. Karel knew about her older hostility towards him, and the reasons for it. To be free of him would be to shake off a burden that she had carried unwillingly for two years. And Grendon was a burden to Karel, too. As an Arraigner he had been invaluable, for how better to go about rooting out the last of the Sanctifieds than by using the powers of one of their own kind? But though he did what he was commanded to do, Grendon's attitude had never changed. He loathed the new order, and if the chance ever came to take vengeance, he would grasp it with both hands. Karel had always known that. To be rid of him now, once and for all, would relieve the king of the feeling that one day he would look over his shoulder just a moment too late.

'My sweet.' He returned to the table, sat down again and refilled his glass. 'You know that the promises I make to *you*' – the emphasis was slight but unmistakable – 'are not broken.'

She smiled hesitantly. 'Yes. I know that.'

'Then I'll make you a promise now. I will not endanger myself in this, and I will not endanger you. Everything will be done properly and with the utmost caution. I wish your brother no harm,' (the lie came glibly) 'but I would be a fool if I allowed myself to remain beholden to him for one moment longer than I need to. Don't you agree?'

Mischane remembered her last conversation with Grendon, and nodded. 'Yes. Yes, I do.'

'Then we'll drink a small toast. To success, and the future.'

Her glass was untouched, but slowly, almost diffidently, she raised it. Eagerness and dread were struggling for precedence in her mind, but eagerness, fuelled by a resentment that reached back far into the past, was gaining the upper hand.

'Yes,' she repeated slowly. 'To success, and the future.'

The clink of the glasses as they touched masked another, even smaller sound, like the faint, sweet chime of a bell. They didn't feel the cold breath that whisked across the room to the window, though from the corner of his eye Karel saw two of the candle flames gutter briefly. He thought nothing of it. The palace was full of draughts.

And Xai, who was rapidly discovering the value of subtlety,

was content to leave them to their intimacy, for she had learned all that she wanted to know.

Grendon returned from delivering his note to find Sefira sound asleep. He was surprised – she had, after all, been complaining increasingly that she slept too much – but the surprise was eclipsed by relief. He didn't want the strain of her presence tonight; for some reason he felt drained and more than a little depressed, and would be glad of a chance to sit alone with a flask of wine and only his thoughts for company.

He had delivered his note to Perlion, and must now wait to see whether it bore fruit. It had been a brief message, asking the Lander to meet him at a certain inn near the city's main market tomorrow at the fourth evening hour. He had a personal matter to discuss, he had said, which he believed was of interest to them both, and Perlion would either grasp the chance eagerly, or baulk. Grendon had a shrewd idea of which way he would swing, and he looked forward to the encounter with interest.

He changed his clothes for more comfortable garments, made up the fire and then went in search of the duty cellar-master, who provided him with two flasks, the second a temptation that for once in his life Grendon didn't feel like resisting. As he walked back to the apartment he reminded himself that he hadn't made contact with Arrine since the wedding. That must be rectified; though at the moment it was perhaps kinder – and safer – to keep her out of the picture. But he should at least send some message, even if it was just a few words to reassure her that all was well.

He sank on to the couch, broached the first flagon and drank it steadily and levelly, gazing into the fire and letting his imagination form images in the flames. It was a way of relaxing, and it had the desired effect; before long he opened the second flask, finished one glass, then lay back and allowed his eyes to close. He would sleep soon, and he hoped that the sleep would be dreamless. It would be a much needed respite.

* * *

Sefira opened her eyes to see that her room was dark save for a thin bar of sullen orange firelight seeping under the door. For a minute or two she lay motionless, scanning the gloom. Her mouth moved, her tongue appearing and flicking as though she were tasting the air, and around her, though she had no knowledge of it, a dim grey haze hovered like condensed breath. Then, with a stealth and silence that wasn't quite natural, she slid out of bed and started to dress. Underclothes, gown, wimple; then outdoor shoes and her hooded cloak, and quietly, surreptitiously, she went through to the outer room.

She could see Grendon's shape on the couch, his hair faintly tinted by the glow from the fire's embers. Powerful feelings welled up within her – *contempt, hatred, hunger, FEED* – and she paused, thinking to move towards him. But an inner voice whispered, '*No, Sefi. Not him. Not yet*', and reluctantly she abandoned the thought and glided to the door.

The bolt unfastened without a sound. Outside, the corridor was empty, and a sure instinct told her that the hour was too late for anyone to be about. Sefira closed the door softly behind her and moved like a phantom away towards one of the palace's back exits.

Kessie had been woken shortly after midnight by a hammering on her door, and had found a dishevelled and distraught young man on her step. His wife; the baby; too early; something wrong – he was sorry, he was *sorry* to come at such an hour, but *please*. She soothed him, assuring him that she expected such untimely disruptions as a natural part of her work, and within minutes she was hurrying beside him through Tourmon's quiet streets.

To her relief, the matter wasn't as serious as the young husband had feared. If the child was early it was only by a matter of days, and once the terrified wife had been calmed – it was her first confinement, and in Kessie's experience that often created a lot of unnecessary panic in all concerned – the whole thing was over very quickly and with no damage that wouldn't heal soon enough. Kessie accepted the young man's profuse and inarticulate thanks, and, leaving the couple safe in the care of several neighbours who had been woken by the commotion, departed for her own home and bed. She refused the offer of an escort; the night was dry, the walk would help her to relax, and with the King's Watch so reliable these days a lone woman was perfectly safe in the streets.

She hummed a little tune to the beat of her own footsteps as she made her way back through the deserted thoroughfares. The Evening Market was long closed, the stalls shuttered and only a few torches burning on their high poles. Kessie's shadow danced in a circle around her as she passed first one light and then another.

And then she saw another shadow move.

She stopped by one of the larger market booths. Her caution was only a habit from the more hazardous past, she knew, but habits were hard to break . . . besides, there was something furtive about the way that shadow crept over the ground. Whoever cast it was hidden from her view behind another of the stalls. A scavenger, possibly? There were always some about when the market closed, pitiable creatures for the most part. But then the shadow's owner came into view – and Kessie almost laughed aloud at her foolishness, for her 'prowler' was merely another solitary woman, wrapped in a cloak and with a wimple over her hair. Kessie wondered what her business was at this time of night, and wryly imagined some clandestine and forbidden tryst from which she was now hurrying home and which would explain her stealth.

She made to walk on, thinking to call out a pleasant 'goodnight' to show that she presented no threat. But the other woman was moving into the circle of torchlight, and suddenly Kessie paused again as she saw her face more clearly. Her features were familiar. Did they know each other?

Then an image came out of memory, of the Purging in

Victory Square and the girl who had fainted. The Arraigner's wife. Or Perlion's daughter . . .

She felt her pulse quicken, and it was an extremely unpleasant sensation. There was no doubt in her mind now: it *was* the girl, Sefira. She was crossing the square with quick, light steps, and there was something very peculiar about the way she moved; hesitant, casting this way and that, like a hunting animal sniffing after its prey.

The truth dawned on Kessie with an appalling sense of inevitability. She shrank back against the booth, suddenly desperate not to be seen, not to be *noticed*, and watched as Sefira continued her bizarre progress across the square. She was heading for the docks, the midwife realised. Oh yes, oh *yes*; that made a dreadful kind of sense. For all the king's reforms there was still human flotsam to be found in Tourmon, and the docks were a natural magnet to such creatures; the feckless, the hopeless, the mindless . . . A violent death or two among those discards of society would arouse no outcry. It wouldn't even be entered in the records.

Sefira was heading now, unmistakably, for a narrow lane that led off the square and wound its way to the riverside. What to *do*? Kessie asked herself desperately. She could – and should – alert the watch, and tell them that a murder was about to be committed. But how could she explain the fact that she knew what Sefira was? To fail to denounce a criminal was punishable by imprisonment, and there could be no excuses. Then there was Perlion. What would he feel, what would he do, if Sefira was taken?

Perlion. Kessie grasped at the thought. She must tell Perlion what she had seen. Above all, she must *warn* him. He fondly believed that the soul-invader had not yet begun to work its corrupting will on his daughter. She must break the news to him that he was utterly and horribly wrong.

Sefira had merged with the darkness on the far side of the square, and Kessie could no longer glimpse her. It was safe to move out of hiding now . . . Gathering her skirt and cloak, she started rapidly away in the opposite direction. She didn't look back; didn't dare look back.

But by the dock lane entrance, a shape paused in its progress. It turned. It saw her. And briefly, shockingly, Sefira's dark eyes flared zircon blue as an alien intelligence registered and recognised the woman who had helped bring it into the mortal world.

The remains of the vagabond who died at an out-of-the-way wharf that night would never be found. If others of his kind heard the distant screaming they thought nothing of it, for there were always a few madmen among their number who yelled at the moon, or at the slap of water against the piers, or at something in their own twisted imaginations. The noise soon stopped. And though Sefira alone would not have had the strength to drag the bloodstained corpse to the riverside and push it over the jetty's edge, with Xai to goad and guide her the task was easily accomplished. Xai's strength was growing. And tonight's work had added to that strength in formidable measure.

Afterwards, she found a ramp that sloped down to the water's edge, and bathed herself in the river. The cold meant nothing to her, as it had meant nothing when she stripped off her clothes before attacking her victim. It was better to do what she did naked, for stains on fabric were harder to remove than those on skin, and there had been no one to see her. Then she gathered up her clothes, which lay neatly folded a short distance away, and walked calmly, sedately from the scene, back into the civilised surroundings of the city. She encountered no one in the streets, and the guards at the great wall took one look into the hypnotic blue eyes that fixed on their faces and, as they had done before, simply opened the gate and let her through. On along the road to the hub of the palace. Passing the Scholarly quarter she thought briefly and malevolently of Arrine, but the hunger in her was sated and she was prudent enough to move on. The palace was as easy to enter as it had been to leave; as was the sanctuary of the apartment. Grendon still slept, and she slipped out of her clothes and into her bed with no one the wiser.

In the morning, Grendon couldn't wake her. He had let her sleep on, but when noon approached and still she hadn't emerged, he went into the bedchamber and shook her by the shoulder.

'Sefira. Sefira, wake up.'

No response. Frowning, Grendon mentally probed the atmosphere for any trace of Xai's presence, but found nothing. Sefira's breathing was quiet and steady; her skin felt clammy and her hair was a little damp, but that was no signal of anything untoward. Yet she wouldn't stir, and that made Grendon uneasy.

He could, he thought, easily find out if Xai had been making mischief. Just a simple piece of sorcery; it wasn't something he would normally countenance in the palace, but this time . . .

His thoughts were interrupted by a knock at the door. Muttering an imprecation Grendon went to answer it, and found a liveried lackey standing outside.

'Arraigner Grendon?' The man had a squint and an arrogant manner to go with it. One of the new breed of servants; Grendon couldn't remember having seen him before.

'Yes.' He didn't bother with pleasantries.

'His Majesty commands you to attend him in the small council chamber.'

Damn the man, Grendon thought. Aloud, he said curtly, 'Very well,' and made to shut the door. The servant jammed it with his foot and added, 'His Majesty used the word, *immediately*.'

Grendon said nothing, but the look he gave the man was glacial. His probing would have to wait. He slid out of the room – the lackey tried to peer inside but Grendon deliberately blocked any view – and made a pointed show of closing the door very firmly. The servant glided away, satisfied that his errand had been completed, and Grendon headed for the council chamber.

Karel was sitting at one end of the chamber's long table with two of his senior ministers, and as Grendon entered he looked up. 'Ah, Grendon. I have a commission for you.' He beckoned, and Grendon approached the table. 'This is normally Arraigner Erys's field rather than yours, but Erys is away in the north at the moment and I don't want to leave the matter unresolved until he can deal with it.'

He pushed a document in Grendon's direction. 'A major defraudment trial has been dragging on in Emelian; it's a highly complex case involving two branches of a Mercantile family, and though a verdict has been reached, six justices have so far been unable to agree on proper compensation. There's obviously some secondary corruption at work, and the only way to put an end to it is for a king's man to unravel the knots and settle the whole tiresome business once and for all. If you leave early tomorrow you should reach Emelian in four or five days, weather permitting, and if fortune smiles, the protagonists won't have crippled or poisoned each other by then.'

Grendon stared at the document, dismayed and not entirely comprehending. 'You want *me* to oversee this, sir?'

'That is what I just said, Grendon.' Karel gazed levelly at him. 'Does that cause you a problem?'

It did, though Grendon wasn't about to admit it. But there was another reason for his surprise and he glanced quickly, expressively at the two ministers, indicating that he had something to say that Karel might not wish them to hear.

The king took his meaning. 'Gentlemen,' he said, nodding to the pair, 'I think that will be all for the time being. You are excused.'

They left, taking their time over it, and when they were gone Karel said, 'Well? What is the problem?'

'I would have thought, sir,' Grendon replied, 'that I might serve you better by staying here and using . . . other methods.'

'Ah; you mean Sefira. No, Grendon, not this time. The facts of this case have already been established; her talents would be superfluous.'

'Perhaps, then,' Grendon persisted carefully, 'I should take her with me simply as a—'

Karel interrupted, smiling. 'I don't think that will be necessary. In fact, I would prefer it if she stays here.'

'Stays here . . . ?'

The king shrugged. 'You'll travel faster without a woman to take care of. And the experience would probably unsettle her; she hasn't yet gained the confidence to go about much in public, as was proved in Victory Square.'

Grendon's eyes narrowed. In one sense he couldn't dispute Karel's logic, but in another he was suddenly deeply suspicious. It felt to him as if Karel had a purpose in wanting Sefira to stay behind at the palace. As if he wanted to separate her and Grendon for some reason of his own.

The king, still smiling, continued. 'You'll pardon my indelicacy, I trust, but I imagine that you've now been wed long enough not to feel too greatly . . . disappointed, shall we say, at having to part from your bride for a little while?'

Grendon said, 'Yes, sir. Of course.' His face was composed, but he knew that he had been neatly cornered. He couldn't refuse the commission; if he tried, he would simply be ordered to go and that would be that. But he didn't trust this. Something was going on.

'Well, then,' Karel gathered up the remaining papers, looking pleased with life at large. 'You'd best see Tomany and acquaint yourself with the facts of the case; he has all the details and will give you a full report. The treasury will issue you with an unrestricted fiscal warrant; that will save the inconvenience of having to carry too much coin with you. Speak to the duty officer and tell him to refer to me for authorisation. Then you'd best see about your means of travel; I'd recommend going by river at this season, but you may make whatever arrangements you prefer.' He sighed, just a little theatrically. 'These minutiae eat into your time, I know, but they have to be attended to.'

In other words, Grendon thought, Karel meant to ensure that he would be kept busy before his departure, and so would not have the chance to think too much about what might or might not be at the back of this move. It was an obvious ploy, but there was nothing he could do about it.

Then he remembered his appointment with Perlion. Sense and lack of time dictated that he should cancel it – but suddenly it seemed very important not to do so. It was possible, he told himself, that what he learned tonight would be of value to him, or to Sefira, during his enforced absence, and though the hope was a slender one he couldn't let it pass. Somehow he must keep that rendezvous, and hope that Perlion wouldn't let him down.

He said, 'Then, sir, if I may be excused I'll begin my preparations.'

'Do that,' Karel agreed equably. 'And I wish you a comfortable journey.'

Grendon had the distinct feeling that in reality the king wished him anything but, but he merely bowed slightly from the waist, and left the council chamber.

A smile still hovered on Karel's lips as he, too, made to leave. With Grendon out of the way for ten days at the very least, there would be plenty of time to carry out the next stage of his scheme. Mischane, despite her misgivings, would play her part and cultivate Sefira's company and friendship; then when some rapport was established between the two women, they would dine together one evening and Karel would make an apparently coincidental appearance. The next step would be more difficult, for even though Mischane was a Sanctified she had no idea of how to make contact with the soul-invader. But Karel had read what little public information there was on the subject, and there had, of course, been that sorcerer unmasked in Tourmon a few months ago, who had had a few of his secrets wrung out of him before he went to the pyre. With one and the other, the king was confident of success. To gain a valuable resource and remove a long-standing and potentially harmful nuisance at the same time would please him greatly. If fortune smiled – and he saw no reason why it should not – then Grendon would return from Emelian to a very unexpected welcome, and one he would not enjoy at all.

Chapter XVI

Grendon returned briefly to the apartment, and found Sefira awake but in a quiet, almost surly mood. He cursed the fact that there would be no time now to delve into the cause of her earlier torpor, but there was no help for it; the king's order had to be obeyed.

He told her, brusquely, about the commission, and was gratified, albeit ironically, to see the look of dismay on her face.

'Away?' Her voice rose in a nervous waver. 'But what shall I do? What if the king summons me and wants me to answer more questions?'

'It can't be done without me to invoke the trance,' Grendon told her, 'and the king knows that.' Or did Karel think otherwise? he wondered suddenly. Was *that* his motive – to try to use Sefira himself? The thought turned him cold as he realised what such an attempt might lead to. If Karel should uncover any sign of Xai's existence . . . or, worse, if the soul-invader should take it in mind to manifest directly . . .

Sefira said suddenly, 'What?' and he realised that in his consternation he had sworn aloud. He shook his head, making a negating gesture. 'Nothing – it was nothing. I must go; I have to see that sly-eyed crawler Tomany.'

He found relief in vitriol, and she knew it and was puzzled. She started to say, 'Grendon, I—' but he cut across her.

'Later. I've no time now.' And he was gone.

Sefira blinked as the slam of the door echoed through the room. What was amiss with him? He seemed angry, but intuition told her that there was more to it than that, and in her stomach an unpleasant sensation started to churn. For all his professed disinterest, she had the distinct feeling that Grendon did not want to leave her behind when he departed for Emelian. It was as if he was *afraid* to go.

She pressed her fingertips to her temples, massaging them and wishing she could think more clearly. She had had a bad headache when she woke, and despite a herbal draught it still persisted, making her feel sluggish and a little sick. Such *dreams* last night. She couldn't remember any details but knew she had suffered nightmare after formless nightmare. She had wanted to talk to Grendon about that, too, and ask him if there was anything he could do to help her stop the dreams. But yet again he had given her no chance. It was unfair. *She wanted to retaliate, wanted to teach him a lesson, hurt him, make him suffer!*

The pain in her head flared and she gasped with the unexpected shock of it. Then it loosed its grip and dazedly Sefira stared at the room around her, which suddenly looked a little unreal. Something was wrong with the colours; there seemed to be a rust-red haze over everything and she rubbed fiercely at her eyes, thinking her vision was at fault. But the haze remained. And sound was fading; moments ago she could hear voices outside quite clearly; now, they had dulled to a distant and barely distinguishable blur.

Then, by the hearth, she saw a glimmer of light that hadn't been there a few moments earlier.

Sefira stared in astonishment which quickly flowered into fascination. She wasn't afraid – though on a detached level it occurred to her that perhaps she should be – and as the light grew stronger she felt a stirring of excitement.

Then, so gradually that at first she thought she must be imagining it, a figure took form in the light. Everything about it was silver grey, and its eyes were closed as though in sleep. For some inexplicable reason Sefira remembered the dream she had had at Arrine's house, when she thought that someone had stolen her own eyes, and a surge of indignant sympathy rose in her. *Had someone robbed this vision of her eyes, too? That was wrong. It deserved punishment. It deserved—*

The deranged chain of thought broke as the figure's eyes flicked open.

Blue. Sefira had never seen eyes as blue as these were. They captivated her, held her entranced. They were *wonderful.* Then the apparition smiled at her, and a voice that somehow she knew as well as she knew her own, spoke to her.

'*Sefi. I am strong now, Sefi. I will help you. I will show you how to stop those who wish us harm. We are more powerful than they are, and we will prove it. We must prove it, or everything will be ruined. We do not want that, Sefi. We must not let it happen to us.*'

Somewhere, far, far away, a part of Sefira was struggling to make itself heard, protesting that this was a dream, an hallucination, madness. But it couldn't combat Xai. Sustained and strengthened by a human victim, her hold on Sefira's mind was complete.

'*Tonight, Sefi,*' she said, '*we shall feed again. We shall make ourselves stronger still. And we shall eliminate something that would do us harm. Send it away. Send it to oblivion. We shall help each other. Tonight . . .*'

The voice was diminishing, dwindling into the background. Sefira tried to speak, but her throat and tongue wouldn't obey her. She could only continue to stare at Xai, not knowing what she was, not knowing what she meant, yet filled with a craving ache for something that she couldn't even name. She watched as the alien yet eerily familiar face began to evaporate, too, and though she didn't know it her eyes were wide, unblinking, and blank as the glass of the window. The last thing she was conscious of was a final, gentle whisper in her mind.

'*Trust me, Sefi. Let me guide you, and we will continue to thrive . . .*'

The light dulled to grey, and vanished. The rusty haze was gone, and Sefira's head no longer ached.

Abruptly her vision snapped back into focus. For a few seconds she was motionless – then she moved, smoothly and lithely and with a new air of purpose, towards the inner room. Methodically she removed her clothes, folded them tidily and put them away. Then she climbed into bed and lay down to wait for night.

Grendon returned just after sunset, feeling ruffled and under pressure. The treasury's duty officer, typically, had dragged his heels over the fiscal warrant, checking and re-checking every detail with ploddingly unrelenting precision. Then Tomany had insisted on going over the minutiae of the commission with him; work that he could have done for himself on the journey with a good deal less trouble. Everyone seemed bent on wasting as much of his time as possible, and Grendon wondered distrustfully if they did so at Karel's order, to keep him too occupied to indulge his suspicions. Now, he had to pack what he needed before the hour came to meet Perlion. There would be no chance to do anything about Xai for a while yet.

But something *would* be done. Grendon had decided on his plan while he waited for bureaucracy to take its course, and it gave him some measure of comfort to think that he wouldn't be leaving Sefira completely unprotected. Tonight, when he returned, he would wake her and make her drink a concoction of his own devising, which would render her ill enough to be of no use whatever to Karel until his return. It was a drastic measure, and its crudeness offended him, but it would ensure that Sefira wouldn't become a pawn in some new game of Karel's devising. And that Xai could not take advantage of the situation.

He looked in on her before he began to pack, standing for a few moments in the bedroom doorway and gazing at her still form under the blankets. The room was unlit and he couldn't see her face clearly, so he was unaware, as he turned away again, that her eyes were open and watching him. As the door closed, a smile formed on Sefira's lips, and she felt a writhing of impatience in her stomach.

Not yet, Sefi. Not yet.

She could hear Grendon moving about in the adjoining room. Very well; she would be patient. She would wait. It would be worthwhile.

Grendon finished his preparations with half an hour to spare before he must leave for the rendezvous. That suited him well, for it allowed enough time to fetch what he needed from the palace kitchens and prepare the mixture that he would give to Sefira on his return. The errand took some degree of subterfuge, for the kitchen servants were notorious gossips, but a few skilled lies and a small show of authority produced results, and he returned to the apartment with several items from pantry and spice cupboard, together with a new flask of wine.

In the outer room he locked his prizes away in a cupboard, then donned his outdoor clothes; dark garments, to make him as inconspicuous as possible in the streets. He doused all but one of the lamps, then, as an afterthought, picked up the last and went to the inner door. Just a final check, to be sure all was well . . .

The door creaked open and he looked in. Then tensed and held the lamp higher, thrusting it into the room.

Something inside him turned cold and sick as the light pushed back shadows and destroyed any possibility, any hope that his first impression had been wrong. It wasn't wrong. The bed was empty; there was just a discarded nightgown lying on the rumpled sheet.

Sefira had gone.

Kessie's fists were clenched with tension as she slammed her front door and hurried to put away her scrip and change her soaking clothes. The day had been one of the most fraught and hectic she could remember, and the plans she had so carefully worked out last night had been flung into disarray.

She had been called out after only three hours' sleep to the wife of a justicer's clerk who lived on the city outskirts; no complications, but the child had taken its time in coming. She had finally returned home in the early afternoon, and after a belated and hasty lunch was about to leave again in search of Perlion when another message came, this time from a well-to-do Mercantile family whose daughter, according to one of the most notable city physicians, was to bear twins. Now her time had come, and the physician could not be found, and she was a fragile creature and in need of help.

Kessie could not refuse the appeal either on compassionate or fiscal grounds, and so she had spent the afternoon and early evening at the nervous girl's bedside, hindered by her husband, mother and sister, until finally the physician arrived and, shortly afterwards, two healthy daughters were delivered. The rain had begun by the time she left; now it was a downpour, but if she had to go out in it again, then go she must. This was too important. She only prayed that she would find Perlion at his cousin's house.

She put on dry garments, then hastened to the kitchen to cut a slice of bread and a piece of cheese. Her stomach was gnawing hungrily but there was no time for a proper meal. Hoping wryly that tonight she would be allowed an uninterrupted night's sleep, Kessie ate the makeshift supper as quickly as she could, then stood up to leave.

And someone hammered on her front door.

She stared towards the little hallway, her heart sinking. Not another – it wasn't *possible* for fate to be so capricious! Then her resolve hardened. She had delayed too long already; this time, even if the message came from the king's palace itself, mother and babe and all who had anything to do with them would simply have to wait!

She hurried along the hall, swiftly rehearsing what she would say, how she would refuse. Hand on the door latch; it swung open.

A heavily cloaked and hooded figure stood on the doorstep.

218

Kessie said, 'I'm sorry, but I can't help you now – I have been called out, and I'm already late. I'm sorry—'

Then she stopped in mid-sentence, for the figure had pushed its hood back, and Sefira's face stared steadily at her from among the folds.

Kessie uttered a shocked oath and took a pace backwards. Sefira smiled, and to the midwife's mind it seemed that her dark eyes briefly flared vivid blue. Then, without a word and before Kessie could stop her, she stepped over the threshold and into the house.

Grendon knelt in the middle of the bedroom floor, the heels of his hands pressed hard to his temples as he focused his concentration. In his inner vision he had seen the black oval form, had willed the silver striations to crack across it and open the gateway, and now his mind was probing the eerie, colourless dimensions of the astral plane, searching for any trace of Sefira – and of Xai.

Something in the wind. He had known it since the encounter when Xai had sullenly refused to show herself. *I protect Sefi,* the soul-invader had said; *I protect my own.* And on the next occasion when he had summoned her, he had been met with mocking taunts: *What did the Lander see? What did he hear? Who knows what he will find out?*

Now Sefira was missing, and though he had no evidence that Xai was behind her disappearance, in his own mind Grendon was certain of it. He cursed himself for not having carried out his resolve to force the truth from Xai. Lack of time was no excuse; he had procrastinated, and now he might well be regretting his error too late. He knew that the demonic parasite had been trying to build and conserve her strength; that was why Sefira had been sleeping so much this last day or two. But as to why . . . his thoughts were racing to a horrible conclusion, and if he was right, then he had to stop her.

If he could. For Xai had been cunning, and as he probed the astral he had so far found only false trails at every turn.

He needed more strength, more *will*. He needed a man with the power and skill of Lendrer. *But Lendrer had died at the stake two years ago, and he had watched him die, and been forced to speak the words that condemned him.*

Blind, bitter rage at that memory swelled violently in Grendon's mind, and on its heels came a rush of physical sensation, as if the blood had caught fire in his arteries. He almost cried out with the shock and pain of it, but it triggered something else within him, and suddenly he felt his consciousness plunge deeper into the astral realm. Colour flared where there had been nothing but grey-shot darkness – he saw a glitter of blue, a flash of silver . . . and then a thin, scarlet thread, vibrating like a plucked string, stretching away across the shifting mindscape.

He had found her. The trace, the track, was unmistakable; and now more cogent shapes were starting to coalesce from the stuff of illusion. A wide city street, filled with market stalls. He knew it instantly. Small houses on either side. And an inn . . .

Grendon snapped his psyche out of the dark plane and back to the physical world with a jolt that seared every nerve in his body. He scrambled to his feet, made for the door, and was striding along the passage by the time his reeling head cleared. A rapid calculation told him that it would be quicker to go on foot rather than lose time in fetching his horse from the stables. Time was imperative, secrecy vital – it wasn't only Perlion's life that depended on both.

Two minor courtiers saw him and called out, a languidly amused greeting and an enquiry into his haste. Grendon ignored them, increasing his pace as he approached the nearest outside door. A torrent of rain slammed into his face as he emerged from the palace; the sky was teeming, water bouncing from the ground with a noise like drums. He ducked into it, wrapping the folds of his cloak more tightly around him, and began to run.

★ ★ ★

The sound of her own front door closing at Sefira's back was one of the most portentous noises that Kessie had ever heard in her life, and when the inner door closed too, caging them both in the small, private confines of the kitchen, she felt that her legs would give way under her from sheer terror. There was no other door, no other way out; she had allowed herself to be cornered like a hunted animal, and the look in Sefira's eyes told her that the hunter was about to move in for the kill.

The table legs scraped on the stone floor as she tried to edge herself behind it, striving to create a barrier between herself and the woman, the *thing*, pacing slowly towards her across the room. Kessie's mouth worked, but she knew that no words would have any effect. Sefira was beyond reason. She was no longer human.

Kessie shut her eyes and heard the moan that broke from her own lips. It was a word, of sorts, but long-drawn and broken and barely recognisable:

'Pl . . . lea . . . leas . . . *p-p-please* . . .'

The slide of feet on stone ceased, though she could still hear the creature breathing, a rough, ragged, *hungry* sound. Then Sefira spoke.

'You know about us.'

Kessie's lungs heaved. 'Unnh – nnh – no! I know nothing, nothing—'

'*Lie.*' Another step, and it was as though a wall of ice began to press in on Kessie. 'You know. You will tell.'

'I will not! I swear it, by all I've ever held dear! Oh please, don't hurt me, don't hurt me!'

Sefira continued to stare at the cowering, whimpering midwife, and suddenly a glimmer of uncertainty fought through the red haze of her mind. She didn't understand – this woman was a stranger, harmless, inoffensive. She had no wish to hurt her.

But then something else grasped hold of the doubt and crushed it. *No, Sefi! She is not harmless. She is the one we came to find. And you know what we must do.*

221

A part of Sefira that still struggled to be human tried to protest that she didn't *want* to do it, but the voice in her head whispered a relentless denial.

But we must. Or she will tell. The tone now was sweet and silvery, and so persuasive that the little sanity Sefira had left began to slip away.

Think, Sefi. Think how strong we shall be when this is done. Stronger than the king. Stronger than Grendon. Strong enough to take vengeance on the ones who betray us and use us and want to destroy our kind . . .

Oh, but that was *right*! Sefira sucked breath into her lungs in a harsh, rattling hiss. Kessie made a dreadful, inarticulate noise and backed violently away, colliding with a dresser. A plate fell and smashed on the floor.

Now, Sefi. I am so hungry. Feed me. Strengthen us . . .

Slowly, Sefira's mouth curved in a smile. She gripped the edge of the table, and began to push it steadily, inexorably aside, clearing the way between herself and her victim.

Kessie saw her own death mirrored in the girl's demented eyes, and suddenly a spark of self-preservation ignited within her. The bread knife was on the dresser, only inches from her hand. If she could reach it . . . Her fingers groped, sliding along the wooden surface. She felt the bone of the handle. Sefira had not noticed; her gaze was still fixed unwaveringly on the midwife's face.

Feed me, Sefi. Give us the power we crave . . .

With a convulsive movement Kessie snatched up the knife and, screaming, lunged for Sefira's heart. She saw a blur of movement, felt the smacking impact of another forearm striking hers as her attack was deflected, and her fingers lost their grip on the knife. She had one instant to glimpse the blade spinning away across the kitchen, then a body hit her with stunning force and the room spun sideways as she was thrown off her feet. There was a rush of arctic coldness – she tried to thrust her hands out and ward it off, but they were flung aside and Sefira's weight crashed down on top of her, pinning her to the floor.

They struggled together in a tangle of limbs and cloaks. Kessie kicked wildly; her fingers, flailing, clamped round a leg of the table and she strove to pull it over on to her attacker. But as it started to tilt, Sefira snarled and something smashed down ferociously on Kessie's wrist, breaking the grip, snapping a bone and sending pain raging through her. She writhed and twisted, her mouth contorting as the first shriek of hysteria tore from her, though it was muffled by the wet mass of Sefira's cloak. Hands ripped her wimple away, snatched at her hair; then her head was slammed savagely against the flagstones and starbursts of light and blackness erupted across her eyes, blotting out all else. Then vision came back, and for perhaps three seconds there was an eerie, horrible hiatus as shock numbed the pain, numbed the terror, and Kessie lay motionless, staring into the eyes of her nemesis like a child gazing in awe at some incredible toy. And Sefira gazed back with the calm, cold-blooded and psychotic self-assurance of the demon within her. Her spiritual sister. A part of her soul. A part that wanted to *feed* . . .

Her lips parted, and her tongue touched her teeth, first above, then below. Her gaze slid to Kessie's throat. She smiled.

And her head speared down.

Chapter XVII

In his determination not to be late for a second rendezvous, Perlion had arrived at the inn far too early. He bought a glass of porter to calm his nervousness, and took a seat by one of the large windows that overlooked the market place.

Though the market traded until midnight, the weather had kept all but the hardiest customers away and there were far fewer stalls than usual. In fact the wide thoroughfare was all but deserted. The downpour had extinguished some of the torches on their high poles, but enough still burned, mostly on the far side of the street and thus in the lee of the weather, to give Perlion a good if rain-blurred view in both directions. A few hunched figures hurried by; one or two turned towards the inn, making him half rise in anticipation, but so far he had been disappointed. Grendon, it seemed, was going to be on time, or late.

To keep his mind from dwelling on what might or might not result from this meeting, he played a game with himself, picking out some of the scurrying passers-by and trying to guess what their Fellowships and occupations might be. That man with a limp was probably a Functional, and a lowly one at that. And the couple, both quite unsuitably dressed for the weather, who so loftily looked the other way as their paths crossed his: Creatives, no possible doubt of it. Perlion could always tell a Creative at a glance. And the woman on the far side of the street . . . impossible to tell what she was, or even judge her age, for her voluminous cloak and hood made her utterly anonymous. She seemed wholly untroubled by the rain though, walking as if the evening were as pleasant as summer. Extraordinary. Perlion watched as she hesitated outside a row of modest houses, then saw her choose one of the doors, approach it and knock. Had he but known it, the address of the house was familiar to him. But words on a piece of paper did not relate to physical reality, and he had met Kessie only on neutral ground . . .

Then a brewman's cart making a late delivery captured his attention; the wheels and the horse's great hoofs were flinging up a spray of water from the road and two men and a woman in sober black – Scholarlies, at a guess – started to shout and shake their fists as they were soaked. Perlion looked on, amused by their annoyance; after all, weren't they too wet already to worry about a little more? Then suddenly the inn door banged as a newcomer entered, and with a start he came out of his reverie and saw Grendon.

He realised at once that something was wrong. There was a wild, haggard cast to Grendon's face behind the streaming tendrils of his hair; he looked urgently around, then saw Perlion and barged unceremoniously through the busy taproom towards him. Perlion stood up as he approached, his own face creasing anxiously.

'Arraigner Grendon – is something wrong? What's happened? Is it—'

The questions broke off as Grendon grabbed hold of his arm. 'Perlion – you're all right?'

Baffled, Perlion said, 'Yes, yes, of course. Why should I not be? What has *happened*?'

But Grendon paid no heed, for his mind was racing ahead. He had been wrong. With the start she had over him Sefira would have reached this inn by now, and he had dreaded what he might find on his arrival. Not a scene of mayhem; Xai wasn't so foolish as to goad Sefira into attacking her victim in a public place. But he had anticipated finding the Lander gone, lured away unsuspectingly to a violent and ugly death in some back street. The fact that it had not happened was a great relief – but it also filled him with horror, as it could only mean that Perlion was not Xai's intended target.

So where in the realms of every nightmare ever created was she, and what did she intend? The confines of the taproom suddenly felt monstrously oppressive, and he peered out of the window, scanning the street quickly. Nothing there to give any clues, but his intuition was stirring, ringing a warning bell, and abruptly he turned again to Perlion.

'I have to leave. Come with me, if you will.' Sheer instinct, but he trusted this man, and any help he could find now would be desperately welcome.

'Arraigner, I don't understand—' Perlion began, but Grendon interrupted.

'I'll explain as we go. I have to find Sefira.'

'Sefira?' Perlion echoed in dismay. 'Has something happened to her?'

Not to her, Grendon thought, and made a cancelling gesture. 'I'll *explain*. But time is vital. Move, man!'

Perlion moved, confounded yet impelled by the imperative in Grendon's voice. They pushed their way back to the door and through it into the hammering rain. As they emerged, the sky lit briefly but violently, and moments later a roar of thunder echoed high above the rooftops. Grendon's mind flicked back to the night when he had found Sefira on the moor and, remembering her cringing terror of storms, he scanned the scene around them more intently. She was somewhere hereabouts, he was certain of it. But the storm would work against him, for it would drive her under cover rather than into the open. He might have tried other means to trace her, but he couldn't concentrate; his mind was too chaotic.

'*Damn her*,' he said under his breath. '*Damn her to perdition and back . . .*'

Perlion grabbed his arm and shook it. 'Sir, what *is* this? Please – if it has some connection with Sefira, you *must* tell me what's going on!'

Had he been less preoccupied, Grendon might have seen the tension that was suddenly in Perlion's face, and heard the new note of fear in his voice. But it skimmed over him, not registering. He still watched the street, hoping, *willing*.

Lightning flashed again. This time the thunder was more distant, but as it rolled away a door slammed somewhere. Just a small sound amidst the noise of rain and the thunder's last echoes and the spitting of the struggling torches, but it alerted him. His head turned. Someone emerging from a house. The slammed door rebounding, juddering back on its hinges and swinging open again. A figure running.

'This way!' His fist thumped across Perlion's shoulder to alert him, and he pointed to the fleeing shape, cloak flying, hood back, wimple awry, that was heading away towards the docks at a stumbling rush. *'Catch her!'*

Perlion's eyes widened and he made a choked sound. Then with a speed that he didn't know was in him, he pelted in Grendon's wake.

Red haze. Red, like blood. It filled her vision, turning everything around her to a dim, displaced blur of vague shapes with no sense to them. There was an odour in her nostrils, familiar, ugly. And a taste in her mouth that made her stomach clench and recoil . . . yet only moments ago that same smell and taste had fired such a *craving* in her.

She felt as though her mind was coming up from a bottomless black well. Slowly, agonisingly slowly, reason and consciousness were returning to her, though she didn't know how or when or why she had lost them. She had no awareness of her body; didn't know whether she was standing or sitting or lying. No idea of where she was. No idea of what she was *doing*.

My name is Sefira and I have lost my memory and I am frightened, so frightened, of the storm . . . Her face felt wet. Was it the rain?

It was raining in the streets. When I—

She heard a peculiar little whimpering sound and realised that she had made it. But no one answered. Was she alone, then? If only the haze would clear and allow her to *see*.

Tentatively she tried to move, and found to her surprise that she could. For the first time she felt contact with her own limbs, and realised that she was crouching on all fours on a hard floor. A hard, wet floor, for she could feel slickness under her hands.

Rain . . . ?

Then the red fog that shrouded everything lit livid violet, and the first clap of thunder boomed on its heels. Sefira cried out as the old fear erupted in her, and with a convulsive jerk tried to scrabble away. She collided with something hard, fell back, felt herself slip in wetness and heard a clatter as something fell past her head.

And the next time she blinked, the haze and the last of Xai's influence vanished.

Astonishment mingled with disbelief as by the light of an oil lamp fixed to a bracket on the wall she saw where she was. Someone's *kitchen*. Scrabbling across the floor, she had blundered into a table leg and the impact had knocked two spoons and a small copper dish off the table and on to the flagstones beside her. Questions tumbled through Sefira's mind – where was this place, what was it, how had she come here, *why* was she here? – and bewilderedly she stared down at the implements, as though they could provide answers. Her own distorted face leered back from the bowl's curved surface. The metal made her skin look red. And the flagstones were red, too; there were thick smears of it everywhere, crimson on the grey . . .

Then she registered a darker bulk lying a few feet away.

Realisation came like the onset of a crawling nightmare as Sefira raised her head and saw the thing on the floor for the first time. It wasn't human, not any more. It was only a grotesque and misshapen travesty of humanity; a tangle of limbs and torso and torn garments and wrenched-out hair, all soaked in the blood that had pumped from the artery in its mangled throat. The face was a wet, red mask, mouth agape, tongue bulging, and the eyes were fixed on the ceiling in a dead, void, witless stare, like the eyes of a dead fish.

And though she had no memory of the act, Sefira knew that this was her handiwork.

The noise began somewhere in the pit of her stomach and rose through her lungs and into her throat in a thin, bubbling whine that climbed up and up the scale. *Blood on her hands – there was blood on her hands, and on her clothes, and she could taste the warm saltiness in her mouth for she had lapped it, drunk it, relished it* . . . Suddenly, violently, her stomach heaved and she vomited a scarlet cascade that cut off the whining in retching, choking horror. Her limbs were moving, utterly beyond her control; she was scrabbling backwards, grabbing at the table, staggering to her feet. There was blood *everywhere*. The floor, the table, the walls – blindly Sefira groped for a door, a window, *anything* that would let her flee from this charnel house. She crashed into the door, clawed at it, dragged it open and fell through into the hall. *Where was she?* Didn't know, didn't care; just had to get *away*!

Thunder sounded again, and she was crawling on hands and knees towards another door that seemed to tower ahead of her like a mocking promise, one moment swelling towards her, the next receding into hallucinatory distance. Then she was there, her fingers clamping round the latch. No sound from her throat now but the stertorous, hectic rush of her breathing; she could make no sound, for shock had driven the capability too deep in her and there was only the mad, bleak vista of dementia in her mind. *Murderer. She had killed. She had slaughtered. She was insane. Murderer.*

The door swung open and she swung herself upright again. Outside was a street, torchlight, battering rain. It meant nothing. Even the storm meant nothing.

Sefira flung herself out into the teeming night.

* * *

'We've lost her!' Perlion slithered to a winded halt on the slick paving. 'It's no use, Grendon – she's gone into that maze and it would need a miracle to find her!'

Grendon stared through the downpour at the black mouth of the alley network that confronted them, and knew Perlion was right. To follow Sefira through that tangle of lanes and yards and shambles would be utterly futile; she could take any one of twenty different directions, and in the darkness they might pass within two paces of her and never know it.

Lightning flickered again, momentarily and starkly illuminating Perlion's face. The Lander looked at Grendon, drew his own conclusion from what he saw in his expression, and said with a strange, calm authority, 'You have to tell me, Grendon. If you know what this means – and I believe you do – then you have to tell me the truth.'

For a few moments Grendon looked back at him. Then he replied, 'I don't know the truth, Perlion. Not yet.'

Before the other man could reply, he turned and strode quickly back the way they had come.

He knew Perlion was following him, but there was nothing he could do to prevent that, and he wasn't even sure that he wanted to prevent it. To trust the Lander was theoretically the act of a fool, but Grendon had learned long ago to put instinct before logic, and in this his instinct was strong. What, if anything, he would find when he reached the house from which Sefira had emerged, he didn't know. But instinct was goading him in that, too, and he quickened his pace as the market stalls came in sight. *Expect the worst, hope against all reason for the best* . . . The door of the house was still open. He ran towards it.

'Grendon!'

Perlion was almost up with him, but the rest of what he called out was lost under a new bawl of thunder.

'Wait!' Grendon made a gesture that clearly told him not to follow any further. 'Stay here – I'll be back!'

Through the door – getting out of the rain was like coming

up from under water – and into a dark, narrow hall. No sound from anywhere in the house, and when he called out a sharp challenge there was no answer. But the door at the end of the passage stood ajar, and there was a glimmer of light from the room beyond.

Dreading to speculate, and trying to prepare himself for anything he might find, Grendon moved quietly to the door and pushed it fully open.

The lamplight was gentle, but it was more than enough. He felt his mind turn numb as he stared at the carnage, at the dead, blank face of the woman on the floor, and at the ruin that Xai, through Sefira, had made of her. On a dreadful, detached level he registered the fact that her face, at least, was undamaged enough to show that she was a stranger to him. On another level, something inside him was starting to scream.

The slam of the front door broke the hiatus, and quick footsteps approached along the hall. Perlion – Grendon's paralysis lost its grip and he swung round, calling a sharp order.

'Stay back, man! Don't—'

He was too late. The kitchen door was pushed open again, and Perlion appeared.

'Grendon, what—' The Lander stopped. Froze. Then, hoarsely, he uttered a filthy oath and swung away, pressing his forehead against the door jamb.

Grendon said grimly, 'I told you not to come in.'

Perlion was still swearing, but softly now, using the profanities in an effort to bring himself under control. His self-possession was commendable, Grendon thought bleakly; even among the Arraigners few men would have the stomach to cope with a sight like this.

Then Perlion stopped cursing and sucked in breath with a rough, dank sound. His mouth worked for a few moments, before he said, 'I know her.'

'What?' An icy sensation clutched at Grendon's gut.

'I said . . . I know her.' A pause while Perlion struggled for another breath. 'Kessie. She is – was – a midwife. Years ago, she . . . she helped, you see, to . . .' But he either couldn't or wouldn't finish.

Putting the gist together but not yet grasping its significance, Grendon said very quietly, 'And Sefira. Did she know her, too?'

Perlion uttered an extraordinary noise that, he realised, was an attempt at a laugh. 'No. No, no. Not in th-the way that you mean.' Another hesitation, and then, with a great effort, he made himself look up and his gaze focused on Grendon's face. 'Did Sefira do this? *Did* she?'

Everything about his demeanour begged Grendon to deny it, but Grendon was so taken aback by the fact that Perlion had made the connection that he couldn't speak. Then the entreaty in Perlion's eyes faded, and in its place grew a profound, almost childlike sadness.

'I think,' he went on softly, 'that it's time for honesty, my friend. For I see from your chagrin that you know the answer to my question.'

Grendon continued to stare at him. 'And you . . .'

'Yes. I know about the soul-invader. I have always known.' He clenched his hands together until the knuckles whitened. 'I'm Sefira's father.'

At last, Grendon understood what had motivated Perlion. In other circumstances the revelation might not have come as such a surprise to him, for if he had thought it through – if there had been *time* to think it through – it would have been an obvious conclusion to draw. But here, now, in a bloodstained room and with the mutilated corpse of Xai's newest victim lying not two paces away, there was no chance for reasoning. All he could do was accept the knowledge, and its implications.

Perlion said in a strange, dead voice, 'Kessie was there. She assisted at the birth. I sent Sefira away. I told the midwife to take her, to find some good family who did not . . . could

232

not . . . have children of their own. Isbel never knew the truth. She thought . . . there were normal twins, and that they both died.' A long, ragged breath. 'I should have killed her. I know that; I knew it then. But I hoped . . .' He swallowed, looked beseechingly at Grendon again. 'Can you understand?'

'Yes,' Grendon said very quietly, 'I can understand.'

'And now . . . now *this*.' Suddenly Perlion covered his face with both hands, and his voice broke. 'Oh, Fates, what have I done?'

You took a rash and irresponsible risk, Grendon thought, *and that makes you the same manner of fool as I am.* But he didn't voice his thoughts, only said, 'We have to find her, Perlion.'

'Yes.' With a struggle the Lander collected himself and his hands dropped to his sides once more. His cheeks bore red indentations where his fingers had pressed hard. 'And then . . . ?'

He was helpless, desperate for guidance, and Grendon could give him none. There was one possibility in his mind but it was crazed, unthinkable, and he thrust it savagely away. 'She'll still be in the lanes,' he said. 'And I think I can trace her.'

'Do you think she – knows what she did?'

'It's likely.' Although why Xai would have allowed her to know it was a mystery that Grendon couldn't yet unravel. 'Come on,' he added abruptly. 'We're wasting time.'

He started for the door, but Perlion hung back, forcing himself to look again at Kessie. 'We can't leave the poor creature like this . . .'

'We have to. She'll be discovered soon enough.' Grendon took his arm in a fierce grip. 'Come. *Move*.'

Perlion made a noise that sounded like a sob, and stumbled before him out of the kitchen.

It took Grendon two hours to find Sefira. He led the now shaking Perlion into the alleyways, and when they were far enough into the maze to be sure of privacy, he crouched down in the deepest shadows and probed the astral plane. Only an old and long-ingrained discipline enabled him to work under such fraught circumstances, and the trace he picked up was far from explicit. But it proved to be enough.

He knew that by performing sorcery in Perlion's presence he had given away a dangerous secret, but if the Lander was shocked by the realisation of what he truly was, he was too concerned for Sefira to show it. A pragmatist, Grendon thought. It reassured him.

They forged on into the network of twisting streets, between crowded buildings whose upper levels almost met across the thoroughfares and blotted out the sky. The rain still fell, but the storm had moved on and could only be heard grumbling in the far distance when at last they came to the place where she was hiding. A storehouse, disused and left to decay into a haven for rats and other vermin. And in the rank, foul-smelling gloom of its doorway, something far larger than a rat huddled against a crumbling lintel and mumbled, mumbled, just one word, over and over again.

'No . . . no . . . no . . .'

Perlion cried in an agony of pity, 'Sefira!' and started forward, Grendon only a pace behind him. Sefira's babbling turned to a strangled scream, and her blood-smeared face looked wildly up at the two figures bearing down on her.

'It's all right, it's all right!' Perlion tried to clasp her to him, but she screamed again and fought him off, kicking and clawing. 'No-no-no-NO—'

'Sefira!' Pushing Perlion aside, Grendon swooped on the girl, pinning her arms and giving her a single, violent shake. 'Sefira, it's Grendon! Look at me!'

Her cries collapsed to a whimpering, then into nothing. Spittle ran down her chin, diluting Kessie's blood. Her teeth and tongue were crimson, and for a horrible instant she looked so like Xai that he recoiled.

But then the semblance vanished. She recognised him and her eyes widened, bulging in their sockets. Her mouth began to chatter soundlessly – then suddenly she reached out, her fingers locked on his biceps in a desperate grip, and words came bubbling from her.

'Grendon, help me! Oh please, oh please, *help me*!'

Chapter XVIII

If the guards on the gate to the city's royal quarter were surprised to see a litter coming in at this hour, they showed no outward sign of it but only stepped forward, nodded to the hired bearers and then peered between the sodden leather curtains to check on the occupant.

'The king's peace to you, gentlemen,' Perlion smiled at them, thankful that the litter's gloom hid the fact that his self-assurance was a very thin veneer indeed.

'King's peace to you, sir.' The senior guard identified him as a visitor staying somewhere in the quarter, though he couldn't put a name to the face. Then he saw the dark, motionless and vaguely human shape beyond Perlion, and his eyes narrowed with a trace of suspicion. 'Is all well?'

'Yes, yes, thank you,' Perlion raised wry eyebrows and gestured expressively to the huddled shape. 'My eldest girl . . . over-excitement, you know, and a little too much wine. Nothing that a night's sleep and a lecture from her mother won't put to rights.'

The guard grinned in sympathy; he too had a wayward daughter. The gate was pulled open, and Perlion returned the man's salute with a wave of thanks as the litter-bearers jogged through.

Grendon watched it disappear, then waited a few minutes before emerging from the shadows and making his own way to the gate. To enter separately had probably been a needless precaution, but he had wanted to take no chances. The guards had seen him leave alone; better that he returned the same way. And Perlion's story, which in one sense was the truth anyway, was plausible enough to arouse no curiosity.

The guards recognised him, and they exchanged a greeting and the customary comments about the weather before Grendon slipped through the gate. He couldn't see the litter, but the bearers at the hiring-stand had been disgruntled at having to turn out and didn't want to get any wetter than necessary; they had set a rapid pace through the city and weren't about to slack now. Perlion had given them a double fee and the same story about his daughter being the worse for drink, and apart from a few grumbles about inconsiderate customers they would have nothing to tattle about later.

Grendon only hoped that nothing untoward would happen before the litter and its passengers reached Arrine's house. He believed that Xai, sated now, had withdrawn far enough from the physical world not to present any further threat, but tonight's calamity had proved that it was dangerous to make any assumptions. Why she had driven Sefira to attack the midwife was a mystery. Logically, Perlion himself would have been a far more likely target, for Xai must know that Sefira's natural father could present a very serious threat. Yet it seemed she had no interest in him, and that didn't make sense.

His judgement could be wrong, however, and thinking of Perlion alone with Sefira and possibly vulnerable, he quickened his pace to a loping, ground-eating stride. The litter came into view ahead as he neared the entrance to the mews square where Arrine lived; it had halted, and to his relief he saw that Perlion had instructed the bearers not to enter the square but to set him down under the arch. Grendon stopped, stepped into a doorway and waited; within another minute the litter-bearers hurried past on their homeward journey, and as they merged into the streaming darkness he went to join Perlion and Sefira.

The Lander had lifted Sefira bodily out of the litter and now stood in the arch's shelter, holding her in his arms as though she was still a small child. Sefira offered no resistance, and didn't even stir as Grendon arrived. They had pulled her hood up to cowl her, and from its folds her eyes stared into the darkness, unblinking, with the wide, blank look of total shock.

Perlion said: 'How far now?'

Grendon nodded through the arch. 'There's a square beyond. Arrine's house is the fourth from the left on the south side; she always leaves a lamp burning over the door.'

Perlion nodded. At the end of the long road the palace with its myriad glowing lights glared at them, and the Lander gave a shiver as he glanced towards it.

'All those windows . . . I can't help the fear that there are eyes in every one of them, observing us . . .'

Grendon knew that feeling well and didn't comment. He moved ahead of Perlion, through the archway and into the square. They emerged into a scene of darkness and silence; Perlion saw Arrine's lamp burning and whispered uneasily, 'If we knock, we'll rouse half the inhabitants.'

'I can get us in.' Arrine had shown him the trick a long time ago, Grendon recalled, though he had never before had to use it. He simply hoped that they wouldn't wake Getha.

They moved across the square. Grendon thought of offering to carry Sefira, but a glimpse of Perlion's set face told him that the offer would be refused. As they neared the door, Perlion spoke again, softly.

'Grendon . . . you're sure of this? Sure that your friend can be trusted?'

This wasn't the time to explain why Arrine was the one person alive who could be trusted, so Grendon only said, 'She can. Believe it.'

Perlion gave a peculiar little snort. 'I've no choice, I suppose. We could hardly have taken her to Vinor's house.'

Grendon didn't reply, and they approached the door. There was a certain pane in one of the ground floor windows that, with a little ingenuity, could be slid from its place and removed, allowing the window catch to be reached. Perlion watched edgily as Grendon eased the window open, saw him climb on to the sill and soundlessly disappear into the house. Seconds later the front door swung back on well-oiled hinges, and they were all inside.

'I'll wake Arrine,' Grendon said quietly. 'Take Sefira in there,' nodding towards a door, 'and we'll both join you shortly.'

He glided away up the staircase. For a moment Perlion stared after him, his mind filled with misgivings and forebodings and an ache of misery that lodged in him like a leaden weight. Then he turned with his burden and went through into Arrine's sitting room.

Karel stared out of the window at the dawning day, deliberately keeping his back to the other two men in the audience room so that one of them, at least, would not see the smile that played about his mouth.

'A midwife, you say.' His tone was dispassionate.

The sergeant of the watch glanced nervously at Tomany, received an encouraging nod and replied, 'Yes, sir, Your Majesty. A widow, sir, living alone.'

'And there is no obvious motive for the outrage?'

'None that we can see, Majesty.' The man was baffled as to why the king should be taking such an interest. This murder was an exceptional and particularly macabre case, true, but the victim had been no one of importance, and thus of no obvious relevance to the monarch. But a new standing order said that any crime with certain distinguishing peculiarities must be reported at once to the palace, and when the night patrol had seen and investigated the house with the open door, and found what they had found in the kitchen, his task had been to obey that order without questioning it.

The reaction when he arrived at the palace had astonished him, for the Arbitrator on duty had sent immediately for the king's own secretary, and the secretary had woken the king, and now the sergeant found himself summoned to Karel's presence to tell the tale again. It occurred to him on an uneasy level that perhaps there was something afoot in the city which, for reasons known only to themselves, the court hierarchy had so far kept from the populace. A madman on the loose, or some such. It had happened before, when he was a raw recruit; a very ugly murder had been committed, and the culprit was one of the king's ministers, whom the king himself had tried to protect from justice. But that had been in the old days, of course, and King Karel was not that kind of a man . . .

Karel turned at last from the window, gave the sergeant a long, assessing look, and said, 'Thank you, sergeant. Your report has been most helpful, and I appreciate your diligence in delivering it so quickly. You'll be commended to your superiors.'

Astonished and delighted, the sergeant drew himself to full attention. 'Majesty. Thank *you*, sir.'

'You may go. And I'd suggest that you take a little time off before resuming your duties. This discovery can't have been a pleasant experience.'

'No, sir. Thank you, sir. Thank you again.'

The sergeant left in a daze of pride and confusion, and when he had gone Karel turned to Tomany.

'I think there's little room for doubt, don't you?'

Tomany inclined his head, half bow and half concurrence. 'I must agree with you, my lord. The comparison with the case in Emelian is too great for coincidence.'

'Only this time the perpetrator was away and gone before her savagery was discovered.' Which, he appended silently, probably meant that the soul-invader was learning to use guile more effectively. 'Very well, then. Dawn has broken, though you'd hardly know it in this filthy weather. Wake Grendon, and send him to me here.'

'Yes, my lord.' Tomany paused. 'And may I presume that you wish me to be discreet?'

Karel smiled. Tomany was fully in tune with his own mode

of thought. It was one of the reasons why his help had been enlisted. 'Indeed,' he said. '*Very* discreet.'

It took Tomany only a matter of minutes to discover that neither Grendon nor Sefira was in the apartment. Suspicious, but not at first unduly troubled, he investigated the rooms more thoroughly. He was an observant man, the kind who noted and remembered the smallest details, and it didn't take him long to realise that the cloak Sefira wore, and certain outdoor clothes of Grendon's – though not any part of his uniform – were missing. Suspicion then became certainty, and he reported back to his master.

Karel was silent for some time when he heard what Tomany had to say. His face was very still, very thoughtful, and the secretary hovered while he considered, waiting for a decision and the instructions that would follow.

At last Karel's eyes re-focused on him. 'I think,' he said calmly, 'that we shall wait for a little while, and see if Arraigner Grendon and his young wife return.'

'And if they do not, my lord . . . ?'

Karel smiled. If they did not, then it would be evidence enough that Sefira was guilty of this new murder and that Grendon knew it. That would give the king a useful advantage in his next move . . .

He didn't answer Tomany's question but only said, 'Have them watched for, and if either or both of them should enter the palace, detain them and inform me at once.' He would see Mischane, he thought. She would be able to answer one or two more small but revealing questions about Grendon which he had not yet troubled to ask, and that, too, would be productive. Satisfied that he had chosen the best course of action, at least for the time being, he started to walk towards the door, then as an afterthought added:

'And if I have any appointments for this morning, cancel them.'

He went out, leaving Tomany alone in the room.

* * *

Sefira stared at Grendon as though he were a complete stranger, and said in a dull, mechanical voice, 'I don't believe you. I don't. I *don't.*'

Perlion, on a chair beside the couch, bit back an unhappy sound and shook his head despairingly. Grendon and Arrine both cast a swift, sympathetic glance at his slumped figure, then Arrine said, 'My dear, I'm sorry. But it's the truth. And however much we all might want to deny it—'

'I *do* deny it!' Flinging aside the blanket in which they had wrapped her, Sefira tried to get to her feet, wanting to escape from them and from the room and from the hideous impossibility that they were trying to force her to confront. Grendon moved quickly, catching hold of her arms and restraining her; she struggled, but he was far the stronger and he forced her to sit down again.

Then suddenly Sefira's resistance crumpled and she burst into violent tears.

'Let her cry,' Arrine said as both Perlion and Grendon seemed about to intervene, Perlion to comfort and Grendon . . . well, Arrine thought, it was impossible to know what Grendon intended, for he seemed almost as confused and unhappy as Sefira. They subsided, and all three watched helplessly as Sefira doubled over, hands clasped to her skull, rocking back and forth and sobbing with a deep, intense and tortured sound. Arrine's heart twisted within her, for she knew what the girl was suffering; knew what it was like to cry from the pit of her soul, without hope and without the smallest possibility of solace. At this moment Sefira wanted only to die. Arrine understood only too well, and turned away, blinking back tears from her own eyes and wishing that she had not lied to this child about Lendrer.

Sefira cried for a long time. Once, Getha, who had been woken by the sound of voices in the house, put her head round the door, but a look and a quick shake of the head from Arrine sent her away again with her questions unasked. Outside, the

242

sky was lightening – though the word was barely appropriate – from black to a dismal and oppressive pewter grey as daylight grew behind the dense cloud pall. It was still raining. Then finally the sobbing began to subside. Sefira was shaking uncontrollably and made no attempt to raise her head, but by degrees the dreadful sounds she was making lessened. Grendon, who had been watching her intently and unremittingly, moved on to the couch at her side and put his arms around her. For a moment Sefira tensed, then she sagged into his embrace and buried her face against him, crying quietly now. Grendon stroked her hair, smoothing it back. Beneath its wet tendrils her cheeks were blotched and puffy, eyes rimmed with crimson; her whole face had a bruised look, as though her injuries were physical.

From her own chair Arrine watched the effect that Grendon's soothing was having on Sefira. She seemed instinctively to trust him, which surprised Arrine; and just as surprising was Grendon's gentleness with her. She was silent now but for an occasional whimper, then at last her eyes closed and her breathing became more even.

Grendon said, 'She's asleep.' He had been sharply alert for any sign of trouble, but it seemed that Xai had indeed withdrawn as he had hoped. Carefully, he stood up and rearranged Sefira's limbs so that she was lying full length on the couch. She curled into a foetal position, hugging herself, but it was a reflex. She was already sleeping deeply, almost comatose, and Grendon knew that shock and exhaustion would keep her in that state for some time to come.

Arrine said, 'I'll fetch her another blanket,' and went quietly out of the room.

'She'll sleep for several hours.' Grendon straightened and looked at Perlion, who nodded.

'It's the best thing for her.' He pressed fingertips to his forehead. 'If I had a flask of wine, I'd be sorely tempted to drink myself insensible now. Just to make this nightmare go *away* for a little while . . .' A long loud sniff, then he squared his shoulders and looked up again. 'But it won't, will it?'

'No. It won't.'

The Lander nodded again. 'I don't know what to do, Grendon. I know – the four winds help me, I know what I *should* do. But she's my daughter. And your wife. We can't . . . we just can't abandon her to – to—'

There was so much Perlion didn't yet know, and Grendon was horribly torn. His conscience told him that it was only right to reveal everything; Perlion deserved that at very least. But arguing against conscience was a cold, hard streak of self-preservation; for if Perlion learned the truth about his relationship with Sefira, there was no telling how he might react. At present he was a staunch ally, not only to Sefira but to Grendon as well. But if the whole story was told, then where Grendon was concerned he might turn from ally to enemy.

Then it occurred to Grendon that he did still hold one trump card. To play it would be a dishonourable act. But honour was something he had not been able to afford for a long time . . .

'Perlion . . .'

The change in his voice alerted the Lander instantly, and he tensed.

'Perlion, there's something more you should know about Sefira. Or rather, about the soul-invader. But the knowledge must form my side of a pact between us. For there's something I want from you in return.'

Perlion didn't even think of hesitating. 'Name it,' he said. 'Anything.'

'I want your oath that, whatever you might learn, you will continue to accept that I have Sefira's best interests at heart, and act accordingly.'

Perlion understood, and felt an uncomfortable war between dread and hope stir within himself. He had to trust. There was no other option.

'If it will help my daughter,' he told Grendon, 'I'll take any oath that will satisfy you, without qualification.'

It was enough, Grendon knew. Perlion was not a man to give his word lightly, and once given, he wouldn't break it.

'Very well.' He looked towards the window, where a narrow gap in the curtains showed that the morning was advancing. 'I have to return to the palace for a short while, and you too should return to your cousin's house. Your family must be worried.'

Surprised, Perlion looked over his shoulder and uttered an imprecation. 'By all powers, is it so late? Isbel will be frantic!'

'Then walk back with me, and I'll explain as we go.'

'Yes . . . yes, I will.' He shivered. 'We don't want to arouse any suspicions, do we, by too prolonged an absence . . . Yes, I'll come with you; I'll tell Isbel that I stayed overnight with a business acquaintance, and must return to complete our transactions. It will give me time. Time to think what to do . . .'

Arrine returned then with the blanket, and the two men watched as she laid it over Sefira. Swiftly Grendon explained what he and Perlion intended, and Arrine nodded assent.

'And if Sefira should wake?' she asked.

'It's unlikely that she will; but if she does . . .' Grendon hesitated, then voiced the decision which he had, in his heart, made some hours ago. 'Tell her everything about Xai, Arrine. And tell her my own story.'

Arrine's eyes met his levelly. 'Are you sure?'

'Yes. Yes, I am.'

'And Perlion . . . ?' She glanced to where the Lander stood looking down at Sefira, oblivious to their exchange.

'He, too, has a right to know. I think . . .' Another pause. 'I think it's the only just course to take.'

It was still early enough for there to be little activity in the palace grounds as Grendon walked towards the great, sprawling building. He had parted from Perlion near his cousin's house, leaving him with a good deal to ponder on before they met again under Arrine's roof – and also with a new ray of hope. For as they walked, Grendon had told him that there might, just might, be a remote possibility that Sefira could be freed from Xai, and the vampiric demon destroyed.

He still didn't know why he had said it. It had been an impulse, a decision taken without time for thought, and he was already starting to regret having spoken. But Perlion's misery and helplessness had been so profound that something in Grendon had been moved to more than pity. He had felt a sense of comradeship with the Lander, and also, strange though it might seem, a sense of gratitude towards him. For Perlion was one of the few people he had ever met who did not instantly and innately turn against another human being cursed with the taint of the soul-invader. The fact that Sefira was his daughter made a difference, of course; but even allowing for that, it was a rare individual who had such strength and charity in his heart.

Grendon remembered his own parents, and the atmosphere of distaste, antipathy and bitterness in which he had grown up. Unlike some others in their predicament, they had not had him drowned – though Grendon knew full well that it was only the intervention of Lendrer and Arrine that had stopped them from doing so – but they had never allowed him to forget the stigma of his birth. Even when Lendrer had succeeded in freeing him from it, they had never forgiven him until the day they died. Only Mischane had understood, he told himself. He owed her a deeply felt debt for that; now he owed another to Perlion. And whatever caution might warn to the contrary, he trusted the man implicitly.

He had, however, refused to say any more than that there was a chance, and a very slender one, to help Sefira. Perlion probed, but Grendon would give no details of how he knew, or what the breaking of the link with Xai might entail. Perlion knew now that he was a Sanctified, and that alone could be enough to damn him if anything went wrong. The Lander would doubtless learn the rest of the story before long, but for the present it was better left untold.

As for Sefira . . . Grendon's thoughts about her were still turbulently unresolved, but his conscience was starting to take more and more of a hand. He pitied her, and always had; now, though, another feeling was clouding the issue. Anger. Anger at the capricious turn of fate that had turned an innocent child into something monstrous; anger at Karel and all his sycophants who sneered behind their hands at her gauche and gamine manner. (It would give him such dark satisfaction to let them know what she truly was . . .) But above all, the anger was directed at himself, and with it came a keen and painful measure of disgust. He had intended to use Sefira, cold-bloodedly and without her knowledge, to further his own cause, and had been ready to pay any price for that usage. He had married her for the cause's sake, though he felt no love for her, or she for him. He had taken absolute control of her and forced her into a way of life that she did not want, using fear as his weapon. Oh, he had saved her from the execution pyre, that was true. But his motive had been entirely selfish; had she been any ordinary murderer, he would have delivered her back to the justices and never thought of her again.

Now he was facing the consequences of his own scheming. Another innocent victim on Xai's list, and Sefira driven into deep shock, possibly into insanity, by the realisation of what she had done. He could see now why she had lost her memory. It had been her mind's own defence, no doubt further manipulated by Xai to keep her functioning. She had probably attacked the guards who were taking her to her execution, and killed them too. How else could she have escaped to be found wandering on the moor? Shock and revulsion had switched off her reasoning powers and driven her memory away, deep enough for it to be lost; and little wonder.

What had he said to Arrine soon after their arrival in Tourmon? That a few lives lost counted for nothing against the others that might be saved if his plan succeeded. Those words sounded hollow now, hollow and hypocritical. Moral principles became a mockery when they were sustained by immoral means. And the one image he couldn't banish from his mind was of Sefira's bloodstained face looking up at him from the doorway of the rotting storehouse, and her voice as she pleaded, *Oh please, oh please, help me . . .*

He had reached the palace now, and entered by a side door which would lead him by a circuitous route to his rooms. Trying to push away the uglier thoughts, he concentrated on the moves he must make in the next few minutes. To all intents and purposes he would appear to leave for Emelian as arranged, and that would buy him time. The murdered woman had probably been discovered by now, but it was unlikely that news of the crime would reach Karel's ears, and even if it did, he would have no reason whatever to suspect any connection with Sefira. Her absence from the palace would cause some outcry, of course. But that could be dealt with when the first crisis was over.

He climbed a flight of back stairs, then turned into a narrow corridor that joined up with one of the main passages on the first floor. Emerging into the passage, he saw Tomany coming towards him, and quickly masked the sour expression that came instinctively to his face.

Tomany saw him and slowed down. 'Arraigner Grendon . . .'

'Good morning, Tomany. No further minutiae for me, before I take the next tide for Emelian?'

Tomany's mouth pursed. 'No, Arraigner. Not in that sense.' Then his eyes focused over Grendon's right shoulder and he nodded.

Grendon heard the scuffle of feet in the split second before he turned and realised what was afoot. Two of the king's guard were coming up behind him. They were armed, and their faces bore set, hostile expressions.

Grendon said explosively, 'What is this?'

'The king wishes to see you, Arraigner Grendon,' Tomany replied smoothly. 'At once, if you please. These men will escort you.'

A tight, queasy sensation gripped Grendon's stomach, and

suddenly he found breathing difficult. Mustering his self-control he said in a low-pitched, dangerous voice:

'Tomany, if this is your idea of mischief—'

'I assure you, Arraigner, I have far better things to do than play petty games with anyone,' Tomany told him with cool asperity. 'If you wish me to be blunt, I shall be. You are under arrest.'

'*What?*'

'I said—'

'I heard you, damn your tongue! What's this nonsense about?'

'I'm sure His Majesty will explain the nature of it to you soon enough, for he gave the order himself,' Tomany said. 'Now, if you please . . . It wouldn't be advisable to keep him waiting.'

One of the guards shifted, and Grendon heard the slide of a blade being fidgeted in its sheath. He flung one wild glance past the two men to the side passage and the stairs, but the impulse to run died stillborn. This was some new, twisted joke on Karel's part; it *had* to be. Better to find out what was afoot and have done with it.

'Very well.' He gave Tomany a searingly contemptuous look, then addressed the guards. 'Lead the way. *If* you please.'

Chapter XIX

As soon as he saw Karel's face, Grendon knew that this was no trivial matter.

The guards had escorted him to the audience room, where from the look of it the king had been waiting for some time. That in itself was an ominous sign, and as Karel looked up and gestured for him to take the uncomfortable looking chair placed on the near side of his desk, Grendon felt a twinge of apprehension.

The guards left, and Karel steepled his fingers and looked at Grendon over them. His pale eyes, not warm at the best of times, had an arctic edge to them. Then at last he said:

'Where is your wife?'

Grendon was too skilled to show his chagrin. 'She is unwell, sir,' he replied.

'Is she? I'm sorry to hear it. But I imagine it's not surprising, under the circumstances.'

'I'm afraid I don't understand you, my lord.'

'Really? Then I shall explain myself. Or perhaps I'll ask another question. What's amiss with her?' His eyes grew steely. 'Is her malady simply exhaustion after her night's activities? Or is it the physical result of drinking her victim's blood?'

Grendon felt as if his own blood had turned to ice. He didn't speak, couldn't speak, and after a few moments Karel, whose gaze hadn't wavered from his face, said, 'I'm waiting for your answer, Grendon.'

There was no answer he could give, and the king knew it. The hiatus held for a few seconds more, then suddenly Karel stood, thrust his own chair back and strode to a side table where a leather folder lay. He picked it up, riffled through its contents, then walked more slowly and deliberately back to the desk.

'I have,' he said in a soft, dangerous voice, 'a report from the watch concerning an incident, shall we call it, that took place in a certain house in a certain street in Tourmon last night. A very *unpleasant* incident.'

He dropped a sheet of paper on to the desk in front of Grendon. Grendon looked at it but couldn't take in the words, and Karel continued.

'The victim was found in her own kitchen, which had been turned into a charnel house. Her throat seems to have been the killer's main target; although there was, I gather, a considerable amount of mutilation, and a prodigious loss of blood.' He started to pace out a circle around Grendon's chair. 'The most interesting thing about this report is that it bears an extraordinary – indeed, I might go so far as to say uncanny – resemblance to a certain deposition lodged in the records by the justices in Emelian. That, too, concerns an unusually brutal murder, but there is one major difference. In the Emelian case the perpetrator was found at the scene of the crime. In fact it took four men to tear her away from the corpse, which she seemed to be trying to devour, and subdue her.' Now he stopped, staring down at Grendon from behind the chair as if challenging him to turn and meet his gaze. Grendon didn't move a muscle.

'I think,' Karel said softly, 'that you have no more to gain from dissembling, Grendon. I don't need to look at your face to know that you're well aware of the truth about Sefira, so it seems a little futile, not to mention a waste of everyone's time, for us to play genteel fencing games with each other. To save you the dilemma of deciding whether or not to lie to me, I shall say this bluntly. I know about the soul-invader.'

Grendon's quick, sharp intake of breath was clearly audible in the room, and Karel smiled a hard, relentless smile.

'Ah, yes; the raw nerve is touched. Well, the scheme you devised has rather rebounded on you, hasn't it? You don't love Sefira, and you most certainly wouldn't have married her unless I had forced your hand. That was a childish joke, I admit, but it amused me at the time. Now, though, the jest seems a little less lighthearted, for you've tied yourself to a murderess and – somewhat more seriously from my point of view – you have also persuaded me to unwittingly harbour an extremely dangerous and unpredictable power under my roof. I do not find *that* amusing in the least.'

The sound of Karel's footsteps set Grendon's teeth on edge as he moved again, this time round to the far side of the desk from where he could study Grendon's face once more. After a few moments, apparently satisfied with what he saw, he continued.

'It may be, however, that this unfortunate situation can be salvaged to the advantage of us both.' A pause, then his voice became harsher. 'Where is she?'

Grendon stared back at him. 'Do you intend to execute her?'

'Not necessarily. It rather depends on how willing she and you are to cooperate with what I have in mind.'

The tip of Grendon's tongue touched his lips, which felt cracked and dry. 'Then what—'

'What do I have in mind? It's quite simple. I want to make direct contact with the creature that controls her.'

This time Grendon couldn't hide his reaction. He half rose from the chair and his voice was incredulous. '*What?*'

'Sit down. And I don't need to repeat myself; you heard me perfectly well. I want to parley with this – this blood-sucking leech, or parasite, or whatever esoteric term you choose for it. You withheld information from me, Grendon. You told me that Sefira had powers, but you allowed me to think that they extended no further than a few clairvoyant tricks. From what I've recently learned of them, I now know that a soul-invader can achieve a great deal more than that.

252

And in my quest to reform this land of ours, those achievements could prove very helpful indeed.'

From what I've recently learned . . . The words echoed in Grendon's mind and sounded an alarm, and he started to demand sharply, 'How did you learn—'

'About these creatures? Ah yes, I understand your surprise. You Sanctifieds kept such information strictly to yourselves, didn't you; and the only written records don't tell more than a crumb of the truth. Yet I, a mere Lander,' vitriol laced his voice, 'have been able to probe the occult secrets of your Fellowship, and pluck some ripe fruits from the thicket you set up around yourselves.' He smiled, enjoying Grendon's consternation, then slipped in the verbal knife that he had been waiting to use; the one that would pierce the fatal flaw in his opponent's defences. 'Your sister was very helpful indeed.'

Mischane . . . a feeling of cold dread lodged in Grendon. Throat constricting, he said hoarsely, 'What have you done to her?'

'My dear Grendon, I'm not *that* crude. I merely pointed out to the lady Mischane that with such a creature as Sefira in our midst it might be safer if I were to be aware of a few salient facts.' His mouth widened in a predatory smile. 'The more I know, the better I can protect both her and her beloved brother. She saw the wisdom of my argument, and cooperated.'

Grendon remained outwardly calm, but inwardly he was seething with a churning mix of fury and fear. Oh, Karel wouldn't have hurt Mischane; as he said, he wasn't that crude. But the threat of what he *might* do if his will was not acceded to, was clearly implicit. And from his own bitter experience during and after the war, Grendon knew that when it came to getting what he wanted, Karel had no scruples whatever.

Which makes you two of a kind, said a small inner voice. Grendon crushed it, telling himself savagely that comparisons couldn't be made. He had to protect Mischane. And there were still so many others of their own kind, innocent of any crime but hunted relentlessly, and tormented, and given a barbaric death . . .

And Sefira, pleading with him: 'Oh, please, help me . . .'

Karel's voice cut into the chaos of his mind. 'Where is she, Grendon? You know the answer. Tell me.'

Grendon drew breath. 'No,' he said.

There was silence. Karel sat down, drew the paper he had dropped on the desk towards himself and scanned it significantly. Then: 'You won't succeed in keeping her hidden. I'll find her.'

'I doubt that.' But his pulse was thick in his veins as he thought of Arrine. Karel knew all about that old friendship, and her house was the first place that he would search. He had to *warn* her . . .

Karel glanced at the document again. 'Ah, well,' he said, almost carelessly, 'if you're unwilling to help me, I must make other arrangements. A pity; I would have preferred to save time and trouble. But possibly the lady Mischane can be of further assistance.'

Grendon started to rise again. 'If you—'

'If I what, my friend?' Suddenly Karel braced his hands on the desk and leaned threateningly towards Grendon. 'If I harm her? Oh, no, no; I don't intend to play my trump card, not yet. Mischane and I will simply have another little talk. In fact, I may allow her to visit you, to see if she can talk sense into you where I have failed.'

Hope quickened in Grendon. If he could speak with Mischane . . . he had resolved not to tell her his ultimate plan, for the sake of her own safety. But there was nothing to be lost now. And if, between them, they could devise a way of misleading Karel, the tables might still be turned . . .

'In the meantime, however,' Karel went on, unaware of the direction Grendon's thoughts were taking, 'I think it would be as well if your freedom was curtailed. We don't want you taking any action that might be construed as hostile, do we?' Reaching across the desk he picked up the bell that stood there and rang it. Grendon heard the door behind him open but forced himself not to turn round. Two sets of footsteps. The guards . . .

Karel's eyes focused beyond him. 'Confine Arraigner Grendon to one of the holding rooms until further notice,' he said crisply, then looked at Grendon again. 'Unless you have anything further to say to me . . . ?'

There was war in Grendon's mind, but it lasted only a moment. To capitulate now would be disastrous – and it was unnecessary. Mischane was not yet in danger. Sefira was not yet captured. And even if he was imprisoned, there might still be a way to get a warning to Arrine.

His gaze met Karel's with a steadiness that held just a hint of contempt. 'I have nothing to say.'

The guards stayed closer to him this time, and outside the audience room they were joined by a third who fell mutely into line behind them. The holding rooms. The name was a veiled reference to the larger chamber nearby, where the shabby, self-effacing little man known as The Confessor carried out his trade. Officially it was pretended that the chamber was never used now; unofficially, the entire court knew better. Grendon, however, wouldn't be meeting the Confessor. Instead, he would be given time to consider his predicament in solitude, which in Karel's experience was more often than not an excellent way to persuade a stubborn adversary to see sense.

The route took them out of the main bulk of the palace and through a bare courtyard to a group of lesser buildings on the north side. Windows overlooked the courtyard, among them the window of a small antechamber that adjoined the audience room. Glancing up, Grendon saw that Karel had moved into the antechamber; back to the window, he appeared to be speaking to someone else who wasn't visible. Then the room's other occupant came into view. It was a woman, and to Grendon's surprise Karel took her into his arms in an unmistakably amorous embrace. So reality didn't quite match the king's carefully maintained public image as a man devoted to his work and with no interest in frivolity . . . Grendon wanted to laugh aloud at such a petty deceit.

But then the laughter died stillborn as the woman moved closer to the window and he saw her face.

The guards didn't notice the tension that gripped him with such sudden violence, nor the pallor that drained his skin of colour and left it grey. They merely walked on. And Grendon went with them, compelled by a tide he couldn't control, as the mental wall he had built to defend his codes and his goals, the whole foundation of his unswerving resolution, began to collapse.

With Isbel soothed and his explanation accepted and oil poured on the troubled waters caused by his absence, Perlion returned to Arrine's house within two hours. Sefira was still asleep on the couch, and on entering the sitting room Perlion hurried to gaze down at her with anxious fondness.

'She hasn't stirred?' he asked.

'Not yet.' Arrine came to stand beside him, and he looked at her keenly.

'I'm so sorry that we embroiled you in this, Arrine. We had no right to ask it, but Grendon said . . . and I knew of no safe place, and . . .' His throat worked as he swallowed. 'I will be eternally in your debt. *Eternally.*'

Arrine was beginning to realise why Grendon had instinctively trusted Perlion. Beneath his outward manner, which at present seemed to swing between calm strength and clumsy confusion, she could see the warmth and honesty and loyalty that had driven him in his bid to be reconciled with his long-lost daughter. She had heard the bones of the whole story in the first disordered minutes after waking to find Grendon at her bedside, and when Perlion had realised that she was ready to help them, the desperate profundity of his gratitude had touched her to the core. He would do anything to save Sefira, for by his reckoning she was as much an innocent victim as the woman so brutally murdered last night. To him, it was Xai alone who stood to answer for the crime. And despite her shock at what had happened, Arrine remembered the events of the past and could not but agree with him.

She said, 'There's no question of debt, Perlion. Grendon and I are old friends, and we . . . well, let's say that our loyalty is strong.'

Perlion paused for a moment. Then he asked gently, 'Is that a part of the Sanctified code?' She stared at him, shocked, and he smiled an open smile. 'Grendon told me. He had to use his skills, you see, to find Sefira when she fled. I'm not unworldly; I recognised what was afoot, and it's only logical that he should have sought help among his own kind. Please, Arrine, don't fear that I'll betray your secret.' He looked at Sefira again. 'After the way in which you have helped my child, I would *never* do that.'

It was a promise Arrine knew she could trust – but she wondered uneasily if he would have made it had he known of Grendon's ultimate plan for Sefira. *He has a right to know the truth*, Grendon had said to her before he left. Very well; then she would tell him the truth if he asked it of her. But not that part.

There was a sound from the couch, and they both turned in time to see Sefira shifting restlessly under her blankets. Her eyelids fluttered and she gave a sigh; then one hand appeared and reached up to rub vaguely at her face.

'She's waking!' Perlion dropped to a crouch beside her and took hold of her fingers. 'Sefira – Sefira, my child, can you hear me?'

Sefira stirred, opened her eyes and looked bewilderedly at him. 'Who . . . ?' she began. Then abruptly she recognised him, and shrank back with a cry of alarm.

'Sefira.' Arrine moved forward. 'It's all right. You're safe in my house.'

Sefira's head jerked quickly towards the direction of her voice, and the bewilderment was replaced by hesitant relief.

But that lasted only a moment before something new crept into her eyes. A memory, of the night and the rain and the anonymous kitchen of the anonymous house . . . and of Grendon, crouching before her in this room as he told her something that was too hideous to accept, too hideous to bear, yet which she knew in the darkest pit of her soul was the truth . . .

Arrine saw, and knew what was dawning in her mind. Quickly she crossed to the door and opened it, calling to Getha, then she hastened back to the couch, where Perlion was restraining Sefira as she tried to struggle to her feet.

'Please . . .' Sefira's voice shook with impending hysteria. 'Let me go. I must go. I must go.'

'Sefira, sit down.' Arrine spoke so authoritatively that Perlion blinked in surprise. But the tactic worked, startling Sefira enough to break the hold that panic was gaining on her. Arrine knew this symptom; knew what the girl's damaged mind was goading her to do, and she took her by the shoulders and looked hard into her eyes.

'Listen to me. You are not going to run out of this house and put an end to your own life. Do you understand me, Sefira? Do you?'

Perlion said, aghast, 'Is that what she wants to do?'

'Yes, it is. Not that Xai would permit it, but she doesn't know that.' Arrine looked at Sefira again, saw that her words had sunk in, and continued, 'Are you so weak that you'll let this parasite have its way without even attempting to fight it?'

Sefira shook her head. 'I can't. I c-c-can't . . .'

'You can. I know it, and so does Grendon.' Arrine hesitated, then decided to follow the instinct that was goading her. She would be lying to Sefira again – but this time, for the first time, her conscience was clear. 'Don't you realise,' she said, 'that that was the *real* reason why Grendon took you under his wing?'

It worked. Sefira's eyes widened, her jaw dropped, and she breathed, 'The – the real reason—?'

'Yes.' Arrine was horribly aware of Perlion watching her, holding his breath, and when she flicked a rapid glance in his direction she saw ardent excitement in his face. He was expecting this, had been waiting for it . . . *by the fates*, she thought, *what has Grendon promised him?*

Getha appeared then, causing a distraction for which Arrine was thankful. She gave the servant swift but precise instructions for a tisane that had a strong calming effect; it gave her time to regain her wits and consider, and by the time Getha departed on her errand she had come to a decision.

'Perlion,' she said quietly, 'please, sit down. And Sefira. I want you to pay me very close attention, for I am going to tell you the whole truth about yourself, and about the creature called Xai.'

Perlion couldn't contain his eagerness. 'Arrine – Grendon said there was a way to destroy this thing; to rid Sefira of it forever. Is it possible? You *must* tell me!'

'Yes, it's possible.' She regarded him sombrely. 'My late husband achieved it. I assisted him, and witnessed what took place.'

'And the victim; the one who was afflicted – has that person survived?'

'Yes,' Arrine replied. 'He is still alive, and I know him well.'

It was the clearest indication she could have given without saying it directly, and realisation dawned in Perlion's face. He uttered a stifled gasp and said softly, 'Oh . . . I was a *fool* not to see it . . . I didn't think; I simply didn't *think* . . .'

'Please.' Arrine interrupted him before the flow of words could distract her. 'Hear me out, Perlion, for I need to tell the story in my own way.' Sefira, she saw, had not yet grasped what Perlion had understood, and was watching them both with hazy bewilderment. Arrine turned to her once more.

'I'll reveal all I know of the soul-invader, Sefira,' she said gently. 'And I'll also explain to you about Grendon. You see, he knows better than any of us what you are suffering, because for the first seventeen years of his life he, too, was a victim of that same curse . . .'

Arrine stood by the window, looking out at the square but not seeing it. Well, it was done. She had told them everything . . . or everything that, now, could possibly have any relevance. Sefira knew the truth about her own affliction and the power that Xai wielded over her; knew, too, that as time went by the demonic parasite's influence would become stronger and stronger, until one day it would integrate fully with her, and she would lose not only her mind but also her soul. Cruel words, but what was the point in kindness? She needed to know. Needed to be aware of what the future might hold.

And she had told them Grendon's story, as he had asked. Another newborn fallen prey to one of Xai's kind; a child who grew up in the shadow of his parents' abhorrence and resentment. They had had such plans for their only son, and those plans had been thwarted. So it was to Arrine and Lendrer that the young Grendon had turned for the affection his own family could or would not give, and they had come to love him as if he was their own. They knew his secret, and they kept it . . . until, as he neared maturity, the soul-invader began to make itself known more forcefully.

It was possible, Arrine thought, that Grendon still didn't realise the full extent of his predations during that nightmare time; and certainly she would never reveal them to him. But then the last and worst onslaught had happened. And vivid in her memory was the night when Grendon had arrived at their door, his skin and his clothes crimson with blood and his eyes wild as a hunted animal's, and on his knees on the threshold he had begged Lendrer to free him from what he had become by putting a knife through his heart.

Arrine gave a small shiver, then looked over her shoulder to where Sefira and Perlion sat, she on the couch and he on the chair close by. There was a look of peace on Perlion's face, for he had told his story, too, and when she discovered who he was Sefira had cried a little, and hugged him, and that had gladdened his heart. Now, he was content simply to gaze at her; for a little while at least, nothing else mattered to him.

Sefira leaned against the couch's high back, her eyes closed and her breathing steady. Arrine suspected she had fallen asleep again, and was relieved. With the help of the tisane she had become calm enough to absorb all that was said to her and there had been no more hysteria. But she was still too shocked to react in any but a passive, almost apathetic way, and the strain of recent events was showing in her pallor and in the dark, bruise-like crescents under her eyes. She had asked only one question, and it had pierced Arrine's defences like a spear. Hearing how Lendrer had taken the decision to try to rid Grendon of his own demonic parasite and, against all odds, had succeeded, her dark eyes had taken on a strange, haunted look and she had said simply, 'Will Grendon do it for me, Arrine? *Will* he?' Arrine had faltered, not knowing what she could say, and Sefira, understanding, turned her head away and said no more.

So doubtless she had been a fool, Arrine told herself. But the impulse had overtaken her before she could stop it and, unprompted, she had promised to do everything in her power to persuade Grendon to try. She had no right to make that promise, and she doubted if Sefira believed her. But she knew deep down that she would strive to keep it.

Perlion moved at last, rising quietly from the chair and walking slowly to join Arrine at the window. 'You must be very tired,' he said.

She smiled. 'I am. But it's of no importance. When Grendon returns I'll sleep for a while.'

Perlion was about to say something more, but abruptly stopped and frowned. Then he looked out of the window, peering at the sky as though trying to gauge the angle of the sun, though cloud made it impossible.

'Touching on that . . .' he said, and there was a glimmer of unease in his voice, 'I'd wager that the morning's half over.

And it occurs to me that Grendon should have been back by now . . .'

Arrine stood very still. She hadn't thought to consider it before, but she realised suddenly that Grendon had indeed been gone for a long time. Two or three hours at most should have been enough for him to lay the false trail and avert any suspicions at the palace, and suddenly, intuitively, she knew that something was wrong.

Perlion saw his own rising fear mirrored in her eyes. 'I think,' he said quietly and deliberately, 'that perhaps I should investigate.'

Arrine felt relief and gratitude; he was keeping his composure and that enabled her to retain a grip on her own. With his cousin in favour at the palace it wouldn't be difficult for Perlion to make a few discreet enquiries, and she nodded.

'If fortune smiles, you'll probably meet him on his way here. I'm sure there's nothing amiss.'

'So am I. But it will put both our minds at rest.'

She saw him to the door, then returned to the sitting room. Sefira hadn't moved, and Arrine sat down in her own old and comfortable chair by the hearth. Head back, she allowed her eyelids to droop. She wouldn't sit for long. She would merely try to relax for a few minutes . . .

Her eyes closed, and in seconds she was soundly asleep.

Chapter XX

Sefira counted to a hundred before opening her eyes. Without turning her head she looked at Arrine supine in the chair, then cautiously sat up.

Her head felt extraordinarily clear. Shock and bewilderment had receded, and her mind was filled with all she had learned, and its implications.

Bizarrely, all her horror at the crime she had committed had vanished without trace. It didn't occur to her to wonder why that should be; she simply accepted the fact and was thankful for it. Instead, she was thinking of Grendon.

If Arrine was to be believed, then she had indeed misjudged him. She understood now the terrible choice he had been forced to make after the war was over; and the reason why, though loathing the duties he must perform, he continued to work in the king's service. Mischane was the key. The only other survivor from his family; for his parents had been among the first Sanctifieds to die a protracted, agonising and public death in the early days of Karel's reign. Grendon, though, had been permitted to survive, and Mischane was the key to his cooperation with the new regime. 'A thief is best caught by one of his own kind,' Arrine had said, bitterly repeating the king's own sardonic words to Grendon when the one-sided bargain had been struck. A Sanctified to recognise and unmask other Sanctifieds. A useful weapon in Karel's hands. And Karel had used Grendon, while his sister lived as a captive in the palace with her life as the forfeit should Grendon ever fail to obey.

Grendon had obeyed. He had overseen the capture and execution of other Sanctifieds, serving Karel in his drive to eradicate the fallen Fellowship from the land. He had watched friends and strangers alike go to the pyre . . . and he had stood on the Arraigner's platform in Victory Square to read the official charges against Lendrer, Arrine's husband and his own mentor and saviour, and had seen him burn. That – and here Arrine's voice had become very soft – was the king's ultimate revenge on Grendon; a way of venting his bitter resentment at the fact that he was obliged to rely on his skills. The choice was stark: if Grendon did not comply, then he would have joined Lendrer at the stake, and Mischane with them. Some who knew what Grendon had done had never forgiven him, and he had never forgiven himself. But Arrine viewed things differently. She owed her own life to Grendon, for he had bargained desperately on her behalf and at last – perhaps discomforted by the thought of burning an ageing woman against whom even he could have no personal grudge – Karel had graciously granted the favour and spared her. To Arrine, he was the betrayer, not Grendon.

Just as my crime, Sefira thought, *was committed not by me, but by . . . someone else*. That was what Arrine had told her, and what Grendon also believed. For the sake of her own sanity she had to believe it, too. Above all else she had to put her trust in the people who could help her. In Arrine. In Perlion . . . and oh it was strange, so *strange*, to know Perlion, to discover who he was . . .

And that he abandoned you when you were born.

The words slipped slyly into her mind, catching her by surprise. Sefira pushed them away. What else could Perlion have done? It changed nothing; he was still her father. And with so much of her memory lost, the gap of many years' separation didn't seem to matter. Kinship was the strongest tie of all, and she *trusted* him.

Fool. Fool to trust any of them. Perlion and Arrine and Grendon . . .

Sefira jumped violently at the second incursion into her mind, and with a sense of foreboding realised that the insidious thought wasn't of her own making. Skin crawling, she turned her head slowly and surveyed the quiet room, but there was only the fire and the gloomy daylight and Arrine sleeping in her chair.

What of Arrine, Sefi? She lied to you before; why should she be telling the truth now? Remember what she said to you about her husband and the fever? A pretty tale, Sefi. And none of it true. Is this true? Or does she have something else in mind for you?

Sefira heard a small, nervous sound break from her lips and quickly stifled it. Arrine slept on. But there was suddenly a sense in the room of *something* awake and aware, and horribly, surely, her mind grasped at the truth.

She whispered softly: 'Xai . . .'

An unnerving sensation, heat and cold together, seemed to flood through her mind and body, and the voice in her head replied, *That is the first time you have ever addressed me by my name, Sefi. Yes, I am here. I am here for you, as I always have been. I protect my own.*

Sefira glanced in terror at Arrine. Should she wake her?

No! Don't wake her. We don't want her; we don't need her. We have each other, and that is enough.

The creature could hear her thoughts . . . A feeling that blended fear and anger and fascination in a confused tangle filled Sefira. Then she remembered Arrine's stern challenge to her: 'Are you so weak that you'll let this parasite have its way without even attempting to fight it?' She wasn't weak. She *would* fight. She would show this depraved *thing* that she wasn't about to be its puppet . . .

Grendon used you as his puppet, Sefi. Doesn't that make you angry?

'I know the truth now,' Sefira whispered furiously.

Oh, the truth, the truth . . . What is the truth? I know the truth; I know. Hate him, Sefi. Hate them all. They will not help us. They have poisoned you against the king with their pretty stories, but

*what harm has the king ever done to you? His word is law. He can
protect you. Perlion cannot. Grendon will not. Perlion abandoned
you, and Grendon and Arrine have told you lies. They are not your
friends. But the king . . .*

The perfidious words were becoming hypnotic, seeping
into her like a weird litany. Though she tried to resist, a part
of her was listening avidly, absorbing, *wanting* to believe.

*Yes, Sefi, yes . . . you want to believe because you know that
only I tell you the truth. I am your friend. I am your sister. I am
with you always, and we shall never be parted, for you do not want
to be parted from me . . .*

It was so strong, so *strong* – Sefira clapped her hands to her
skull and cried aloud, 'No! Get out of my mind! Leave me!'

'Unhh?' With a start Arrine woke. 'Sefira, what—' She
stopped. Sefira was staring at her. For an instant the girl's
eyes pleaded in mute terror for help, then a violent shudder
went through her and all traces of recognition vanished like a
shutter slamming down. And her eyes changed colour from
dark brown to zircon blue.

'Sefira . . .' Slowly Arrine rose to her feet. *Where was Grendon?*
She couldn't cope with this; didn't have the skill. 'Sefira, do
you know me? It's Arrine. Arrine, your friend—'

She is no friend to us!

Sefira uttered an extraordinary mewing sound, as though
she were struggling to express something but had forgotten
how to speak. Xai was tightening her hold and her mind was
drowning; she was losing control.

*She is no friend, Sefi. Not she, not Grendon, not Perlion. But
the king . . .*

Arrine was backing away, her gaze transfixed on Sefira's
eyes. There was no sanity there, no trace of humanity, and
Arrine felt the creeping, paralysing certainty that within the
next few minutes she was going to die.

Then Sefira's head began to turn from side to side, a
strange, sinuous motion like something blind and half-sentient,
casting about for the scent of prey. Two words were echoing

and re-echoing through her fractured mind: *The king. The king. The king* . . .

She moved, and Arrine's lungs heaved with the beginnings of a scream. But Sefira did not attack. Calmly, smoothly, she glided towards the door, opened it quietly, went out. *The king. Yes, Sefi, yes. The king.*

The front door slammed with a noise that brought Getha running from the kitchen. She found her mistress gasping for breath, clutching the back of the chair and staring as if mesmerised towards the window. Alarmed, Getha looked out, but saw only an indistinct figure in a long cloak walking across the square towards the arch.

'Madam?' She hastened back to Arrine's side. 'Madam, what is it? Here, now; sit down. I'll fetch you a glass of wine . . .'

Perlion was leaving the palace by a side entrance, his mind in turmoil, when he saw the detachment of guards walking down the road ahead of him. There was a purposeful air about them, and in the light of what he had just learned Perlion had a dreadful feeling that he knew the nature of their mission.

He quickened his own pace, wanting to catch up though with no idea of what that might achieve. Then at a barked word from their sergeant the detachment halted. The sergeant was giving orders; Perlion hurried past, remembering to look curiously at them as others in the street were doing, but he couldn't overhear what was being said.

The men started to move again. Three had headed away in another direction – he didn't know why – but the rest were marching behind him now. Marching, he was certain, towards Arrine's house.

Sweat broke out on him despite the chill of the day. What to *do*? He knew no short cuts to the square, and even if he did there would be no time to warn Arrine and get Sefira away before the guards arrived. He was almost running now, not caring if he drew attention to himself. Then in the distance ahead he saw a solitary, cloaked figure approaching.

Perlion slid to a halt and stared in disbelief, convinced his eyes must be deceiving him. But as the figure came closer his doubts fell away. It *was* Sefira. She was walking steadily towards him. Towards the palace and the oncoming guards.

Perlion thought, *What in all the realms of madness* . . . and started to hurry towards her. Her face was a white mask in the frame of her hood, and as he drew nearer he saw that her eyes had a blank, glazed look.

And they were blue.

He could hear the tramp of the guards' feet behind him. Perlion didn't pause to think; he ran the last few paces, placed himself squarely in Sefira's path and said in a stern voice, '*Daughter!*'

She stopped abruptly and looked up at him. For a moment there was such contemptuous fury in the look that he shrank back; then it vanished and was replaced by a small, unpleasant smile.

'I am going,' she said, 'to see the king.'

'The *king*?' Perlion was appalled, then his own anger rose, impelled by fear of her dreadful transformation and what it implied. 'Damn my sight, you're doing no such thing!'

The cold blue eyes stared at him. 'Move out of my way.' Then she smiled again; not her own smile but Xai's. 'Or I shall make you move. I can. I have the power now.'

The guards were almost upon them. Praying that they hadn't yet recognised Sefira as their quarry, Perlion gambled. His hands shot out, he grabbed hold of Sefira's arms and roared in the most outraged voice he could summon, 'Disobedient girl! To think that I should ever hear such a thing from a daughter of mine – you are coming home with me, madam, and we'll see what your mother has to say about it!'

The guards marched past them as he whirled the astonished Sefira around and hustled her willy-nilly towards an arched side alley. He heard a chuckle of wry laughter, and to keep up the masquerade shook her so hard that he nearly knocked her off her feet. 'There'll be no more of this nonsense, you wretched child; not while I am head of the household!'

The detachment went by. And before Sefira – or Xai – could recover and resist him, Perlion dragged her into the alley and out of sight of the main thoroughfare.

They stumbled together under the arch, and suddenly Sefira's wits came back. She uttered a furious screech and twisted in his grasp, so suddenly and so fast that Perlion was caught unawares. He lost his hold; she lunged to get away, and he made a desperate grab for her. His fingers closed on a fold of her cloak and she lurched backwards, off balance, and fell to the ground. Perlion pounced, kneeling over her and pinning her arms, and she glared up at him with a mad malevolence that seemed to drill through his skull.

'Let me go. *Let me go, or I will kill you!*'

Perlion's lip curled. 'I'm not frightened of you, Xai.' And, incredibly, he wasn't, for Sefira meant far more to him than his own safety. 'You won't have her,' he continued, breathing hard. 'I'll see her destroyed rather than let you and your filthy taint take her over!'

Sefira was suddenly quiet in his grip. She looked at him, and the blue faded from her eyes, leaving them brown and familiar and . . . beseeching.

'Father . . .' she said in a tremulous voice. 'Father, please . . . don't let her control me. It hurts so . . . Oh, Father, *help me . . .*'

Compassion and relief flooded through Perlion. He relaxed his hold, started to sit up—

And with a rabid snarl Sefira jackknifed, her fingernails slashing out at his unprotected eyes.

Perlion yelled, and only pure reflex saved him as he thrust her arms backwards so that the savage strike went wide. Sefira writhed with unhuman strength; she was breaking his grasp on her, and in the heat of the moment there was only one thing he could do. Chivalry and principle forgotten, one fist snapped back and he flung a full-blooded punch at her jaw.

Sefira dropped like a sack of flour, and Perlion nursed his knuckles and stared down at her, bemused and chagrined. To hit a woman . . . but he shook the self-disgust off, reminding himself of what he had been dealing with. Grendon, he gathered, had been forced to do the same once . . .

Thought of Grendon brought back his sense of urgency, and he looked quickly along the alley in both directions. No one in sight; well and good. Further along, deeper in the gloom, some barrels had been stacked and left. From the look of them they had been there a long time, so it would take an especially capricious turn of chance for anyone to disturb them now.

He carried Sefira along the alley, hauled the lid off one of the largest barrels and, ignoring his irrational pangs of guilt at this indignity, put her inside. The lid went back on – there was enough holes to allow her to breathe – and he lifted another cask and placed it on top. Even Xai, he thought, couldn't give Sefira the strength to escape from this, and with fortune on his side she would stay unconscious for a good while anyway.

He glanced uneasily over his shoulder several times as he moved away down the alley, half-expecting to see the top cask crash to the ground and Sefira appear. But she didn't; and other fears were claiming his attention, demanding, imperative.

Perlion put Sefira from his mind and hastened away to the main thoroughfare and the mews square.

'They searched the house from top to bottom,' Arrine said, shivering. 'They were civil enough; I have to grant them that. But they expected to find her, and when they didn't, they tried to intimidate me into telling them where she is.'

'But you convinced them you didn't know?' Perlion took hold of her hand and squeezed it, trying to reassure.

'Yes, I think that finally they believed me. And Getha played her part very well; she put on a good show of outrage and that helped.'

Perlion nodded. 'Nonetheless, I don't think it would be wise to bring her back here; or at least not for long. Even if the house isn't searched again, you'll be watched from now on.'

He was right, Arrine knew. But where else could they find a safe hiding place? Sefira was their responsibility now, and she didn't know what to do.

Perlion had learned enough at the palace to allow them to piece the rest of the story together. Grendon had been imprisoned, and the hunt was on for his wife, who had disappeared. No one knew what their supposed crime was, though wild rumours were rife, but King Karel had ordered that the search should take priority over everything else. To Arrine, that could only mean one thing: somehow, Karel had found out the truth about Sefira.

And Sefira had tried to go to the palace. *I'm going to see the king*, she had told Perlion. It could only be Xai's doing. But what did she *want*?

Perlion was speaking again, and with an effort Arrine made herself snap out of her thoughts and listen.

'. . . and I learned from Grendon that sleeping is one matter, but if she is completely unconscious the demon can't reach her mind at all.'

'What?' Arrine floundered, then caught the gist of his words. 'Oh – oh, yes. Xai can control her in sleep, but not, as you say, while she is unconscious. If her mind is closed down, the demon has no power at all.'

'Ah. So when she comes round – that will be the dangerous time.'

She saw what he was implying. As soon as she had control of Sefira again, Xai would be out for vengeance . . .

'She must be kept unconscious,' Perlion said urgently. 'A herb, a tincture – anything that will work. Do you have such things?'

'Nothing strong enough; only sleeping draughts.' Arrine frowned, thinking. Something in the past, a memory of what Lendrer had done . . .

'Wine!' she said suddenly. 'The strongest wine, and as much as we can make her drink – that will work. If the host is drunk, the parasite is kept at bay, for the mind it tries to influence is too befogged to function. Sefira doesn't drink; Xai has seen to that. So it should be easy enough to intoxicate her.'

'The fumes in the barrel will probably have done that already,' Perlion said, wryly but with a degree of relief. 'However, that still leaves the question of where to hide her.' He spread his hands helplessly. 'If we were in Chalce it would be different, but here I have nowhere.'

'Nor I. There are Grendon's old rooms, of course, but they will be watched as surely as this house.'

'There must be *something* . . .' Perlion began in frustration.

Suddenly Arrine's face lit eagerly. 'There is!'

'What? Where?'

She turned to him. 'Perlion, your cousin's estates supply wine among other things, do they not?'

'Yes; though grain is their mainstay. I'm sorry, Arrine, I don't—'

'The wine season hasn't quite ended, so there must still be some transportation to and from the city. How is it carried?'

'By wagon,' Perlion told her. 'In . . .' His voice tailed off and his eyes widened. 'In *casks* . . .'

'A wagon,' she said. 'A wagon, and a single load of casks. Can you procure them without arousing your cousin's suspicions?'

Pulse quickening, Perlion waved the question away. 'I don't need to go to such lengths. Empty casks are sent back to Vinor's estates almost daily, to be re-used.' He smiled. 'Vinor does not believe in waste. And one more barrel among so many will not be noticed.' Then his face clouded. 'But where can she be taken, Arrine?'

'As to that,' Arrine said, remembering the tale Grendon had told her of his first meeting with Sefira, 'I have an answer.'

The holding room had one small, barred window at ground

level, enough to let in a miserable trickle of daylight but not sufficient for Grendon to judge how much time had passed. Not that he cared about time, for since the door had been closed and locked on him he had merely sat on the grimy floor, back to the wall, staring across the room at nothing.

Sefira, Arrine, Perlion and everything to do with them had been swept from his mind, and he could think, obsessively, only of one thing – Mischane, and the depth of her betrayal.

His sister; Karel's lover. He didn't doubt it; that one glimpse of them in the window of the anteroom had told the truth as clearly as if they had both screamed it in his face. How *long* had they been duping him? Could it be that they had deceived him from the start, and that all along he had been carrying out Karel's filthy work while the blackmail Karel used against him was a fiction?

There was such a fury in him that he couldn't even reach into his soul and grasp hold of it; it was rooted too deeply. His ribs ached with it, a physical pain and a black sickness in his stomach. And only one thing would ease it, he knew. To be even with them. To have revenge.

But this was not the revenge of the past; the cause for which he had intended to use Sefira. Suddenly that old desire seemed to be nothing more than an empty, profitless and abhorrent ambition; a plan created in cold blood, to be carried out equally coldly. Grendon's blood was burning now. And Sefira had no part to play; he would not manipulate her as he had been manipulated. When Karel died, *he* would be the one to strike the fatal blow.

When Karel died . . . Grendon sighed with savage contempt at himself and tilted his head back so that his skull pressed hard against the cold wall. Fine words and fine promises – but he was a prisoner, and Sefira a fugitive, and if Karel once made contact with Xai and agreed a bargain with her, the future implications for anyone who ever crossed him in the smallest way were too grotesque to think of.

And the future for Sefira was worse still.

Suddenly unable to bear the tension building up in him, Grendon got to his feet and paced across the room. Five steps. That was all he could take. Five. And the window was barred, and the door was locked, and unless he could think of *something* soon, then—

The thought collapsed as he heard a grating sound from outside. He spun round, and saw that the door was shifting on its hinges, as though someone was wrestling with the rusty bolt on the far side. Hope flared irrationally; he froze, waiting . . .

The bolt was released with a clang, and two armed and uniformed men came in. One hung back while the other beckoned impatiently.

'You're to come out. His Majesty wants to see you.'

What now? Grendon thought edgily. But it hardly mattered. At least he would be free from this cell, and that would lessen the odds against him.

'I said, out!' The guard wasn't in a mood to be patient. Grendon nodded, and with a lurching heart fell into step beside them as they marched him away.

Chapter XXI

The start of it had been unequivocally spectacular. Karel had opened the door of his private sitting room, and as he stepped over the threshold something came hurtling through the air at him, missed his left ear by a hair's breadth and smashed explosively against the wall. From behind the door, where he had instinctively ducked, Karel saw the great flower of the wine stain lose cohesion and run down the wall like blood, while a litter of shattered glass winked firelight reflections from the flagstones.

He drew a quick, trained breath, then looked rapidly round the room. It was empty. There was no assassin waiting for him. For an illogical moment he wondered if he had done something to anger Mischane . . . but that idea was ridiculous. And the room was *empty*.

The wind, he tried to tell himself. A gust had blown the curtains, knocked the flagon – *damn it, man, don't be ridiculous! The window's closed, and that flagon wasn't knocked, it was violently hurled!*

Cautiously, bewildered but keeping the feeling firmly repressed, he started to straighten.

From the fireplace came a metallic scraping noise, and Karel's eyes widened as he saw a poker rise into the air with no hand to touch it. It hovered unsteadily for a second or two, then dropped with a raucous clatter and rolled across the hearth and under the firebasket. Karel's heart pounded as he stared incredulously. *What in all the names of a hundred demons was going on?*

He turned, meaning to reach for the bell on his table and summon servants and guards. The bell was snatched away as his fingers touched it – it flew across the room, straight at the window; he heard the dull crunch of the impact, saw the bell spin in one direction and the clapper ricochet in another, and then with a noise like madly flapping wings the papers on his table were flung into the air and came raining down on him, together with a quill stand and the box of drying sand. The inkwell tipped up; Karel tried to catch it but was too late, and an indigo flood cascaded across the table's polished surface.

'What are you?' He found his voice at last, struggling against shock. 'What do you think you're about? Stop this, damn you!'

For answer, the curtains heaved as though a gale had blown in, then the rail that held them was torn from its bracket, and rail and curtains together crashed down, breaking the slender stem of a smaller table as they fell. Outside in the passage running feet sounded; Karel's voice and the falling curtains had alerted the servants, and as they approached, calling anxiously to each other and their master, Karel heard something else. A thin, high-pitched whine that seemed to come from somewhere above his head. A sound of frustration . . . and it almost, but not quite, formed recognisable words.
'*I want . . . I want . . .*'

Four servants burst in, armed with makeshift weapons. Their expressions when they saw Karel amid the chaos were so comical that the king felt a crazed urge to laugh. He forced it down and, breathing hard, said, 'Fetch the guards on duty. Tell them to bring Grendon here to me. *Now!*'

When Grendon entered the room, he was greeted by the basket of logs. Karel had seen it rise, hesitate as though the invisible hand were aiming it, and it gave him bleak satisfaction to witness Grendon's shock as the entire basket, logs spinning everywhere, was flung straight at his head. With an oath Grendon dodged, fending the basket off with one arm. And a shrill, angry buzzing swelled deafeningly for a second or two before fading into silence.

Grendon and the king stared at each other. Karel was breathless, dishevelled. One sleeve of his shirt was torn – something had grabbed it and ripped it from shoulder to elbow – and there was sand in his hair and wine on his clothing – three flagons had so far been smashed – and scorch marks on his hands from where he had thrust two blazing logs back into the fire when they were hurled out. The room was a wreckage of strewn papers and broken furniture and glass. And Grendon knew instantly what had happened.

Karel glared ferociously at him and snarled, 'Can you stop this?'

Grendon's eyes narrowed. 'If I choose to.'

'Damn you, if you don't then I'll—' He got no further, for the poker, now red-hot under the firebasket, suddenly hurtled across the room at ankle level, and both men leaped, startled, out of its path. It landed on a rug, which began to smoulder, and with a foul oath Karel kicked it on to the stone floor where it could do no harm.

'Do something,' he said to Grendon, 'or I'll kill you myself!'

For a moment their gazes held and clashed. Then Grendon said curtly, 'Move back. As close to the wall as you can.'

As Karel obeyed, Grendon focused his mind. This would be relatively easy to deal with, for he knew full well why and how it had happened. Xai had been trying to communicate with the king, but had found she could not break through to the mortal world. Thwarted, she had gone into a frenzy, trying to attract Karel's attention and at the same time vent her frustration on anything and everything she could reach. But the one thing she wanted to control – Sefira – was beyond her power. Sefira's mind must be closed down . . . and that led him to an unpleasant but, he believed, inevitable conclusion. Karel's searchers had found her, and in the struggle to capture her she had been hurt. She must be under guard somewhere in the palace, senseless and helpless. His anger rekindled, and he wanted to strangle Karel with his own hands. But to try would be futile; he must deal with Xai, and only then might there be a chance to salvage this situation.

It took him a little over five minutes to break the link that the demon had managed to form. Without Sefira to act as her medium Xai was weak; bar a few more abortive sallies she put up no resistance, and Grendon was able to astrally seal the room. When it was done, he looked at Karel and said:

'She won't return.'

Karel licked his lips uneasily. 'She . . . ?'

'Xai. The soul-invader whose acquaintance you're so anxious to make.'

Karel sucked air into his lungs. 'If you were responsible—'

'The responsibility's yours, not mine. It was you she was trying to reach. No doubt she's as eager as you are to make a bargain; but unfortunately, at the moment, she's unable to manifest directly, so she decided to take out her temper on this room instead.'

Karel's eyes narrowed. 'Why can't she manifest?'

'You should know.' Grendon's anger rekindled. 'It must have been your men who knocked Sefira unconscious.'

'My men who—?' Karel stopped then, but too late; he hadn't been able to mask his surprise in time, and Grendon realised that his own assumption had been wrong. Sefira had not been captured. Instead, Arrine must have realised the danger that Xai posed, and had done something to render Sefira senseless. Silently praising her wisdom, Grendon thought rapidly. Arrine's house must have been searched by now, so where had Sefira been taken? There was only one way to find out. He had to regain his freedom.

Karel was walking slowly around his desk, looking with distaste at the debris of Xai's tantrum. 'Don't think,' he said in a carefully controlled voice, 'that I won't find her.'

Grendon made a sceptical sound at the back of his throat. 'And when you do, Karel, what then? How do you intend to control what you unleash?'

The king stopped, turned and regarded him with open enmity. There was no pretence between them now; Grendon had dropped the mask of subservience together with the dropping of his title, and for the first time in two years they were facing each other on straightforward terms.

'The cold fact is,' Grendon went on, 'that you need me, because you can't cope with Xai alone. This,' he indicated the demolished furnishings, 'is nothing by comparison to what she's really capable of. Cross her once, and you'll find that out for yourself. So I have a hold over you. Of course, you could have me put to death, and I don't doubt you're considering it right at this moment. However, if you kill me you'll have to kill Sefira too, or she might run amok one day and there'll be no one to help you. But . . .' He was gambling, he knew; putting this idea into Karel's head might be the most foolish move he had ever made. Yet intuition said otherwise, and as always he trusted intuition. 'But I think she's just a little too useful to you. Just a little too *tempting.*'

For a while there was no other sound but the hiss of Karel's breathing. Then, tightly, he said, 'What do you want?'

'Freedom to find Sefira, without the intervention of you and your men.'

'I see. And when you find her?'

Grendon knew he had to act his part convincingly. Karel wasn't aware of what he had seen in the window of the anteroom, and provided he could keep his anger in check, that little deception could now be turned back upon him. He paused, giving the impression that he was reluctant to admit to something and that the words he was about to speak would cost him dearly. Then he said, slipping what he hoped was a plausible note of resentment into his voice:

'I want our original bargain kept. *All* of it.'

'Our orig—' Then Karel stopped. He smiled, and as Grendon saw the gleam of triumph that crept into his eyes, he knew that the ploy had worked. 'Ah, yes,' the king said.

'The lady Mischane . . . So you want her freedom in exchange for Sefira's.'

'If you care to phrase it like that.'

'I do. And I think I can be accommodating; although perhaps there will need to be one or two little . . . adjustments to our pact, simply as a precaution.' He raised a querying eyebrow, challenging Grendon to argue, but Grendon said nothing.

'Very well.' Karel picked up an ink-soaked scroll, looking at it for a moment then dropped it back on the table. 'I'll not have you followed. Bring Sefira back to the palace, and we'll talk again. But Grendon . . . don't try to trick me. It would not be good for your sister's welfare.'

Grendon didn't even answer that, but turned on his heel and walked to the door. The guards were outside; they moved to bar his way but Karel called to them. 'Let him go. He is a free man.'

They fell back, and the slam of the door echoed in Karel's ears.

How to make contact; that was the problem. Karel wouldn't keep his promise; there would be surveillance, and the moment he showed any sign of leading the watchers to Sefira, they would close in. As he rode along the street from the palace Grendon was sharply alert for any sign of followers, but he knew that for every one he was able to identify, there was likely to be another he would miss. Arrine's house would already be watched and he dared not go there. How, then?

His horse was excitable after days of inactivity, and now that the rain had finally stopped it resented the slow pace to which Grendon kept it. Several times it snatched the reins through his hands and performed a skittish, sidelong dance across the road, shaking its head irritably, and on the fourth occasion Grendon was still wresting it back under control when someone hurrying along the pavement veered suddenly into his path. Horse and hastening figure collided and rebounded, and Grendon was about to demand what in the name of perdition the stranger thought he was doing when the man looked up and he saw his face.

'*Perlion!*' Fortunately Grendon had the wit to mute his shocked exclamation to a whisper, and Perlion made a show of stumbling backwards and almost losing his balance.

'Have a care, sir!' he said loudly and indignantly. 'That horse should be under better control!' And in an undertone he added, '*Dismount – pretend to be helping me!*'

Grendon sprang down from the saddle. '*Perlion, what—*'

He was interrupted in an urgent hiss. '*Are you being followed?*'

'*I've no doubt of it.*' Grendon yanked on the reins, making the horse jump and skitter in protest, then raised his voice. 'Sir, my apologies! The damned animal hasn't been exercised for days. Are you hurt? *Perlion, there's no time to explain everything. Where's Sefira?*'

'*Safe. She left the city an hour ago. In a wine barrel.*'

'*What?*'

'*Never mind, never mind.* No, sir, I'm well enough; and the fault was entirely mine. I thought to cross to the other side of the street, and I neglected to look . . . *Do you know the old watchtower south of the city, a mile from the curve in the river?*'

'*I know it.*'

'*Sefira's there. It was Arrine's idea, and she's gone with her.*' He brushed energetically at his sleeve. 'No, no; it's nothing that won't come off. No damage, I assure you. *Can you evade your watchers and join them?*'

He didn't know, but . . . '*Yes.*'

'*I'll be there later this evening. Good luck, my friend.*'

They exchanged another courteous apology for appearances' sake, then Grendon remounted and they went their separate ways. As the horse clattered on down the paved road Grendon felt sweat on his face and neck. Perlion must have been looking out for him. And as Karel knew nothing of his connection with the Lander, it had been a simple matter for him to engineer the collision and pass on his hasty message.

The old watchtower . . . Grendon knew it well. Since the war it had fallen into disuse. It was the perfect hiding place.

Now, though, he had the problem of getting out of the city with Karel's men none the wiser. As he rode his mind worked on the problem, and by the time the surrounding wall of the royal quarter came in sight he had the outline of a scheme. Whether or not it would work was uncertain. But if anything went wrong, he could always turn to more drastic measures . . .

The guards had seen him and were opening the gate. With a nod of acknowledgement Grendon rode through and out into the city streets.

The inn wasn't far from the docks, and was large enough and crowded enough to arouse suspicion in Karel's spies, as Grendon intended. He ordered a mug of ale and sat drinking it near the window, feigning to watch surreptitiously for someone or something. Then after a while he rose casually and went to speak with the innmaster. Money changed hands, and when the innmaster was questioned after Grendon's departure he would say truthfully that his customer had asked him to pass on a passage fee to a certain barger who was sailing upriver on the late afternoon tide. That would take the hunt in the opposite direction from the watchtower. Now, all Grendon had to do was get away from the inn undetected.

It proved easier than he had feared. His horse was in the adjoining stables, and to keep up the fiction he had created he went out to the yard and negotiated a few days' livery fee with the head stableman. He had no doubt that the youth loitering at the yard entrance was a king's man and that he had overheard the discussion, so when Grendon disappeared into the stable, ostensibly to see his horse settled, the watcher didn't follow him.

There was a boy forking hay in the stable, but he was half-witted and only grinned foolishly, tongue lolling, as Grendon took off his horse's harness and settled it into a stall. No danger there . . . Grendon looked around at the other animals and saw a tall, grey mare at the far end of the line, with a green blanket flung over her back. The mare's colour was a complete contrast to that of his own horse, and the blanket could easily be made to look like a cloak . . .

Minutes later, the grey and her rider left. The loitering youth glanced up, but briefly; the hooded figure on the mare's back wore green, not black, and from the look of his belly he'd been overfeeding himself for years past. Yawning, he resumed his stance as Grendon rode sedately out of the yard.

As they left the last straggling buildings of Tourmon behind, Grendon gave thanks for the fact that the city's outer wall had not been rebuilt after the war. Karel professed not to believe in walls and curfews and their like – though the wall around the royal quarter seemed to be a convenient exception to that rule – and no one had challenged him or even given him more than a passing glance. Now, finally, he was clear of the city. He felt queasy with relief.

Half a mile from the perimeter he stopped for long enough to remove the straw that he had stuffed under his clothes to give him a portly shape, then he remounted and set the mare at an efficient but careful pace over the darkening landscape. Thunder was muttering far away to the west, and from the feel of the wind the storm would head this way. No matter; he would reach shelter before then.

The watchtower came in sight as the last of the light faded. By this time the thunder was louder and an occasional flicker of lightning showed on the horizon. Grendon recalled Sefira's terror of storms and smiled a little grimly. By the time tonight was over, she would have experienced something far worse. If she survived it – if either of them survived it – then she would never fear mere weather again.

He had reached his final decision almost unconsciously as he rode. In reality he suspected that his mind had resolved on it long before then; possibly since the moment when he had realised the truth about Mischane. The bitter anger that gnawed at him through the hours of his imprisonment had not only swept away the detritus of confusion, it had also clarified his conscience. His *principles*. Not the principles of family loyalty, nor of fealty to a Fellowship. Though he would never before have admitted it, there had been as much corruption among the Sanctifieds as among any other caste; if not more. It didn't even have more than the most tenuous connection with Karel and his ruthless methods. No; this was something still more personal. His own code. His own sense of what was *right*. And at the hub of it was one memory that he could not shake off. Sefira's face in the crumbling doorway, and her desperate plea as she recognised that he was the only human being in the world who could help her.

The tower loomed above him as he slowed the mare to a walk and then to a halt. The thunder had ceased temporarily, and only the soft voice of the wind broke the silence as he carefully surveyed the scene. The tower's windows were shuttered, but a chink of light showed. And the door stood ajar. Grendon slid from the saddle, suddenly weary to the bone, and led the mare through the entrance. As he entered, a trapdoor was lifted above his head and a voice called softly, 'Who's there?'

'It's Grendon, Arrine.'

'Grendon . . . oh, thank the fates you're safe! Come up, quickly!'

He climbed the rickety steps, and emerged into a scene of strange, almost domestic comfort. Arrine had brought blankets, candles, food, utensils; the bare tower room was transformed into a small haven. And in the midst of it all lay Sefira. She was, Grendon realised, dead drunk.

'It was the only thing I could think of,' Arrine said apologetically. 'I was so afraid that Xai would return.'

'She did, after a fashion. It was what gained me my freedom.' Grendon told her the story of Xai's attack on Karel and what it had led to. And he told her about Mischane. Arrine listened, her eyes solemn, and when he finished she shook her head sadly.

'Oh, my dear, I'm sorry. So sorry. That she should prove so treacherous . . .' She laid a gentle hand on his arm. 'Truly, Grendon, I don't know what to say.'

He uttered a short, self-conscious laugh. 'Please, Arrine; I don't want sympathy. I don't *need* it.' He scrubbed at his face with a tired hand. 'In one sense, I owe Mischane a debt. You see, thanks to her I've decided what to do about Sefira.'

Arrine stilled. She remembered Sefira's one question, and the answer she had been unable to give. 'What do you mean?' she asked softly.

Grendon looked at the girl lying so inert and silent. 'I talk of debts,' he said. 'This is another. The debt I owe to Lendrer, and to you.'

'I don't understand.'

'Don't you? You should, Arrine. You and he saved my life when I was seventeen. Years later, when Lendrer was taken, I wasn't able to . . . to return that favour. But now, I can repay you in another way. By giving to Sefira what Lendrer gave to me.' A ghost of a wry smile caught at his mouth. 'Or trying to.'

Arrine's eyes were steady on his face. 'You're going to try to destroy Xai . . .'

'Yes. I know I've a slender chance of succeeding; I don't have the half of Lendrer's skill. But I'm going to *try*. And if it kills us both, well . . .' He looked at her, a strangely candid look. 'As matters stand, we both have short lives to look forward to anyway.'

Most people who loved him as Arrine did, he knew, would have tried to dissuade him. But Arrine made no protest. She only smiled warmly, proudly at him, and said, 'I understand now, my dear. Only tell me what you want of me, and I will do it.'

For some moments they were still, silent, simply looking into each other's faces without need for words. Then Grendon sighed softly and his gaze fell away.

'Perlion should be here soon,' he said. 'We'll wait until he comes. And then I'll begin . . .'

Chapter XXII

'It's no use,' Grendon said. 'Her mind's too far out of Xai's reach: I can't get through.'

Arrine and Perlion exchanged a troubled look, and Sefira rolled over and muttered something incoherent.

'It's my fault,' Arrine said unhappily. 'I gave her too much wine.'

Grendon shook his head. 'You couldn't have judged; no one could. And too much was safer than too little.' He sighed and flexed his shoulders, forcing some of the tension out of them. 'I'll simply have to wait a little longer, and then try again.'

He moved back to where he could lean against the tower wall, and closed his eyes. He was in no fit state for this; too tired and not sufficiently prepared. But if he let the moment pass, he was afraid that doubt would set in, and where doubt took root it was a sure road to failure.

He had heard the whole story of Sefira's and Arrine's escape from Tourmon, and under other circumstances it would have been absurdly comical. A consignment of empty casks bound for Vinor's estates, and Perlion had spun both his cousin and the wagon driver a fine tale about a surprise present for Isbel which must be hidden in some out-of-the-way place until he was ready to reveal it. Thus two heavy casks had been loaded along with the lighter ones, and Perlion had cheerfully supervised the loading whilst talking of weather and money and the fine sights of Tourmon, aware that Arrine was huddled in one barrel and Sefira, kept senseless by the whole flagon of

287

wine that he had forced down her throat, lay oblivious of the world in another. Amid much jesting and mock secrecy the wagon had been sent on its way, and the driver had delivered his extra consignment to the watchtower, hauled the two barrels up the stairs with a great deal of colourful cursing, and resumed his journey happy in the knowledge that Perlion's generous bonus was safe in his pocket.

Now, it was nearly midnight. Perlion had arrived later than promised – some small difficulty in making his excuses, he explained – and Grendon had made his first attempt to rouse Sefira from her stupor sufficiently for Xai to manifest. It would be, he suspected, an hour or two yet before she would be coherent again, and the prospect of trying to stay awake until then wasn't one he relished. Yet he didn't want to sleep. Sleep would fog his mind, and that, like doubt, would be disastrous.

Perlion, who had watched him for the last few minutes and had a shrewd idea of his condition, said suddenly, 'Grendon, I think I'd like to walk outside; get a little air. Will you join me?'

Grendon raised his head and rubbed at sore eyes. 'Yes. Yes, I will. Arrine, if you don't mind . . . ?'

'Of course not. Don't fear; I'll keep a close watch on Sefira.'

The two men went down the stairs, checked briefly on their horses, then walked a little stiffly outside into the night. The storm had passed by some miles to the north and now seemed to have dispersed, and the land was still and quiet and peaceful. They wandered slowly, not speaking but with a companionable mood between them, across the turf, not with any destination in mind but simply appreciating the refreshing chill, until at length Perlion broke the silence.

'Grendon, when this is over . . . and if, of course, it's successful . . . what will you do?'

By 'you' he meant primarily Sefira, Grendon knew; but the question applied to them both. It was ironic, he thought. He was still legally Sefira's husband, and so her future was theoretically in his hands. But Perlion had a much older and more rightful claim. Besides, the marriage was a sham, and they both knew it; Sefira would not want to stay with him, nor he with her.

Yet how in all conscience could he surrender her to Perlion? Whatever the outcome of this, if she survived tonight she would be a fugitive, and though he knew the Lander wanted desperately to take responsibility for her, to do so would be to put himself and the rest of his family in jeopardy. Grendon, too, would have no future in this country, and the plan he had made to take Mischane far enough away from Karel's influence to be able to begin a new life was now his only hope of redemption.

And possibly Sefira's.

He said, 'I truly don't know, Perlion.' Nor did he even want to try to answer the question; not yet. In the faint nightglow he glanced at the Lander's face, saw the thoughtfulness and apprehension and uncertainty mirrored there, and smiled. 'But I make you one pledge now. Sefira's future will be as much yours to decide as it is mine.'

Perlion returned the smile with hesitant appreciation. 'Thank you,' he said. 'That is – very generous.'

Grendon was about to reply that it was nothing of the kind, but as he opened his mouth something made him pause. A flicker of faint light in the distance, towards Tourmon. No more than a will-o'-the-wisp over marshy ground probably, but nonetheless he felt a faint stirring of disquiet.

'Perlion.' He touched the other man's shoulder, nodding in the direction where the glimmer had shown. 'Over there; a mile or so distant at a guess. Do you see anything?'

Perlion peered. 'No, I don't think . . .' Then he tensed. 'Wait – I saw a light. Very faint, but . . . look, there it is again! Like a reflection of water.'

On his way to the tower, Grendon had ridden through several wide, shallow sheets of water that the rain had left lying where the ground was low. Even under the cloud the splashes kicked up by the grey mare's hoofs had refracted into a thousand glittering droplets, and the spectral glimmer in the distance looked unnervingly like that same phenomenon.

Perlion said uneasily, 'You don't think . . .'

'I don't know. But I don't like the sign.' Grendon looked swiftly at him. 'Your wagon driver – was he trustworthy?'

'So far as it's ever possible to tell with his kind. But he went on southwards, not back to the city, so even if he had suspected anything amiss he wasn't there for the king's men to question.' Then Perlion tensed. 'But the other servant . . . oh, by the fates! He was hovering about while the loading was going on; I sent him away because he's well-known as a snooper and a gossip. It's possible – just possible – that he might have seen something.'

Grendon stared out over the grass. The glimmering was perceptibly closer, and he thought of what one tattling servant and a stolen grey mare could add up to in Karel's mind. The barge on which he had booked passage might have been searched before it left the docks, and no trace of its supposed passenger found. And Karel wouldn't fail to follow up even the most unlikely clues.

Abruptly, he made a decision. This might be nothing; just the wind ruffling the shallow pools' surface. But he didn't think so, for the movement wasn't random enough. And he wasn't about to take any chances.

'Perlion.' Though they were too far away to be glimpsed as yet, he started to draw the Lander back towards the tower. 'I think we should prepare a contingency, and quickly.'

Perlion nodded. They had discussed the outline of a strategy earlier, agreeing that although it had its risks it was probably the best that could be achieved if anything went awry. Now, it seemed, it was about to be put to the test.

They backed a few more paces, still watching. Then at a quiet word from Grendon they turned and ran back towards the tower.

Sefira pushed Arrine's arm away with a petulant movement

and said indistinctly, 'Nuh . . . leavemelone . . . want to *sleep*.'

She curled up again into a tight huddle, and Arrine looked helplessly at Grendon. 'I can't make her understand!'

Grendon suspected that there was a little more to Sefira's stubbornness than met the eye. She was recovering rapidly from her stupor; enough to have paved the way for Xai's return. And Xai had her own reasons for wanting the approaching horsemen to find them.

There was no doubt now that their whereabouts had been discovered. A minute ago the cloud had broken briefly, allowing the moon to shine through, and by its light they had seen the silhouettes on the moor. Some eight or ten mounted figures, riding cautiously but covering the ground fast enough to give them little time to escape. Thankfully the cloud cover had thickened again and the tower had a second door on its south side; when they made their break its bulk would shield them – but not for long.

Perlion, hovering near the top of the stairway, said agitatedly, 'They'll be here within minutes – we *must* make her move!'

Sefira uttered an ugly sound halfway between a scream and a laugh. She would fight them again if they tried to force her into action, and there was no more wine left to give her. Grendon reached out, meaning to grasp her arms and make one last attempt – then stopped, realising that this was futile and they were losing valuable moments. They must take another course.

'Arrine.' His voice was suddenly curt. 'You used to ride. Can you still sit a horse at speed?'

She was startled by the question. 'Yes – I think so. I'm fit enough for my age.'

'Then you and Perlion must go without us. They're probably not expecting to see more than two horses, so if you make a break in sight of them, most will follow you. One or two might investigate the tower, but I'll deal with them.'

Arrine looked at him fearfully. 'It's a terrible risk, Grendon.

If you're wrong, and they all turn here instead—'

'They'll do that anyway unless they have another quarry, and with Sefira as she is we'll all be trapped. Don't argue with me, either of you. Go, *now!*'

Perlion said, 'Arrine, he's right. It's our only hope.'

Arrine hesitated. Then her uncertainty gave way to something stronger, and her face set resolutely. 'Good fortune go with you,' she said, and made a sign in Grendon's direction. Then she and Perlion were gone, as Grendon moved to snuff out the candles.

Karel stared ahead at the ponderous mass of the tower, and tried to quell the belligerent excitement that was building in him. The pursuit wasn't over yet, and it was still possible that this would prove to be a wild-goose chase. But his doubts were small. The theft at the inn had given them the first clue, then there had been a valuable snippet concerning a wagon that had recently left the city, and lastly Arrine's servant, Getha, had proved to be exceedingly cooperative once faced with the Confessor and his implements. He was glad that words alone had been enough to convince her of wisdom. And what she revealed had been enough to complete a likely picture.

Karel had been unable to resist the temptation to ride with the search party. He wanted not only to witness the outcome but to be the prime mover in its achievement. Seven men rode with him, and now, as they neared the tower, their leader looked to his liege for instructions. At a nod the troop was waved from their rapid trot to a slow walk, and Karel studied the building carefully. No gleam of light anywhere, but that proved nothing. A pity that there was no way to judge whether their approach had been seen, or—

His musing was shattered as one of the men gave a yell, and from the far side of the tower two shapes erupted. One light, one dark – horses; a grey and a bay, with muffled figures hunched on their backs, spurring them into a desperate gallop away from the tower and the oncoming men.

Karel bellowed, 'TAKE THEM!' and the troop surged forward with the king in the lead. As they swept round the curve of the stone wall Karel shouted to the nearest rider, 'The tower, man! Check the tower, then follow us!' and two horses peeled off and slithered to a halt, their riders scrambling down and running towards the door as the rest of the party vanished into the night.

Inside the tower, in the deepest darkness between the empty stalls and the ladder of the stairs, Grendon held his breath and listened to the approaching footfalls. His hand flexed around the short but heavy metal bar he held, and he waited, tense but motionless. The door opened; two figures were silhouetted against the night sky. One started to explore the stalls, while the other moved towards the stairs, looking upwards.

From above came a thud, and Sefira's voice rose in a strange, shrill giggle.

With an oath the men both ran for stairs. They were completely unaware of Grendon's presence until the moment when he slid out from behind them and brought the metal bar down with a dull, sick sound, first on one head and then, before the second man could turn in shock, on the other. They slumped, and Grendon stared down at their vague shapes huddled on the floor. It was as likely as not that he had killed them, for he had struck hard, but he was past caring. All he could think of was Arrine and Perlion fleeing into the night in their attempt to lead the other pursuers away. That, and what awaited him on the upper level . . .

Another thud overhead was followed by a slithering sound, as though Sefira was trying to drag something across the floor. Grendon turned, and moved quickly and quietly back up the stairs. He had closed the trapdoor, and when he tried to push it open, it resisted. Sefira – or Xai – was trying to shut him out, barricade herself away from him, and tensing his muscles Grendon shoved, violently, against the door. There was a cry of anger, the noise of something shifting, and the door jolted

open. Grendon scrambled up the last few steps into the room
– and stopped.

Sefira was in the middle of the floor, braced on hands and
knees. Even in the gloom he could see that she had stripped
off her clothing and crouched naked, like an animal, her shorn
hair falling unkempt over her face and her skin glistening with
sweat. She breathed harshly, steadily, each exhalation rattling
in her throat and echoing ominously in the tower's close
confines, and through her hair's tendrils he saw that her eyes
were glittering a hard, unnatural blue.

He still held the metal bar, and his gaze slid to it, though to
use it would be a last and desperate resort. Then, carefully, he
moved one foot forward.

She snarled like a rabid dog, a warning and a threat, and
he saw her hands tense as though she was about to spring.

'Sefira.' He kept his voice level. 'Sefira, listen to me. Try
to—'

'*I listen to no one!*' The voice was ferocious, and so unlike
Sefira's own that he knew he would not be able to reach even
a part of her mind. In the brief minutes of his absence Xai
had made her move, and had crushed her host's will so
completely that she was beyond help. He was not dealing
with Sefira now. He was dealing only with the demon.

He spoke again. 'Very well, Xai. There's no point in fencing,
is there? You know why Sefira was brought here, and what I
intend to do.'

Sefira's body quivered and a low, rumbling growl began
somewhere deep in her throat. '*I will kill you, Grendon,*' she
said thickly. '*I have been waiting for this moment – and I will kill
you!*'

'I don't think so. I've seen your kind destroyed before,
remember.'

She uttered a truncated shriek. '*I know that! I know! But
this time you will not succeed! Sefi will strike! Sefi will kill!*'

'Sefi will not!' Grendon snapped back, deliberately lacing
his voice with a sneer. 'For if she does, if you goad her to try,'

– for the first time he showed the bar in his hand, though he was careful to keep it out of Sefira's range – 'then I will use *this*. I will smash her skull, Xai. *I* will kill *her*. Do you understand?'

Yes, he thought; threaten her. Taunt and anger her. It was dangerous, for if she called his bluff she would soon learn that he wasn't prepared to translate the threat into reality. But, knowing what he did of the parasite, he thought she would not quite dare to take the risk.

'What will you do then, Xai?' he continued. 'You can't survive without Sefira to feed you and nurture you and provide you with a link to this world. You'll wither. You'll shrivel. You'll follow where the filth that infected me went, into oblivion! And all I have to do . . .' He hefted the bar. 'All I have to do is strike *once*.'

For a single instant, no more, the aberrant blue of the crouching girl's eyes wavered, and in that moment Grendon saw Sefira's dark gaze, filled with terror and pain and bewilderment, break through. Then it vanished, and Xai said ferociously:

'*You will not dare . . . I know. I know you.*'

'You know *nothing*,' Grendon countered scornfully. 'What is your precious Sefira to me? I was willing to pay any price to save my own life from your kind once; do you think I'd not do the same again? Don't doubt me, Xai. It makes no difference to me whether Sefira lives or dies – all I care about is ridding the world of you!'

Yet even as he spoke he knew that this verbal circling and sparring was leading him inexorably towards an impasse. Xai's strength had increased greatly with the murder of Kessie; in the past he could have fought her on the astral plane, but now if he tried she would certainly defeat him. The binding and the destruction must be done in the physical world. But for that, he had to have Sefira's cooperation – and Xai's hold on her host was too powerful now for that to be possible. The link between them had to be weakened, and short of killing

Sefira he could think of no way to achieve it.

Sefira was breathing more rapidly now, as though the creature within her was becoming excited. Xai hadn't responded to Grendon's last taunt, but suddenly she said, '*I see into your heart, Grendon. I see what is there. For all your brave words, you are afraid of us now.*' She giggled shrilly. '*When your friends killed the other one of my kind, they first made him weak. They would not allow him to feed. You would like to do that to me. Days. It would take many days, and Sefi would scream and cry and plead, just as you did all those years ago. You might do that, Grendon; you might be ready to watch her suffering like that. But you haven't enough time, have you? The men will come back. The king will come back. He will catch you. He will kill you. And he will take Sefi to the palace again, and then we will be safe!*'

She was enjoying her mockery and his discomfort – but abruptly Grendon realised that she had inadvertently let something slip. Just a hint, and he couldn't be certain, but . . .

He chose his words very carefully, aware that his pulse had started to race at a disconcerting speed. 'The king?' he said derisively. 'The king isn't interested in you. He has better things to concern him.'

'*Oh, you think. You say. But I know.*'

Grendon laughed and, as he had hoped, it provoked Xai to anger. '*I KNOW!*' she shouted; then her voice took on a smugly challenging note. '*If the king is not interested in me, why does he ride with his men now? For he does, Grendon. He is with them. He is taking a very great interest indeed!*'

Karel, with the guardsmen? The possibility hadn't occurred to Grendon before, but it made sense. Karel would want to ensure that nothing went wrong. More to the point, he would want to savour the triumph of the capture personally.

Suddenly, through the mad eyes and twisted expression of the creature crouching on the floor, he saw in his mind something else; an image of the real Sefira overlaid on the mask Xai was forcing her to wear. Just a woman. His wife. Once, just once, he had truly reached her, when she cried out to him for help and reached out willingly to cling to him. If he could make that happen again . . .

He smiled a slow, almost lazy smile. 'Xai,' he said softly. 'You are a fool.'

She hissed. '*Not so!*'

'It is so. You've given something away that it would have been wiser not to reveal. You've told me that the king is riding with his men, and that is very useful to me.' He paused. 'Do you remember what I told you I wished to do to the king?'

Sefira's eyes narrowed. Xai said ominously. '*Ah, no . . .*'

'Ah, *yes.* I shall prepare a welcome for him. One he won't live long enough to remember.'

Sefira's mouth opened and she started to growl again. The threatening sound built up; he saw her arm and leg muscles tense, her shoulders go back.

'No, Xai! Not if you value your life!' He swung the bar, gripping it in both hands and brandishing it challengingly. Sefira's eyes fixed on it, then the snarl rose to a frustrated scream and she hunched back, angrily defensive. *Good*, he thought, *good . . .*

Xai said, '*You will not kill the king.*'

'Him, or Sefira. It doesn't matter to me. Or perhaps both – then I can be rid of two evils.'

She spat at him. '*No!*'

He shrugged, laughed. But he was still watching Sefira carefully, and from her changing face could see that the demon was in a quandary. She looked on Karel's protection as a safe haven from where she could continue her predations unchecked, and the prospect of losing that haven alarmed her. *If only*, he thought, *she will do what I want her to . . .*

Suddenly Sefira's mouth opened wide; she tilted her head up, shut her eyes and uttered a yell of blind fury that reverberated through the tower. The psychic force of it made Grendon rock backwards – then a grey, translucent cone of mist streamed from Sefira and whirled towards the window. An ice-cold gust knifed across the room; the shutters rattled violently – and with a gasp Sefira collapsed to the floor.

'Sefira!' Dropping the metal bar Grendon ran to her and knelt at her side, cupping one hand under her head and lifting it gently. 'Sefira, can you hear me? Can you speak?'

Her eyes opened. They were brown again, and filled with pain, shock and confusion. She said unsteadily, 'Grendon . . . ?' Then her mouth distorted and tears welled.

'There's no time for that!' He gripped her shoulders and pulled her into a sitting position. '*Listen* to me! Do you want to be free of Xai? Do you want to see her destroyed?'

A new intensity crept into her look as she took in his words. Then: 'Y-yes. *Yes!*' A violent shudder went through her. 'I remember, Grendon. I remember what she did. But I couldn't stop her . . .'

'I know; I know. She's released you for the moment, but she'll return soon.' How long would it take the demon to warn Karel? he asked himself. Minutes? Less? So much depended on how willing he was to listen – or how she chose to manifest to him. Another outburst like the one in the palace would buy valuable time. He had to work fast, while her attention was divided. Divide and conquer . . .

'Sefira, look at me.' She did, and her look was so innocent and trusting that doubt assailed him. Could he *do* this? He wasn't a violent man, not in the sense that would be demanded of him now. She would fight him, and she must not be allowed to win; though he would take no pleasure in her fear. *Could* take no pleasure in it. Yet there must *be* pleasure, or their last hope would crumble into ruins . . .

'Sefira,' he said, striving to control his voice, 'when we were forced to marry, I made you a promise. I promised that I would never touch you, never demand a husband's rights from you. I must break that promise. For your sake, I must break it!'

Her eyes widened. Trust vanished, and astonished disbelief took its place. Then, as she realised that this was no game, no jest, all other emotions were eclipsed by fear.

'Grendon, no – you can't! *Grendon!*'

She could say no more, for he caught hold of her hair, pulled her head towards his and kissed her so furiously, so savagely, that her body writhed with shock. *Her mouth, sweet and warm, tasting of wine . . . her hair was in his eyes, her breasts crushed against his ribs where he could feel their soft contours . . .* Grendon shut his eyes, willing his own body to respond, to rouse. He had never before taken a woman against her will; but he must, *must*—

She broke free from the kiss, gasping, trying to flail at him with her hands. 'No, Grendon, *no! Let me go!*'

'I can't!' Grabbing her wrists he pinned them against the floor. He was lying on top of her, one knee forcing between her thighs. *He must respond! She was young, ripe, desirable – she was his wife.*

'Sefira, don't fight me! Please, you have to understand – there's no time for orthodox ways, no time for what Lendrer and Arrine did for me! This is the only way to save you from Xai!'

She couldn't or wouldn't heed him. She was crying now, hysterically, squirming and struggling under him.

'Sefira—' Grendon fought to be rid of his own clothes, wanting the touch of skin on skin, the warmth, the supple softness. She was so *young* . . . and her body was beautiful. Not Xai; not a demon; just a young and lovely mortal woman. His wife. His own . . .

Suddenly he was kissing her face, her hair, her neck, her shoulders and breasts and arms; and the kisses were wild, frenetic. There was hunger in him, a longing, a craving – heat swept through him in a stunning wave, and she was so pliant under him, her writhing movements stirring him to a pitch. He knew she was struggling but told himself she was not; this wasn't fear, it was excitement, desire; she wanted him as he wanted her, *he had to make himself believe that!*

His hips were between her thighs now and her legs were convulsing; she was drawing them up in her frantic battle to throw him off, but he felt only the clasping sensation of her flesh, of his pelvis pressing into softness. He blotted from his mind her cries and pleas and sobs; they were sounds of pleasure, of *pleasure*, and together they were going to break the link and defeat Xai and see the monstrous creature turned to dust and scattered on the four winds.

'Sefira.' He uttered her name in a long-drawn groan. 'Sefira, forgive me . . . forgive me, and try to understand!'

Perhaps some import of what he was trying to tell her got through her fear and confusion, for suddenly, briefly, Sefira was still. Their eyes met. What she saw in his gaze he would never know, but in hers he recognised the pain and misery of what she believed to be the ultimate betrayal.

'It isn't a betrayal, Sefira,' he said softly. 'Never, *never* that.'

His mouth covered hers again, cherishing the kiss now with a passion that swamped his mind. He moved carefully, smoothly; for a moment there was resistance, and then with a sigh that fanned warm breath across her face he entered her, breaking the chain with which Xai had bound her.

And a shriek like the voice of a hurricane, deranged, tumultuous, insane with rage, exploded out of the astral world and stunningly into his mind.

Chapter XXIII

When Karel's horse suddenly whinnied in terror and reared high, Karel was almost unseated. With a yell he wrenched on the reins, dragging the animal back under control and groping for a lost stirrup, and heard his sergeant's shout of alarmed query from a short way off.

'Sir! Are you all right?'

Mouth opening to call back, Karel froze as he felt something touch his waist. *Fingers* . . . Then, stunning him, a voice whispered out of the air at his back.

'*King Karel . . . King Karel . . .*'

Very, very slowly, Karel turned his head, and saw what was sitting behind him on the horse's saddle, lit by an eerily glowing aura.

White skin. Silvery hair, fine and soft as thistledown. A shift so filmy that he could clearly see the contours of the rake-thin body beneath. And the eyes . . . huge eyes, blue and deep and hungry . . .

The apparition's lips parted, showing a bright scarlet tongue, and it said, '*King Karel . . . help us.*'

'Sir?' the sergeant shouted again. But Karel was staring mesmerised at the vision. And for one moment he saw another face superimposed on the stark, pale features. The face of Sefira.

'*Sefi needs you, King Karel. We need you.*' Xai smiled at him, a peculiarly conspiratorial smile. '*Sefi is in the tower.*'

Hoofs thumped, and the sergeant's voice rang out a third time. 'My lord, is—'

Karel interrupted him. 'All's well, sergeant. Wait where you are.' At last he found the wherewithal to blink, and it snapped the spell's paralysis. 'You,' he said, 'are Xai . . .'

'*Yes, I am Xai.*' She smiled again. '*Grendon wants to destroy me. He wants to stop me from helping Sefi . . . and from helping you.*'

The king's hands tightened on the reins. His horse was shifting nervously, snorting; a vicious jerk brought it under control again and he continued to stare at the soul-invader. 'How will you help me?'

'*As we have done before. Sefi and I. But without Grendon. We do not need Grendon.*'

No, Karel thought; we do not . . . Speculatively, he touched his tongue to his lips. 'And where is Grendon now?'

'*With Sefi. He threatens to kill her. And,*' Xai shrugged, not anxious to admit that she had mistakenly given away more than was wise, '*he knows that you are here. With the searchers.*'

So the two riders had been a decoy . . . Karel looked over his shoulder to where the rest of the search party were vague, milling shapes in the dimness, and barked out, 'Sergeant! Line the men up for further instructions!'

'Sir!' The sergeant was baffled but didn't dare question the order. Karel turned to Xai again.

'Then Grendon will be waiting for me.'

'*He waits. He expects you to come.*'

And would doubtless have set a trap. Well, Karel thought, the mouse could play that game as well as the cat. And he had a new weapon . . .

Understanding, Xai gave a soft little laugh, sweet and melodious but with an undercurrent of pure malignance. '*I will help you,*' she said. '*I will help you to kill him. For I have been waiting, King Karel. I have been waiting for a long time to take my revenge on Grendon.*'

Karel returned her smile with one in which the hunter's instinct was slowly and surely rising. 'That pleases me, Xai,' he said. 'And if—'

He stopped as Xai gave a strange cry. The demon's eyes widened hugely, unnaturally, and their colour flared into blue fire. '*No! NO!*'

'What?' Karel demanded. His horse squealed and started to prance wildly. And Xai was changing, her form fluctuating like a mirage. Sefira's face appeared again, her eyes filled with terror and her mouth contorted in a silent scream, and Xai screeched, '*NO, NO, NO!! YOU CANNOT! YOU WOULD NOT DARE!*' Her figure lost all cohesion, and Karel recoiled as she coalesced into a spinning column of mist, spitting with tongues of sapphire flame.

'*Come back!*' he yelled at her. But Xai only shrieked again. '*THE TOWER! THE TOWER! HURRY!*'

With a crack like lightning the column arrowed away northwards and Karel's horse reared again. He wrenched its head round, dug his heels into its flanks and spurred it to where his men waited.

'Sergeant! Did you *see*?'

The man looked at him blankly and said, 'See what, my lord?'

They knew nothing, Karel realised. To them, Xai had been invisible and inaudible, and the chances were that they hadn't even heard his side of the exchange. For a moment he stared at them – then his mind snapped into focus.

'Northward,' he said crisply. 'To the watchtower.'

The sergeant baulked. 'But sir, the runaways—'

'Let them go; they're of no importance.' Even their identities were irrelevant, he thought. He was only interested in one quarry. 'Stir the men, sergeant. *Move!*'

Grendon was crawling across the tower room, too stunned to stagger upright but knowing that he had only seconds to prepare for what was about to happen. Candles – had to reach the candles, and light four of them, and surround them both with a protective square.

He was dragging Sefira with him, but though she still

kicked she was also clinging to his arm, using her feet to try to propel them both across the floor. He heard her voice, ragged and indistinct, 'Grendon, what's happening, what are you doing—'

He could see the bruises flowering on her skin and knew that he must have suffered the same from the psychic kickback of Xai's fury. It had hit them with the force of a physical blow, stunning them and sending them rolling together across the floor. But Xai had realised the truth too late; distracted by her hunt for Karel she had not known what was happening in the tower. Her rage had erupted instinctively, without thought, and the shock of it had hurled Grendon's pent-up reflexes into a violent involuntary spasm that completed what had been begun, and irrevocably shattered the demon's most powerful link with Sefira.

As for Sefira – he didn't know if she hated him, was terrified of him, understood, even *comprehended* what had happened, and there was no time to find out. His hand, clawing, snatched at the first of the candles and he scrabbled to light it, cursing damp tinder and his own shaking fingers. Sefira had sprawled as he let go of her, and now she raised her head and stared bemusedly at his efforts. Grendon flung her a searing glance and said, 'Four – we need four!' Then, 'Sefira, we've weakened her! Don't you realise? But she'll attack – *help me!*'

Frantic words, and incoherent, but Sefira seemed to grasp their meaning, and with a cry she took hold of another candle. *Xai, weakened – it was true, she felt it. Grendon had had no choice. He had broken the demon's sway. Oh, Xai still lived; and while she did Sefira would never be truly free, for the soul-invader's strength would grow again, and her own will would start to weaken, and the cycle would begin once more. But not yet. Not yet . . .*

She returned an extraordinary look that he couldn't interpret, and as the second candle caught and began to burn they lit two more and Grendon thrust them into place, forming a rough square. Outside, there was a sound. Like the wind rising . . .

'Over here!' He yanked at her arm and dragged her to him. 'Keep inside the candles' boundaries!' She huddled in an effort to obey, and he scrambled to his feet and stood straddling her, facing out into the room. *That noise wasn't the wind . . .*

Grendon shut his eyes and summoned all the will he could muster. *The words – he knew them so well, but suddenly they were gone . . .* Then out of the abyss of memory came a vision of Lendrer, standing as he stood now, his voice ringing with stern authority through the confines of a dank, noisome and hidden room. The old language, the arcane tongue . . .

'*Aeno te. Halkut te. Te arkora, te geneka, te ir issidul . . .*' He heard Sefira's grating intake of breath, felt the energy rise, the protective circle forming . . .

The wind that was not a wind rose to a shriek of insane proportions. Then the tower rocked as the shutters smashed inward and a hurricane exploded into the room. Grendon reeled back, thrown off balance by the blast; the candles whirled away and were pulverised against the wall, and a tide of detritus, Arrine's small home comforts, swept past and over him in their wake. Grendon could hear Sefira screaming; through the flying strands of his hair he saw her huddling, covering her head with her arms in a desperate effort to protect herself. But the circle was holding; he felt it, knew it, grasped at the lifeline it offered.

'Sefira!' He yelled her name above the roaring din. 'Sefira, it isn't real! It's Xai, and she can't control us! Will it to stop – compel it, compel it, *help me*!'

He thought at first that she couldn't hear him, or didn't comprehend, for she only screamed again. But then her scream took on a new note. A note of defiance. Of resolution. Of *loathing*.

'*NO!*' Sefira's voice rose shrill and wild, challenging the mayhem, driving against it with a passion that fired Grendon's own will. '*NO! I SHALL NOT SUBMIT TO YOU, XAI! YOU CANNOT CONQUER ME!* **I WILL SEE YOU TURNED TO DUST!!**'

The supernatural gale howled anew, but Grendon no longer felt its onslaught. He was strong – she was giving him strength, melding her spirit to his, joining with him in mind as they had joined in body. Above the tumult of Xai's shrieking and Sefira's furious answering defiance, he drew on all his strength, called back into his past and his memory – *Lendrer, good friend and mentor, this repayment has been so long in coming* – and the words of the ritual, the ceremony that would wipe Xai from the face of the earth, began to ring out through the pandemonium.

Karel saw the incredible spectacle as he and his party pelted over the turf. The entire watchtower was wreathed in blue light, a huge, translucent column that roared skywards like fire. The horses screamed as they felt the colossal backlash of the wind; they were rearing, bucking, out of control, and Karel flung himself from the saddle, yelling for the men to join him as he raced towards the tower door.

'*Sir, no!*' the sergeant bawled. '*Stay back!*' But Karel ignored him. The sergeant turned to exhort the others to follow, but terror had swamped them and they were scattering like leaves, shouting to their horses, kicking them, spurring them into a wild gallop away from this nightmare. The sergeant's own horse fought against the bit, then suddenly the reins were snatched from his hands and the animal bolted, carrying him helplessly with it.

'*Cowards!*' Karel's voice screamed through the night in their wake, but his fury was lost in the din of the gale. Staggering, hair streaming, Karel turned towards the tower again and ran on.

'Sefira, no! Hold her back – *hold her back*!' But Sefira was twisting and writhing in his grip, her body bending into an appalling contortion as she fought him, fought the agony, fought the whole horror of Xai's onslaught on her mind. *Xai was punishing her for this betrayal, and it wouldn't stop until she yielded, until she let the demon possess her again; and she couldn't bear the pain, she couldn't, she couldn't . . .*

Sefira howled like a banshee, and Grendon felt her spine arch further, impossibly far. He was trying to pull her upright, but bone and muscle were locked against his efforts, and her bloodshot eyes bulged in their sockets as her agony increased.

'*Lesthu te – an . . . anuka, arkora, imbrimir . . .*' But he couldn't hold the power and hold Sefira; and Xai was trying to pull her from him, pull her across the floor and out of the astral barricade's protection. Blood was running from Sefira's mouth where she had bitten her tongue in her torment, and she was trying to speak, to plead.

'Let me . . . go . . . oh, please . . . oh, please . . . I can't; I can't endure it . . .'

The last fragment of the ritual – that was all that remained between him and Xai's destruction! But he couldn't summon the focus, couldn't form the words! 'Sefira, hold on! Hold on to me!' Memory was surging through him again; the memory of his own agony, his own panic. He had prevailed; he had overcome. But he had had Lendrer's power to help him, and Lendrer was not here, he was dead, he was gone, burned, *ashes* – Grendon was losing Sefira and there was nothing he could do. *Let her go, or see her die in agony!* his mind screamed at him. *There's no third choice!*

Without conscious volition his fingers started to slacken their hold. Xai screeched in triumph, and Sefira moaned, a lost, accursed sound.

And the trapdoor in the floor smacked open with a noise like a whiplash as Karel hurled himself into the room.

In the split second that he had to register what was happening, Grendon saw the king's shocked face and saw him reel backwards, one flailing foot kicking the trapdoor shut again. As Karel staggered against the wall the demon's attention riveted for a single instant on him, and in that instant a great, sucking rattle came from Sefira's throat as the air she had been unable to breathe rushed suddenly into her lungs. Her body flexed with a huge convulsion, and she doubled up in Grendon's arms, slamming against him as Xai's power ricocheted from her. Grendon's eyes widened; for a heartbeat he was paralysed.

Then the paralysis broke, and with a last thundering surge of energy from his mind he roared the final words of the rite.

'ANU KIRAH! ANU, TE INKHAMINEI, TE SUKOR! *LAMAL! LAMAL! LAMAL!*'

There was a sound that went beyond sound, blasting through the audible spectrum and into insanity. Grendon clapped both hands to his ears, oblivious to Sefira slumping heavily to the floor, oblivious to the fact that he too was falling, crashing down on top of her, as a vast wall of pressure came thundering at him out of the sky, out of the earth, out of a dimension beyond imagining . . . Madly, a part of his mind that seemed to have been torn from him and was roiling and spinning away with a life of its own, saw Karel wreathed in a savage fire of pulsating blue light, and somewhere in another, impossible world he heard the king and Xai screaming in appalling disharmony as the demon tried to tear into Karel's soul in its last, hopeless bid for refuge. But there was no refuge. There was only blackness, non-being, *destruction*.

Then came the final, shattering concussion . . . and utter silence.

For some time nothing in the tower moved. Then, at last, there was a stirring near the trapdoor. Slowly, groggily, Karel raised his head. He could see little in the gloom, but for some obscure reason that didn't seem to matter.

He stared into the dimness, listening to the sound of his own breathing. He felt sick. Where were his men? Cowards, they'd proved themselves. They would suffer for that; he would see that they suffered. They had lost him the greatest prize of all; and for that they would *die*.

Carefully, he rose to his feet and with a bizarrely commonplace gesture brushed the worst of the dust and grime from his clothes. Cloak. He had left his cloak somewhere. Where? It didn't matter; he would have a new one made. And one for Mischane. And one for . . .

But no; not for *her*. She was gone. Dead. Destroyed. Again, no matter. *Or did it matter so much to him, so much, that his mind was seething with a rage that would never, ever loose its grip . . . ?*

New cloaks he would have, for him and for Mischane. From the cowards' flayed skins. It seemed fitting, did it not? Karel laughed at the thought, then stared at the smashed shutters and the window gaping open to the night. Time to leave. No point in staying; his own private chambers in the palace at Tourmon were far more comfortable than this squalid place.

It took him a minute or two to locate the trapdoor, but at last he found it, lifted it and eased himself stiffly through and down the steps to ground level. He hadn't earlier noticed the two men Grendon had felled, and he didn't notice them now. He simply walked outside, closing the door very carefully behind him.

The sergeant had finally got his horse under control and had managed to round up two others of the search party. At the last they had proved more terrified of their officer than of the watchtower, and the trio arrived minutes after Karel's emergence. They found their king sitting on the grass, systematically pulling the gold braid from the edge of his jerkin and shredding it. Karel looked up at them and said contemptuously, 'Cowardice. There is no defence, sergeant. You will present yourself at the guardhouse for trial one hour after dawn.'

The men looked uneasily at each other, then the sergeant ventured, 'My lord . . . perhaps you'd care to ride my horse back to the city . . . ? I think we should go, sir. There's nothing more to be done here.'

That was true enough. Karel glanced with faint regret at the tower, and shrugged.

'Is there . . . anyone else in there, sir?' the sergeant asked.

Karel considered. Grendon. Sefira. Just names. They meant nothing. 'No,' he said, and walked across the turf to take the reins of the sergeant's horse and swing himself into the saddle.

Grendon watched them leave. He had not moved while

Karel was still in the room, but he had listened, and what he had heard gave him a chilly sense of satisfaction. Karel was unaware that he had voiced his thoughts; and when he went out to meet his men Grendon had crouched by the window and gleaned the gist of the conversation between them. In what was perhaps the ultimate irony, Xai's last, doomed battle to survive had granted both him and Sefira a boon which he could never have foreseen. She had given them sanctuary from Karel's retribution. For in her attempt to possess his soul, she had driven him over the brink of madness, and into a world of his own from which he would never return.

He moved from the window, suddenly conscious of the cold night air chilling his naked body. Every muscle and sinew seemed to ache as he straightened; every bone felt as though it had been bruised. Behind him Sefira lay prone, arms flung out, hair soaked with sweat. She looked like a child's discarded doll, and he crossed the room to kneel beside her. One finger lightly traced down her spine. He could feel no real damage, though she would ache for some time to come.

'Sefira?' He spoke her name in the quiet, but she didn't stir. She was unconscious, and that, he thought, was probably for the best. Let her rest; let her mind begin to recuperate in darkness and silence. Grendon leaned down, and planted a kiss on the nape of her neck.

'You're free,' he told her, though she could not hear him.

Then he lay down beside her and closed his eyes.

'It's one of Vinor's hunting lodges, but he rarely uses it.' Perlion turned from the window, which looked on to a vista of rolling downs. 'And what Vinor doesn't know can't hurt him, eh?'

Arrine looked at Grendon and saw that he was smiling in response. 'You're a generous man, Perlion,' he said.

'Oh, nonsense. What father – or father-in-law for that matter – wouldn't do the same for his own child and her husband?'

Grendon could have disputed that, and with evidence, but

held his tongue. He owed Perlion too much to quibble with him, even in jest.

Perlion and Arrine had woken him from a deep sleep shortly before dawn. From the vantage point of a low hill crowned with trees they had seen their pursuers stop and then turn back towards the watchtower, and a little later had witnessed, though at a great distance, the eerie spectacle of Xai's final attack. It was some time before they dared return to the tower, but when they did they found Grendon and Sefira amid the wreckage of the room. Grendon had supplied the bones of the story when they woke him, and Perlion, ever resourceful, had returned immediately to Tourmon and hired a carriage which he himself drove back to the tower to collect them all. Now, the whole of the tale had been told, and Grendon was still trying to adjust to the strangeness of being warm and comfortable and relaxed in the homely surroundings of Vinor's lodge. It all felt very unreal.

Sefira had not yet woken. She lay in a comfortable bed in the adjoining room; for most of the day Arrine had sat with her, and every few minutes now she rose to look in and see that all was well. No one quite knew what to expect of Sefira when she finally regained consciousness, and thus far they had all carefully avoided the subject. But there were other matters to be resolved, and now, gently, Arrine broached the one that was foremost in her mind.

'Grendon . . . what will you do?'

Grendon had been waiting for this, and he sighed. 'I don't know.'

'You could return to Tourmon. You know that.'

He laughed bitterly. 'And take royal service again?'

'Karel won't last as king. What afflicts him can't be cured, and who knows what manner of ruler will take his place?'

A short time ago, Grendon reflected, that would have mattered to him. He would have fought for a Sanctified ruler, as in the old days. He would have fought to restore the established ways. Now, though, it didn't seem relevant. Power corrupted, no matter who wielded it, and he didn't want to be a part of that world any more.

He said, 'No, Arrine; I don't think I'll ever return.' He looked keenly at her. 'I think I'm too proud.' Then an image of Mischane rose in his mind and, surprised at the sudden lack of bitterness in himself, he added, 'Or maybe I've finally learned the *real* meaning of self-respect.'

Perlion made a noise in his throat that might have been agreement or embarrassment. Three deer were walking gracefully across the vista, and he was very partial to venison, but at present he had other preoccupations.

'Before the search party intervened,' he said carefully, 'we were talking, Grendon. And you said—'

'I remember.' Grendon flexed an aching leg. 'And I meant what I said, Perlion.'

The Lander nodded. 'Then I have a suggestion to make. We don't yet know what we will meet in Sefira when she wakes.' He turned round. 'To put it more harshly, what will be left of her now that the soul-invader is finally gone forever. So would it not be wise to defer any decision until we *do* know?' He smiled self-consciously. 'I have my own interests at heart, I admit. I want – I so much *want* – the chance to know my child. And then there is Isbel; and Sefira's brothers and sisters . . . Fates help me, it will be hard to admit the truth after all this time; but I want them to know her, too.' A little impatiently he put a hand to his eyes, pretending it was only a stray lock of hair that made him blink so rapidly. 'So I would ask you, Grendon; wait a little while before deciding your future. And until that time comes, feel content to accept the hospitality of my family.' A small laugh escaped him. 'We are, after all, your family. If you and Sefira wish us to be.'

There was silence. Then Arrine, sensing that she was suddenly an intruder, rose quietly and said, 'I'll go to Sefira . . .'

She left the room, and Grendon and Perlion regarded each other for a long time. At last Grendon said, 'Perlion, I'm bereft of words. By rights you should hate me.'

'Hate you? My dear friend, why?'

'Because of what I am.'

'A Sanctified? Oh, no; you misjudge me. In truth I don't care about the Fellowships. I never have – and I'll give Karel his due; in that, if in nothing else, his professed aims for our land were good and worthy, even if his methods left much to be desired.' He moved to a chair and sat down, giving a contented sigh as he did so. 'Times are changing, Grendon, and with a little fortune to aid us they will change more surely and for the better before long. Karel's day is over. We needed him as a reformer, but not as a king. And I think that whoever follows him will learn a lesson from his mistakes.'

Would he? Grendon wondered. Knowing human nature as he did, he doubted it. But then perhaps his view was clouded . . .

The door opened then and Arrine returned. There was an odd look in her eyes and she said, 'Grendon, Perlion . . . She is awake.'

They rose together, and quickly. Perlion said, 'May we—?'

'Of course.' Arrine stood aside to let them through. 'But . . .'

Grendon looked at her. 'But what?'

A slight hesitation, then Arrine shook her head. 'No matter. You'll see for yourselves soon enough. Go through.'

They entered Sefira's room together. She was propped up with pillows, and she looked very small and pale and vulnerable. Seeing them she smiled hesitantly, and Perlion hurried to her side.

'Sefira!' Relief suffused his voice. 'You've recovered!'

Her eyes searched his face, and she seemed to have a little difficulty in focusing. Then at last she said, 'You are . . . Perlion? My father . . . ?'

'Yes, child, I am. We've been parted for many years, but now that I've found you again—'

Sefira interrupted. She was looking at Grendon, and when she spoke he felt something turn over within him.

313

'And you,' she said tentatively, 'are my husband . . . ?'

Grendon couldn't reply. He could only stare at her, confounded by the strange, shy, warm note that was in her voice. Then she said, 'Arrine told me . . . you see, I seem to have . . .' she shook her head. 'Oh dear. This isn't easy.'

'She has lost her memory,' Arrine said gently.

The words went through Grendon like a hot tide. Perlion was looking at him, his expression hovering between shock, uncertainty and hope. 'Grendon . . .' he said.

Sefira smiled again at Grendon. 'I knew I was married,' she said, and held up her wrists. 'The bracelets. You see; I've not forgotten everything. And your faces *are* a little familiar to me. Enough for me to understand that I know and trust and love you all. But . . .'

'Child,' Arrine said softly, 'that is *more* than enough. We know. We understand.'

'And, daughter, we will help you,' Perlion added. He sat down on the bed and took a tight hold of Sefira's hands. Then he looked at Grendon again.

Grendon stood very still. For the first time, he realised, he was seeing Sefira as she truly was. Not Xai's victim. Not a hunted killer. Simply a woman, almost a stranger, to whom he owed an obligation. And, though he couldn't yet tell the reason why, it wasn't one that he wished to shrink from.

New beginnings. The tide of change. It was a cleansing force, and he knew he would be a fool if he turned his back on it. What would happen in the future he did not know and would not yet speculate upon. But this was a chance. And he wanted – for her sake, for Perlion's and Arrine's and possibly even his own – to take it.

He sat beside Sefira; looked into her eyes. For a moment she returned the look; then she cast her gaze down, and her lips smiled. Lightly, gently, Grendon leaned forward to kiss her brow. Her skin had a faint, sweet scent to it.

'My love,' he said. 'There is time to learn. There is all the time in the world.'